There's No Place Like Here

Also by Cecelia Ahern

There's No Place Like Here

Cecelia Ahern

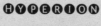

NEW YORK

Mass Market ISBN: 978-0-7868-9131-3

Hyperion books are available for special promotions and premiums.
For details contact the HarperCollins Special Markets Department
in the New York office at 212-207-7528, fax 212-207-7222, or email
spsales@harpercollins.com.

FIRST U.S. MASS MARKET EDITION

10 9 8 7 6 5 4 3 2 1

For you, Dad—with all my love.
Per ardua surgo.

"A missing person is anyone whose whereabouts are unknown whatever the circumstances of disappearance. The person will be considered missing until located and his/her well-being, or otherwise, established."

An Gardai Siochana

Jenny-May Butler, the little girl who lived across the road from me, went missing when I was a child.

The Gardaí launched an investigation, which led to a lengthy public search for her. For months every night the story was on the news, every day it was on the front pages of the papers, everywhere it was discussed in every conversation. The entire country pitched in to help; it was the biggest search for a missing person I, at ten years of age, had ever seen, and it seemed to affect everyone.

Jenny-May Butler was a blond-haired blue-eyed beauty whose smiling face was beamed from the TV screen into the living rooms of every home around the country, causing eyes to fill with tears and parents to hug their children that extra bit tighter before they sent them off to bed. She was in everyone's dreams and everyone's prayers.

She too was ten years old and in my class at school. I used to stare at the pretty photograph of her on the news every day and listen to them speak about her as though she were an angel. From the way they described her, you never would have known that she threw stones at Fiona

Brady during recess when the teacher wasn't looking, or that she called me a frizzy-haired cow in front of Stephen Spencer just so he would fancy her instead of me. No, for those few months she had become the perfect being and I didn't think it fair to ruin that. After a while even I forgot about all the bad things she'd done because she wasn't just Jenny-May anymore: she was Jenny-May Butler, the sweet missing girl whose nice family cried on the nine o'clock news every night.

She was never found, not her body, not a trace; it was as though she had disappeared into thin air. No suspicious characters had been seen lurking around, no CCTV was available to show her last movements. There were no witnesses, no suspects; the Gardaí questioned everyone possible. The street became suspicious, its inhabitants calling friendly hellos to one another on the way to their cars in the early morning but all the time wondering, second-guessing, and visualizing dark, distorted scenarios implicating their neighbors. Washing cars, painting picket fences, weeding the flowerbeds, and mowing lawns on Saturday mornings while surreptitiously looking around the neighborhood conjured up shameful thoughts. People were shocked at themselves, angry that this incident had perverted their minds.

Pointed fingers behind closed doors couldn't give the Gardaí any leads; they had absolutely nothing to go on but a pretty picture.

I always wondered where Jenny-May went, where she had disappeared to, how on earth anyone could just vanish into thin air without a trace, without *someone* knowing *something*.

At night I would look out my bedroom window and stare at her house. The porch light was always on, acting as a beacon to guide Jenny-May home. Mrs. Butler couldn't sleep anymore and I could see her perpetually perched on the edge of her couch, as though she was on her marks waiting for the pistol to be fired. She would sit in her living room, looking out the window, waiting for someone to call or come by with news. Sometimes I would wave at her and she'd give me a half-hearted wave back. Most of the time she couldn't see past her tears.

Like Mrs. Butler, I wasn't happy with not having any answers. I liked Jenny-May Butler a lot more when she was gone than when she was here and that also interested me. I missed her, the *idea* of her, and wondered if she was somewhere nearby, throwing stones at someone else and laughing loudly, but that we just couldn't find her or hear her. I took to searching thoroughly for everything I'd mislaid after that. When my favorite pair of socks went missing I turned the house upside down while my worried parents looked on, not knowing what to do but eventually settling on helping me.

It disturbed me that frequently my missing possessions were nowhere to be found and on the odd occasion that I did find them, it disturbed me that, as in the case of the socks, I could only ever find one. Then I'd picture Jenny-May Butler somewhere, throwing stones, laughing, and wearing my favorite socks.

I never wanted anything new; from the age of ten, I was convinced that you couldn't replace what was lost. I insisted on things having to be found.

I think I wondered about all those odd pairs of socks

as much as Mrs. Butler worried about her daughter. I too stayed awake at night running through all the unanswerable questions. Each time my lids grew heavy and neared closing, another question would be flung from the depths of my mind, forcing my lids to open again. This process kept much-needed sleep at bay and left me each morning more tired yet none the wiser.

Perhaps this is why it happened to me. Perhaps because I had spent so many years turning my own life upside down and looking for everything, I had forgotten to look for myself. Somewhere along the line I had forgotten to figure out who and where I was.

Twenty-four years after Jenny-May Butler disappeared, I went missing too.

This is my story.

My life has been made up of a great many ironies; my going missing only added to an already very long list.

First, I'm six foot one. Ever since I was a child I've been towering over just about everyone. I could never get lost in a shopping center like other kids, I could never hide properly when playing games, I was never asked to dance at discos, I was the only teenager that wasn't aching to buy her first pair of high heels. Jenny-May Butler's favorite name for me, well, certainly one of her top ten, was "Daddy-longlegs," which she liked to call me in front of large crowds of her friends and admirers. Believe me, I've heard them all. I was the kind of person you could see coming from a mile away. I was the awkward dancer on the dance floor, the girl at the cinema that nobody wanted to sit behind, the one in the shop that rooted for the extra-long-legged trousers, the girl in the back row of every photograph. You see, I stick out like a sore thumb. Everyone who passes me registers me and remembers me. But despite all that, I went missing. Never mind the odd socks, never mind Jenny-May Butler; how a throbbing sore thumb on a hand so bland couldn't be seen was the ultimate icing on the cake. The mystery that beat all mysteries was my own.

The second irony is that my job was to *search* for missing persons. For years I worked as a garda. With a desire to work solely on missing persons but without working in an actual division assigned to these, I had to rely solely upon the "luck" of being assigned these cases. You see, the Jenny-May Butler situation really sparked off something inside me. I wanted answers, I wanted solutions, and I wanted to find them all myself. I suppose my searching became an obsession. I looked around the outside world for so many clues I don't think that I once thought about what was going on inside my own head.

In the Gardaí sometimes we found missing people in conditions I won't ever forget, not for the rest of this life and far into the next, and then there were people who just didn't want to be found. Often we uncovered only a trace, too often not even that. Those were the moments that drove me to keep looking far beyond my call of duty. I would investigate cases long after they were closed, stay in touch with families long after I should have. I realized I couldn't go on to the next case without solving the previous, with the result that there was too much paperwork and too little action. And so knowing that my heart lay only in finding the missing, I left the Gardaí and I searched in my own time.

The families always wondered what drove me to do this. They had a reason, a link, a love for the missing, whereas my fees were barely enough for me to get by on.

So, what was my motivation? Peace of mind, I suppose. A way to help me close my eyes and sleep at night.

But all of this begs the question: how can someone like me, with my physical attributes and my mental attitude, go missing?

I've just realized that I haven't even told you my name. It's Sandy Shortt. It's OK, you can laugh. I know you want to. I would too if it wasn't so bloody heartbreaking. My parents called me Sandy because I was born with a head of sandy-colored hair. Pity they didn't foresee that my hair would turn as black as coal. They didn't know either that those cute pudgy little legs would soon stop kicking and start growing at such a fast rate, for so long. So Sandy Shortt is my name. That is who I am supposed to be, how I am identified and recorded for all time. But I am neither of those things. The contradiction often makes people laugh during introductions. Normally I respond to their amusement with a shrug and a smile. But not now. You see, there's nothing funny about being missing. I also quickly realized there's little difference between being missing and looking for the missing: every day I search. Same as I did when I was working. Only this time I search for a way back to be found.

I have learned one thing worth mentioning. There is one huge difference in my life from before, one vital piece of evidence. For once in my life I want to go home.

What bad timing to realize such a thing. The biggest irony of all.

I was born and reared in County Leitrim in Ireland, which with a population of about 25,000, is the smallest county in the country. Once the county town, Leitrim has the remains of a castle and some other ancient buildings, but it has lost its former importance and dwindled to a village. The landscape ranges from bushy brown hills to majestic mountains with yawning valleys and countless picturesque lakes. Leitrim is all but landlocked, having a coastal outlet to the Atlantic only two miles long. When there, I feel it brings on a sudden feeling of claustrophobia and an overwhelming desire for solid flat ground.

There's a saying about Leitrim and that is that the best thing to come out of Leitrim is the road to Dublin. I finished school when I was seventeen, applied for the Guards, and I eventually got myself on that road to Dublin. Since then I have rarely traveled back. A few times a year I would visit my parents in the three-bedroom terraced house in a small cul-de-sac of twelve houses where I grew up. The usual intention was to stay for the weekend but most of the time I only lasted a day, using an emergency at work as the excuse to grab my unpacked bag by the door and drive, drive, drive very fast on the best thing to come out of Leitrim.

I didn't have a bad relationship with my parents. They were always supportive, ever ready to dive in front of bullets, into fires and off mountains if it meant my happiness. The truth is, they made me uneasy. In their eyes I could see who they saw and I didn't like it. I saw my reflection in their expressions more than in any mirror. Some people have the power to do that, to look at you and their faces let you know exactly how you're behaving. I suppose it was because they loved me, but I couldn't spend too much time with people who loved me because of those eyes, because of that reflection.

When I was ten—after Jenny-May went missing—my parents began to tiptoe around me, watching me warily. They had pretend conversations and false laughs that echoed around the house. They would try to distract me, create a false sense of ease and normality in the atmosphere, but I knew that they were doing it and why and it only made me aware that something was wrong.

They were so supportive, they loved me so much, and each time the house was about to be turned upside down for yet another grueling search, they never gave in without a pleasant fight. Milk and cookies at the kitchen table, the radio on in the background, and the washing machine going, all to break the uncomfortable silence that would inevitably ensue.

Mum would give me that smile, that smile that didn't reach her eyes, that smile that made her back teeth clench and grind when she thought I wasn't looking. With forced easiness in her voice and a forced face of happiness, she would cock her head to one side, try not to let me know she was studying me intently, and say, "Why do you want to search the house again, honey?" She always called me honey, like she knew as much as I did that I was no more Sandy Shortt than Jenny-May Butler was an angel.

No matter how much action and noise had been created in the kitchen to avoid the uncomfortable silence, it didn't seem to work. The silence drowned it all out.

My answer: "Because I can't find it, Mum."

"What pair are they?"

The easy smile, the pretense that this was a casual conversation and not a desperate attempt at interrogation to find out how my mind worked.

"My blue ones with the white stripes," I answered on one particular occasion. I insisted on bright-colored socks, bright and identifiable so that they could be easily found.

"Well, maybe you didn't put both of them in the linen basket, honey. Maybe the one you're looking for is somewhere in your room." A smile, trying not to fidget, swallowing hard.

I shook my head. "I put them both in the basket, I saw you put them both in the machine and only one came back out. It's not in the machine and it's not in the basket."

The plan to have the washing machine switched on as a distraction backfired and was then the focus of attention. My mum tried not to lose that placid smile as she glanced at the overturned basket on the kitchen floor, all her folded clothes scattered and rolled in messy piles. For one second she let the façade drop. I could have missed it with a blink but I didn't. I saw the look on her face when she glanced down. It was fear. Not for the missing sock, but for me. She quickly plastered on the smile again, shrugging like it was all no big deal.

"Perhaps it blew away in the wind, I had the patio door open."

I shook my head.

"Or it could have fallen out of the basket when I carried it over from there to there."

I shook my head again.

She swallowed and her smile tightened. "Maybe it's caught up in the sheets. Those sheets are so big; you'd never see a little sock hidden in there."

"I already checked."

She took a cookie from the center of the table and bit down hard, anything to take the smile off her aching face. She chewed for a while, pretending not to be thinking, pretending to listen to the radio and humming a song she didn't even know. All to fool me into thinking there was nothing to be worried about.

"Honey," she said, smiling, "sometimes things just get lost."

"Where do they go when they're lost?"

"They don't *go* anywhere." She smiled. "They are always in the place we dropped them or left them behind. We're just not looking in the right area when we can't find them."

"But I've looked in *all* the places, Mum. I *always* do."

I had; I always did. I turned everything upside down; there was no place in the small house that ever went untouched.

"A sock can't just get up and walk away without a foot in it." Mum false-laughed.

You see, the way Mum gave up right there, that's the point when most people stop wondering, when most people stop caring. You can't find something, you know it's somewhere, and, even though you've looked *everywhere*, there's still no sign. So you put it down to your own madness, blame yourself for losing it, and eventually you forget about it. I couldn't do that.

I remember my dad returning from work that evening to a house that had been literally turned upside down.

"Lose something, honey?"

"My blue sock with the white stripes," came my muffled reply from under the couch.

"Just the one again?"

I nodded.

"Left foot or right foot?"

"Left."

"OK, I'll look upstairs." He hung his coat on the rack by the door, placed his umbrella in the stand, gave his flustered wife a tender kiss on the cheek and an encouraging rub on the back, and then made his way upstairs. For two hours he stayed in my parents' room, looking, but I couldn't hear him moving around. One peep through the keyhole revealed a man lying on his back on the bed with a wash-cloth over his eyes.

On my visits in later years they would ask the same easygoing questions that were never intended to be intrusive, but to someone who was already armored up to her eyeballs they felt as such.

"Any interesting cases at work?"

"What's going on in Dublin?"

"How's the apartment?"

"Any boyfriends?"

There were never any boyfriends; I didn't want another pair of eyes haunting me day in and day out. I'd had lovers and fighters, short-term boyfriends, men-friends and one-night-only friends. I'd tried enough to know that anything long term wasn't going to work. I couldn't be intimate; I couldn't care enough, give enough, or want enough. I had no desire for what these men offered, they had no understanding of what I wanted, so it was tight smiles all round while I told my parents that work was fine, Dublin was busy, the apartment was great, and no, no boyfriends.

Every single time I left the house, even when I cut my visits short, Dad would announce proudly that I was the best thing to come out of Leitrim.

The fault never lay with Leitrim, nor did it with my parents. They were so supportive, and I only realize it now. I'm finding that with every passing day, that realization is so much more frustrating than never finding anything.

When Jenny-May Butler went missing, her final insult was to take a part of me with her. The older I got, the taller I got, the more that hole within me stretched, an abyss that continued to grow as I got older. But how did I physically go missing? How did I get to where I am now? First question, and most important, *where* am I now?

I'm here and that's all I know.

I look around and search for familiarity. I wander constantly and search for the road that leads out of here, though there isn't one. Where is *here*? I wish I knew. It's cluttered with personal possessions: car keys, house keys, cell phones, handbags, coats, suitcases adorned with airport baggage tickets, odd shoes, business files, photographs, can openers, scissors, earrings scattered among the piles of missing items that glisten occasionally in the light. And there are socks—lots of odd socks. Everywhere I walk, I trip over the things that people are probably still tearing their hair out to find.

There are animals, too. Lots of cats and dogs with bewildered little faces and withering whiskers, no longer identical to their photos on small-town telephone poles. No offers of rewards can bring them back.

How can I describe this place? It's an in-between place. It's like a grand hallway that leads you nowhere, it's like a banquet dinner of leftovers, a sports team made up of the people never picked, a mother without her child, it's a body without its heart. It's almost there but not quite. It's filled to the brim with personal items yet it's empty because the people who own them aren't here to love them.

How did I get here? I was one of those disappearing joggers. How pathetic. I used to watch those B-movie thrillers and groan every time the credits opened at the early-morning crime scene, the murdered body lying on the ground in workout clothes. I thought it foolish that women went running down quiet alleyways during the dark hours of the night, or during the quiet hours of the early morning *especially* when a known serial killer was on the prowl. But that's what happened to me. I was a predictable, pathetic, tragically naive early-morning jogger, in a gray sweatsuit and blaring headphones, running alongside a canal in the very early hours of the morning. I wasn't abducted, though; I just wandered onto the wrong path.

I was running along a canal, my feet pounding angrily against the ground as they always did, causing vibrations to jolt through my body. I remember feeling beads of sweat trickling down my forehead, the center of my chest, and down my back. The cool breeze caused a light shiver to course through my body. Every single time I remember that morning I have to fight the urge to call out and warn myself not to make the same mistake. Sometimes in that memory, on more blissful days, I stay on the same path, but hindsight is a wonderful thing. How often we wish we'd stayed on the same path.

It was five forty-five on a bright summer morning; silent apart from the music from my iPod spurring me on. Although I couldn't hear myself I knew my breathing was heavy. I always pushed myself. Whenever I felt I needed to stop, I made myself run faster. I don't know if it was a daily punishment or the part of me that was keen to investigate, to go new places, to force my body to achieve things it had never achieved before.

Through the darkness of the green-and-black ditch beside me, I spotted a water-violet up ahead, submerged. I remember my dad telling me when I was a little girl, lanky, with black hair and embarrassed by my contradictory name, that the water-violet was misnamed too because it wasn't violet at all—it was lilac-pink with a yellow throat—but nevertheless, wasn't it beautiful and didn't that make me want to laugh? Of course not, I'd shaken my head. I watched it from far away as it got closer and closer, telling it in my mind, *I know how you feel.* As I ran I felt my watch slide off my wrist and fall against the trees on the left. I'd broken the clasp of the watch the very first moment I'd wrapped it around my wrist, and since then it occasionally unhooked itself and fell to the floor. I stopped running and turned back, spotting it lying on the damp estuary bank. I leaned my back against the rugged dark brown bark of an alder and, while taking a breather, noticed a small track veering off to the left. It wasn't welcoming, it wasn't developed as a rambler's path, but my investigative side took over; my enquiring mind told me to see where it led.

It led me here.

I ran so far and so fast that by the time the playlist had ended on my iPod I looked around and didn't recognize the landscape. I was surrounded by a thick mist and was so high up in what seemed like a pine-covered mountain. The trees stood erect, like needles at attention, immediately on the defensive the way a hedgehog bristles under threat. I slowly lifted the earphones from my ears, my panting echoing around the majestic mountains, and I knew immediately that I was no longer in the small town of Glin. I wasn't even in Ireland.

I was just here. That was a day ago and I'm still here.

I'm in the business of searching and I know how it works. I'm a woman who packs her own bags and doesn't tell anyone where she's going for a whole week. I disappear regularly, I lose contact regularly, no one checks up on me. I come and go as I please and I like it that way. I travel a lot to the destinations where the missing were last seen, I check out the area, ask around. The only problem was, I had just arrived in this town that morning, driven straight to Shannon Estuary, and gone for a jog. I'd spoken to no one, hadn't yet checked into a B&B, nor walked down a busy street. I know what they'll be saying, I know I won't even be a case. I'll just be another person that's walked away from her life without wanting to be found; it happens all the time. If this had happened to me last week they probably would have been right.

I'll eventually belong to the category of disappearance where there is no apparent danger to either the missing person or the public: for example, persons aged eighteen and over who have decided to start a new life. I'm thirty-four, and in the eyes of others, have wanted out for a long, long time now.

This all means one thing: right now nobody out there is even looking for me.

How long will that last? What happens when they find the battered, red 1991 Ford Fiesta along the estuary with a packed bag in the trunk and a missing-persons file, a cup of, by then, cold not-yet-sipped coffee, and a cell phone, probably with missed calls, on the dashboard?

What then?

Wait a minute.

The coffee. I've just remembered the coffee.

On my journey from Dublin, I stopped at a closed garage to get a coffee from the outside dispenser and he saw me; the man filling his tires with air saw me.

It was out in the middle of nowhere, in the midst of the countryside at five fifteen in the morning, when the birds were singing and the cows mooing so loudly I could barely hear myself think. The smell of manure was thick but sweetened with the scent of honeysuckle waving in the light morning breeze.

This stranger and I were both so far from everything but yet right in the middle of something. The mere fact that we were the only two people around for miles was enough for our eyes to meet and to feel connected.

He was tall but not as tall as I am; they never are. Five eleven, with a round face, red cheeks, strawberry-blond hair, and bright blue eyes I felt I'd seen before, which looked tired at that early hour. He was dressed in a pair of worn-looking blue denims, his blue-and-white-check cotton shirt crumpled from his drive, his hair disheveled, his jaw unshaven, his gut expanding as his years moved on. I guessed he was in his mid to late thirties, although he looked older, with stress lines along his brow and laugh lines—no, I could tell from the sadness emanating from him that they weren't from laughter. A few gray hairs had crept into the side of his temples, fresh on his young head, every strand the result of a harsh lesson learned. Despite the extra weight, he looked strong, muscular. He was someone who did a lot of physical work, my assumption backed up by the heavy work boots he wore. His hands were large, weather-beaten but strong. I could see the veins on his forearms protruding as he moved, his sleeves rolled up messily to below his elbows as he lifted the air pump from its stand. But he wasn't going to work, not dressed like that, not in that shirt. For him this was his good wear.

I studied him as I made my way back to my car.

"Excuse me, you dropped something," he called out.

I stopped in my tracks and looked behind me. There on the tarmac sat my watch, the silver glistening under the sun. "Bloody watch," I mumbled, checking to see that it wasn't damaged.

"Thank you." I smiled, sliding it back onto my wrist.

"No problem. Lovely day, isn't it?"

A familiar voice to match the familiar eyes. I studied him for a while before answering. Some guy I'd met in a bar previously, a drunken fling, an old lover, a past colleague, client, neighbor, or school friend? I went through the regular checklist in my mind. There was no further recognition on either side. If he wasn't a previous fling, I was thinking I'd like to make him one.

"Gorgeous." I returned the smile.

His eyebrows rose in surprise first and then fell again, his face settling in obvious pleasure as he understood the compliment. But as much as I would have loved to stay and perhaps arrange a date for sometime in the future, I had a meeting with Jack Ruttle, the nice man I had promised to help, the man I was driving from Dublin to Limerick to see.

Oh, please, handsome man from the garage that day, please remember me, wonder about me, look for me, find me.

Yes, I know; another irony. Me, wanting a man to call? My parents would be so proud.

Jack Ruttle trailed slowly behind an HGV along the N69, the coast road that led from North Kerry to where he lived in Foynes, a small town in County Limerick a half-hour's drive from Limerick city. It was five A.M. as he traveled the only route to Shannon Foynes Port, Limerick's only seaport. Staring at the speedometer, he telepathically urged the truck to go faster while he gripped the steering wheel so tightly his knuckles turned white. Ignoring the advice of the dentist he had seen just the previous day in Tralee, he began to grind his back teeth. The constant grinding was wearing down his teeth and weakening his gums, causing his mouth to throb and ache. His cheeks were red and swollen, and matched his tired eyes. He'd left the friend's couch he was sleeping on in Tralee to drive home through the night. Sleep wasn't coming easily to him these days.

"Are you under any stress?" the dentist had asked him while studying the inside of Jack's mouth.

An open-mouthed Jack had swallowed a curse and fought the urge to clamp his teeth down on the white surgical finger in his mouth. *Stressed* was an understatement.

His brother Donal had disappeared on his twenty-fourth birthday after a night out with friends in Limerick city. Following a late-night snack of burger and chips in a fast-food restaurant, he had separated himself from his friends and staggered off alone. The joint was too packed for any particular person to be noticed; his four friends were too drunk and too distracted by their attempts to bring a female home for the night to care.

CCTV showed him taking €30 out of an ATM on O'Connell Street at 3:08 A.M. on a Friday night, and later he was caught on camera stumbling in the direction of Arthur's Quay. After that, his trail was lost. It was almost as if his feet had left the earth and he'd floated up toward the sky. Jack prepared himself for the fact that, in a way, maybe he had. His death was a concept he knew he could eventually accept if only there was a shred of evidence to support it.

It was the not knowing that tortured him. It was the worry that kept him awake and the fear that drove him from his bed at night to the toilet to be physically ill. But it was the inconclusive search of the Gardaí that fueled his continuous search. He had combined his trip to the dentist in Tralee with a visit to one of Donal's friends who had been with him the night he went missing. Like the other crowd that were there that night, he was a person Jack felt like punching and hugging all at the same time. He wanted to shout at him, yet console him for his loss of a friend. He never wanted to see him again, yet he didn't want to leave his side in case he remembered something, something he'd previously forgotten that would suddenly be the clue they were all looking for.

He stayed awake at nights looking through maps, rereading reports, double-checking times and statements while, beside him, Gloria's chest rose and fell with her silent breathing, her sweet breath sometimes blowing the corners of his papers as her sleeping world crept in on his.

Gloria, his girlfriend of eight years, always slept. She had slept soundly through the entire year of Jack's horrid nightmare, and still she dreamed. Still, she had hopes for tomorrow.

She had fallen into a deep sleep after hours spent at the garda station, the first day they worried about not hearing from Donal after four days of silence. She slept after the Gardaí had spent the day searching the river for his body. She slept after the day they'd spent hours attaching photos of Donal to shop windows, supermarket notice boards, and lampposts. She slept the night they thought they had found his body down an alley in the town and slept the next night when they discovered it wasn't him. She slept the night the Gardaí said there was nothing more they could do after months of searching. She slept the night of his mother's funeral, after seeing the coffin of a grief-stricken mother being lowered into the dirt to join her husband at long last after twenty years in this life without him.

It frustrated Jack, but he knew it wasn't a lack of caring that caused Gloria's lids to close. He knew this because she held his hand when they sat through the questions at the garda station that first time. She stood beside him as the wind and rain lashed at their faces, by the river, watching the divers appear on the surface of the gray murky water with faces more gloomy than when they had disappeared into the world below. She had helped him stick posters of Donal to windows and poles. She had held him tightly when he cried the day the Gardaí stopped looking and she stood in the front row of the church and waited for him while he helped carry his mother's coffin to the altar.

She cared all right, but one year on, she still slept at night during the longest hours of his life. The hours when Jack cared most about everything but the hours when deep in her sleep, Gloria didn't and couldn't care at all. Every night he felt the distance grow between her sleeping world and his.

He didn't tell her about coming across the woman, Sandy Shortt, from the missing persons agency in the Yellow Pages. He didn't tell her he had called her. He didn't tell her about the late-night phone calls all last week and the new sense of hope this woman's determination and belief had filled his head and heart with.

And he didn't tell her that they had arranged to meet on this very day in the next town because . . . well, because she was sleeping.

Jack finally managed to overtake the long vehicles, and as he neared home he found himself alone on the now quiet country road in his twelve-year-old rusting Nissan. The interior of his car was silent. Over the past year he found he was intolerant of unwanted noise; the sound of a TV or a radio in the background was merely a distraction to his pursuit of answers. Inside his mind was manic: shouting, screaming, replays of previous conversations, imaginings of future ones all leaped around his head like a bluebottle fly trapped in a jam jar.

Outside the car the engine roared, the metal rattled, the wheels bounced and fell over every pothole and bump in the surface. His mind was noisy in the silent car, his car clattered in the quiet countryside. It was five fifteen on a sunny Sunday morning in July and he needed to stop for air, for his lungs, and for the front deflated wheel.

He pulled over at the deserted gas station which would be closed until later in the morning, and parked beside the air pump. He allowed the birdsong to fill his head temporarily and push out his thoughts while he rolled up his sleeves and stretched his limbs from the long journey. The bluebottle momentarily settled.

Beside him a car pulled up and parked. The population of the area was so small he could spot an alien car a mile away . . . and the Dublin license plate gave it away too. Out of the tiny battered car, two long legs dressed in gray sweatpants appeared, followed by a long body. Jack stopped himself from gawking but from the corner of his eye he watched the curly-black-haired woman taking long strides to the coffee dispenser by the door of the shuttered garage. He was surprised that someone of her height could even fit into such a small car. He noticed something fall from her hand and heard the sound of metal against the ground.

"Excuse me, you dropped something," he called out.

She looked behind her in confusion and walked back to where the metal was glistening on the ground.

"Thank you." She smiled, sliding what looked like a bracelet or a watch onto her wrist.

"No problem. Lovely day, isn't it?" Jack felt the pain in his swollen cheeks worsen as they lifted in a smile.

Her green eyes sparkled like emeralds against her snow-white skin and glinted as they caught the sunlight streaming through the tall trees. Her jet-black curls twirled around her face playfully, revealing parts of her features, hiding others. She looked him up and down, taking him in as though analyzing every inch of him. Finally she raised an eyebrow. "Gorgeous," she replied and returned the smile. She, her jet-black curly hair, the Styrofoam cup of coffee, legs and all, disappeared into the tiny car like a butterfly into a Venus flytrap.

Jack watched the Ford Fiesta drive into the distance, wanting her to have stayed, and once again he noted how things between him and Gloria, or perhaps just his feelings for her, were changing. But he hadn't time to think about that now. Instead he returned to his car and leafed through his files in preparation for his meeting later that morning with Sandy Shortt.

Jack wasn't religious; he hadn't been to church for more than twenty years. In the last twelve months he had prayed three times. Once for Donal not to be found when they were searching the river for his body, the second time for the body in the alley not to be him, and the third time for his mother to survive her second stroke in six years. Two out of three prayers had been answered.

He prayed again today for the fourth time. He prayed for Sandy Shortt to take him from the place he was in and to be the one to bring him the answers he needed.

The porch light was still on when Jack arrived home. He insisted on it being left on all night for Donal's sake, as a beacon to guide his brother home. He turned it off now that it was bright outside and tiptoed around quietly, careful not to wake Gloria, who was enjoying her Sunday lie-in. Scouring through the linen basket of dirty clothes, he grabbed the least crumpled garment he could find and quickly changed out of one check shirt and into another. He hadn't washed as he didn't want the electric ceiling fan in the bathroom to wake her. He'd even held back from flushing the toilet. He knew it wasn't his overflowing generosity that was causing him to behave that way and yet he couldn't quite summon the shame in knowing that it was exactly the opposite. He was deliberately keeping his meeting with Sandy Shortt a secret from Gloria and the rest of his family.

It was as much to help them as it was to help him. In their hearts, they were beginning to move on. They were trying their utmost to settle back into their lives after the major upheaval and upset of suffering the loss of not one but two family members in one year. Jack under-

stood their positions. They had all reached a point where
no more days off work could be taken, sympathetic smiles
were being replaced by everyday greetings, and conversations with neighbors were returning to normal. Imagine, people were actually talking about other things and
not asking questions or offering advice. Cards filled with
comforting words had stopped landing on his doormat.
People had gone back about their own lives, employers
had moved around shifts as much as possible, and now it
was back to business for all concerned. But to Jack it felt
wrong and awkward for life to resume without Donal.

Truthfully it wasn't Donal's absence that held Jack
back from joining his family in bravely carrying on with
the rest of his life. Of course he missed him. His heart
ached from how much he missed him. But, as with the
death of his mother, he could and would eventually get
through the grief. Instead it was the mystery that surrounded his disappearance; all the unanswered questions left question marks dotting his vision like the
aftermath of flash photography.

He closed behind him the door to the cluttered one-
bedroom bungalow where he and Gloria had lived for
five years. Just like his father, Jack had worked as a cargo
handler at Shannon Foynes Port his entire working
life.

He had chosen Glin village, thirteen kilometers west
of Foynes, for the meeting point with Sandy Shortt as it
was a place none of his family inhabited. He sat in a small
café at nine A.M., a half hour before they were due to
meet. Sandy had said on the phone that she was always
early and he was eager, fidgety, and more than willing to

give this fresh idea a go. The more time they had together, the better. He ordered a coffee and stared at the most recent photograph of Donal on the table before him. It had been printed in almost every newspaper in Ireland and seen on notice boards and shop windows for the past year. In the background of the photo was the fake white Christmas tree his mother had set up in the living room every year. The baubles caught the flash of the camera and the tinsel twinkled. Donal's mischievous smile grinned up at Jack as though he was taunting him, daring him to find him. Donal had always loved playing hide-and-seek as a child. He would stay hidden for hours if it meant winning. Everyone would become impatient and declare loudly that Donal was the winner just so that he could leave his place with a proud beaming smile. This was the longest search Jack had ever endured and he wished his brother would come out of his hiding place now, show himself with that proud smile and end the game.

Donal's blue eyes, the only similar feature between the two brothers, sparkled up at Jack and he almost expected him to wink. No matter how long and hard he had stared at the photograph, he couldn't inject any life into it. He couldn't reach into the print and pull his brother out; he couldn't smell the aftershave he used to engulf himself in, he couldn't ruffle his brown hair and ruin his hairstyle as he annoyingly had, and he couldn't hear his voice as he helped their mother around the house. One year on he could still remember the touch and smell of him, though, unlike the rest of his family, to him the memory alone wasn't enough.

The photo had been taken the Christmas before last, just six months before he went missing. Once a week, Jack would call around to his mother's house, where Donal lived—the only one of six siblings who remained. Apart from the small talk between Jack and Donal that lasted for no more than two minutes at a time, that Christmas was the last occasion Jack had spoken to Donal properly. Donal had given him the usual present of socks and Jack had given him the box of handkerchiefs his oldest sister had given him the year before. They'd both laughed at the thoughtlessness of their gifts.

That day, Donal had been animated, happy with his new job as a computer technician. He'd begun it in September after graduating from Limerick University; a ceremony at which their mother had almost toppled off her chair, such was the weight of her pride for her baby. Donal had spoken confidently about how he enjoyed the work, and Jack could see how much he had matured and become more comfortable after leaving student life behind.

They had never been particularly close. In the family of six children, Donal was the surprise baby, nobody more surprised than their mother, Frances, who was forty-seven at the time she learned of the pregnancy. Being twelve years older than Donal meant that Jack had moved out of the house by the time Donal was six. He lost out in knowing the secret sides to his brother that only living with someone brought, and so for the past eighteen years they had been brothers, but not friends.

Jack wondered not for the first time whether, if he had known Donal better, he could have solved part of the mystery. Maybe if he'd worked harder at getting to know his little brother or had had more conversations about something rather than nothing, then perhaps he could have been out with him on the night of his birthday. Maybe he could have prevented him from leaving that fast-food restaurant or maybe he could have left with him and shared a taxi.

Or maybe Jack would have found himself in the same place as Donal was right now. Wherever that place was.

— 8 —

Jack slugged back his third cup of coffee and looked at his watch. Ten fifteen.

Sandy Shortt was late. His legs bounced up and down nervously beneath the table, his left hand drummed on the wood and his right hand signaled for another coffee. His mind stayed positive. She was coming. He knew she would come.

Eleven A.M., he tried calling her mobile number for the fifth time. It rang and rang and finally, "Hello, this is Sandy Shortt. Sorry I'm not available at the moment. Leave a message and I'll call you back as soon as I can."

Jack hung up.

Eleven thirty, she was two hours late and once again Jack listened to the voice message Sandy had left the previous night.

"Hi, Jack, Sandy Shortt here. I'm ringing to confirm our meeting tomorrow at nine thirty A.M. in Kitty's Café in Glin. I'm driving down tonight." Her tone softened. "As you know, I don't sleep," she laughed lightly. "So I'll be there early tomorrow. After all our conversations I look forward to finally speaking with you in person, and Jack"—she paused—"I promise you I'll do my best to help you. We won't give up on Donal."

Twelve o'clock, Jack played it again.

At one o'clock, after countless cups of coffee, Jack's fingers stopped drumming and instead made a fist for his chin to rest on. He had felt the café owner's gaze on his back as he sat for hours waiting nervously, watching the clock, and not giving up his table to a group willing to spend more money than he. Tables filled and emptied around him; his head snapped up every time the bell over the door rang. He didn't know what Sandy Shortt looked like; all she had said was that he couldn't miss her. He didn't know what to expect but each time the bell tinkled, his head and his heart both lifted with hope and then fell as the newcomer's gaze flitted past his and settled on another.

At two thirty, the bell rang once more.

After five and a half hours of waiting, it was the sound of the door opening and closing behind Jack.

9

For almost two days I'd stayed in the same wooded area, jogging back and forth trying to re-create my movements and somehow reverse my arrival here. I ran up and down the mountainside, testing different speeds as I struggled to remember how fast I'd been running, what song I'd been listening to, what I'd been thinking of, and what arca I was in when I first noticed the change in my location. As though any of those things had any part in what happened. I walked up and down, down and up, searching for the point of entry and, more importantly, the point of exit. I didn't want to sleep, I wanted to keep busy. I didn't want to settle like the personal possessions scattered around; I didn't want to end up like the backless earrings that glinted from the long grass.

Thinking you're missing is a bizarre conclusion to arrive at. I'm well aware of that. But it wasn't a sudden conclusion, believe me. I was hugely confused and frustrated for those first few hours but I knew that something more extraordinary than taking a wrong turn had occurred because geographically, a mountain couldn't just rise from the ground in a matter of seconds, trees that had never grown before in Ireland couldn't all of a sudden sprout from the ground, and the Shannon Estuary couldn't dry up and disappear. I wasn't simply lost—I was somewhere else.

I did, of course, contemplate the fact that I was dreaming, that I had fallen and hit my head and was currently in a coma or that I'd died. I did wonder about whether the anomalous nature of the countryside was pointing toward the end of the world and I questioned my knowledge of the geography of West Limerick. I did indeed consider very strongly the fact that I'd lost my mind. This was number one on the list of possibilities.

But when I sat alone for those days and thought rationally, surrounded by the most beautiful scenery I'd ever seen, I realized that I was most certainly alive, the world had not ended, mass panic hadn't taken over, and I was not just another occupant of a junk-yard. I realized that my searching for a way out was clouding my view of where exactly I was. I wasn't going to hide behind the lie that I could find a way out by running up and down a hill. No deliberate distractions to block out the voice of reason for me. I am a logical person and the most logical explanation out of all of the incredible possibilities was that I was alive and well but missing. Things are as they are, no matter how bizarre.

Just as it was beginning to get dark on my second day, I decided to explore this curious new place by walking deeper through the pine trees. Sticks cracked beneath my sneakers, the ground was soft and bouncy, covered with layers of fallen, now decayed leaves, bark, pine cones, and velvet-like moss. Mist hovered like wispy cotton above my head and stretched to the tips of the trees. The lofty, thin trunks extended up like towering wooden pencils that colored the sky. During the day they tinted the ceiling a clear blue, shading wispy clouds and orange pigment, and now by night the charcoaled tips, burned from the hot sun, darkened the heavens. The sky twinkled with a million stars, all winking at me, sharing a secret between them, of the world I could never know.

I should have been afraid, walking through a mountainside in the dark by myself. Instead I felt safe, surrounded by the songs of birds, engulfed by the scents of sweet moss and pine, and cocooned in a mist that contained a little bit of magic. I had been in many unusual situations before: the dangerous and the plain bizarre. In my line of work I followed all leads, wandered down all paths and never allowed fear to cause me to turn away from a direction that could lead me to finding someone. I wasn't afraid to turn over every stone that lay in my path or hurl them and my questions around atmospheres with the fragility of glass houses. When individuals go missing it's usually under dark circumstances most people don't want to know about. Compared to the previous experiences of delving into the underworld, this new project was literally a walk in the park. Yes, my finding my way back into my life had become a project.

The sound of murmuring voices up ahead stopped me in my tracks. I hadn't had human contact for days and wasn't at all sure if these people would be friendly. The flickering light of a campfire cast shadows around the woods, and as I quietly neared, I could see a clearing. The trees fell away to a large circle where five people sat laughing, joking, and singing to music. I stood hidden in the shadows of the giant conifer, but like a hesitant moth being drawn to a flame. Irish accents were audible and I questioned my ludicrous assessment of being outside the country and of being outside my life. In those few seconds I questioned everything.

A branch snapped loudly beneath my foot and it echoed around the forest. The music immediately stopped and the voices quietened.

"Someone's there," a woman whispered loudly.

All heads turned toward me.

"Hello, there!" a jovial man called excitedly. "Come! Join us! We're just about to sing 'This Little Light of Mine.'" There was a groan from the group.

The man jumped up from his seat on a fallen tree trunk and came closer to me with his arms held open in welcome. His head was bald apart from four strands of hair, which hung spaghettilike in a comb-over style. He had a friendly moon-shaped face and so I stepped into the light and instantly felt the warmth of the fire against my skin.

"It's a woman," the woman's voice whispered loudly again.

I wasn't sure what to say and the man who had approached me looked now uncertainly back to his group.

"Maybe she doesn't speak English," the woman hissed loudly.

"Ah," the man turned back to me, "Doooo yooooou speeeeeaaaaak Eng-a-lish?"

There was a grumble from the group, "*The Oxford English Dictionary* wouldn't understand that, Bernard."

I smiled and nodded. The group had quietened and were studying me and I knew what they were all thinking: she's tall.

"Ah, great." His hands clapped together and remained clasped close to his chest. His face broke into an even more welcoming smile. "Where are you from?"

I didn't know whether to say Earth, Ireland, or Leitrim. I went with my gut instincts and "Ireland" was all that came out of my mouth, which hadn't spoken for days.

"Splendid!" The cheery fellow's smile was so bright and I couldn't help but return it. "What a coincidence! Please come and join us." He excitedly led me toward the group with a hop, skip, and a jump.

"My name is Bernard," he beamed like the Cheshire cat, "and heartiest welcome to the Irish contingency. We're frightfully outnumbered here," he said, frowning, "although it seems that the numbers are rising. Excuse me, where are my manners?" His cheeks flushed.

"Underneath that sock over there."

I turned to look at the source of the smart comment to see an attractive woman in her fifties, tight salt-and-pepper hair, with a lilac pashmina shawl draped around her shoulders. She was staring distantly into the center fire, the dancing flames reflecting in her dark eyes, her comments flowing out of her mouth as though she were on autopilot.

"Who have I the pleasure of being acquainted with?" Bernard beamed with excitement; his neck craned up to look at me.

"My name is Sandy," I replied, "Sandy Shortt."

"Splendid." His cheeks flushed again and he shook my outstretched hand, "It's a pleasure to meet you. Allow me to introduce you to the rest of the gang, as they say."

"As who say?" the woman grumbled irately.

"That's Helena. She loves to chat. Always has something to say, don't you, Helena?" Bernard looked at her for an answer.

The wrinkles around her mouth deepened as she pursed her lips.

"Ah." He wiped his brow and turned to introduce me to a woman named Joan; Derek, the long-haired hippie playing the guitar; and Marcus, who was sitting quietly in the corner. I took them in quickly: they were all of a similar age and seemed very comfortable with one another. Not even Helena's sarcastic comments were causing any friction.

"Why don't you take a seat and I'll get you a drink of some sort—"

"Where are we?" I cut in, unable to take his bumbling pleasantries any longer.

All other conversation around the fire stopped suddenly and even Helena raised her head to stare at me. She took me in, a quick glance up and down, and I felt like my soul had been absorbed. Derek stopped strumming his guitar, Marcus smiled lightly and looked away, Joan and Bernard stared at me with wide frightened Bambi eyes. All that could be heard was the sound of the campfire crackling and popping as sparks sprang out and spiraled their way up to the sky. Owls hooted and there was the distant snap of branches being stepped on by wanderers beyond.

There was a deathly silence around the campfire.

"Is anyone going to answer the girl?" Helena looked around with an amused expression. Nobody spoke. "Well, if nobody speaks up," she wrapped her shawl tighter around her shoulders and grasped it at her chest, "I'm going to give my opinion."

Voices of objection rose from the circle and I immediately wanted to hear Helena's opinion all the more. Her eyes danced, enjoying the choir of disapproval.

"Tell me, Helena," I interrupted, feeling my usual impatience with people return. I always wanted to get to the point. I hated pussyfooting around.

"Oh, you don't want that, trust me," Bernard fluffed, his double chin wobbling as he spoke.

Helena lifted her silver-haired head in defiance and her dark eyes glistened as she looked at me directly. Her mouth twitched at the side. "We're dead."

Two words said coolly, calmly, crisply.

"Now, now, don't you mind her," Bernard said in what I imagined was his best angry voice.

"Helena," Joan admonished, "we've been through this before. You shouldn't scare Sandy like that."

"She doesn't look scared to me," Helena said, still with that amused expression, her eyes unmoving.

"Well," Marcus finally spoke after his long silence since I'd joined the group, "she may have a point. We may very well be dead."

Bernard and Joan groaned, and Derek began strumming lightly on his guitar and singing softly, "We're dead, we may very well be dead."

Bernard tutted, then poured tea from a china pot into

a cup and handed it to me on a saucer. In the middle of the woods, I couldn't help but smile.

"If we're dead, then where are my parents, Helena?" Joan scolded, emptying a packet of biscuits onto a china plate and placing them before me. "Where are all the other dead people?"

"In hell," Helena said in a singsong voice.

Marcus smiled and looked away so that Joan wouldn't see his face.

"And what makes you think we're in heaven? What makes you think *you'd* get into heaven?" Joan huffed, dunking her biscuit into her tea and pulling it up before the soggy end fell in.

Derek strummed and sang gruffly, "Is this heaven or is this hell? I look around and I can't tell."

"Didn't anybody else notice the Pearly Gates and the choir of angels as they entered, or was it just me?" Helena smirked.

"You didn't enter through Pearly Gates." Bernard shook his head wildly, his neck wobbling from side to side. He looked at me and his neck continued to shake. "She didn't enter through Pearly Gates."

Derek strummed, "I didn't pass the Pearly Gate nor felt the burning flames of hate."

"Oh, stop it," Joan huffed.

"Stop it," he sang.

"I can't bear any more."

"I can't bear any more, someone please show me the door . . ."

"I'll show you the door," Helena warned, but with less conviction.

He continued strumming and they all fell silent, contemplating his last few lyrics.

"Little June, Pauline O'Connor's daughter, was only ten when she died, Helena," Bernard continued. "Surely a little angel like her would be in heaven and she's not here, so there goes your theory." He held his head high and Joan nodded in agreement. "We're not dead."

"Sorry, it's over-eighteens only," Helena said in a bored tone. "Saint Peter's down at the gate with his arms folded and an earpiece in his ear, taking instructions from God."

"You can't say that, Helena," Joan snapped.

"I can't get in, I can't get out, Saint Peter, what's it all about?" Derek sang in a gravelly voice. Suddenly he stopped strumming and finally spoke. "It's definitely not heaven. Elvis isn't here."

"Oh, *well then*." Helena rolled her eyes.

"We've got our own Elvis here, haven't we?" Bernard said, chuckling, changing the subject. "Sandy, did you know that Derek used to be in a band?"

"How would she know that, Bernard?" Helena said, exasperated.

Bernard ignored her again. "Derek Cummings," he announced, "the hottest property in St. Kevin's back in the sixties."

They all laughed.

My body turned cold.

"What was it you were called, Derek? I've forgotten now," Joan said with a laugh.

"The Wonder Boys, Joan, the Wonder Boys," Derek said fondly, reminiscing.

"Remember the dances on a Friday night?" Bernard asked excitedly. "Derek would be up there on the stage, playing rock and roll, and Father Martin would be almost having a heart attack at him shaking his pelvis." They all laughed again.

"Now, what was the name of the dance hall?" Joan thought aloud.

"Oh, gosh . . ." Bernard closed his eyes and tried to remember.

Derek stopped strumming and thought hard.

Helena kept staring at me, watching my reactions. "Are you cold, Sandy?" Her voice sounded far away.

Finbar's Hall. The name jumped into my head. They had all loved going to Finbar's Hall every Friday night.

"Finbar's Hall," Marcus finally remembered.

"Ah, that was it." They all looked relieved and Derek's strumming continued.

Goose pimples formed on my skin. I shivered.

I looked around at the faces of the group, studied their eyes, their familiar features, and I allowed all I had learned as a little girl to come flooding back to me. I could see it now as clearly as I had then, when I came across the story in the computer archives while researching a project for school. I had immediately taken interest, had followed up on the story and was more than familiar with it. I saw the young teenage faces smiling up from the newspaper's front page and I saw those same faces around me now.

Derek Cummings, Joan Hatchard, Bernard Lynch, Marcus Flynn, and Helena Dickens. Five students from

St. Kevin's Boarding School. They disappeared during a school camping trip in the sixties and were never found. But here they were now, older, wiser, and their innocence lost.

I had found them.

10

When I was fourteen, my parents talked me into seeing a counselor after school on Mondays. They didn't have to do much convincing. As soon as they told me I'd be able to ask all the questions I wanted and that this person was qualified enough to answer, I practically drove myself to school.

I knew they felt that they had failed me. I could tell that by their expressions when they sat me down at the kitchen table, with the milk and cookies in the center and the washing machine going in the background as the usual distraction. Mum held a rolled tissue tightly in her hands as though she had used it earlier to dab away tears. That was the thing with my parents: they would never let me see their weaknesses, yet they would forget to get rid of the proof of them. I didn't see Mum's tears but I saw the tissue. I didn't hear Dad's anger at having failed to help me but I saw it in his eyes.

"Is everything OK?" I looked from one strong face to the other. The only time two people can look so confident and as though they can face anything is when something bad happens. "Did something happen?"

Dad smiled. "No, honey, don't worry, nothing bad happened."

Mum's eyebrow lifted when he said that and I knew she didn't agree. I knew Dad didn't agree with his words either but he was saying them nonetheless. There was nothing wrong with sending me to a counselor, nothing wrong at all, but I knew that they had wanted to help me themselves. They had wanted their answers to my questions to be enough. I overheard their endless discussions about the correct method of dealing with my behavior. They had helped me in every way they could and now I could feel their disappointment in themselves and I hated myself for making them feel that way.

"You know the way you have so many questions, honey?" Dad explained.

I nodded.

"Well, your mum and I"—he looked to her for support and her eyes softened immediately as she glanced at him—"well, your mum and I have found someone that you'll be able to talk to about all of those questions."

"This person will be able to answer my questions?" I felt my eyes widen and my heart quicken as though all of life's mysteries were about to be answered.

"I hope so, honey," Mum answered. "I hope that by talking to him, you won't have any more questions that will bother you. He'll know far more about all the things you worry about than we do."

Then it was time for my lightning round. Fingers on the buzzers.

"Who is he?"

"Mr. Burton." Dad.

"What's his first name?"

"Gregory." Mum.

"Where does he work?"

"At the school." Mum.

"When will I see him?"

"Mondays after school. For an hour." Mum. She was better at this than Dad. She was used to these discussions while Dad was out working.

"He's a psychiatrist, isn't he?" They never lied to me.

"Yes, honey." Dad.

I think that's the moment I began to hate seeing myself in their eyes, and unfortunately it was when I began to dislike being in their company.

Mr. Burton's office was in a room the size of a closet, just about big enough for two armchairs. I chose to sit in the dirty olive-green-velvet-covered chair with dark wooden handles, as opposed to the stained brown-velvet-covered chair. They both looked like they dated from the forties and hadn't been washed or removed from the small room since. There was a little window so high up on the back wall that all I could see was the sky. The first day I met Mr. Burton it was a clear blue. Every now and then a cloud passed, filling the entire window with white before moving on.

On the walls were posters of school kids looking happy and declaring to the empty room how they had said no to drugs, spoke out against bullying, coped with exam stress, had beaten eating disorders, dealt with grief, were clever enough to not have to face teenage pregnancy because they didn't have sex, but on the off chance that they did, there was another poster of the same girl and boy saying how they used condoms. Saints, the lot of them. The room was so positive I thought I was going to be ejected from my chair like a rocket. Mr. Burton the magnificent had helped them all.

I expected Mr. Burton to be a wise old man with a head of wild gray hair, a monocle in one eye, a waistcoat with a pocket watch attached by a chain, a brain exploding with knowledge after years of extensive research into the human mind. I expected Yoda of the Western world, cloaked in wisdom, who spoke in riddles and tried to convince me that the Force in me was strong.

When the real Mr. Burton entered the room I had mixed feelings. The inquisitive side of me was disappointed; the fourteen-year-old in me positively delighted. He was more of a Gregory than a Mr. Burton. He was young and handsome, sexy and gorgeous. He looked like he had just walked out of college that very day, in his jeans and T-shirt and fashionable haircut. I did my usual calculations: twice my age could work. In a few years it would be legal and I would be out of school. My whole life was mapped out before he had even closed the door behind him.

"Hello, Sandy." His voice was bright and cheery. He shook my hand and I vowed to lick it when I got home and never wash it again. He sat on the brown velvet armchair across from me. I bet all those girls in the posters invented all those problems just to come into this office.

"I hope you're comfortable in our designer, top-of-the-line furniture?" He wrinkled his nose in disgust as he settled into the chair, which had burst at the side and had foam spilling out.

I laughed. Oh, he was so cool. "Yes, thanks. I was wondering what you would think my choice of chair says about me."

"Well," he said with a smile, "it says one of two things."

I listened intently.

"First, that you don't like brown, or second, that you like green."

"Neither." I smiled. "I just wanted to face the window."

"A-ha." he grinned. "You are what we call at the lab a 'window facer.'"

"Ah, I'm one of *those*."

He looked at me with amusement for a second, then placed a pen and pad on his lap and a tape recorder on the arm of the chair. "Do you mind if I record this?"

"Why?"

"So I can remember everything that you say. Sometimes I don't pick up on things until I listen back over the conversation."

"OK, what's the pen and pad for, then?"

"Doodling. In case I get bored listening to you." He pressed RECORD and said that day's date and time.

"I feel like I'm at a police station, about to be interrogated."

"Has that ever happened before?"

I nodded. "When Jenny-May Butler went missing, we were asked to give any information we had at the school." How quickly talk had come around to her. She would have been delighted at the attention.

"Ah," he nodded. "Jenny-May was your friend, wasn't she?"

I thought about that. I looked at the anti-bullying posters on the wall and wondered how to answer. I didn't want to seem insensitive to this gorgeous man by saying no, but she wasn't my friend. Jenny-May hated me. But she was missing and I probably shouldn't speak badly of her because, after all, everyone thought she was an angel. Mr. Burton mistook my silence for being upset, which was embarrassing, and the next question he asked, his voice was so gentle I almost burst out laughing.

"Do you miss her?"

I thought about that one, too. *Would you miss a slap across the face every day?* I felt like asking him. Once again I didn't want him to think I was insensitive by saying no. He'd never fall in love with me and take me away from Leitrim then.

He leaned forward in his chair. Oh, his eyes were so blue.

"Your mum and dad told me you want to find Jenny-May, is this true?"

Wow. Talk about getting the wrong end of the stick. I rolled my eyes, OK, enough of this crap. "Mr. Burton, I don't want to seem rude or insensitive here because I know Jenny-May is missing and everyone is sad but . . ."

"Go on," he encouraged me, and I wanted to jump on him and kiss him.

"Well, me and Jenny-May were never friends. She hated me. I miss her in a way that I notice she's gone but not in a way that I want her back. And I don't want her back or to find her. Just knowing where she is would be enough."

He raised his eyebrows.

"Now, I know you probably thought that because Jenny-May was my friend and she went missing, that every time I lose something, like a sock, and try to find it, it's like my way of finding Jenny-May and bringing her back."

His mouth dropped open a little.

"Well, it's a reasonable assumption, I suppose, Mr. Burton, but it's just not me. I'm really not that complicated. It's just annoying that when things go missing, I don't know where they go. Take, for instance, the Scotch tape. Last night Mum was trying to wrap a present for Aunt Deirdre's birthday but she couldn't find the Scotch tape. Now, we always leave it in the second drawer under the cutlery drawer. It's always there, we never put it anywhere else, and my mum and dad know how I am about things like that and so they really do put everything in their places. Our house is really tidy, honestly, so it's not like things just get lost all the time in a mess. Anyway I used the Scotch tape on Saturday when I was doing my art homework, for which I got a crappy C today, by the way, even though Tracey Tinsleton got an A for drawing what looks like a squashed fly on a windscreen and that's considered 'real art,' but I promise I put it back in the drawer. Dad didn't use it, Mum didn't use it, and I'm almost certain no one broke into the house just to steal some Scotch tape. So I searched all evening for it but I couldn't find it. Where is it?"

Mr. Burton was silent and slowly moved back and settled into his chair.

"So let me get this straight," he said slowly. "You don't miss Jenny-May Butler."

We both started laughing and for the first time ever, I didn't feel bad about it.

"Why do you think you're here?" Mr. Burton got serious again after our bout of laughter.

"Because I need answers."

"Answers like . . . ?"

I thought about it. "Where is the Scotch tape that we couldn't find last night? Where is Jenny-May Butler? Why does one of my socks always go missing in the washing machine?"

"You think I can tell you where all these things are?"

"Not specifics, Mr. Burton, but a general indication would be fine."

He smiled at me. "Why don't you let me ask you the questions for a moment, and maybe through your answers, we'll find the answers you want."

"OK, if you think that'll work." Weirdo.

"Why do you feel the need to know where things are?"

"I have to know."

"Why do you feel you have to know?"

"Why do you feel you have to ask me questions?"

Mr. Burton blinked and was silent for a second longer than he wanted, I could tell. "It's my job and I get paid to do it."

"Paid to do it." I rolled my eyes. "Mr. Burton, you

could have my Saturday job stacking toilet rolls and get paid but you chose to study for what, ten million years? To get all of those scrolls you've hung on the walls." I looked around at his framed qualifications. "I'd say you went through all of that studying, all of those exams, and ask all these questions for more reasons than just getting paid."

He smiled lightly and watched me. I don't think he knew what else to say. And so there was a two-minute silence while he thought. Finally he put down his pen and paper and leaned toward me, resting his elbows on his knees.

"I like to have conversations with people, I always have. I find that through talking about themselves people learn things that they didn't know before. It's a kind of self-healing. I ask questions because I like to help people."

"And so do I."

"You feel by asking questions about Jenny-May, you're helping her or maybe her parents?" He tried to hide the confusion from his eyes.

"No, I'm helping myself."

"How does it help you? Isn't *not* getting the answers frustrating you even more?"

"Sometimes I find things, Mr. Burton. I find the things that have just been misplaced."

"Isn't everything that's lost, misplaced?"

"To misplace something is to lose it temporarily by forgetting where you put it. I always remember where I put things. It's the things that I *don't* misplace that I try to find—the things that grow legs and walk away all by themselves—that annoy me."

"Do you think it's possible that somebody else, other than you, moves all these things?"

"Like who?"

"I'm asking you."

"Well, in the case of the Scotch tape the answer is clearly no. In the case of the socks, unless somebody reaches into the washing machine and takes out my socks, then the answer is no. Mr. Burton, my parents want to help me. I don't think that they would move things and then forget about it every single time. If anything, they are more aware of exactly where they put things."

"So what is your assumption? Where do you think these things are?"

"Mr. Burton, if I had an assumption, then I wouldn't be here."

"You have no idea, then? Even in your wildest dreams, during your most frustrating times when you're vigorously searching into the early hours of the morning and you still can't find it, have you any opinion *at all* as to where you think the missing things are?"

Well, he'd clearly learned more about me from my parents than I thought, but having to answer this question truthfully, I feared, would mean he'd never fall in love with me. But I took a deep breath and told the truth anyway. "At times like that I'm convinced they are in a place where missing things go."

He didn't miss a beat. "Do you think Jenny-May is there? Does it make you feel better to think that she's there?"

"Oh, God." I rolled my eyes. "If someone killed her,

Mr. Burton, they killed her. I'm not trying to create imaginary worlds to make myself feel better."

He tried very hard not to move a muscle in his face.

"But whether she's alive now or not, why haven't the Gardaí been able to find her?"

"Would it make you feel better to just accept that sometimes there are mysteries?"

"You don't accept that, why should I?"

"What makes you think I don't?"

"You're a counselor. You believe that every action has a reaction and all that kind of stuff, I read up on it before I came here. Everything that I do now is because of something that happened, something somebody said or did. You believe there are answers to everything and ways of solving everything."

"That's not necessarily true. I can't fix everything, Sandy."

"Can you fix me?"

"You're not broken."

"Is that your medical opinion?"

"I'm not a doctor."

"Aren't you a 'doctor of the mind'?" I held up my fingers in quotation marks and rolled my eyes.

Silence.

"How do you feel when you are searching and searching but you still can't find whatever it is that you're looking for?"

I could tell this was the weirdest conversation he had ever had.

"Have you a girlfriend, Mr. Burton?"

His forehead creased. "Sandy, I'm not sure that this is relevant." When I didn't answer, he sighed. "No, I don't."

"Do you want one?"

He was contemplative. "Are you saying that the feeling of searching for a missing sock is like searching for love?" He tried to ask the question without making me sound stupid but he failed miserably.

I rolled my eyes again. He was making me do that a lot. "No, it's a feeling of knowing something is missing in your life but not being able to find it, no matter how hard you look."

He cleared his throat awkwardly, picked up his pen and paper and pretended to write something.

Doodle time. "Boring you, am I?"

He laughed and it broke the tension.

I tried to explain again. "Perhaps it would have been easier if I said that not being able to find something is like suddenly not remembering the words to your favorite song that you knew by heart. It's like suddenly forgetting the name of someone you know really well and see every day, or the name of a television show you watched for years. It's something so frustrating that it plays on your mind over and over again because you know there's an answer but no one can tell you it. It niggles and niggles at me and I can't rest until I know the answers."

"I understand," he said softly.

"Well, then, multiply that feeling by one hundred."

He was contemplative. "You're mature for your age, Sandy."

"Funny, because I was hoping you'd know an awful lot more for yours."

He laughed until our time was up.

That night at dinner Dad asked me how it went.

"He couldn't answer my questions," I replied, slurping on my soup.

Dad looked like his heart was going to break. "So I suppose you don't want to go back."

"No!" I said quickly and my mum tried to hide her smile by taking a sip of water.

Dad looked back and forth from her face to mine questioningly.

"He has nice eyes," I offered by way of explanation, slurping again.

His eyebrows rose and he looked to my mum, who had a grin from ear to ear and flushed cheeks. "That's true, Harold. He has very nice eyes."

"Ah, *well then*!" He threw his arms up. "If the man has nice eyes for Christ's sake, who am I to argue?"

Later that night I lay on my bed and thought about my conversation with Mr. Burton. He may not have had answers for me but he sure cured me of searching for one thing.

— 11 —

I went to see Mr. Burton every week while I was at St. Mary's Secondary School. We even met up during the summer months when the school remained open to the rest of the town for summer activities. The last time I went to see him was when I had just turned eighteen. I'd finished my leaving certificate the previous year and I'd found out that morning I'd been accepted into the Gardaí Síochana. I was due to move to Cork in a few months to train at Templemore.

"Hello, Mr. Burton," I said as he entered the small office that hadn't changed one bit since the first day we met. He was still young and handsome and I loved every inch of him.

"Sandy, for the hundredth time, stop calling me Mr. Burton. You make me sound like an old man."

"You are an old man," I teased.

"Which makes you an old woman," he said lightly, and a silence fell between us. "So"—he became businesslike—"what's on your mind this week?"

"I got accepted into the Gardaí today."

His eyes widened. Happiness? Sadness? "Wow, Sandy,

congratulations. You did it!" He came over and gave me a hug. We held on a second longer than we should have.

"How do your mum and dad feel?"

"They don't know yet."

"They'll be sad to see you go."

"It's for the best." I looked away.

"You won't leave all your problems behind in Leitrim, you know," he said gently.

"No, but I'll leave behind the people who know about them."

"Do you plan on coming back to visit?"

I stared him directly in the eyes. Were we still talking about my parents? "As much as I can."

"How much will that be?"

I shrugged.

"They have always supported you, Sandy."

"I can't be who they want me to be, Mr. Burton. I make them uncomfortable."

He rolled his eyes at me calling him that, at my deliberate attempts to build a wall between us. "They just want you to be you, you know that. Don't be ashamed of the way you are. They love you for who you are."

The way he looked at me made me wonder again if we were talking about my parents at all. I looked around the room. He knew everything about me, absolutely everything, and I sensed everything about him. He was still single and living alone, despite every girl in Leitrim town chasing him. He tried to tell me week after week to accept things as they were and move on with life, but if there was one man who had put his life on hold to wait for something, or someone, it was him.

He cleared his throat. "I heard you went out with Andy McCarthy this weekend."

"And?"

He rubbed his face wearily and allowed a silence to fall between us. We were both good at that. Four years of therapy, of me baring my soul, yet every new word was a word farther from discussing the very thing that consumed my thoughts most moments of most days.

"So come on, talk to me," he said softly.

Our last session and I couldn't think of anything. He still had no answers for me.

"Are you going to the costume party on Friday?" He picked up the mood of the atmosphere.

"Yes," I smiled. "I can't think of a better way to say good-bye to this place than to walk out being dressed as something else."

"What are you dressing up as?"

"A sock."

He laughed so hard. I knew he, of all people, would get the joke. "Andy isn't going with you?"

"Do my socks ever come as a pair?"

He raised his eyebrows, indicating he wanted to know more.

"He didn't 'get' why I turned his flat upside down when I couldn't find the invite."

"Where do you think it is?"

"With everything else. With my mind." I rubbed my eyes wearily.

"You haven't lost your mind, Sandy. So you're going to be a garda." His smile was shaky.

"Worried about the future of our country?"

"No." He smiled. "At least I know we'll be in safe hands. You'll be questioning criminals to death."

"I learned from the best." I forced myself to smile.

Mr. Burton turned up at the costume party that Friday night—dressed as a sock. I'd laughed so hard. He drove me home that night and we sat in silence. After so many years of talking, neither of us knew what to say. Outside my house he leaned over and kissed my lips hungrily; long and hard. It was like our hello and a good-bye all at once.

"Pity we're not the same pattern, Gregory. We would have made a good pair," I said sadly.

I wanted him to tell me that we'd make the most perfect odd pair around but I think he agreed because I watched him drive away.

The more partners I had, the more I realized Gregory and I were the best pair I'd ever come across. But in my pursuit of answers to all the difficult questions in my life, I missed out on the obvious ones right in front of my very eyes.

12

Helena was watching me curiously through the amber blaze of the campfire, the shadow of the flames dancing upward to lick her face. The other members of the group had continued with their reminiscing of Derek's rock-and-roll days, happy to move the subject away from my question about where we were. Excited chatter had resumed but I remained on the outside, though I was not alone. Finally, I lifted my eyes from the ash floor and allowed them to meet Helena's.

She waited for a silence to fall among the group before asking, "What do you do for a living, Sandy?"

"Oooh, yes," Joan said excitedly, warming her hands around her teacup. "Do tell us."

I had everyone's attention and so I considered my options. Why lie?

"I run an agency," I began and then stopped.

"What kind of an agency?" Bernard asked.

"A modeling agency is it?" Joan asked in hushed tones. "With long legs like yours, I'll bet it is." Her teacup rested in her hands not far below her lips, her pinky erect and standing tall like a dog on the hunt.

"Joan, she said she *runs* the agency, not is a *member* of one." Bernard shook his head and his chin wobbled.

"Actually, it's a missing-persons agency."

There was a silence as they searched my face. I shrugged as if to say "Yes, I'm aware of the irony," and when they all looked at each other, they erupted in laughter. All except Helena.

"Oh, Sandy, that was a good one." Bernard wiped the corners of his eyes with his handkerchief. "What kind of agency is it really?"

"Acting." Helena jumped in before I had a chance to answer.

"How do you know?" Bernard asked her, rather in a huff that she knew something before him. "You're the one who asked the question in the first place."

"She told me while you were all laughing." She waved her hand dismissively.

"An acting agency." Joan looked at me with wide eyes. "How wonderful. We had some excellent plays in Finbar's Hall," Joan explained. "Do you remember that?" She looked around at her friends. "*Julius Caesar, Romeo and Juliet*, to name but two of Shakespeare's finest works. Bernard was—"

Bernard coughed loudly.

"Oh, I'm sorry," Joan blushed, "Bernard *is* a fantastic actor. He played quite a convincing Bottom in *A Midsummer Night's Dream*. No doubt you would love him to be in your agency."

And they fell into their usual chatter of swapping old stories. Helena made her way round the fire and sat next to me.

"I must say, you excel in your occupation," Helena chuckled.

"Why did you do that?" I referred to her interjection.

"Oh, you don't want to tell them that, especially Joan, with her voice so hushed she feels the need to tell everybody everything just to make sure she's heard," she teased, but watched her friend fondly. "If anyone finds out you run a missing-persons agency you'll be swamped with questions. Everyone will think you'll have come to bring us all home." I wasn't sure whether she was joking or asking me a question. Either way, she didn't laugh and I didn't answer.

"Who else is there to tell around here?" I stared into the silent black woods. I hadn't come across any others for two days.

Helena looked at me curiously again. "Sandy, there *are* others, you know."

Apart from Ewoks, I found it hard to believe anybody else inhabited these dark and silent surroundings.

"You know our story, don't you?" Helena kept her voice low so that the others couldn't hear.

I nodded, took a deep breath, and recited, "'Five students are missing after disappearing during a school camping trip in Roundwood, County Wicklow. Sixteen-year-olds Derek Cummings, Helena Dickens, Marcus Flynn, Joan Hatchard, and Bernard Lynch from St. Kevin's Boarding School for Girls and Boys in Blackrock were due to visit Glendalough but were missing from their tents that morning.'"

Helena was gazing at me with such childlike intent and tear-filled eyes I felt a duty to recite the newspaper article word for word, pitch-perfect. I wanted to express the feeling in the country during that initial week; on behalf of the country, I wanted to convey accurately the outpour of love and support complete strangers had displayed toward the missing five students. I felt I owed it to all those people who prayed for their return. I felt Helena deserved to hear it.

" 'The Gardaí today said that they were following leads although they couldn't confirm ruling out foul play. They ask for anyone with any information to contact the Roundwood or Blackrock Gardaí. The students of St. Kevin's have all gathered to pray for their fellow students and locals have been placing flowers near the scene.' "

I was silent.

"What's wrong with your eyes, Helena?" Bernard asked worriedly.

"Oh," Helena said and sniffed, "it's nothing. Just a spark from the fire jumped into my eye, that's all." She dabbed her eyes with the corner of her pashmina.

"Oh, dear," Joan said, moving over and peering in her eye. "No, it looks fine to me, just red and watery. It probably just stings a bit."

"I'm fine, thanks," Helena dismissed them all, embarrassed by their care, and the others continued chatting among themselves.

"With acting like that you could join my agency," I smiled.

Helena laughed and fell silent again. I felt I should say something.

"They never gave up looking for you, you know."

Her mouth let out a tiny sound. A sound that was beyond her control to stop, a sound that had worked its way up straight from her heart.

"Your father championed every new Garda Commissioner and Minister for Justice that took office. He knocked on every door and searched between every blade of grass to find you. He made sure they searched the entire area with a fine-tooth comb. As for your mother, your amazing mother . . ."

Helena smiled at the mention of her mother.

"She set up an organization to help counsel families suffering the effects of missing loved ones, named Porch Light, as many families of the missing leave their front lights on as a beacon, hoping that someday their loved ones will return. She was tireless in her charity work, setting up bases all around the country. Your parents never, ever gave up. Your mother still hasn't."

"She's alive?" Her eyes widened and filled once again.

"Your father, I'm sorry, passed away some years ago." I allowed her to process the information before moving on. "Your mother is still actively involved with Porch Light. I attended their annual lunch last year and had the pleasure of meeting her and telling her how wonderful I thought she was." I looked down at my hands and cleared my throat, the role of messenger not always proving easy. "She told me to continue with my efforts, as she wished I could find her beloved daughter for her."

Helena's voice was barely a whisper. "Tell me about her."

And so I forgot about my own worries and settled down by the warmth of the campfire to do just that.

"I never wanted to go on the camping trip." Helena was exhilarated and full of emotion after I had filled her with knowledge of her mother. "I pleaded with them not to make me go."

I knew all this but I listened intently, fascinated to hear the story I knew so well, from one of its main characters. It was like seeing my favorite book come alive on stage.

"I'd wanted to go home that weekend. There was a boy . . ." She laughed and looked at me. "Isn't it always about a boy?"

I couldn't relate but smiled all the same.

"A new boy had moved into the house next door to us. Samuel James was his name, the most beautiful creature alive." Her eyes were bright, as though the fire's sparks had leaped in and set her pupils alight. "I met him that summer and fell in love and we had the most wonderful time together. *Sinful.*" She raised her eyebrows and I smiled. "I'd been back at school for two months and I missed him dreadfully. I begged and pleaded with my parents to let me go home but to no avail. They were punishing me," she said with a sad smile, "I'd been caught cheating in my history exam in the same week I'd been caught smoking behind the gymnasium. Unacceptable, even by my standards." She looked around the group, "And so I was stuck going away with this lot, as though separating me from my best friends would suddenly make me an angel. All the same, it turned out to be a punishment I don't think I entirely deserved."

"Of course not," I empathized. "How did you get here?"

Helena sighed, "Marcus and I made arrangements early in the evening to meet up when everyone had gone to sleep. He was the only one who had a packet of cigarettes so the other two boys went with him and, well, Joan"— Helena looked at her friend on the other side of the campfire with fondness—"she was afraid to stay in the tent by herself so she came too. We moved away from the camp so our teachers wouldn't see the cigarettes alight or smell the smoke. We didn't walk that far at all, just a few minutes or so, but we found ourselves here." She shrugged. "I can't really explain it any other way."

"That must have been terrifying for you all."

"No more than it was for you." She looked at me. "And at least we had each other, I couldn't imagine going through it all alone."

She wanted me to talk but I wouldn't. It wasn't in my nature to open up. Not unless it was with Gregory.

"You can't even have been born when we went missing. How do you know so much?"

"Let's just say I was an inquisitive child."

"Inquisitive indeed." She studied me again and I looked away, finding her glare intrusive. "Do you know what has happened to everybody's family here?" She nodded at the rest of the group.

"Yes." I looked around them all, seeing their parents' faces in each of them. "I made it my life's work to know. I followed up on all of you every year, wanting to see if anyone came home."

"Well, thank you for helping me feel one step closer to it now."

A silence fell between us, Helena no doubt lost in her memories of home.

Eventually she spoke again. "My grandmother was a proud woman, Sandy. She married my grandfather when she was eighteen years old and they had six children. Her younger sister, who they could never seem to marry off, embarked on a mysterious affair with a man she would never name and, to everybody's shock, gave birth to a baby boy." She chuckled. "That my grandfather's face was written all over that child was not lost on my grandmother, nor were the shillings that disappeared from their savings just as the new clothes appeared on the child. Of course, those things are entirely coincidental," she said in a singsong voice, stretching her legs out in front of her. "There are a great many brown-haired, blue-eyed men in the country, and the fact my grandfather had a fondness for drinking would explain the dents in their savings." Her eyes twinkled at me.

I looked at Helena in confusion. "I'm sorry, Helena, I'm not sure why you're telling me this."

She laughed. "That you have ended up here with us could be one of life's great coincidences."

I nodded.

"But my grandmother didn't believe in coincidences. And neither do I. You're here for a reason, Sandy."

13

Helena added another log to the dying fire and its weight sent a pile of adolescent ashes racing one another down the side of the burning tower. The flames were awakened from the embers and sleepily began to climb up the log, giving off heat to Helena and me.

I had been talking to her for hours, filling her in on all the details of her family life that I knew of. An unusual feeling had stirred within me, as soon as I'd realized whose company I was keeping. It washed over me in waves, each wave relaxing me, making my eyes that little bit heavier, causing my mind to tick that little bit slower, and for the tension in my muscles to relax just a little bit more. It was just a little bit, mind you, but it was something.

Throughout my life people had told me that my questions were irrelevant, my over-interest in cases of missing persons unnecessary, but right there in the woods every stupid, embarrassing, irrelevant, and unnecessary question I had ever asked about Helena Dickens meant the world to her. I knew there had been a reason for my endless searches, my infinite interrogations of myself and of others. And the greatest thing of all was that there wasn't just one reason for it all; sitting next to me by the campfire there were four others.

Oh, the relief. That's what the feeling was. The first sense of relief my mind had felt since I was ten years old.

The sky was growing brighter; the tips of the trees that had been burned by the sun by day had been cooled by the night and now shaded the cool blue sky. The birds that had been silent during the dark hours were now warming their vocal cords, like the idiosyncratic rendition of an orchestra tuning, pre-performance. Bernard, Derek, Marcus, and Joan lay asleep in their sleeping bags, covered by blankets and looking how they should have the night of their school camping trip. I wondered, had they slept soundly through that night instead of venturing into the woods, would they have been back in their families' arms all those years ago or would the secret door to this world have welcomed them in regardless?

Was it an accident that we were all here? Did we stumble upon a blip in the earth's creation, a black hole on the surface, or was this just a part of life that remained unspoken throughout the centuries? Were we lost and unaccounted for, or was this where we truly belonged and our normal lives the original error? Was this a place for those who felt like outsiders in life to belong, to finally feel relief? Despite my own relief, my questions kept flowing. The world around me had changed but some things remained constant.

"Were you happy?" I looked around at the others sleeping. "Was everybody happy?"

Helena smiled softly. "We've all asked the question

of why, and there is no answer that we know of. Yes, we were happy. We were all very, very happy in our lives." She paused. "Sandy . . ." She broke the silence again, watching me with that amused expression as if enjoying a private joke. "Believe it or not we're very happy here too. We've spent more years living here than anywhere else. The past is a distant but pleasurable memory for us."

I looked around the campfire. They had nothing. Nothing but small overnight bags packed with teabags, unnecessary chinaware and biscuits, blankets and sleeping bags, wraps and jumpers to keep warm, all of which they undoubtedly retrieved from the piles of belongings scattered around us. These five people had slept under the stars, swathed in blankets with a fire and a sun as their only source of light and heat. For forty years. How could they be truly happy? How could they not be clawing their way back to existence, back to material belongings and craving the companionship of others?

I shook my head as I looked around.

Helena laughed at me, "Why are you shaking your head?"

"I'm sorry." I was embarrassed at being caught pitying a life they seemed content with. "It's just that forty years is such a long time to settle"—I looked around at the clearing—"well . . . here."

Helena's face opened in surprise.

"Oh, I'm so sorry." I backtracked. "I didn't mean to offend you—"

"Sandy, Sandy," she interrupted, "*this* is not our whole world."

"I know, I know." I backed off. "You have each other and—"

"No." Helena started laughing and her forehead crumpled in confusion. "I'm sorry, I thought you knew this wasn't a permanent thing. We go camping together once a year on the anniversary of our disappearance. I thought you would recognize the date. This clearing is the first place we arrived at forty years ago—well, the first area where we *realized* we weren't at home anymore. We all stay in touch during the year but we live more or less separate lives."

"What?" I was confused.

"People go missing all the time, you know that. Wherever people gather, life begins, civilization exists. Sandy, fifteen minutes' walk from here, the woods end and a whole new life begins."

I was stunned. My mouth opened and closed but no words would come out.

"Interesting you should arrive here today of all days," Helena said, deep in thought.

I scrambled to my feet. "Come on, let's go now. Show me this place you're talking about. We won't disturb the others."

"No." Helena's voice was hard and her smile quickly faded. Her hand sprang up to grab my arm. I flinched and tried to pull away, not liking the human contact, but this did not rattle her. I couldn't move; the force of her hold was so strong. Her face was stony. "We do not just leave each other like that, we do not disappear from one another. We will sit here until they wake."

She loosened her grip on my arm and wrapped her

pashmina tighter around her body, retreating to the guarded woman she had been earlier in the evening. She watched her friends intently as though on duty and I realized it wasn't just me that had been keeping her awake all night. It was just her turn.

"We stay until they wake," she repeated firmly.

Jack sat on the corner of the bed and watched Gloria sleeping with a small smile on her face. It was the early hours of Monday morning and he had just returned home. After Sandy Shortt's no-show he had spent the entire day checking B&Bs and hotels in all the nearby towns to see if she had checked in anywhere. There were so many things that could have prevented her from arriving at the café; he convinced himself her no-show that morning didn't mean it was the end of their search. She could have just overslept and missed their meeting or gotten caught up in Dublin and couldn't leave for Limerick that night. There could have been a death in the family or a sudden lead in another case that took her away from Limerick. She could be heading toward him now, driving through the night to get to Glin. He had thought of endless possibilities, but not one of those theories was the idea that she could have deliberately let him down.

A mistake had been made, that was all. He would return to Glin later today on his lunch break to see if she had arrived. He had lived all week for that meeting and he wasn't going to give up now. Sandy had given him more hope in one week during a few phone conversations than anyone else had succeeded in doing over the entire year. He knew from their talks that she wouldn't let him down.

He was going to tell Gloria, he really was. He reached out to touch her shoulder and shake her gently but his hand stopped in midair. Maybe he should hold off on telling her until he made contact with Sandy again. Gloria sighed sleepily, stretched her body, and turned over.

She eventually settled on her side, her back toward Jack and his outstretched hand.

14

O nly a week before Sandy's no-show, Jack had quietly closed the bedroom door adjoining the living room so as not to disturb a sleeping Gloria. The Yellow Pages lying open on the couch stared back at him as he paced the far side of the room, one eye on the phone book, the other eye on the bedroom door. He stopped and traced his finger down the page until he came across the ad for Porch Light, the organization that helped counsel friends and relatives of the missing. Jack and his sister Judith had tried to convince their mother to talk to Porch Light after Donal's disappearance, but her old Irish ways of refusing to speak her private thoughts to a stranger held her back. Below the ad was the number for Sandy Shortt's missing-persons agency. He picked up his cell phone and switched on the television so as to cover the sound of his voice in case Gloria awoke. He dialed the number he had memorized when he first came across the advertisement. It rang twice before a female answered.

"Hello?"

Jack suddenly couldn't remember what to say.

"Hello?" The voice was softer this time. "Gregory, is that you?"

"No." Jack finally found his voice. "My name is Jack, Jack Ruttle. I got your number from the Yellow Pages."

"Oh, I'm sorry," the woman apologized and returned to her original businesslike tone. "I was expecting someone else. I'm Sandy Shortt," she said.

"Hello, Sandy." Jack paced the small cluttered living room, tripping over the unevenly rolled, mismatching rugs that adorned the old wooden floors. "I'm sorry to call so late." Get to the point, he hurried himself, pacing faster while he watched the bedroom door.

"Don't worry. A call at this hour of the night is an insomniac's dream, pardon the joke. How can I help you?"

He stopped pacing and held his head in his hand. What was he doing?

Sandy's voice was gentle again. "Is somebody you know missing?"

"Yes," was all Jack could reply.

"How long ago?" He could hear her rooting for paper.

"A year." He settled on the arm of the couch.

"What is this person's name?"

"Donal Ruttle." He swallowed the lump in his throat.

She paused, then: "Yes, Donal," a tone of recognition in her voice. "You're a relative?"

"Brother . . ." Jack's voice cracked and he knew he couldn't go on. He needed to stop now; he needed to move on like the rest of his family. He was stupid to think that an insomniac from the phone book with too much time on her hands could succeed where an entire garda search hadn't. "I'm sorry, I'm very, very sorry. This phone call was a mistake," he forced out. "I'm sorry for wasting your time." He quickly hung up the phone and fell back on the couch, embarrassed and exhausted, knocking against his files and sending pictures of a smiling Donal floating to the ground.

Moments later his mobile rang. He dived for it, not wanting the ring tone to waken Gloria.

"Donal?" he breathed, jumping to his feet.

"Jack, it's Sandy Shortt."

Silence.

"Is that how you usually answer the phone?" she asked gently.

He was lost for words.

"Because if it is and you're still expecting your brother to call, I don't think your phone call to me was a mistake, do you?"

His heart was hammering in his chest. "How did you get my number?"

"Caller ID."

"My number is blocked."

"I find people, Jack. That's what I do. And there's a chance that I can find Donal for you."

He glanced at all the photographs scattered around him, the cheeky smile of his younger brother staring up at him, silently daring him to seek him out as he had when he was a child.

"Are you back in?" she asked.

"I'm in," he replied, and he headed to the kitchen for a cup of coffee in preparation of the long night ahead.

The following night at two A.M., as Gloria lay asleep in bed, Jack lay on the couch, on the phone to Sandy, his hundreds of pages of garda reports scattered around him.

"You've spoken to Donal's friends, I see," Sandy said, and he could hear her leafing through the pages he'd faxed to her earlier in the day.

"Over and over again," he said wearily. "In fact, I'm going to call in to one of his friends again on Saturday while I'm in Tralee. I've got a dental appointment," he added casually and then wondered why.

"The dentist, yuck, I'd rather have my eyes gouged out," she murmured.

Jack laughed.

"Don't they have dentists in Foynes?"

"I have to see a specialist."

He could hear the smile in her voice. "Don't they have specialists in Limerick?"

"OK, OK," he said, laughing. "So I wanted to ask Donal's friend a few more questions."

"Tralee, Tralee," she repeated, rustling through paper. "A-ha." The paper rustling stopped. "Andrew in Tralee, friend from college, works as a Web designer."

"That's him."

"I don't think Andrew knows anything more, Jack."

"How do you know?"

"Judging by his answers during questioning."

"I didn't give you that file." Jack sat upright.

"I used to be a garda. Conveniently for me, it's about the only place I managed to make friends."

"I need to see those files." Jack's heart raced. There was something new, something more for him to stay awake at night analyzing.

"We can meet up soon," she dismissed him politely. "I suppose talking to Andrew again wouldn't hurt." There was a sound of her leafing through more pages and she was silent for a long time.

"What are you looking at?"

"Donal's photograph."

Jack picked it up from his pile and stared at it too. It was becoming too familiar to him; it was looking more like just a photograph and less like his brother every day.

"Good-looking guy," Sandy complimented. "Nice eyes. Do you two look alike?"

Jack laughed. "I feel inclined to say yes after that."

They continued studying the pages.

"You don't sleep?" Sandy asked.

"No, not since Donal went missing. What about you?"

"I've just never been a great sleeper."

He laughed.

"What?" she asked defensively.

"Nothing. You being a light sleeper is a great answer," he said playfully, dropping the pages onto his lap. In the deathly silence of the cottage he listened to the sound of Sandy's breathing and her voice and tried to imagine what she looked like, where she was, and what she was thinking.

After a long silence her voice was gentler. "I've a lot of

missing people on my mind. There's too much to think about, too many places to look to allow sleep to come. You can't find anyone or anything in dreams."

Jack looked toward the closed bedroom door and agreed.

"But why I told you that, I have no idea," she grumbled to the sound of more paper being shifted.

"Tell me honestly, Sandy, what's your success rate?"

Paper rustling stopped. "It depends of the level of the missing case. I'll be honest with you, cases like Donal's are difficult. There has already been a large-scale search and it's rare that I have found someone under these circumstances. But with general missing cases I find people around forty percent of the time. You should know that not all the people I find return to their families. You have to be prepared for that."

"I am prepared. If Donal's lying in a ditch somewhere I want him back here so we can bury him and give him a proper funeral."

"That's not what I mean. Sometimes people go missing deliberately."

"Donal wouldn't do that," Jack said dismissively.

"Perhaps not. But there have been situations, just like this, that I've learned that people, just like Donal, from families, just like yours, voluntarily move on from their lives without a word to anyone close to them."

Jack digested this. It hadn't occurred to him that Donal would take off of his own free will and he found this scenario hugely improbable. "Would you tell me where he was if you found him?"

"If he didn't want to be found? No, I couldn't tell you that."

"Would you tell me *if* you found him?"

"It depends on how prepared you are to accept being unable to know where he is."

"All I would want to know is that wherever he is, he's safe and happy."

"Well, then I would tell you."

After a long silence, Jack asked, "Is there much work for you? On the rare occasions that people go missing, don't their families turn to the Gardaí to deal with it?"

"That's true. There aren't many severe cases for me like Donal's, but there's always something or someone to find. There are categories of missing people that the Gardaí can't and won't investigate."

"Like what?"

"You really want to know this?"

"I want to know everything about it." Jack looked at the clock: two thirty A.M. "And besides, I've nothing better to do at this time of night."

"Well, sometimes I find people that others have merely lost contact with, long-lost relatives, old school friends, or adopted children trying to find their biological parents, that kind of thing. I work quite a lot alongside the Salvation Army, trying to trace people. Then there are the more serious cases such as people who have disappeared, many of them of their own volition, and families just want to know where they are."

"But how would the Gardaí know it was their choice?"

"Some people leave messages behind saying they don't

want to return." He could hear her unwrapping something in the background. "Sometimes they take their personal effects with them or sometimes people have previously expressed dissatisfaction with their situation."

"What are you eating?"

"A chocolate muffin," she replied with her mouth full. She swallowed. "Sorry, did you hear me properly?"

"Yeah, you're eating a chocolate muffin."

"No, not that." She laughed.

Jack smiled. "So the families come to you for cases the Gardaí can't deal with."

"Exactly. A lot of my work, using the help of other missing-persons agencies in Ireland, is in specifically tracking cases that aren't classed as high risk. If a person has left home of their own accord they won't be accepted as missing but it doesn't ease the worries of their families and friends."

"So they're just forgotten about?"

"No, a record will be made at the station but the extent of the enquiries is left to the discretion of the garda in charge of the station."

"What if somebody who was incredibly unhappy with his life packed his bags to be alone for a while, but then went missing? Nobody would look for him because he previously expressed a dislike of his life. And haven't we all done that at some point?"

Sandy was silent.

"Am I wrong in thinking that? Wouldn't you want to be found?"

"Jack, I can only assume that there's only one thing *more* frustrating than not being able to find someone, and that's not being found. I would want someone to find me, more than anything," she said firmly.

They both thought it over.

"I'd better go now." Jack yawned. "I've to be up for work in a few hours. Will you sleep now?"

"After I go through all these files again."

He shook his head in wonder. "Just so you know, if you'd told me you'd never found anyone, I'd still be on this phone."

She was quiet for a moment. "And if I'd never found anyone, I would be too."

15

Jack woke up earlier than Gloria, as usual. Her head rested on his chest, her long brown hair spread across his skin, tickling where it fell down alongside his ribs. He silently and very slowly moved his body from under hers and slipped out of bed. Gloria moaned sleepily and settled back down with a peaceful look on her face. He showered and dressed and left the bungalow before she had even stirred.

Every morning he left their home before she did to be at work at eight A.M. Gloria didn't start work as a guide in Foynes Flying Boat Museum until ten o'clock. The museum was Foynes' number-one tourist attraction, celebrating the era between 1939 and 1945 when Foynes was the center of the aviation world, with air traffic between the U.S. and Europe. Gloria, always more than willing and happy to talk and help people, worked as a multilingual guide in the museum from March until October.

Apart from the museum, Foynes was famous for one other thing: the invention of Irish coffee. During cold and rainy weather, people waiting at the air terminal needed something stronger than coffee to keep them warm. Thus Irish coffee was born.

In a matter of days from now, Foynes would be overrun by bands playing music on the festival stage; the farmers' market in museum square; the regatta; and the children's street art would decorate the town for the Irish Coffee Summer Festival. As usual the celebratory fireworks would be sponsored by Shannon Foynes Port Company, which was exactly where Jack was headed that morning.

After greeting and consulting his colleagues, Jack took his place in the gigantic metal crane and got to work loading cargo. He enjoyed his job and felt a sense of satisfaction knowing that someone just like him, somewhere on foreign soil, would unload the gift he had helped wrap. He enjoyed placing things where they belonged. He knew everything and everyone had a place in life: every piece of cargo that lay stocked up on the docks and every man and woman who worked alongside him had a space to slot into and a part to play. Every day he had the same goal: moving things and putting them where they belonged.

He could hear Sandy's voice in his head, repeating the same sentence over and over again: *I can only assume that there's only one thing more frustrating than not being able to find someone, and that's not being found. I would want someone to find me, more than anything.*

He carefully placed the cargo onto the ship, lowered himself to the ground, to the surprise of his watching colleagues, took off his helmet, threw it to the ground, and ran. Some watched in confusion, some in anger, but those closest to him viewed his exit with sympathy, for they guessed that even a year on, Jack could no longer sit in his perch high above the ground, so high he felt he could see the entire county and all that was in it, except his brother.

For Jack, running down to his car, all he could think about was finding Sandy, so she could bring Donal back to where he belonged.

Jack's continuous questions about Sandy Shortt to the hotels, inns, and bed and breakfasts in Glin were beginning to raise eyebrows. Impatience was entering the voices of the once-friendly staff, and his phone calls to duty managers were becoming more frequent. Now, with still no clues as to where Sandy was, Jack found himself taking deep breaths of fresh air down by the Shannon Estuary. The River Shannon was a special place to Jack. He had always felt a connection with the river and wanted to be a part of helping all it carried.

His mother and father had brought the family to Leitrim on a summer holiday one year, the holiday that remained more vivid in Jack's mind than any other. It was before Donal's birth, when Jack was barely ten years old. It was on that holiday he learned where and how the great river began, slowly and quietly at first in County Cavan before it picked up speed, gathering the secrets and spirit of each county, with each part of soil it eroded. Each tributary was like an artery being pumped from the heart of the country, whispering its secrets silently in hushed and excited babbles until it eventually carried them to the Atlantic where they were lost with the rest of the world's whispered hopes and regrets. It was like Chinese whispers, starting out small but eventually growing and becoming exaggerated, from the freshly painted wooden boats that bobbed on the surface in Carrick-on-Shannon to finally carrying steel and metal ships alongside cranes and warehouses that was the grand excitement of Shannon Foynes Port.

Jack rambled aimlessly down a quiet road along Shannon Estuary, grateful for the peace and quiet. Glin Castle disappeared behind the trees as he walked farther down the track. A splash of bright red glowed from behind the greenery in an area that had long ago been used as a parking lot but was now overgrown and merely used as a walk-through area for ramblers and birdwatchers. The gravel was uneven, the white lines had faded, and weeds grew from between every crack. There sat an old red Fiesta, battered and dented, its gleam long ago rubbed away. Jack stopped in his tracks. He knew this car. It was the Venus flytrap that had captured the long-legged beauty from the garage the previous morning.

His heart quickened as he looked around to find her but there was no sight or sound of any other presence. A coffee-filled Styrofoam cup sat on the dashboard, newspapers piled up on the passenger seat alongside a towel, which led his already overactive imagination to believe she was jogging nearby. He moved away from the car in fear she would return to find him peering through the windows. The coincidence of them meeting once again in another deserted area filled him with far too much curiosity for him to walk away. And saying hello to her again would be a welcome joy to a day lacking in results.

After forty-five minutes of waiting around, Jack began to feel bored and foolish. The car looked as though it had been abandoned years ago in the forgotten area yet he knew for sure that he had seen it being driven yesterday morning. He moved closer to the car and pressed his face against the glass.

His heart almost stopped. Goose bumps rose on his skin as a shiver ran through his body. There on the dashboard, beside the cup of coffee and a cell phone with missed calls, was a thick brown file with DONAL RUTTLE written in neat handwriting across the front.

16

I tapped my shoe against the plate that once held the chocolate digestives, causing a loud tinkling to echo through the clearing. Around me the four sleeping bodies were lazily stretched out on the forest floor, and Bernard's snores seemed to be getting louder with every minute that passed. I sighed loudly, feeling like a pesky hormonal teenager who couldn't get her way. Helena, whom I hadn't spoken to for an hour, raised her eyebrows at me, trying to show her lack of amusement, although I knew well that she was enjoying every second of my torture. Over the past hour I had "accidentally" knocked over the china, dropped a packet of biscuits on Joan, and had a rather loud bout of coughing. Still, they slept and Helena refused to lead or even direct me out of the woods to the other life she had spoken of.

Hearing laughter, I had attempted to make my own way out but, finding my way blocked by thousands of identical leering pines, I decided that getting lost once was enough, to get lost a second time in already unusual circumstances would be just plain stupid.

"How long do they usually sleep for?" I asked loudly in a bored tone, hoping my voice would disturb them.

"They like to get a good eight hours."

"Do they eat?"

"Three times a day; usually solids. I walk them twice a day. Bernard in particular loves the leash." She smiled into the distance as though remembering. "And then they partake in the occasional personal grooming."

"I meant, do they eat here?" I looked around the clearing in disgust, no longer caring if I insulted their annual camping resort. I couldn't help my agitation but I hated to be pinned down. Usually I came and went in my life as I pleased, in and out of others'. I never even succeeded in staying in my own parents' house for very long, usually grabbing my bag and running out the door. But here, I had no place to go.

Laughter echoed in the distance once again.

"What is that noise?"

"People call it laughter, I think." Helena settled down in her sleeping bag looking snug and smug at the same time.

"Have you always had an attitude problem?" I asked.

"Have you?"

"Yes," I said firmly and she laughed. I let go of my frown and smiled. "It's just that I've been sitting in these woods for two entire days now."

"Is that an apology?"

"I don't apologize. Not unless I really need to."

"You remind me of me when I was young. Young*er*. I'm still young. What has you so irritable at such a young age?"

"I'm not a people person." I looked around as I heard another bout of laughing.

Helena continued talking as though she hadn't even heard it. "Of course you're not. You've just spent the guts of your life working to find them."

I registered her statement but decided not to respond to it. "Do you not hear these sounds?"

"I grew up beside a train station. When friends stayed over they'd be kept awake all night by the noise and the vibrations. I was so used to it I couldn't hear a thing, yet the creaking on the stairs when my parents went to bed woke me every time. Are you married?"

I rolled my eyes.

"I'll take that as a no. Do you have a boyfriend?"

"Sometimes."

"Have you got children?"

"I'm not interested in children." I sniffed the air, "What is that smell? And who is laughing? Is there somebody nearby?"

My head whizzed around like a dog trying to snap at a fly. I couldn't discern where the sounds were coming from. They had seemed to be coming from behind me but when I'd turned around the noise appeared to be louder in the other direction.

"It's everywhere," Helena explained lazily. "What the new people here compare to a surround-sound system. You probably understand that more than I."

"Who's making that noise and is someone smoking a cigar?" I sniffed the air again.

"You ask a lot of questions."

"And you didn't when you first arrived here? Helena, I

don't know where I am and what's going on, and you're not being much help."

Helena at least had the honesty to look embarrassed. "I'm sorry. I'd forgotten what it's like." She stopped and listened to the sounds. "The laughter and these smells are just entering our atmosphere now. So far, what do you know about people who come here?"

"That they're missing."

"Exactly. So the laughter, cries, and scents that arrive are missing too."

"How can that be?" I asked, utterly confused.

"Sometimes people lose more than just socks, Sandy. You can forget where you put them first of all. Forgetting things is just parts of your memory missing, that's all."

"You can remember again, though."

"Yes, but you don't remember *all* things and you don't find *all* things. Those things end up here, like the touch and smell of someone, the memory of their exact face and the sound of their voice."

"That's bizarre." I shook my head, unable to take it all in.

"It's really very simple if you remember it like this. Everything in life has a place, and when one thing moves, it must go somewhere else. Here is the place that all those things move to." She held her hands up to display our surroundings.

A thought suddenly occurred to me. "Have you ever heard your own laughter or cries?"

Helena nodded sadly. "Many times."

"*Many* times?" I asked in surprise.

She smiled. "Well, I had the great privilege of being

loved by many people. The more people who love you, the more people you have out there to lose memories of you. Don't make that face, Sandy. It's not as desperate as it sounds. People don't intend to lose memories. Although there are always some things that we would rather forget." She winked. "It could be that the real sound of my laughter has been replaced by a new memory, or that, when a few months after I went missing my scent left my bedroom and my clothes, the scent they tried so hard to remember was altered. I'm sure the image I have of my own mother's face is very different from how she actually looked but, forty years on and no reminder, how is my mind to know, exactly? You can't hold on to all things forever, no matter how hard you grip them."

I thought of the day I'd hear the sound of my own laughter drifting overhead, and I knew it would happen only once because there was only one person who knew the true sound of my laughter and my cries.

"All the same"—Helena looked up to the now bright sky with tears in her eyes—"you do sometimes feel like catching them and throwing them back to where they came from. Our memories are the only contact we have. We can hug, kiss, laugh, and cry with them over and over again in our minds. They're very precious things to have."

Chuckles, hisses, snorts, and giggles filtered through the air, floating by our ears on the wind, the light breeze carrying the faint scents like the forgotten smell of a childhood home; a kitchen after a day's baking. There's a mother's forgotten smell of her baby, now grown up: baby powder, skin cream, candy-smelling skin. There are older, musty smells of favorite grandparents: lavender for

Grandma; cigar, cigarette, and pipe smoke for Grand-dad. There are the smells of lost lovers: sweet perfumes and aftershaves, the scent of sleepy morning lie-ins or simply the unexplainable individual scent left behind in a room. Personal smells as precious as the people themselves. All the aromas that had gone missing in people's lives had ended up here. I couldn't help but close my eyes and breathe in those scents and laugh along with the sounds.

Joan stirred in her sleeping bag and I snapped out of my trance. My heart began to race in anticipation of finally seeing beyond the woods.

"Good morning, Joan." Helena sang so loudly she succeeded in waking Bernard, too. He awoke with a start, raising his head and revealing his spaghetti-strip hair hanging to the wrong side. He looked around sleepily, his hand feeling for his glasses.

"Good morning, Bernard," Helena said so loudly she succeeded in waking both Marcus and Derek.

I stifled a laugh.

"Here you go, a nice hot cup of coffee to wake you up." She thrust steaming mugs in their faces.

They looked at her sleepily in confusion. As soon as they'd taken their first sip of coffee Helena threw off her blanket and rose to her feet.

"Well, that's enough hanging around, now. Let's go, everybody." She started folding her blanket neatly and packing away the utensils.

"Why are you talking so loudly and what's the rush?" Joan held her messy bed head and whispered as though she was suffering a hangover.

"It's a brand-new day so let's drink up and we'll head back as soon as you're all done."

"Why?" Joan asked, sipping quickly.

"What about breakfast?" Bernard moaned like a child.

"We'll have that when we get back." Helena grabbed his mug from him, threw the remainder of the coffee over her shoulder and packed the mug in a bag. I had to look away out of fear of laughing.

"What's the rush?" Marcus asked. "Is everything OK?" He watched her intently, still unsure of my presence.

"Everything's fine, Marcus." She placed a hand on his shoulder caringly. "Sandy just has some work to do." She smiled at me.

I did?

"Oh, how lovely. Are you staging a play? It's been such a long time since we've done a play," Joan said excitedly.

"I do hope you give us notice of the auditions well in advance because we'll need time to prepare. It's been awhile," Bernard said worriedly.

"Don't worry," Helena jumped in to say, "she will."

My mouth dropped open but Helena held a hand up to stop me from protesting.

"Have you ever thought of doing a musical?" Derek asked, packing away his guitar. "There would be huge interest in taking part in a musical."

"That's a very strong possibility." Helena spoke as though dismissing a child.

"Will there be group auditions?" Bernard asked, a little panicked.

"No, no," Helena said, smiling, and I finally knew what she was up to. "I think Sandy will want to spend a little time with everyone alone. Well"—she lifted Bernard's blanket from off his shoulders and began folding it while he watched open-mouthed—"let's get ourselves ready so we can show Sandy around. She'll need to find a good venue for the show."

How quickly Bernard and Joan got ready.

"By the way, I meant to ask you," Helena whispered, "were you working when you arrived here?"

"What do you mean exactly?"

"Were you on a job or following the trail of somebody at the time you arrived here? It's such an important question but I forgot to ask it."

"Yes and no," I replied. "I was jogging by Shannon Estuary when I found myself here but my reason for being in Limerick was work-related. I had just taken on a new case five days beforehand." I thought back to the phone call that I'd received from Jack Ruttle late one night.

"The reason I ask is because I wonder what it was about *that* person out of all the missing people you've searched for, that brought you here. Had you a strong link to him?"

I shook my head but knew I wasn't quite telling the truth. The late-night phone calls with Jack Ruttle had been very different from all my other cases. They were phone calls I enjoyed receiving, he was someone I could talk with about other things besides business. The more I spoke to the likable Jack, the harder I worked trying to find his brother. There was only one other person in my life who could allow me to feel similarly.

"What was the missing person's name?"

"Donal Ruttle," I said, remembering the playful blue eyes from the photograph.

Helena thought about it. "Well, we might as well start now. Anyone here know a Donal Ruttle?" She looked around.

17

Jack paced alongside the red Ford Fiesta, feeling a mixture of impatience, frustration, and anxiety. Occasionally he would stop, stare in the passenger window, and will the door to open so he could grab the file and hungrily scoff the information on the pages. Then he'd calm down and pace again. He looked around, not wanting to venture far from the car in case Sandy Shortt returned and drove off without him.

He couldn't believe Sandy was the woman from the petrol station. They had passed by each other as though they were strangers, but just as when he'd been speaking over the phone, he had felt something when he saw her, a bond that linked them. At the time he had thought it was because they were the only two in the place so early in the morning, but now he knew that connection was more. And now, here again, he had come across her in a hidden place. Something was drawing him to her. What he'd give to go back to that moment so he could talk to her about Donal. So she had come to Glin after all. He knew she wouldn't have let him down, and she had driven through the night just as she'd promised. Finding her car in this desolate spot only raised more questions than he already had. If she was in Glin, where had she been on Sunday when they were due to meet?

He looked at his watch. Three hours had passed since he'd come across the car and there was still no sign of her. A more important question reared its ugly head: Where was she now?

He sat down on the dilapidated curb by the car and did what he had become accustomed to doing over the past year. He waited. And he wasn't going to budge an inch until Sandy Shortt came back to her car.

I followed the group through the trees, my heart beating so loudly I could barely hear Bernard, who was chatting to me constantly about his previous years' acting experience. I nodded now and then when I felt his eyes on me. Disappointingly, there had been no reaction to Donal's name when asked; just shrugged shoulders and mumbles of "I don't know." But a reaction had stirred within me as soon as Helena mentioned his name to the others because hearing it made it all become real to me. I would be seeing people I had been searching for for years.

I felt as though all my life's work led up to this moment. Nights of no sleep, distancing myself from possible friends and caring parents had left me living a solitary life I had been content with, but it was a life haunted by friendships and relationships with people I'd never met. I knew everything about them: their favorite colors, their best friends' names, their favorite bands—and I felt that with every step I took I was closer to meeting my long-lost friends, my missing parents, uncles, aunts, and family. Recognizing these emotions alerted me to the island I had become. None of those missing people I thought of so fondly would even know me. When their eyes fell upon me they would see a stranger, yet my eyes would see anything but. Though we had never met, family photos of past Christmases, birthdays and weddings, first days of school, debutante balls were firmly imprinted in my memory. I had sat with crying parents and been shown photo album after photo album, yet I couldn't remember a day when I had shared a couch with my own family and had done the same. The people I lived for didn't even know of my existence and I hadn't acknowledged that of the people who lived for me.

I could see up ahead where the trees ended. The stillness of the woods was dissipating and instead there was lots of movement, noise, and color. So many people. I stopped walking with the group and shakily held out my hand to hold on to the trunk of a pine.

"Sandy, are you OK?" Bernard asked, stopping beside me.

The group stopped walking and turned to look at me. I couldn't even smile. I couldn't pretend everything was OK. The master of lying was caught in a web of lies I'd weaved myself. Helena pushed her way from the front of the group and rushed over to me.

"Go ahead, all of you. We'll meet you later on." She dismissed them, and when they didn't move: "Go on!" Slowly they turned round and reluctantly left the shade for the light.

"Sandy." Helena softly placed her hand on my shoulder.

"You're trembling." She put her arm around my shoulders and held me to her. "It's OK, you've nothing to fear here. It's perfectly safe."

It wasn't the safety of the place my body shook for. It was the fact that I had never felt as if I belonged anywhere. I had spent my life detaching myself from anyone who wanted to be close, dissociating myself from friends and lovers because they never answered my questions, nor tolerated or understood my searches. They made me feel like I was wrong and, without them knowing it, maybe even a little crazy, but I had a passion to just *find*. Finding this place was just one big answer to a life-long question that had caused me to sacrifice everything. I'd hurt so many people who loved me in order to help those whom I couldn't see, and now as I was just about to see them I was afraid to let them in, too. I used to think that I was a saint, just like Jenny-May Butler on the nine-o'clock news; I thought I was Mother Teresa with a missing-persons file, making sacrifices to help others. In reality I'd sacrificed nothing. My behavior suited me and only me.

The people in this place were the people I had clung to. When I grabbed my bag by the door of my family home in Leitrim it was for these people. When I ended relationships and turned down invitations to nights out it was for these people.

But now that I'd found them, I had no idea what to do.

18

Helena and I stepped out of the darkness of the shaded woods and entered a world of color. I held my breath at the sight before me. It was as though grand red curtains had parted to welcome a production on such a scale I could barely focus on one thing for long enough. What welcomed my eyes was an entire bustling village of nations gathering. Some people were walking alone, others gathering in twos, threes, groups, and in crowds. Sights of traditional costumes, sounds of combined languages, scents of cuisines from all over the world. It was rich and alive, bursting at the seams with color and sound as though we'd followed the path of a pulse to reach the heart of the woods. And there it pumped, people flowing here, there, and everywhere.

Sophisticated wooden buildings lined the street with doors and windows decorated with ornate carvings. Each building was constructed from a different timber, the varying shades and grains camouflaging the village so that it and the woods were combined and almost one. Solar panels lined the roofs, and the hundreds of roofs extending into the distance. All around were wind turbines, up to one hundred feet tall, with blades going around and around in the blue skies, their dark shadows circling on rooftops and roadways. The village was nestled among the trees, among mountains, among wind machines. Before me, hundreds of people, dressed in traditional costumes from all eras, *lived* in a lost place that looked real and smelled real and, when I held out my hand and felt the fabric of someone rush by, felt real. I fought with myself to believe it.

It was a scene I was familiar yet unfamiliar with all at the same time because everything I could see was composed of recognizable elements from home, but used in such very different ways. We hadn't stepped backward or forward, we had entered a whole new time. A great big melting pot of nations, cultures, design, and sound mixed to create a new world. Children played; market stalls decorated the road and customers swarmed around them. So much color, so many new sounds, unlike any country I'd been in. A sign beside us said HERE.

Helena linked my arm, a gesture I would normally have shrugged off had I not physically needed her to prop me up. I was stunned. I was Ali Baba who'd stumbled across the cave of treasures, Galileo after his discoveries through the telescope. More important, I was a ten-year-old girl who had found all her socks.

"Every day is market day," Helena explained softly. "Some people like to trade whatever bits they've found for things of value. Sometimes they're of no value at all but it's become a bit of a sport now. Money is worthless here; all we need is found readily on the streets. There is, however, a requirement to help the village. Our occupations are more in the nature of community service rather than for self-gain—age, health, and other personal reasons permitting."

I looked around in awe. Helena continued talking softly in my ear, holding my arm as my body shook.

"The turbines are something you will see throughout the land. We have many wind plants, most of them among the mountain gaps that produce wind funnelling. One wind machine can produce enough electricity for up to four hundred homes a year, and the solar panels on the buildings also help generate energy."

I listened to her but barely heard a word. My ears were tuned in to the conversations around me, to the sounds of the monstrous wind-turbine blades breaking through the air. My nose was adjusting to the crisp freshness that seemed to fill my lungs with cool air in one small breath. My attention turned to the market stall closest to us.

"It's a mobile phone," a British gentleman explained to an elderly stall owner.

"What use have I for a mobile phone?" The Caribbean stall owner dismissed him, laughing. "I've heard those things don't even work here."

"They don't, but—"

"But nothing. I have been here forty-five years, three months, and ten days." He held his head high. "And I don't see how this music box is a fair trade for a phone that doesn't work."

The customer stopped fuming and appeared to view him with more respect. "Well, I've been here only four years," he explained politely, "so let me show you what phones can do now." He held the phone up in the air, pointed it at the stall owner and it made a clicking sound. He showed the screen to the salesman.

"Ah!" He started laughing. "It's a camera! Why didn't you say?"

"Well, it's a camera *phone* but, even better, look at this. The person who owned it took a whole pile of photos of themselves and whatever country they live in." He scrolled down the phone.

The stall owner handled it gently.

"Somebody here might know these people," the customer said softly.

"Ah, yes, mon," the salesman replied gently, nodding. "This is very precious indeed."

"Come on, let's go," Helena whispered, leading me by the arm.

I began to move as though on autopilot, looking around openmouthed at all the people. We passed the customer and stall owner; they both nodded and smiled. "Welcome."

I just stared back.

Two children playing hopscotch stopped their game on hearing the men's salutation. "Welcome." They both gave me toothless grins.

Helena led me through the crowd, through the choruses of welcomes, the nods and smiles of well-wishers. Helena acknowledged them all politely for me. We walked across the street toward the large wooden two-story building with a decked porch across the front. An intricate carving of a scroll and theatrical feathered pen decorated the door. Helena pushed the door open and the scroll and feather halved as though bowing and holding out their arms to make way for us.

"This is the registry. Everyone comes here when they first arrive," Helena explained patiently. "Everybody's name and details are logged in these books so that we can keep track of who is who and how many people are here."

"In case anybody goes missing," I said smartly.

"I think you'll find that nothing goes missing here, Sandy." Helena was serious. "Things have no place else to go and so they stay here."

I ignored the chill of her implication and instead tried unsuccessfully to inject humor into the situation. "What will I do with myself if I've nothing to look for?"

"You'll do what you've always wanted; you'll seek out those you searched for. Finish the job you started."

"Then what?"

She was silent.

"Then you'll help me get home, right?" I asked rather forcefully.

She didn't respond.

"Helena," a cheery fellow called out from where he was sitting behind a desk. On the desk a series of numbers was displayed. Beside the main door there was a board with all the countries of the world, their associated languages, some of which I'd never even heard of, and their corresponding numbers. I matched one of the numbers on his desk to a familiar one on the board. COUNTRY: IRELAND. LANGUAGES: GAELIC, ENGLISH.

"Hello, Terence." Helen seemed glad of the interruption to our conversation.

It was then that I looked around the room for the first time. There were dozens of desks in the large room. Each desk had a series of numbers and behind each desk sat a person of a different nationality. Lines had formed before the tables. The room was quiet and filled with the tension of hundreds of people who had just arrived, who couldn't yet comprehend their situation. They each looked around the room nervously with wide, terrified eyes as they hugged their own bodies for comfort.

I noticed Helena had joined Terence at his desk.

He looked up as I approached them. "Welcome." He smiled softly. I sensed sympathy in the older man's voice, and his accent revealed his Irish roots.

"Sandy, this is Terence O'Malley. Terence, this is Sandy. Terence has been here for . . . oh gosh, how many years has it been now, Terence?" Helena asked him.

Eleven years, I thought.

"Almost eleven years now," he replied with a smile.

"Terence worked as a—"

"Librarian in Ballina," I cut in before even thinking about it. Ten years on, he was still recognizable as the single, fifty-five-year-old librarian who had disappeared on his way home from work eleven years ago.

Helena froze and Terence looked confused.

"Oh yes, I told you that before we came in," Helena jumped in. "Silly me. I must be getting old, repeating myself like that." She laughed.

"I know the feeling." Terence laughed, pushing his sliding spectacles back up his nose.

I'd always thought his nose was exactly like his sister's. I studied it some more.

"Well." Terence began to fidget under my glare and he turned to Helena for backup, "Let's get down to business now, shall we. If you wouldn't mind taking a seat, Sandy, I'll help you go through this form, it's very simple really."

As I took a seat before the desk I looked at the lines around me; to my right a woman was helping a young boy onto the chair before her desk. *"Permettimi di aiutarti a sederti e mi puoi raccontare tutto su come sei arrivato fin qui. Avresti voglia di un po' di latte con biscotti?"*

He looked at her with big brown eyes, as lost as a puppy, and nodded. She nodded to someone behind her, who disappeared through a door behind the desk and returned moments later with a glass of milk and a plate of cookies.

To my right, a bewildered-looking gentleman stepped up to the front of the line. The man at the desk, name tag reading "MARTIN," smiled at him encouragingly, *"Nehmen Sie doch Platz, bitte, dann helfe ich Ihnen mit den Formularen."*

"Sandy." Terence and Helena were calling me, trying to get my attention.

"Yes, what, sorry." I snapped out of my trance.

"Terence was asking you where you are from."

"Leitrim."

"Is that where you lived?"

"No. Dublin." I looked around as more people were led into the room looking dazed.

"And you went missing in Dublin," Terence confirmed.

"No. Limerick." My voice was quiet as all the thoughts in my head got louder and louder.

". . . you know Jim Gannon . . . Leitrim town? . . ."

"Yes," I replied, watching a young African woman draping her ochre-colored blanket tighter around her body as she looked around at her strange surroundings in fear. Armbands of copper, weaved grasses, and beads decorated her skin. We locked eyes for a moment before she quickly looked away and I continued speaking to Terence as though I wasn't really there. "Jim owns the hardware store. His son taught me geography."

Terence laughed happily about it being a small world.

"A lot bigger than I thought," I replied, my voice sounding like it was coming from somewhere else.

Terence's voice came and went in my head as I looked around at all the faces, all the people who had one moment ago been on their way to work, or walking to the shop, and who had suddenly found themselves here.

". . . for a living?"

"She's involved in theatre, Terence, she runs an acting agency."

Some more mumbling as I tuned out.

". . . is that right, Sandy? You run an agency of your own?"

"Yes," I said absentmindedly, watching as the little boy beside me was led by the hand through a door behind the Italian registry desk.

He watched me with big worried eyes all the way. I smiled at him lightly and his frown softened. The door was closed behind him.

"Where does that door lead?" I asked suddenly in the middle of one of Terence's questions.

He stopped. "Which door?"

I looked around the room and noticed for the first time there was a door behind each desk.

"All of them. Where do they all lead to?" I asked faintly.

"That's where people are briefed on what we know, where we are, and what happens here. There's counseling services and employment opportunities, and we arrange for somebody from here to come to greet them so that they can guide them around for however long they're needed."

I looked at the large solid-oak doors and didn't say anything.

"As you have already met Helena, she will be your guide," Terence said gently. "Now we'll just get through the last of these questions and then you can get out of here, which I'm sure you're anxious to do."

The main door opened and sunlight filled the room again. Terence had asked me another question, but I was distracted by the person in the doorway. I watched as a young girl, no older than ten, with soft, bouncing blond curls and big blue eyes walked into the room. She sniffled and wiped her eyes, following the guide who led her into the room.

"Jenny-May," I whispered, my head becoming dizzy again.

"And your brother's name?" Terence asked working his way down the form.

"No, hold on a minute, she doesn't have a sister," Helena interrupted. "She told me earlier she was an only child."

"No, no," Terence sounded slightly agitated, "I asked her if she had any sisters and she said Jenny-May."

"She mustn't have heard you correctly, Terence," Helena said calmly, and the rest of their sentences turned to murmuring in my ears.

My eyes continued to follow the little girl as she was led through the room; my heart beat faster just as it always did when Jenny-May Butler was within a few feet of me.

"Maybe you could clear this up." Terence looked at me. His face appeared and faded from my vision.

"Maybe she's not well, Terence. In fact she looks very pale." Helena's voice was close to my ear now. "Sandy, would you like to—"

That's when I passed out.

— 19 —

"Sandy." I could hear my name being called and felt a warm breath on my face. The smell was familiar; sweet coffee that sent my heart into its usual flutter, fanning my body and causing excited chills to chase one another just below the surface of my skin.

Gregory's hand softly brushed back strands of hair from my face as though gently brushing away sand on an excavation site to reveal something far more precious than me. But that's what he was, my excavator, the one who unearthed all that was buried beneath to discover my hidden thoughts. One hand was placed at the back of my neck as though I was the most fragile thing he'd ever held; the other softly traced the line of my jaw, occasionally running up my cheeks and through my hair.

"Sandy, honey, open your eyes," the voice whispered close to my ear.

"Move back, everybody!" a louder and more aggressive voice shouted nearby. "Is she OK?" His voice got louder, closer.

The comforting hand moved from my hair to my hand and grasped it tightly, his thumb soothingly stroking my skin as he spoke quietly, "She's not responding, call an ambulance." His voice was distorted and it echoed in my head. My head hurt.

"Oh, mother of Jesus," the voice muttered.

"Sean, get the kids back into the school, don't let them watch this," my savior said calmly.

Sean, Sean, Sean. I knew that name. Knew that voice.

"Where's that blood coming from?" he panicked.

"Her head. Get the kids away." My hand was held tighter.

"He hit her hard, the bastard."

"I know, I saw. I was watching her from the window. Call the ambulance."

Sean's shouts to the kids to go inside moved farther away and I was left in the echoing silence with the angel. I felt soft lips on my hand.

"Open your eyes, Sandy," he whispered. "Please."

I tried to but they felt as if they were glued together, like a lotus nestled in the mud forced to open its petals ahead of time. My head was heavy, my thoughts clumsy and slow, as it throbbed and pulsated repeatedly with abnormally strong force in the protective hand that cradled it. The ground felt cold and rough beneath me. Concrete. Why was I on the ground? I struggled to get up but my body resisted the action, my eyes wouldn't open.

I heard the ambulance in the distance and I fought to

open my eyes. They opened just a slit. *Ah. Mr. Burton. My savior.* He held me in his arms, looking down at me as though he'd just discovered gold in the Leitrim roadway. He had blood on his shirt. He was hurt? His eyes looked hurt as they searched my face. I suddenly remembered the great big pimple on my chin that I wished all day I'd popped that morning. I tried to move my hand to cover it but it felt like my hand had been dipped in concrete and left to dry. "Oh, thank god," he whispered, his hand holding mine tighter. "Don't move yet, the ambulance is almost here."

I had to cover my pimple. I was finally this close to Mr. Burton after four years and I looked a mess, my seventeen-year-old hormones were ruining the moment I'd been dreaming of. Hold on, he'd said "ambulance." What had happened? I tried to speak and a croak passed my lips.

"It's going to be OK." He hushed me, his face close to mine.

I believed him and forgot my pain for a moment while I once again self-consciously felt my face.

"I know what you're trying to do, Sandy, so stop it." Gregory attempted to laugh lightly while carefully removing my arm from my face.

I groaned, words still not coming to me.

"He's not so awful, you know. His name is Henry. He's been keeping me company while you've been so rudely passed out. Henry, meet Sandy, Sandy, meet Henry, although I don't think you're a very welcome guest here." Gregory ran his finger across my chin, lightly brushing the blemish as though it were the most beautiful thing about me.

So there I was with blood running from my head, a pimple named Henry on my chin, and a face so aflame it could have powered the entire town. I began to close my eyes again, the sky seemed so bright it pierced my pupils and sent spears of pain through my sockets and into my already throbbing head.

"Don't close your eyes, Sandy," Gregory said more loudly.

I opened them and caught the worry in his face before he had a chance to hide it.

"I'm tired," I finally whispered.

"I know you are"—he held me tighter—"but stay awake with me for a while, keep me company until the ambulance gets here," he pleaded. "Promise me."

"Promise," I whispered before shutting my eyes again.

A second siren arrived on the scene, a car pulled up nearby, I could feel the vibrations on the concrete near my head and I feared the tires would run over me. Doors opened and slammed.

"He's over there, Garda," Sean was back, shouting. "He drove straight into her, wasn't even looking," he said, panicked. "This man here saw it."

Sean was quieted down, I heard a man crying. Heard garda voices trying to comfort, radios crackling and beeping, Sean being led away. Footsteps came closer to me, there was mumbling above my head of concerned voices. All the time Gregory whispered in my ear words that sounded pretty, the vowels easy in my ringing ears. The sounds shut out the sirens, the cries of fear, the shouts of panic and anger, the feel of the cold concrete and the sticky wet trickling down my ear.

As the ambulance sirens got louder, Gregory's tones became more urgent as I began to drift away in his arms.

"Welcome back," I heard as I awoke to see a worried Helena wafting a fan in my face.

I groaned and my hand flew to my head.

"You've got a nasty bump so I'd advise you not to touch it," she said gently.

My arm kept moving.

"I said don—"

"Ouch."

"Serves you right," she said haughtily and walked away.

I squinted around the unfamiliar room, feeling the egg-sized bump that had formed above my temple. I was on a couch; Helena was at a sink facing a window. The light was bright and illuminated her, blurring her around the edges as though she were a holy vision.

"Where are we?"

"My home." She didn't turn around, continued rinsing a cloth.

I looked around. "Why do you have a couch in the kitchen?"

Helena laughed lightly. "Of all the questions you could have asked, that is the first one you chose."

I was silent.

"It's not a kitchen, it's a family room," was her reply. "I don't cook here."

"I don't suppose you have electricity."

She grunted, "Once you get a chance to look around outside you'll see we have a system of what we call *solar panels*." She dragged out the words as though I was slow. "They're similar to the ones found on pocket calculators and they generate electricity from the sun. Each house has its own power voltage system," she said excitedly.

I lay back in the couch, feeling dizzy and closed my eyes. "I'm aware of how solar panels work."

"They exist there, too?" She was surprised.

I ignored her question. "How did I get here?"

"My husband carried you."

My eyes flew open and I winced with the pain. Helena still didn't turn around and the water still flowed.

"Your husband? You can get married here?"

"You can get married anywhere."

"Not technically true," I protested meekly. "My god, electricity *and* marriage? This is too much for me," I mumbled, the ceiling beginning to swirl above me.

Helena sat beside me on the couch and held a cold washcloth over my forehead and eyes. It felt soothing on my throbbing, burning head.

"I had the most awful dream that I was in a bizarre place where all the missing things and people in the world go," I grumbled. "Please tell me that was a dream, or at least a nervous breakdown. I can handle a nervous breakdown."

"Well, if you can handle *that*, then you can handle the truth."

"What is the truth?" I opened my eyes.

She was silent as she stared at me and sighed. "You know the truth."

I closed my eyes and fought the urge to cry.

Helena grabbed my arm, squeezed it, and leaned in with urgency in her voice. "Hang in there, Sandy, it will make sense to you after a while."

I didn't think that possible.

"If it makes you feel better, I haven't told anybody else what you've told me. *No one.*"

It did make me feel better. I could figure out in my own time whatever it was I had to do.

"Who is Jenny-May?" Helena asked curiously.

I closed my eyes and groaned, remembering the scene at the registry. "Nobody. Well, not nobody, she's somebody. I thought I saw her in the registry, that's all."

"It wasn't her?"

"Not unless she stopped aging the day she arrived here. I don't know what I was thinking." Frowning, I reached to my pounding head again.

There was a light tap on the door and it was gently opened by a man so tall and broad he filled the door frame. White light impatiently squeezed itself through the small spaces he didn't fill, shooting into my eyes like spears of fire direct from the sun. He was of similar age to Helena, with shining ebony skin and intense black eyes. He stood well over my six-foot-two height and for that reason alone I immediately liked him. His figure dominated the room yet brought with it a feeling of safety. A small smile revealed snow-white teeth, while eyeballs like purified sugar melted around pupils of black coffee. He was hard, but softened around the edges. His cheekbones sat high and proud on his face, his jaw square yet, above it, cushioned lips for his words to bounce from and launch themselves into the world.

"How is our *kipepeo* girl doing?" The rhythmic sound of his words revealed his African roots.

In confusion I looked to Helena, who was looking at the man in surprise, the surprise, I could tell, not for his sudden presence but for the words he had spoken. She knew this man and I assumed knew his words. I didn't know what the words meant but I guessed the speaker of them, her husband. Our eyes met and I felt drawn to his gaze, trapped in his and he trapped in mine as though a magnet drew us together. He held a plank of wood in his large hands; sawdust covered his white linen clothes.

"What does *kipepeo* mean?" I asked the room. The room didn't answer, but knew.

"Sandy, this is my husband, Joseph." Helena introduced us. "He's a carpenter," she added, referring to the plank of wood in his hands.

My unusual introduction to Joseph the carpenter was interrupted by a little girl who entered the kitchen through Joseph's legs, giggling while her curly black hair bounced with each childish skip. She ran to Helena and grabbed onto her leg.

"And who's this, the Immaculate Conception?" I asked, the little girl's shrieks sounding like wails in my pounding head.

"Almost." Helena smiled. "She's our daughter's Immaculate Conception. Say hello, Wanda." She ran her hand through the little girl's hair.

A toothless smile greeted me before she shyly ran out of the room under her grandfather's legs. I looked up from where she had disappeared, to Joseph's eyes again. He was still watching me. Helena looked from him back to me, not with suspicion but with . . . I couldn't quite figure it out.

"You must sleep." He gave a single nod.

Under the gaze of Helena and Joseph, I placed the washcloth over my eyes and allowed myself to drift. For once I was too tired to ask questions.

"Ah, there she is now." The sound of my father's voice greeted me as though I was suddenly pulled up out of the water. Muffled sounds gradually became audible, faces eventually recognizable. It was as though I was reborn into the world, facing my loved ones from a hospital bed once again.

"Hello, honey." My mother rushed to my side and took my hand. Her face appeared close to mine, too close for me to focus and so she remained a lavender-scented blur with four eyes. "How do you feel?"

I hadn't yet had time to feel before I was asked, and so concentrated on it before answering. I didn't feel very good.

"OK," I responded.

"Oh, my poor baby." Her cleavage dominated my

view as she leaned over to kiss my forehead, glossy lips
leaving my skin sticky and ticklish. I looked around
the room after she'd moved and saw my father,
scrunched cap in hand and looking older than I remembered. Perhaps I had been underwater longer than
I'd thought. I winked, he smiled, relief written all over
his face. Funny how it was the job of the patient to
make the visitors feel better. It was as though I was on
stage and it was my turn to entertain. The walls of the
hospital had rendered everyone speechless and awkward as though we had met that day for the very first
time.

"What happened?" I asked after sipping water through
a straw from a cup that had been thrust at me by a
nurse.

They looked nervously at each other. Mum decided to
do the honors.

"A car hit you, honey, just as you were walking across
the road from the school. He came around the corner . . .
he was just a young lad only on his provisional license,
his mother didn't know he'd taken the car, bless her
heart. Luckily Mr. Burton saw it all happen and could
give the Gardaí an eyewitness report. He's a good man is
Mr. Burton," she said as she smiled. "Gregory," she added
to me a bit more quietly.

I smiled too.

"He stayed with you all the way into the hospital."

"My head," I whispered, the pain suddenly entering
my body as though hearing the story had reminded it it
needed to do its job.

"Your left arm is broken." Mum's glossy lips glistened in the light as they opened and closed. "And your left leg." Her voice shook lightly. "But apart from that, you're very lucky."

It was only then I noticed my arm in a sling and my left leg in a cast and found it amusing that they thought I was lucky even after being hit by a car. I started to laugh but the pain stopped me.

"Oh, yes, and you've a cracked rib," my father added quickly, looking apologetic for the lack of warning.

When they had left, Gregory rapped lightly on the door. He looked more gorgeous than ever with his tired, concerned eyes and messy hair that I could imagine he ruffled as he paced with worry. He always did that.

"Hi." He smiled walking in and kissed me on the forehead.

"Hi," I whispered back.

"How are you feeling?"

"Like I've been hit by a bus."

"Nah, it was only a mini. Stop looking for attention," he said as a smile tickled the sides of his lips. "You've heard the bad news, I assume?"

"That I have to do my final exams orally?" I lifted up the cast covering my left arm. "I think the guards will still accept me," I said.

"No," he said seriously and took a seat on the bed. "We lost Henry in the ambulance. I think it's the oxygen mask that took him out."

I started laughing but had to stop.

"Oh, shit, sorry." He immediately stopped joking around at seeing me in pain.

"Thanks for staying with me."

"Thanks for staying with me," he replied.

"Well, I did promise." I smiled. "And I'm not planning on disappearing anywhere anytime soon."

20

Jack sat on the gravel surface beside what he assumed to be the now abandoned car. His overactive mind contemplated every possible scenario as to where Sandy Shortt was, why her car was in the middle of the trees in an old parking lot, why she hadn't turned up for their meeting the previous day, and why she hadn't returned to her car for the entire day. Nothing made sense to him anymore. He hadn't moved from the car's vicinity all day. A quick search of the surroundings showed no sign of her or of any other life for that matter. It was late now, the forest area was black, the only lights being those from distant ships out at sea and Glin Castle in the distance behind the tall pines. Jack could barely see past the end of his nose. The blackness of the night was thick and engulfing, yet he was afraid to leave in case he missed her, in case somebody towed the car away, which in turn would take away Donal and all possible traces of him.

The file sat on the dashboard. The mobile phone beside it was the only immediate source of light, flashing every few seconds to signal a dying battery. If Sandy wasn't going to arrive at her car anytime soon, Jack needed to get his hands on that phone to see her recent call list and, with luck, trace somebody from her phonebook who would help find her. If her battery went dead it was possible he wouldn't be able to switch it back on without a PIN code.

His own mobile phone rang again: Gloria looking for him, no doubt. It was eleven o'clock and he couldn't bring himself to answer; he didn't know what he could possibly say to her. He didn't want to lie, so lately he had avoided conversation with her altogether, leaving the house before she woke, arriving home after she had fallen asleep. He knew his behavior would most definitely be upsetting her, sweet, patient Gloria, who never nagged as friends of his claimed their partners did. She always gave him the space he needed, and felt secure enough in herself to know that he wouldn't betray her. But he was; he was betraying her patience now and perhaps even driving her away. Maybe that's what he wanted. Maybe it wasn't. All he knew was that Donal's disappearance had brought an end to talks of family and marriage that had previously seemed so important to him, to them both. Right now he was putting their relationship aside and focusing on finding his missing brother. Somehow he felt that by finding Sandy, he would be one step closer to finding Donal, or perhaps that was just another excuse, another obsession to delay moving on with life, to delay confronting Gloria over a relationship he no longer knew how he felt about.

He did the only thing he could think of. He picked up his phone and rang Graham Turner, the guard Jack and his family had been dealing with during the search for Donal.

"Hello?" Graham answered. The background was noisy with shouts, chatter, and laughter. Pub noises.

"Graham, it's Jack," Jack shouted in the silent wooded area.

"Hello?" Graham shouted again.

"It's Jack." He raised his voice even higher, startling whatever animals had taken refuge in the nearby trees.

"Hold on, I'm going outside," Graham shouted. The voices and noise grew louder as the phone was carried through the pub. Finally there was silence. "Hello?" Graham said more quietly.

"Graham, it's Jack." He kept his voice down now. "Sorry to call you so late."

"No problem, is everything OK?" Graham asked with concern, used to Jack's late-night calls over the past year.

"Yeah, things are OK," Jack lied.

"Any news on Donal?"

"No, no news. Actually I was calling you about something else."

"Sure, what's up?"

How on earth was he going to explain this? "I'm just a bit worried about someone. I was due to meet them yesterday morning in Glin but they didn't show up."

Silence.

"I see."

"A message on my answering machine was left before leaving Dublin to let me know they were on their way down but they never showed and the car is parked down by the Estuary."

Silence.

"Yeah."

"I'm just starting to get worried, you know?"

"Yeah, yeah, I know. You're bound to under the circumstances."

That one statement suddenly made Jack feel like a raving paranoid lunatic. Maybe he was.

"I know it sounds like nothing but I think it's something, you know?"

"Yeah, yeah, of course," Graham said hurriedly. "Sorry, hold on one minute." The phone was covered as voices became muffled. "Yeah, another pint. Cheers, Damian. I'll be in as soon as I finish my smoke," he said, and then came back on the line. "Sorry about that."

"No problem. Look, I know it's late and you're out. I apologize for calling." Jack held his head in his hands, feeling like a fool. His story had sounded stupid and his concern for Sandy unnecessary as soon as he had expressed them but he knew deep down that things weren't right.

"Don't worry about it. What do you want me to do? What's the guy's name and I'll ask around?"

"Sandy Shortt."

"*Sandy* Shortt." Yep, the guy was a woman.

"Yeah."

"Right."

"And you were to meet her . . . ?"

"In Glin yesterday. We passed each other at Lloyds station, you know, the one on—"

"Yeah, I know it."

"Yeah, well, we met there at about five thirty A.M. but she didn't show up later that morning."

"She didn't say where she was going when you met her?"

"No, we hardly spoke."

"What does she look like?"

"Very tall, curly black hair . . ." He trailed off, realizing he had no idea what Sandy Shortt looked like, he had no reason to believe that the woman he had passed at the petrol station even was Sandy Shortt. The only proof he had was a file on the dashboard with Donal's name on it. The driver could have been anyone. He had allowed all the pieces to fit together nicely without even questioning its sense, which right now seemed liked none at all.

"Jack?" Graham was calling him.

"Yeah."

"She's tall with curly black hair. Know anything else? Her age or where she's from or anything?"

"No, I don't know, Graham. I'm not even sure what she looks like. We only ever spoke over the phone, I don't even know if that was her at the station." He suddenly had a thought. "She used to be a garda. In Dublin. She quit four years ago. That's all I know." He gave up.

"OK. Right, well, I'll make a few phone calls and get back to you."

"Thanks." Jack felt humiliated, his story was full of holes. "You'll keep this between us, won't you?" he asked quietly.

"Will do. All well with Gloria?" The tone was accusing. Or maybe it wasn't, it was possible Jack was misjudging everything these days.

"Great, yeah."

"Good. Send her my regards. You've got a saint there, Jack."

"Yeah, I know," he replied defensively.

Silence. Then pub atmosphere.

"I'll get back to you, Jack," Graham shouted. The line went dead.

Jack thumped his head, feeling like an idiot.

At midnight, as he ran a finger up and down the side of the cold metal car as he paced, his phone rang. He had already texted Gloria to let her know he would be home late, and so he knew it wasn't her when he answered.

"Jack, it's Graham here." His tone was gentler than before. "Listen, I made a few calls, asked around the lads to see if any of them knew a Sandy Shortt."

"Go on." His heart thumped.

"You should have told me, Jack," Graham said softly.

Jack nodded in the darkness, though Graham couldn't see him. Graham continued, "Seems you shouldn't worry about her. A good few of the lads knew her." He laughed, and stopped himself. "They said she disappears all the time without letting anyone know. She's a hermit, keeps to herself and comes and goes as she pleases but always comes back within a week or so. I wouldn't worry about her, Jack. This seems to be in keeping with her usual behavior."

"But what about her car?"

"A 1991 red Ford Fiesta?"

"Yeah."

"That's hers, all right. Don't worry about it; she's probably around the area checking out the place. The lads say she's a keen jogger, so she probably parked there and went for a run earlier, or maybe the car wouldn't start or something simple as that. Anyway, it's been a little over twenty-four hours since you were supposed to meet. There's no need to panic."

"I thought the first twenty-four hours were supposed to be the most important," Jack said through gritted teeth.

"In missing-persons cases they are, Jack, but this Sandy Shortt isn't missing. She likes to disappear all the time. I was told that most of the time even her family doesn't know where she is. They called the guards on three occasions years ago but they don't bother anymore. She comes back."

Jack was silent.

"There's not much I can do. There's nothing to go on, nothing to suggest she's in any danger. She'll probably call you in a few days. According to her ex-colleagues, that's the way she works."

"I know, I know." Jack rubbed his eyes wearily.

"As a word of advice, be careful of those kinds of people. Agencies like Sandy Shortt's are just out to make money, you know? I wouldn't be surprised if she's done a runner. There's nothing that they can do that we haven't already done. There aren't any more places to search that we haven't already searched."

Sandy hadn't asked for a cent, knowing that Jack hadn't got a cent to give.

"I had to do something." That was all he could reply. He didn't like how Graham was referring to Sandy. He didn't believe she was crooked, he didn't believe she had gone wandering off on an investigation without her phone, her file, her diary, and her car, or was still jogging at midnight. Nothing Graham said made sense, yet nothing Jack said aloud seemed to make sense either. He was going entirely by instinct alone, instinct that had been affected by Donal's disappearance and a week of nightly phone calls to a woman he had never met.

"I understand," Graham responded. "I'd probably do the same myself if I was in your shoes."

"What about my stuff that's locked in her car?" Jack bluffed.

"What stuff?"

"I sent her Donal's file and a few other things, I can see them sitting in the car. If she's going to take my money and run, I'd at least like my things back."

"I can't help you out in that area, Jack, but I wouldn't be asking any questions if by morning your belongings are back in your possession."

"Thanks, Graham."

"Anything at all to help."

A few hours later, as the sun was rising over the Estuary, casting orange hues on black ripples, Jack found himself sitting in Sandy's car, leafing through Donal's file and through all the pages of Garda reports that only Sandy had been able to retrieve through her contacts. Her diary revealed a plan to go to Limerick city the following day to visit one of Donal's friends, Alan O'Connor, who had been out with Donal the night of his disappearance. Hope returned at the possibility of meeting her there. The cramped car smelled sickeningly sweet of the vanilla-fragrance air freshener that hung from the dashboard mirror, mixed with the tinge of stale coffee from the Styrofoam cup balanced below it. There was nothing about the car that gave him any more clues as to the type of person Sandy was. There were no wrappers left behind, no CDs or cassettes revealing her taste in music. Just an old, cold car with work and cold coffee left behind.

It had no heart; she had taken that part with her.

21

I awoke, I wasn't sure how many hours later, to see a little girl with wild, black frizzy hair perched next to me on the arm of the couch, watching me with the same intense black eyes as her grandfather's.

I jumped.

She smiled. Dimples dented her yellow skin and her eyes softened to a dark brown.

"Hi," she chirped.

I looked around the room that was now almost pitch-black save for the orange light creeping under the kitchen door, lighting the floor just enough for me to be able to make out my surroundings and the little girl half-lit before me. The sky outside the window over the sink was black. Stars, the same stars I never paid the slightest bit of notice to at home, hung above like Christmas lights decorating a toy village.

"Well, aren't you going to say hi?" the little voice again chirped happily.

I sighed; I had never had time for children and had even despised being one myself.

"Hi," I said with disinterest.

"See? That wasn't so hard, was it?"

"Excruciating." I yawned and stretched.

She hopped off the arm of the sofa and bounced onto the end, joining me but crushing my feet in the process.

"Ouch," I moaned, tucking my legs closer to my body.

"That can't have hurt." She lowered her head and viewed me doubtingly.

"How old are you, one hundred and ninety?" I asked, pulling my blanket around me tighter as though it would protect me from her.

"If I was a hundred and ninety, I'd be dead." She rolled her eyes.

"And what a shame that would be."

"You don't like me, do you?"

I thought about that. "Not really."

"Why not?"

"Because you sat on my feet."

"You didn't like me before I sat on your feet."

"True."

"Most people think I'm cute." She sighed.

"Really?" I asked in mock surprise. "I don't get that impression."

"Why not?" She didn't seem to be insulted, just more interested.

"Because you're three feet tall and you have no front teeth." I closed my eyes, wishing she'd go away, and rested my head against the back of the couch. The throbbing in my head had dissipated but the chirping at the end of the couch would no doubt bring it back in full force.

"I won't be like this forever, you know," she said, trying to please me.

"I hope so for your case."

"Me too," she said with a sigh and rested her head on the back of the couch, imitating me.

I stared at her in silence, hoping she'd take the hint and go away. She smiled at me.

"Most people's impression of me is that I don't want to talk to them," I hinted.

"Really? I don't get that impression," she imitated me, saying the words with difficulty in her toothless mouth.

I laughed. "What age are you?"

She held up her hand displaying four fingers and a thumb.

"Four fingers and a thumb?" I asked.

She frowned and looked at her hand again, her lips moving as she counted.

"Is there a special school kids go to, to learn to do that?" I asked. "Can't you just say five?"

"I can say *five*."

"So what, you think holding up a hand is cuter?"

She shrugged.

"Where is everyone?"

"Asleep. Did you used to have a television? We have televisions here but they don't work."

"Bummer for you."

"Yeah, bummer." She sighed dramatically but I don't think she cared. "My grandma says I ask a lot of questions but I think you ask more."

"You like to ask questions?" I was suddenly interested. "What kind of questions?"

She shrugged. "Normal questions."

"About what?"

"Everything."

"You keep on asking them, Wanda, maybe you'll get out of here."

"OK."

Silence.

"Why would I want to get out of here?"

Not such normal questions after all, it appeared. "Do you like it here?"

She looked around the room. "I prefer my own room."

"No, this *village* place." I pointed out the window. "Where you live."

She nodded.

"What do you do all day?"

"Play."

"How tiring for you."

She nodded. "Sometimes it is. I start school soon though."

"There's a school here?"

"Not in here."

She still couldn't get past this room. "What do your parents do all day?"

"Mama works with Granddad."

"She's a carpenter too?"

She shook her head. "We don't have a car."

"What does your dad do?"

She shrugged again. "Mama and Daddy stopped liking each other. Have you got a boyfriend?"

"No."

"Ever had one?"

"I've had more than one."

"At the same time?"

I didn't answer.

"Why aren't you with any of them now?"

"Because I stopped liking them."

"*All* of them?"

"Almost all of them."

"Oh. That's not very nice."

"No." My mind wandered. "I suppose it's not."

"Does it make you sad? It makes Mama sad."

"No, it doesn't make me sad." I laughed awkwardly not feeling comfortable with her gaze or loose tongue.

"You look sad."

"How can I look sad when I'm laughing?"

She shrugged again. That's why I hated children; there were so many empty spaces in their minds and not enough answers, the exact reason why I'd hated being one myself. There was always a lack of knowledge about what was going on and seldom did I come across an adult who could enlighten me.

"Wanda, for someone who asks a lot of questions, you don't know a lot of answers."

"I ask different questions than you do." She frowned. "I know lots of answers."

"Like what?"

"Like . . ." She thought hard. "The reason Mr Ngambao from next door doesn't work in the fields is because he has a sore back."

"Where are the fields?"

She pointed out the window. "That way. That's where

our food grows and then everyone goes to the eatery three times every day to eat it."

"The entire village eats together?"

She nodded. "Petra's mama works there but I don't want to work there when I'm older, or in the fields, I want to work with Bobby," she said dreamily. "My friend Lacey's dad works in the library."

I searched for the importance of her sentence and found none. "Does anybody ever think of spending their time more wisely, like trying to get the hell out of here?" I asked smartly, more to myself.

"People try to leave," she said, "but they can't. There's no way out, but I like it here, so I don't mind." She yawned. "I'm tired. I'm going to bed. 'Night." She climbed down off the couch and made her way to the door dragging a torn blanket behind her. "Is this yours?" She stopped, bending over to pick up something from the floor. She held it up and I saw it shine as the light seeping in from under the door hit it.

"Yes," I said, taking my watch from her hands.

The door opened, orange light filled the room, forcing me to close my eyes, and then I heard it shut again and I was alone in the darkness with the words of a five-year-old ringing in my ears.

"People try to leave but they can't. There's no way out . . ."

That was the other thing I hated about kids; they always said the exact things that deep down you already knew, would never admit to, and most certainly never wanted to hear.

22

"So Joseph is a carpenter. What is it that you do, Mary?" I asked Helena as we strolled along the dusty path of the village.

Helena smiled.

We had walked through the village and now wandered beyond, passing fields of glorious golds and greens, dotted with people of all nationalities who stooped and rose as they worked the farm, growing anything and everything I had ever and never heard of. Dozens of greenhouses speckled the landscape, the villagers taking every opportunity to grow what they could. Like the diverse people, the weather had arrived in this place in all its fiery yet vital forms. Already in just a few days I'd experienced the sweltering heat, a thunderstorm, a spring breeze, and a winter chill, inconsistent weather I presumed to be the explanation for the unusual array of plants, trees, flowers, and crops that all managed to live together successfully in the same environment. The explanation for the humans, I hadn't yet learned of. But it seemed there were no rules regarding nature in this place. Four seasons in one day was accepted, welcomed, and adapted to. It was warm again now as we strolled side by side, me feeling revitalized after sleeping more hours in one night than I had since I was a child. Since Jenny-May.

"Since Jenny-May *what*?" Gregory would always ask me. "Since she went missing?"

"No, just since *Jenny-May*—period," I would reply.

That morning I encountered someone I had been searching for for twelve years. Helena had urged me onward, snapping shut my gaping mouth and clicking fingers before my goggling eyes. I was overwhelmed by her presence, and I was never overwhelmed. I was dumbfounded, and I was never dumbfounded. I suddenly felt lonely, and I was never lonely. But lately I was a lot of things I never used to be. After so many years of looking, it was near impossible to remain as serene as Helena when the faces I saw in my dreams passed me in my waking hours.

"Stay calm," Helena had murmured more than once into my ear.

Robin Geraghty was the first of my ghosts to float by. We had been seated at the eatery, a stunning timber building on two levels, with a balcony around four sides from which the views of forestry, mountains, and fields were displayed to perfection. It wasn't a crammed work cafeteria, as I had imagined; it was a beautiful building that housed the local villagers for breakfast, lunch, and dinner; a scheme created to help ration the food they collected and grew. Money, I recalled, had no value here, not even when wallets filled with it arrived on their doorsteps. "Why spend money on something that arrives in abundance daily?" Helena had asked by way of explanation.

On the front of the building, ornate handcrafted timber decorated the entrance as it did the registry. Owing to the many languages of the village, Helena explained, these carvings were the most productive and attractive methods of exhibiting the use of the building. Oversized grapevines, wine bottles, and bread loaves decorated the front, looking so delectable even in their lumber form that I had to run my hand along the smooth curve of the berry.

I was returning from my trip to the buffet-style counter when I saw Robin, causing me almost to drop my tray of doughnuts and iced coffee. (It appeared that a box of food had gone missing from a Krispy Kreme delivery van and had arrived on the outskirts of the village that morning, much to my delight. I had visions of a delivery man, clipboard in hand, ignoring the insults of a stressed-out store manager, as he scratched his head in wonder and recounted the contents of his van, parked up on a busy loading bay outside a downtown New York store while I, and a line of hungry people behind me, dove into the basket in a long-lost place.) The appearance of Robin almost caused me to douse myself; it was as though my iced coffee got a fright too, wavering slightly in its stance.

Robin Geraghty had disappeared at the age of six. She had gone out to play in her front garden in the suburbs of North Dublin at eleven A.M. but was gone when her mother checked on her at eleven-oh-five. Everyone, and I mean *everyone*, the family, the country, the Gardaí, which at that time included me, all thought she had been abducted by the next-door neighbor. Fifty-five-year-old Dennis Fairman, an odd man, a loner, spoke to nobody but Robin each time he passed her, much to her parents' concern.

He said he didn't do it. He swore to me he didn't do it; he kept on repeating that she was his friend and that he couldn't and wouldn't hurt her. Nobody believed him; *I* didn't believe him; yet we didn't have the proof of his guilt. We didn't even have a body. The man became so tormented by his neighbors, by the media, by the constant Garda questioning that he ended his own life, a sure sign to the parents and everybody else of his guilt. But as a nineteen-year-old Robin walked by me and made her way to the counter, I felt ill.

Although Robin had disappeared at the age of six, I knew it was she the moment I lifted my ogling eyes from the Krispy Kreme to see the young woman walk by. A computer-generated image of her had been made public and updated every few years. I had memorized it, had used it every day as part of my mind checks when I came across familiar faces. And that face was all of a sudden coming toward me. The computer image hadn't been far off, though her face was fuller; her hair was darker; there was a swing in her hips and a knowledge in her eyes as all she had seen and done had altered all but their color. All the things a picture couldn't convey. But it was she.

I'd been unable to eat my breakfast; instead I sat in a daze at the table with Helena's family, while Wanda studied me and impersonated my every move. I ignored her and her constant babbling about somebody called Bobby, instead unable to stop myself from watching Robin while trying to figure out how I felt about seeing this young woman living life as she had done for the past twelve years. My feelings were mixed, my happiness bittersweet, because although all the people I yearned to find surrounded me, it was also the moment I realized that I had spent a colossal portion of my life looking in all the wrong places. It's that moment when you meet your idol, when all your wishes come true; there's a feeling of secret disappointment.

Helena and I stopped walking at an uncultivated multicolored field filled with bright yellow Bermuda buttercups, blue-and-mauve milkwort, daisies, dandelions, and long grasses, the sweet smell reminding me of the last few breaths I had taken in Glin.

"What's up ahead?" I spotted more buildings peeking out behind a gathering of silver birch, the oak visible against the peeling, papery black-and-white bark of the trunk.

"That's another village," Helena explained. "There are so many new arrivals every day, we couldn't possibly fit into this tiny town. Also there are so many cultures that wouldn't and couldn't settle for living in environments like this. Their homes are out there." She nodded toward the faraway trees and mountains.

I hadn't even contemplated that. "So there are more people I've searched for, over there?"

"Possibly," she said in agreement. "They would have registry offices just as we have here so all the names will be logged, although I'm not sure they'll release the information, as it's usually deemed private unless in the case of emergencies. Hopefully, we won't have to go looking for them, they'll find you."

I smiled at the irony. "What exactly is this plan you're hatching?"

"Well," she said, smiling as her eyes sparkled mischievously, "thanks to the list you provided me with, Joan is now taking bookings for private auditions for a new Irish play in about"—she lifted my hand and looked at my watch—"two hours' time."

I felt anxious about meeting people like Robin, but Helena's plan made me laugh. "Surely there could have been an easier way to do this."

"Of course," Helena said, throwing her lemon pashmina over her right shoulder, "but this is so much more fun."

"What makes you think that any of the people on my list will come to these auditions?"

"Are you joking?" She looked surprised, "Didn't you see Bernard and Joan? Most people here really love to get involved in activities, especially ones held by people from home."

"Won't the non-Irish communities be jealous?" I half-joked. "I wouldn't want them to think I'm omitting them from my grand production."

"No." Helena laughed. "Everyone will have a laugh at our expense come show time."

"Show time? You mean we're actually staging a play?" My eyes widened.

"Of course!" Helena laughed again. "We're not dragging

twenty people to the auditions just to tell them there's no play, but what exactly that play will be we've yet to decide."

My headache returned. "As soon as I start talking to them today they're going to realize the likelihood of my running an acting agency is no greater than Bernard's chances of landing a lead role."

Helena laughed. "Don't worry, they won't suspect a thing, and even if they do they won't mind. People tend to reinvent themselves here; they use this experience as a second chance in life. If what you were at home was not an acting agent, it doesn't mean that you're not one here. The longer you're here the more you'll notice that there really is a good atmosphere among everyone."

I had noticed. The atmosphere was relaxed; people were peaceful and went about their daily duties efficiently yet without rushing or panic. There was room to breathe, space to think, time to spend wisely, and lessons to be learned. People who were once lost took time to reflect, to love, to miss, and to remember. Belonging was important, even if it meant joining a hopeless play.

"Won't Joseph mind that he can't take part?"

Helena laughed. "Oh, I don't think that will worry him in the slightest."

"Joseph is from Kenya?"

"Yes." We began walking back toward the village. "Along the coast of Watamu."

"What was it he called me yesterday?"

Helena's expression changed and I knew she was feigning ignorance. "What do you mean?"

"Come on, Helena, I saw your face when he called

me it, you were surprised. I can't remember the word, kalla . . . kappa something; what does it mean?"

Her forehead wrinkled in pretend confusion. "Sorry, Sandy, I've no idea. I honestly can't remember."

I didn't believe her. "Did you tell him what I do for a living?"

Her face changed to that same intrigued look from yesterday. "He knows *now*, of course, but he didn't then."

"He didn't *when*?"

"When he met you."

"Of course he didn't, I don't expect him to be psychic, I just want to know what he said." I stopped walking out of frustration. "Helena, please be straight with me, I can't take riddles."

Her face pinked. "You'll have to ask him, Sandy, because I don't know. Whatever it was, it must have been in his local Kiswahili language, and I'm far from being an expert."

I was convinced she was lying and so we walked in silence. I looked at my watch again, anxious that I would soon be sharing messages from family members at home. Messages they sent off in their prayers every night to land here and be told. I questioned my ability to transmit their sentiments accurately. What I had said to Helena the previous day was true, I *wasn't* a people person; finding them didn't mean wanting to spend time with them. Wondering where Jenny-May went didn't mean wanting to go there or wishing she'd return.

Helena, as usual, in her own instinctive way picked up on my feelings. "It was nice being able to tell Joseph about my family at long last," she said gently. "We spoke about them until my lids closed and I dreamed about them until the sun came up. I dreamed about my mother and her organization, about my father and his searching for me." She closed her eyes. "I woke up in this place this morning hardly knowing where I was after spending hours in my dreams where I grew up."

"I'm sorry if I upset you. I'm not quite sure how to tell people what it is their families would want me to say." I twisted my watch around as we walked, wanting to turn back the time that kept ticking on around my wrist.

Helena's eyes opened and I could see a layer of tears settling on her lower lashes, building up in an invisible reservoir. "Don't think that about yourself, Sandy. I felt soothed by your words, how could I not be?" Her face brightened. "I woke up *knowing* I had a mother out there still minding me. Today I feel protected, like I'm swaddled in an invisible blanket. You know, you're not the only one whose lifelong questions have been answered I now have photographs in my mind that I never had before; an entire catalog has been filed and stored, all in one night."

I just nodded. There was nothing to say.

"You will be fine with these people; I know you will be *more* than fine. The people on the list you have given will be arriving in how long?"

I looked at my watch. "An hour and a half."

"Right, in ninety minutes they'll all be there with the full intention of spending a short while of their lives calling Romeo from a balcony or reenacting the great escape through the art of mime."

I laughed.

"Anything more you tell them will be a bonus, no matter how you phrase it."

"Thank you, Helena."

"No problem." She gave my arm a comforting pat and I tried to stop myself from stiffening.

I looked down at my clothes. "There's just one more problem. I've been wearing this tracksuit for days and I would really love a change of clothes. Is there anything you have that I could borrow?"

"Oh, don't worry about that," Helena said walking off in the direction of the trees. "You wait here; I'll be back in a minute."

"Where are you going?"

"Just a minute . . ." Her voice disappeared, along with her short salt-and-pepper hair and billowing lemon pashmina, into the darkness.

I tapped my foot impatiently, wondering and worrying about where she'd gone. I couldn't lose Helena now. Up ahead I spotted the towering figure of Joseph leaving the woods, carrying logs in one hand, an axe in the other.

"Joseph!" I called.

He looked up and waved with the axe, a motion that wasn't particularly heartwarming, and he made his way toward me. His bald head shone like a polished marble, his flawless skin making him appear younger than his years.

"Everything OK?" he asked with concern.

"Yes, I think so. Well, I don't know," I added with confusion. "Helena just disappeared into the woods and—"

"What?" His eyes darkened.

I realized my error. "I don't mean *disappeared*. She walked, *walked* into the woods a few minutes ago." Disappearing from here was impossible, so no wonder Joseph was alarmed. "She told me to wait here for her."

He set the axe down and watched the woods. "She will return, *kipepeo* girl." His voice was gentle.

"What does that mean?"

"It means she will come back," he said with a smile.

"Not *that*, what does the Kenyan word mean?"

"It is what you are," he said lazily, his eyes not moving from the trees.

"Which is?"

Before he had a chance to answer the question, Helena reappeared tugging what appeared to be luggage behind her. "Found this for you. Oh, hi, sweetheart, I thought I heard you tapping away at the trees. Name on the bag says Barbara Langley from Ohio. Hope for your sake Barbara from Ohio has long legs." She dropped the bag by my feet and dusted off her hands.

"What is this?" I asked open-mouthed, studying the baggage ticket on the handle. "This was bound for New York over twenty years ago."

"Great, you'll have a nice retro look," Helena joked.

"I can't wear someone else's clothes," I protested.

"Why not? You were going to wear mine." Helena laughed.

"But I know you!"

"Yes, but you wouldn't have known the person who wore them before me," she teased, heading off before me.

"Come now, how much time have we left? We're going to the auditions now," she explained to Joseph, who nodded solemnly and picked up his axe again.

I looked at my wrist. My watch was gone.

"Oh, damnit," I grumbled, dropping the bag back down on the ground and searching around my legs.

"What's wrong?" Helena and Joseph stopped walking and turned around.

"My watch fell off my wrist again," I grumbled, standing back and scouring the ground.

"Again?"

"The fastener on it is broken. Sometimes it just opens and falls onto the ground." My voice was muffled as I went down on my knees and searched closer to the ground.

"Well, you were wearing it just a minute ago so it can't have gone far. Just lift the bag," Helena said calmly.

I looked under the bag.

"That's funny." Helena came over to where I stood and leaned over to get a closer look at the ground. "Did you go anywhere when I went into the trees?"

"No, nowhere. I was waiting *right* here with Joseph." I began crawling around the dusty ground.

"It can't have gone missing," Helena said, not at all worried about the situation. "We'll find it, we always do, here."

We all stood still as we looked around the small area I hadn't moved from for over five minutes. There was nowhere else it could have fallen. I shook out my sleeves, emptied my pockets, and checked the bag to see if the watch had got caught up. Nothing, no sign, nowhere.

"Where on earth did it roll to?" Helena muttered, examining the ground.

Joseph, who had barely said a word since he'd joined us, stood still in the same place he had been standing all along. His eyes, as black as coal, appeared to have absorbed all light from around him. They were on me the whole time.

Just watching.

23

I spent the next half hour searching the road for my watch, retracing my steps over and over again in my usual obsessive way. I combed the long grass by the sides of the uncultivated fields and dug my hands deep into the soil lining the forest. The watch was nowhere to be seen but this brought a strange kind of comfort to me. My mind instantly erased where I was and all that had happened, and for those few moments I was me again with one goal. Finding. As a ten-year-old I would hunt for a single sock as though it had the value of the rarest diamond in the world, but this time it was different; the watch was worth far more.

Joseph and Helena watched over me worriedly as I uprooted grass followed by sods, in order to find the precious jewel that had clung to my wrist for thirteen years. Its inability to remain where it should have been for too much of that time pretty much tallied with the inconsistency of the relationship with the person who had given it to me. But even those times when it released itself from my clutches and flew off, drawn in the opposite direction to the one I was heading, I always looked out for it and wanted to be near it. That way too, exactly like the relationship.

Helena and Joseph didn't pretend, as my parents used to when I had a hunting episode. They looked worried and they were right to, because for people who said nothing could or ever had gone missing in this place, they were finding it difficult having to munch on and digest their own words. At least that's what the obsessive side of me thought. The rational side of me reckoned the more obvious cause for their concern may have just been me, on my hands and knees, covered in dust, dirt, grass stains, and muck.

"I think you should stop looking now," Helena said with a hint of amusement on her face. "You have lots of people to meet at the Community Hall, not to mention now needing a shower and change of clothes."

"They can wait," I said, clawing my way through the grass, feeling soil gathering beneath my fingernails.

"They've waited long enough," Helena said forcefully, "and frankly so have you. Now stop trying to avoid the inevitable and come with me now."

I stopped clawing. There was the word I was so used to hearing from Gregory's mouth. *Avoid. Stop avoiding things, Sandy* . . . Was that what I was doing? How I could be avoiding things by concentrating fully on one thing and refusing to leave it had always been beyond me; surely avoidance meant walking in the other direction. It was people like Gregory, my parents, and now Helena and Joseph, who were avoiding dealing with the fact that something had gone missing and couldn't be found. I looked up at Helena, who looked doll-like beside Joseph's huge frame. "I really need to find that watch."

"And you will," she said so easily that I believed her. "Things *always* show up here. Joseph said he would keep an eye out for you and maybe Bobby will know something."

"Who's this Bobby that I keep hearing about?" I asked, getting to my feet.

"He works in Lost and Found," Helena explained, handing me the luggage I had abandoned in the middle of the road.

"Lost and Found." I laughed, shaking my head.

"I'm surprised you didn't end up in the front window," Helena said gently.

"That's Amsterdam you're thinking of," I smiled.

Her forehead wrinkled. "*Amsterdam?* What are you talking about?"

Dusting myself off, I left the search scene behind me. "Helena, you have so much to learn."

"A wonderful piece of advice, coming from someone who spent the last thirty minutes on her hands and knees trawling through muck."

We left Joseph standing in the middle of the road, hands on his hips, logs and axe by his feet, surveying the dusty path.

I arrived at the Community Hall dressed as Barbara Langley from Ohio. Her legs, it seemed, were far from long and had a penchant for miniskirts and leggings I didn't even dare try on. The other items she unfortunately missed out on wearing on her New York trip were stripy sweaters with shoulder pads that brushed my earlobes and jackets covered with badges of peace signs, yin-yang emblems, yellow smiley faces, and American flags. I had hated the eighties the first time round; I had no intention of reliving it.

Helena had laughed when she saw me in skin-tight stonewashed jeans that stopped above my ankles, white socks, my own trainers, and a black T-shirt with a yellow smiley face.

"Do you think Barbara Langley was in *The Breakfast Club*?" I asked, trudging out of the bathroom like a child who had been forced to replace their play clothes with a dress and tights for Sunday dinner of green vegetables aplenty.

Helena looked confused. "I have no idea what clubs she was a member of, although I do see others wearing those kinds of clothes here."

I ended up doing what I had been convinced I would never resort to, grabbing marginally more decent items of clothing lying alongside the roads as we made our way to the village.

"We can go to Bobby's afterward." Helena had tried to cheer me up. "He has a huge collection of clothes to choose from or else there are a few clothes-makers around."

"I'll just get some secondhand clothes," I insisted. "I won't be here by the time they finish making me a wardrobe."

She snorted at that, much to my annoyance.

The Community Hall was a magnificent oak building

with a large double-door entrance similar to the others. On it were larger-than-life carvings of people gathered together, arms and shoulders touching and hands holding while their hair and clothes flapped in a breeze trapped in the walls of wood. Helena pushed open the twelve-foot-tall doors and the crowd parted for us.

A stage stood at the top of the forty-foot-long hall; all around it on three sides were rows of solid oak chairs and the same above on a second gallery level. A red velvet curtain parted and was held back on both sides by a thick golden rope. On the entire length of the back wall on the stage was a canvas covered in handprints created by hands dipped in black paint. They were all of different sizes, representing different ages from babies to the elderly as they lined up in a row of at least one hundred across and one hundred down. Above it were two words written in many languages, but reading the English I saw that they meant *strength* and *hope*. It was so familiar to me.

"They are the handprints of each person that lives and has lived here over the past three years. Each village has the same in its community hall. I suppose it's our emblem now for here."

"I recognize it," I said, thinking aloud.

"Oh no, you couldn't." Helena shook her head. "The Community Hall is the only place you'll see this in the village."

"No, I recognize it from home. There is a national monument just like it on the grounds of Kilkenny Castle. Each hand was cast from the actual hand of a relative of a missing person. Beside it is a stone with an inscription of the words," I said, and closed my eyes and recited the inscription I had run my finger over so many times: *"This sculpture and area of reflection is dedicated to all missing persons. May all relatives and friends who visit find continuing strength and hope. The cast of your mother's hand is there."*

Helena looked as though she was holding her breath as she searched my face, waiting for me to somehow announce that I was joking. I didn't and she exhaled slowly.

"Well, I don't know what to say." Her voice shook and she turned to look at it. "Joseph thought it would be a nice idea for everyone to do that." She shook her head in disbelief. "Wait until he hears what you've told me."

"Wow," I said, looking around the rest of the building. It was more like a theater than a community hall.

"This seats twenty-five hundred people," Helena explained, moving on from what I had told her though understandably seeming somewhat distracted. "The chairs are taken out if we need to hold more but it's very rare that the entire community will attend anything. It's used for lots of different things such as a ballot hall, a discussion forum between the elected council and the community, art galleries, debates, even a theater on the rare occasions that plays are staged. The list goes on."

"Who is on the elected council?"

"A representative from each nation in the village. We have over one hundred nations in this village alone and every village has its own council. There are dozens of villages."

"So what happens at these council meetings?" I asked with amusement.

"The same as everywhere else in the world; everything that needs discussion and decision is discussed and decided."

"What are the crime levels here?"

"Minimal."

"How is it kept that way? I don't recall seeing the long hand of the law patroling the streets on our way here. How is everyone kept on the straight and narrow?"

"There has been a judicial system in place for hundreds of years. We have a courthouse, a rehabilitation institute, and a security council, but getting every nation to abide by the same rules isn't always easy. The council at least encourages talk and debate."

"So this is the sounding house? Do they actually have any power?"

"The power that we have vested in them. Everybody gets one of these in their information pack when they arrive." Helena took a pamphlet from a display on the wall. "You should have got one too, if you bothered to look through your folder. There are voting guidelines."

I flicked through the pamphlet, reading aloud: "Vote for those with the ability to listen and to make decisions on behalf of the people in a manner reflecting consensus and serving the well-being of all." I laughed. "What else is preached, two legs good, four legs bad?"

"They are the basics of good leadership."

"Well, does this pamphlet for how to elect a leader work?" I smirked.

"I should think so." She made her way over to Joan,

who was on the far side of the room. "Seeing as Joseph is on the council."

My mouth dropped as I watched her cross the room. *"Joseph?"*

"You seem surprised."

"Yes, well, I am surprised. He seems so . . ." I searched for the correct way to explain without offending her. "He's a carpenter," I eventually settled on.

"Those on the council are ordinary people with their own day jobs. He's merely called on to voice decisions when decisions need voicing."

I couldn't stop smiling. "I just get the feeling that everybody here is playing 'House,' you know? It's hard to take seriously." I laughed. "Come on, I mean we're in the middle of *nowhere* and you have councils and courthouses and who knows what else?"

"You think it's funny?"

"Yes!" I smiled. "Everywhere I look everyone's playing dress-up in other people's clothes. How can this place, wherever this place *is*, have any kind of order or rules at all? It exists completely without *logic*; it lacks all sense of *practicality*."

Helena seemed offended at first but then became sympathetic, which I hated. "This is *life*, Sandy, *real life*. Sooner or later you'll discover that nobody's playing any games here. We're all just getting on with life and doing what we can to make it as normal as possible, just like everybody else, in every other country, in every other world." She approached Joan. "How did you get on with Sandy's list?" she asked, ending our conversation.

Joan looked up in surprise. "Oh, hello, I didn't hear

you both coming. You look"—she gave my eighties outfit the once-over—"different."

"Did you get in touch with everyone on the list?" I asked, ignoring her disapproving gaze.

"No, not all of them," she said, glancing down at her page.

"Let me see." I grabbed her notepad, my body surged with a sudden rush of adrenalin. My eyes scanned through the list of thirty names I had provided her with: fewer than half of them had ticks beside them. Joan continued talking as I read through the names so quickly I was barely able to take them in. My heart beat wildly and skipped a beat each time my eyes registered a name and I realized that person was alive and well and that soon we would be meeting.

"As I was saying," Joan spoke, angry I had jumped ahead of her story, "Terence at the registry was no help because he couldn't give out any information unless someone from the council requested it for official reasons." She eyed Helena warily. "So I had to just ask around the village, but you'll be pleased to know, Sandy, the Irish community here is so small that everyone knows everyone anyway."

"Go on," Helena urged.

"Well, I got in contact with quite a lot of people, twelve in total," she continued. "Eight are interested in auditioning, the other four said they'd take part in the production in some way but definitely not on stage. But I didn't get the likes of, let me see . . ." She put her glasses on and lifted the page.

"Jenny-May Butler." I finished the sentence for her, my heart plunging into the depths of my stomach.

Helena looked at me, obviously recognizing the name from the time of my collapse.

"Bobby Stanley," I read another name, my hopes dashed. I continued, "James Moore, Clare Steenson . . ." The list of untraceable people went on.

"Well, just because they're not here doesn't mean they're not in the next village," Joan tried reassuring me.

"What are the chances of that?" I asked, feeling hopeful again.

"I won't lie to you, Sandy. The majority of the Irish community are in this village," Helena explained. "Five to fifteen people, at most, arrive each year, and because there are so few of us we tend to stick together."

"So Jenny-May Butler must be here," I said forcefully. "She has to be here."

"What about the others on the list?" Joan said in a quiet voice.

I scanned it quickly, Clare and Peter, Stephanie and Simon . . . I had sat with their relatives long into the night, thumbed through photo albums, and wiped tears through promises of finding their children, brothers, sisters, and friends. If they weren't here then it meant I could only suspect the worst.

"But Jenny-May." I started digging into the facts of the case I'd stored in my brain. "There was no one else. Nobody saw anything or anybody."

Joan looked confused; Helena sad.

"She has to be here. There was nothing sinister at all

about her disappearance," I rambled on to myself. "Unless she's hiding, or else she's in another country; I didn't look into other countries."

"OK, Sandy, why don't you just take a seat now? I think you're burning up," Helena interrupted.

"I'm not burning up." I swatted her hand away. "No, she's not hiding and she can't be in another country. She's my age now." I looked to Joan and everything was clear. "You have to find Jenny-May Butler, tell everyone that she's my age. She's thirty-four years old. She's been here since she was ten, I know it."

Joan nodded her head quickly, almost afraid to say no. Helena held out her hands toward me, afraid to touch me yet afraid to move away. I noticed the faces of the two women as they watched me. Worried. I quickly sat down and drank from a glass of water Helena had thrust into my hands.

"Is she OK?" I heard Joan ask Helena as they moved away.

"She's fine," Helena said calmly. "She just really wanted Jenny-May for the play. Let's do our best to find her, shall we?"

"I don't think she's here," Joan whispered.

"Let's look anyway."

"Can I ask why I was given a list of thirty to find? How does Sandy know they can act? When I contacted them all, they were very surprised. Most of them have never been involved in amateur dramatics. What about all the others who are interested in taking part? They're still allowed to audition, aren't they?"

"Of course, everyone's allowed." Helena pawned her off. "The people on the list were just special, that's all."

Of the two thousand people reported missing in Ireland every year, between five and fifteen will never be found. The thirty people I had chosen were the ones I had spent my entire working life obsessed with finding. Others I had found, others I could give up looking for, knowing something sinister was involved, that harm had sadly come to them or that they'd merely walked away of their own accord. But these thirty on the list, they were the ones who had disappeared without a trace and without reason. These were the thirty who haunted me, the thirty without a crime scene to examine or witnesses to question.

I thought of all their relatives and of how I'd promised I'd find their loved ones. I thought of Jack Ruttle, of how only last week I had made that promise. I thought of how I had failed to show up at our meeting in Glin and how now I had once again failed.

Because according to the list, Donal Ruttle wasn't here.

24

On Tuesday morning, exactly two days since Sandy's no-show, Jack, who had not long returned home with Sandy's file on Donal, stepped out into the fresh July morning air and closed the door to the cottage quietly behind him. Around the town, preparations were being made for the pending Irish Coffee Festival; banners were rolled up beside telegraph poles ready to be hung and the back of a truck had been opened up as a makeshift stage for the outdoor trad-band performances. The town was quiet now, though, everybody still in the comfort of their beds, dreaming of other worlds. Jack started his engine, the noise of it loud enough in the quiet square to wake the entire town, and he made his way into Limerick city where, hopefully, he would meet Sandy at Donal's friend Alan's home. He also wanted to pay a visit to his sister Judith.

Judith was the closest of his siblings. Married with five kids, she was a mother from the moment she arrived kicking and screaming into this world. Eight years older than Jack, she had practiced her skills of obedience training and nurturing on every doll and every child that lived nearby. The common joke on the street was that there wasn't a doll in the city that didn't sit up straight and shut up when Judith was around. As soon as Jack was born, she turned her attention to him, a real baby whom she could mother and often smother from that day until now. She was still the one he ran to for advice and she still always found time between school runs, diaper changing, and breastfeeding to lend an ear.

As he pulled up outside her terraced house, the front door opened and the wail of a thousand banshees flew past his ears, almost blowing his hair.

"Daaa-deee," a banshee yelled.

The banshee's father appeared at the door in an off-white creased shirt with an open top button and a loosened tie in an uneven knot. He held in one hand a mug that he clung to for dear life and gulped on with bulging eyes. His other hand gripped a tattered briefcase while the banshee with white-blond hair, Power Rangers pajamas, and Kermit the Frog slippers clung to his leg.

"Dooon't gooooo," she yelled, wrapping her limbs around one of his legs as though her life depended on his staying.

"I have to go, sweetie. Daddy has to work."

"Nooooooo."

An arm appeared from inside the door, thrusting a slice of toast in Willie's direction. "Eat," said Judith's voice over more wails from a second source.

Willie took a bite, slugged down some more coffee, and gently shook Katie from his leg. His head disappeared from the doorway, kissed the owner of the arm, shouted, "Bye, kids!" and the door was slammed. The screams were still audible, yet Willie kept a smile on his face. It was eight A.M. and he'd already been through an hour or two of what Jack would consider pure torture. Yet he smiled.

"Hiya, Jack." His moon-shaped face beamed.

"Good morning Willie," Jack said, noticing how his shirt buttons strained at his gut, a coffee stain decorated his shirt pocket, and there was toothpaste on his paisley tie.

"Sorry. Can't talk. Escaping," he said with chuckle, patting Jack on the back and squeezing into his car. The tailpipe let out a bang and off he sped.

Jack looked around the housing estate of tightly packed gray houses and noticed a similar scene occurring on each doorstep.

He opened the door tentatively, hoping the madhouse wouldn't swallow him whole. He stepped inside and saw fifteen-month-old Nathan running off down the hall, with a bottle hanging from his lips and naked but for a bulging diaper. Jack followed him. Four-year-old Katie, who only seconds ago had clung to her father as though her world was going to end, was sitting a foot away from the television, cross-legged on the floor, a bowl of cereal spilling onto the already stained carpet, completely captivated by dancing bugs singing about the rainforest.

"Nathan!" Judith called pleasantly from the kitchen, "I have to change your diaper. Come back in here, please!"

She had the patience of a saint, while around her, chaos ensued. Toys cluttered every surface, scribbles and drawings were either pinned to the walls or directly *on* the walls. There were baskets of dirty clothes, baskets of clean clothes, clotheshorses with drying clothes lining the walls. The television was blaring, a baby was wailing, pots and pans were being banged. It was a human zoo; three girls and two boys, a ten-year-old, an eight-year-old, a four-year-old, a fifteen-month-old, and a three-month-old, all running riot and demanding attention, while Judith sat at the kitchen table, dressed in her stained robe, hair wild and unwashed, *things* just everywhere, cluttering every surface, and her face a picture of serenity.

"Hi, Jack." She looked up in surprise. "How did you get in here?"

"The door was open, and I followed your doorman in." He nodded at Nathan, who had taken his position on the floor, stinky diaper and all, and had resumed banging pots with a wooden spoon. Three-month-old Rachel was shocked into silence, her eyes widened and her lips parted, ready to release bubbles. "Don't get up." Jack leaned over Rachel in her cot to kiss Judith.

"Nathan, honey, I told you not to unlock the door without Mammy saying so," Judith explained calmly. "He keeps turning the lock," she explained to Jack.

Nathan stopped banging and looked up at her with big blue eyes, a double chin with drool dripping from it. "Dada," he gurgled in response.

"Yes, you do look like your daddy," Judith replied, getting to her feet. "Can I get you anything, Jack? A cup of tea, coffee, toast, earplugs?"

"Tea and toast, please. I've had enough coffee," Jack replied, rubbing his face wearily as the banging of saucepans became almost unbearable.

"Nathan, stop," Judith said firmly, flicking the switch on the kettle. "Come on, let's change your diaper."

She lifted him onto a diaper-changing facility in the kitchen and got to work, giving Nathan her house keys to amuse himself with.

Jack looked away, no longer feeling hungry.

"So why aren't you at work?" Judith asked, holding two pudgy legs together at the ankles as though she were about to stuff a turkey.

"I took the day off."

"Again?"

He didn't answer.

"I spoke to Gloria yesterday and she said you'd taken the day off," Judith explained.

"How did she know?"

Judith pulled a baby wipe from a container. "Now is not the time to start thinking your intelligent partner of eight years is stupid. Oh, what's that I hear?" She held her hand to her ear and looked off into the distance. Nathan stopped jangling the keys and watched her. "Oh, no, I don't hear it anymore but I used to hear the sound of wedding bells and the pitter-patter of tiny feet."

Nathan laughed and continued jangling his keys. Judith popped Nathan back on the floor again, the sound of his feet on the tiles like a duck stepping on puddles.

"Gee, Jack, you've gone awful quiet," she said sarcastically, washing her hands in the kitchen sink, he noted, over a pile of dirty dishes and cups.

"It's not the right time," Jack said tiredly, taking the wooden spoon from Nathan, who in turn started screaming, which woke Rachel, who started screaming, which caused Katie to turn up the volume of the television instantly in the living room. "Besides, this place alone is enough of a contraceptive for me."

"Yes, well, when you marry a man with the name Willie you pretty much know what you're getting." In less than one minute Judith had calm again, a cup of tea and a slice of toast on the table before Jack. She finally sat down, removed Rachel from her cot, moved her bathrobe to one side and began breastfeeding while Rachel's tiny fingers opened and closed in midair, playing an invisible harp with her eyes closed.

"I've taken the week off work," Jack explained. "Arranged it on the way here this morning."

"You've what?" she took a sip of tea. "They let you have more time off?"

"With a bit of persuasion."

"That's good. You and Gloria need to spend more time together." But she could tell by his face that that wasn't the intention. "What's going on, Jack?"

He sighed, wanting so much to tell her the story but afraid to do so.

"Tell me," she said gently.

"I came across someone," he began. "An agency."

"Yes?" Her voice was low and questioning, like it used to be when he came home from school after being in trouble and was forced to explain such things as why they'd stripped Tommy McGovern naked and tied him to the goalposts in the yard.

"It's a missing persons agency."

"Oh, Jack," she whispered, hand flying to her mouth.

"Well, what harm could it do, Jude? What's the damage in one more person having a look?"

"*This* is the damage, Jack. *You*, taking one more week off from work, *Gloria* ringing me looking for you."

"She rang?"

"Ten o'clock last night."

"Oh."

"So go on, tell me about the agency."

"No." He leaned back in his chair, frustrated. "No, I couldn't be bothered now."

"Jack, don't be such a child and tell me."

He waited to cool down before speaking again. "I came across the ad in the Yellow Pages and I gave her a call."

"Who?"

"Sandy Shortt. I explained the case to her and she told me she'd solved cases like this before. We spoke on the phone until late every night last week. She used to be a garda and she got her hands on a few reports we'd never seen."

Judith raised her eyebrows.

"She wasn't asking for a penny, Judith, and I believed her. I believed she wanted to help and I believed she could find Donal. She was legit, there's no doubt about it."

"Why are you speaking about her like she's dead?" She smiled and then stopped quickly, looking alarmed. "She's not dead, is she?"

"No." Jack shook his head. "But I don't know where she is. We arranged to meet on Sunday morning in Glin, we passed one another at a petrol station but I didn't know it was her until after."

Judith's forehead wrinkled.

"We'd only ever spoken on the phone, you see."

"So how do you know it was her?"

"I found her car down by the estuary."

Judith looked even more flummoxed.

"Look, we were supposed to meet and she left a voice message the night before saying she was on her way over from Dublin, but she didn't show up. So I looked around the town, asked for her in all the B&Bs and when I couldn't find her, I went for a walk by the estuary. That's when I found the car."

"How can you be sure it was her car?"

Jack opened the bag beside him. "Because this was on the dashboard." He placed the file on the kitchen table. "So was this," he said, and placed her diary down. "And this." Her charged mobile phone. "She labels *everything*, absolutely everything, I went through her bag, all her clothes, her socks, *all* labeled. It's like she's afraid of losing things."

Judith was quiet. "You went through her bag?" She shook her head, confused. "But how did you get these from the car? Maybe she was just taking a walk, Jack. What if she returns to her car and all her stuff is missing? Are you crazy taking all this?"

"Then I'll have some apologizing to do, but it's been *two* whole days. That's a long walk."

Silence while they both remembered how their mother had been desperately worried after two days of Donal's silence.

"I rang Graham Turner."

"What did he say?" she asked, hands holding her face. The same scenario all over again.

"He said that as it had only been over twenty-four hours and because it was in keeping with her usual behavior that he didn't think there was any cause to worry."

"Why, what's her usual behavior?"

"That she comes and goes as she pleases, keeps to herself and doesn't tell anyone where she's going," Jack rattled off tiredly.

"Oh." Judith looked relieved.

"But that doesn't mean you park your car in the middle of trees by the estuary and desert it for two days. That's slightly different from coming and going as she pleases."

"So let me get this straight," Judith said slowly. "The missing-persons person is missing?"

Silence.

Judith allowed that thought to roll around in her head, shifting it until it found a place it was comfortable to settle in. She looked contemplative as she moved her jaw from side to side.

Then she snorted and burst out laughing.

Jack sat back in his chair and folded his arms, feeling offended as Judith shook uncontrollably before him. Rachel stopped suckling and watched her bouncing mother, who was now wiping tears from her eyes. Nathan stopped playing with his blocks, stood to watch his mother. His face broke into a gummy smile and he began laughing, clapping his pudgy hands and bouncing his body with delight from the knees up. Eventually, Jack felt the corners of his lips tickle and he joined in, laughing deliriously at the ridiculousness of the situation and feeling such relief to let go after so long, even if only momentarily. Once they'd settled down, Judith began rubbing Rachel gently on her back, so soothingly it made Jack's eyes feel heavy.

"Look, Judith, maybe Graham is right. Maybe she did just walk away. Maybe she just thought to hell with all this and left her car, left her phone, her diary, her life, and gave up. Maybe she's this mad, loony woman who does it all the time with the intention of coming back after a while. Maybe she walked away completely but *I'm* going to find her, *she's* going to find Donal, and *then* she can quit. *Then* I'll let her walk away."

"You really think this woman could find Donal?" Judith was contemplative.

"She believed she could."

"What do you think?"

He nodded.

"So if you find her, you'll be helping to find Donal." She was deep in thought. "You know, Willie and I were going through the photo album last night with the kids and Katie pointed to Donal and asked who he was." Her eyes filled. "Neither Katie or Nathan remember him, they'll *never* have a memory of him and Rachel"—she looked down at her baby in her arms—"she doesn't even know he existed. Life is going on without him and he's missing all this." She shook her head.

Jack couldn't think of anything to say, didn't think

there *was* anything to say. The same thoughts ran through his head every second of every day.

"What makes you so sure that a woman you've never even met, a woman you don't know anything about, has the ability to find Donal?"

"Blind faith." He smiled.

"Since when did you ever have that?"

"Since I spoke to Sandy on the phone," he replied earnestly.

"There was nothing . . ." She paused and decided to ask it anyway. "There was nothing between you two, was there?"

"There was something but it was nothing."

"When is something ever nothing?"

He sighed and decided to avoid the question. "Gloria doesn't know about Sandy, not that there's anything to know, but I don't want her or the rest of the family knowing about the agency."

Judith didn't look happy.

"Please, Jude." He grabbed her hand. "I don't want to bring everyone through all this again, I just want to try by myself. I need to."

"OK, OK." She let go, holding her hand up in defense. "So what are you going to do now?"

"Simple." He put the file, diary, and phone back into his bag. "I'm going to start looking for her."

25

I was sixteen years old, in Mr. Burton's office. I was sitting on one of the burst velvet chairs, the same since the day I'd arrived over two years ago, but for the extra foam on display. I was staring at the same posters on the walls of the cramped room. The bricked walls had been clumsily painted white, some holes still black and naked of paint, others holding clumps of white. It was all or nothing in this room, never even. Blu-Tack clung to parts of the walls, corners of old posters still hung on to the Blu-Tack. Somewhere in the school I imagined a room fully stocked with cornerless posters.

"What are you thinking about?" Mr. Burton finally spoke.

"Cornerless posters," I replied.

"Ah, that old chestnut." He nodded. "How was your week?"

"Crap."

"Why crap?"

"Nothing very exciting happened."

"What did you do?"

"School, ate, slept, school, ate, slept, multiplied by five

more times and to be multiplied by a million more weeks in my life. My future looks bleak."

"Did you go out at the weekend? You were saying last week that you'd been asked out by a group of people."

He always wanted me to make friends. "Yeah, I went out."

"And?"

"And it was OK. There was a house party. Johnny Nugent's parents were away, so we all went there."

"Johnny Nugent?" He raised his eyebrows.

I didn't answer but my cheeks pinked.

"Were you able to forget about Mr. Pobbs and enjoy yourself?"

He asked it so seriously, I studied the Blu-Tack again, feeling slightly embarrassed. I'd had Mr. Pobbs since I was a baby. He was a gray, fluffy, one-eyed teddy bear in blue-striped pajamas, who slept in my bed, and any other bed I stayed in, every night. My parents and I had been away for the week a short time before and as soon as we'd returned I had repacked to go stay with my grandparents for the weekend. Somewhere in changing over my clothes, I'd misplaced Mr. Pobbs. It had upset me deeply all the time I was at my grandparents' and I'd taken to a two-week-long search of the house on my return, much to my parents' dismay. Last week we had discussed my not wanting to go out with Johnny Nugent at the weekend because I'd have preferred to find Mr. Pobbs, my trusted friend, no matter how ridiculous it sounded. It had been difficult leaving the house to go out for the night knowing that somewhere in there, Mr. Pobbs lay hidden.

"So you went out with Johnny Nugent?" Mr. Burton went back to the question.

"Yes, I did."

He smiled awkwardly. He'd obviously heard the rumors too. "Is everything . . . are you . . ." He stopped talking and instead made trumpeting noises with his lips while he thought how to rephrase his question. It was rare to see him awkward, as he always seemed to be in control. He was in this room, anyway; other than the small hints of personal information he revealed mistakenly during our at times candid talks, I knew nothing of his life outside of these four walls. I also knew not to ask any questions, because he wouldn't answer and because I didn't want to know. Not knowing, asking and him not answering, reminded me that we were strangers in a way. Only inside this room were we familiar. We had created our own world, had rules to follow, and had a line between us that, although it couldn't be passed, could be danced upon on playful days.

I jumped in and stopped his trumpeting lips from launching into an orchestra of brass instruments. "Mr. Burton, if you're wondering if I'm OK, then please, don't worry. For once in my life I've lost something and I've no intention of searching for it or expect it to come back. I think I'm cured."

We laughed. And laughed. And when there was an uncomfortable silence while I fantasized about him curing me, too, we laughed again.

"Will you see him again? And by that I mean did you enjoy the company of others? Did you enjoy going out, did you relax, could you forget about all the things that are missing?" He started laughing again. "Did they manage to reach Scathach's island?"

While my head was banging against the headboard in Johnny Nugent's parents' bed, I'd had an epiphany. I'd remembered where I thought I'd put Mr. Pobbs aside in my grandmother's house, before packing my clothes. I had called her the next day and expected Mr. Pobbs to be found, lying under the bed staring with his one eye at the broken springs beneath. But he wasn't and we had arranged for my search of my grandparents' house the following weekend. Even though Johnny Nugent had asked me out. I was going to explain all this when I frowned and asked, "Wait a minute what's Scathach's island?"

Mr. Burton laughed. "Sorry, that just slipped out. It's a bad analogy."

"Explain!" I smiled, watching his face redden.

"I didn't mean to say it. It just popped out. Never mind, let's move on."

"Hold on a minute, you don't let me get away with that! I have to repeat *everything* I mumble." I laughed, watching him squirm for the first time in my life.

He composed himself. "It's an old Celtic story, and it was a stupid comparison."

I motioned for more.

He rubbed his face. "Oh, I can't believe I'm telling you this. Scathach was a great warrior woman who trained many heroes of the time. Legend tells us that it was almost impossible to reach her island, so that anyone who did was considered worthy to be trained in martial arts."

My mouth dropped. "You've named me after a warrior woman who trains martial arts?"

He laughed again. "The point is that she was a woman who was hard to reach." He stopped laughing when he saw my face. He leaned forward and grabbed my hand. "I think you've taken that the wrong way."

"I hope so," I said, slowly shaking my head.

He groaned and thought fast. "It's just that only the strongest, bravest, and most worthy people could reach her."

I relaxed a little, liking the sound of this. "How would they reach her?"

He relaxed a little too. "First they would have to cross the Plain of Ill Luck, where they would be pierced by razor-sharp grass blades." He paused while he studied my face to see whether he should go on or not. Happy that I wasn't about to punch him, he continued. "Then they would face the Perilous Glens with devouring beasts. Their final task was the Bridge of the Cliff, which was a bridge that tilted upward whenever anyone tried to cross."

I pictured the people in my life who tried to approach me, who tried to befriend me, who tried to connect with me. I pictured me knocking them back.

"Only real heroes would get across," he finished.

Goose bumps formed on my skin. My hairs stood up and I hoped he didn't notice.

He ran his hands through his hair and shook his head. "That wasn't part of the . . ." *job*, he almost said. "I shouldn't have said that. Sorry, Sandy."

"It's OK," I decided and he looked relieved. "Just tell me one thing. Where are you on this journey?"

Those gorgeous blue eyes bore into mine. He didn't even need to think about it, didn't even look away. "I'd say I've just passed over the Plain of Ill Luck right this minute."

I pondered that. "I'll go easy with my devouring beasts if you promise to just let me know when you've passed the bridge."

"You'll know." He smiled, reaching for my hand and squeezing it. "You'll know."

Jack pulled up beside Alan's flat and flicked through Sandy's datebook. She had also made an appointment yesterday for one o'clock at a place with a Dublin number, and he needed to know if she had kept it. He was hoping that whoever she was to meet would be able to help him. Though Sandy had made this appointment for yesterday in Dublin, she had planned to visit Alan in Limerick today. It must have been an important appointment in Dublin in order for her to make the journey over and back.

With shaking hands he dialed the Dublin number Sandy had written. A woman answered quickly, sounding distracted as other phones rang in the background.

"Hello, Scathach House."

"Hi, I am wondering if you can help me," Jack said politely. "I have your phone number written down in my datebook and I can't remember why I've made a note to call you."

"Of course," she said politely. "Scathach House is the office of Dr. Gregory Burton. Maybe you wanted to make an appointment?"

I woke up in my Dublin bedsit to the shrill sound of a telephone ringing in my ear. I put the pillow over my head and prayed for the noise to stop, I had a terrible hangover. I peeked over the side of my bed and caught a glimpse of my crumpled garda uniform lying in a ball on the ground. I'd worked a late shift and then gone for a few drinks. A few had clearly turned into a few too many and I had absolutely no memory of coming home. The ringing finally stopped and I breathed a sigh of relief, although it echoed in my head for a few seconds longer. And then it started again. I grabbed the phone from the side of the bed and brought it back under the pillow to my ear.

"Hello," I croaked.

"Happy birthday to yooooou, happy birthday to yooooou, happy birthday dear Sandeeeee, happy birthday to yooou." It was my mother singing so sweetly as though she was in a church choir.

"Hip, hip . . ."

"Hooray!" That was Dad.

"Hip hip . . ."

"Hooray!" He blew a party blower down the receiver, which I instantly held far away from my ear, allowing my arm to hang off the bed. I could still hear them celebrating from under the pillow as I drifted off again.

"Happy twenty-first, honey," Mum said proudly. "Honey? Are you there?"

I put the phone back to my ear. "Thanks, Mum," I mumbled.

"I wish you'd have let us throw you a party," she said wistfully. "It's not every day my baby girl is twenty-one."

"It is, actually," I said tiredly. "I have three hundred and sixty-four more days of being twenty-one, so we've lots of time to celebrate."

"Oh, you know it's not the same."

"You know what I'm like at those things," I said, referring to the party idea.

"I know, I know. Well, I want you to enjoy your day. Would you think about coming home for dinner at all? At the weekend, maybe? We could just do a small thing, just me, you and your dad. We won't even mention the birthday word."

I paused and decided to lie. "No, I can't this weekend, sorry. Things are really busy at work."

"Oh, OK, well, what about if I come to Dublin for a few hours? I won't even stay over; we can have a coffee or something. A quick chat and I'll be gone, I promise." She gave a nervous laugh. "I just want to mark the day with you in some way. I'd love to see you."

"I can't, Mum, sorry."

There was a silence. For far too long.

Dad came on the phone cheerily. "Happy birthday, love. We understand you're busy so we'll let you get back to doing what you were doing."

"Where's Mum?"

"Oh, she, eh, had to answer the door." He was as bad at lying as I was.

She was crying, I knew it.

"OK, well, have a great day, honey. Try to enjoy yourself, OK?" he added softly.

"OK," I said quietly, and the phone clicked and went dead.

I groaned, hung the phone back up on my bedside locker, and threw the pillow off my head. I allowed my eyes to adjust to the bright light my cheap curtains were incapable of keeping out. It was ten A.M. on a Monday morning and I finally had a day off. What I was going to do with it, I had no idea. I would have preferred to work on my birthday, although I would busy myself with working on a missing case that had recently run into a dead end. A little girl named Robin Geraghty had disappeared while playing in her front garden. All the signs were implicating her middle-aged neighbor next door. However, no matter how hard we'd dug into this case, we weren't hitting the treasure chest at the bottom. Recently I had started following up on such cases by myself, unable to switch off the file that was locked away in a cabinet.

I turned to lie on my back and noticed from the corner of my eye a lump beside me in the bed. The lump was on its side, a tousle of dark brown hair lying on the pillow. I jumped, gathering my bedclothes and wrapping them around me tighter. The lump began to move to face me, his eyes opened. Bloodshot, tired eyes.

"I thought you were never going to answer that phone," he said croakily.

"Who are you?" I asked in disgust, clambering out of

bed and taking the covers with me, leaving him lying on the bed spread-eagled and naked. He smiled, rested his hands behind his head sleepily, and winked.

I groaned. It was meant to be a silent, inward groan but it forced its way out of my mouth. "I'm going to the bathroom and when I get back you will be gone." I picked up what I assumed were his clothes and threw them onto the bed. I picked up my own stray clothes that were resting on a chair, hugged them close to me and banged the door shut. Almost immediately I returned and grabbed my wallet, much to his disgust. I wasn't about to leave that there.

Not after the last time.

I stayed in the bathroom down the hall for as long as I could until Mr. Rankin from next door began pounding on the door and telling me and everyone else in the building how he was going to burst an area of his body that I didn't care to think much about. I opened the door immediately and went back to my bedsit hoping the hairy stranger had vanished. No such luck. He was closing the door behind him.

I walked toward him slowly, not knowing what to say. He didn't seem to know either, but nor did he care, his smirk still on his face.

"Did we . . . ?" I asked.

"Twice." He winked and my insides churned. "By the way, before you throw me out of your building, some guy came by when you were in the bathroom. I told him he could wait if he wanted, but you probably wouldn't recognize him when you saw him." He grinned again.

"What guy?" I racked my brain.

"See, I told him you wouldn't remember him."

"Is he in there?" I looked toward the closed door.

"No, I guess he didn't feel like hanging around a bed-sit with a naked hairy man."

"You answered the door naked?" I asked angrily.

"I thought it was you." He shrugged. "Anyway, he left this card for you." He handed me the business card. "I don't suppose there's any point in me giving you my number?"

I shook my head, took the card from his hand. "Thanks, eh . . ." I began weakly.

"Steve," he said, holding out his hand.

"Nice to meet you." I smiled and he laughed. He was kind of cute but still I watched him walk down the stairs.

"We met before, by the way," he called up to me, not turning around as he made his way down the steps.

I was silent while I tried to remember.

"At Louise Drummond's Christmas party last year?" He stopped and looked up hopefully.

I frowned.

"Ah, it doesn't matter." He waved his hand dismissively. "You didn't remember the next morning then, either." Then he smiled and was gone.

There was a moment of guilt until I remembered the business card in my hand and the bad feelings vanished. My knees went weak when I saw the name.

It seemed Mr. Burton had set up a clinic in Dublin, Scathach House on Leeson Street. Wait a minute, *Dr.* Burton; he'd passed his exams at last.

I danced around excitedly on the spot. I heard the

toilet flush and Mr. Rankin left with a newspaper in his hand and caught me dancing.

"You need to go again? I wouldn't go back in there for a while." He wafted the newspaper.

I ignored him and went back into my bedsit. Mr. Burton was here now. He'd found me three years after I'd moved away and that's all that mattered. At last, one odd sock had showed up.

26

"Oh, Dr. Burton." Jack sat up in the car seat and pressed the phone closer to his ear. "I remember why I'd made a note of it now. Actually it's not me that I'm enquiring about. It's about a friend of mine who had an appointment yesterday with Doctor . . ." He stopped, already forgetting the surname.

"Burton," the secretary finished for him, and he could hear another phone ringing in the background. "I'm sorry, could you just hold for a moment, please, sir?"

"Yes." Jack waited and listened to Duran Duran playing over the phone while he tried to formulate some sort of a plan. He scribbled Dr. Gregory Burton's name and address into his notebook. Later he would go through Sandy's missed calls, received calls, and dialed numbers that her phone had recorded over the last few days and he would try to piece together where she had gone, even if it meant ringing everyone in her phonebook.

The secretary returned on the line. "I'm sorry, it's very busy here today. How can I help you?"

"I was wondering if you could tell me whether my

friend Sandy Shortt showed up for her appointment yesterday?"

"I'm sorry, Mr. . . . ?"

Jack thought fast. "Le Bon." Not fast enough. *Le Bon?*

"I'm sorry, Mr. Le Bon, but we can't give out information about our clients."

"Oh, of course you can't, I understand that, but I'm not looking for any personal information. My friend has been terribly sick lately but she has been afraid to do anything about it in case it's more serious than she anticipates. It's her stomach; it's been giving her trouble for months. I made an appointment for her and she says she went to Dr. Burton yesterday but I'm afraid she's lying to us all. The family are all so worried. Could you at least just let us know if she arrived for the appointment? I'm not asking for any personal details."

"You're enquiring about Sandy Shortt?"

He sat back relieved. "Yes, Sandy," he replied happily. "Her appointment was for one o'clock."

"I see. Well, I'm afraid I can't help you as this is not a medical clinic, Mr. Le Bon. It's a counseling center, so you can't have made the appointment for her regarding stomach problems. Is there anything else I can help you with?" Her voice was firm, angry even.

"Em," Jack said, his face red with embarrassment. "No."

"Thank you for calling." She hung up.

He stared in embarrassment at the appointment made for one o'clock in Sandy's diary. Suddenly Sandy's phone began ringing and the name "Gregory B" flashed up on the screen. Jack's heart thumped like a drum. He ignored the ring tone, relieved when it finally stopped and beeped to signal a message. He picked up the phone and dialed into her messaging service.

"Hi, Sandy. Gregory here. I've tried calling you a few times but there's no answer. I presume you've gone wandering the deep abyss again. I was just calling to let you know that a man named . . ." He moved his mouth away from the phone. "Carol, what was his name?"

Jack heard the secretary's voice saying "Mr. Le Bon."

"Right, yeah." Gregory came back on the phone. "A Mr. Le Bon, I assume that's not his real name," he said laughing, "rang our offices looking for you. He was wondering if you'd made your appointment yesterday for your *stomach* problem?" His voice got quieter. "Just be careful, OK? I don't suppose there's any chance you've considered getting a real job yet, waitressing or something. There's little chance nuts would be chasing you then. You could go door-to-door, selling bibles; in fact a nice woman dressed head to toe in tweed came to my door last night, which quite obviously made me immediately think of you, so I took her card. Think about calling her. It's a fine, uplifting card with Our Lord looking miserable on the cross. And it's recycled paper so she really must care." He laughed again. "Anyway, if you don't think you could endure the tweed, get a nine to five. I don't know if you've heard of it, it's this thing that people do. It allows them to have a life outside of work hours. That's 'life,' L-I-F-E, you can look it up in your dictionary when you get the chance. Anyway . . ." He sighed and was quiet for a while as if deciding what to say, or more likely he knew exactly what to say and was deciding whether to say it or not. Jack knew that silence well. "Right," his voice suddenly got louder and more businesslike. "Talk to you soon."

Knuckles rapping loudly on the glass of the passenger side of the car caused Jack to jump and drop the phone. He looked up to see Alan's mother, a round-faced frump of a woman glaring in the window. He leaned over and rolled down the window.

"Hello, Mrs. O'Connor."

"Who's that?" She scrunched up her face and stuck her head in the window. Wiry hairs escaped from her jawline. Her false teeth unclamped themselves from her gums and moved around in her mouth as she spoke. "Do I know you?" she shouted, spit landing on Jack's lip.

"Yes, Mrs. O'Connor." He wiped his lip and raised his voice, knowing she had bad hearing. "I'm Jack Ruttle, Donal's brother."

"Merciful hour, baby Donal's brother. What are you doing sitting out here? Get out and let me have a look at you."

She shuffled away in maroon-colored velvet slippers, her jaw moving as she looked him up and down, teeth still sloshing around in her mouth. She was dressed in the same outfit she appeared to have been wearing since the forties. "Make Do and Mend" had always been a part of the O'Connors' way of life, recycling textiles around the house to clothe the twelve children she had reared without their father, who came for one thing and left when he got it. Jack remembered Alan coming along on a day out with Donal when they were kids, wearing white shorts made from pillowcases. Donal never seemed to care, refusing to mock his friend as the other kids did. Not that Alan endured the taunts, instead choosing to knock the bejaysus out of anyone who even looked at him the wrong way. But he protected Donal from everyone, and his friend's disappearance had hit him particularly hard.

"Com'ere to me, aren't ya all grown up?" She rubbed Jack's hands and tousled his hair as though he had just reached adolescence that very day. "You're the image of your father, God rest his soul," she said, blessing herself.

"Thank you, Mrs. O'Connor. You look great too," he said, though it was a lie.

"Ah, I don't." She waved her hand dismissively and began to shuffle back toward her ground-floor flat in the high-rise building. Two bedrooms and twelve kids; he wondered how she had managed it. No wonder Alan had spent so much time in the Ruttles' house, being satiated with food by Jack's mother.

"Is Alan here? I came to talk to him."

"No, he's not. He finally moved in with that young thing. In a house now, wouldn't you know. He's only with her because of the house but she only gets it because of her kid, mind you. Fancy houses they get nowadays, the single mothers. I had nothin' like it in my day, not that I was single, but I was as good as, and all the better for it," she continued, shuffling to her door.

Jack laughed. Alan was always involved in something, landing on his feet no matter what the circumstances. Donal had named him "The Cat."

"I won't disturb you, Mrs. O'Connor. I'll go over to Alan at the house if that's OK."

"You think he done something wrong?" She looked worried.

"Not to me, anyway." Jack smiled, and she nodded, relief written all over her hard face.

Alan must have received a phone call from his mother, because he was outside in the driveway waiting. He looked thin, thinner than usual, and his face was pale and drawn, paler and more drawn than usual. But didn't they all, hadn't everyone and everything been affected by Donal's disappearance? It was as if, when he left the chipper that night, bumping against the door frames in his drunken state, he had managed to bump the earth off its axis, causing it to swirl at top speed in the wrong direction on the wrong path. Everything felt out of place.

They greeted each other with a hug. Alan immediately began to cry and Jack fought the urge to join him. Instead, he stiffened, allowing the younger man to weep on his shoulder, swallowing back the lump in his throat, blinking back the tears and trying to focus on everything around him that was real and that he could touch— everything except Donal.

They sat in the living room. Alan's hands shook as he tapped ash from his cigarette into one of the empty beer cans piled alongside the couch. The room was deathly silent; Jack wished they could put on the television as a background distraction.

"I came here to see if a woman had called by today, she's helping me out with looking for Donal."

Alan's face brightened. "Yeah?"

"She just wanted to ask you questions about the night, you know go back over everything again."

"I've been through that a million times with the guards, and a million times every day with myself." He inhaled deeply on his cigarette and his nicotine-stained fingers rubbed his eyes wearily.

"I know, but it's good to have a fresh eye and ear go over everything again, maybe there's something they missed."

"Maybe," he said in a small voice, but Jack doubted he believed that; he doubted there was any moment of that night that Alan hadn't analyzed, overanalyzed, and then dissected all over again. To tell him there was maybe something he was forgetting must surely be an insult.

"She didn't call by?"

He shook his head. "I've been here all day, was here all day yesterday, and I'll be here all day tomorrow, too," he said angrily.

"What happened to that last job of yours?"

He made a face and Jack knew not to ask any more questions.

"Do me a favor, will you?" Jack said, and handed Alan his phone. "Ring this number and make an appointment for me with Dr. Burton, I don't want them to recognize my voice."

Alan being Alan, he didn't ask any questions. "Hi, I want to make an appointment with Dr. Burton," he said, opening another beer can.

He raised his eyebrows and looked at Jack. "Yeah, for a counseling session."

Jack nodded.

"When do I want the appointment?" He repeated the secretary's question, looking at Jack.

"As soon as they can," Jack whispered.

"As soon as you can," Alan repeated. He listened and looked at Jack. "Next month?"

Jack shook his head wildly.

"No, I need it sooner than that, my head is really messed up, you never know what I might do."

Jack rolled his eyes.

Seconds later he hung up. "You got a cancellation for noon on Thursday."

"Thursday?" Jack asked, jumping up from his chair as though moving now would have him there on time.

"Well, you said as soon as possible," Alan said, handing him back the phone. "Has that got anything to do with finding Donal, by any chance?"

Jack thought about it. "In a way, yeah."

"I hope you find him, Jack." His eyes filled up again. "I keep going back over that night again and again, wishing I'd left with him. I really thought he'd be OK getting a taxi down that way, you know?" His eyes looked tortured and his hands shook. Around his feet on the floor lay sprinkles of ash he constantly flicked with his nicotine-stained thumb.

"You weren't to know." Jack comforted him. "It's not your fault."

"I hope you find him," Alan repeated, opening another can of beer and slugging it down.

Jack left him sitting there in the silence of the empty house, staring into space, knowing he was rethinking and reliving that night all over again, looking for the vital piece of evidence they had all missed. It was all they could do.

27

M issing person number one, Orla Keane, entered the great Community Hall, the light shining in from the open door spotlighting her presence. She stopped at the entrance, trying to get her bearings, looking like Alice in Wonderland who had just swallowed an "Eat Me" beside the monstrous oak door. I cleared my throat nervously and its amplified sound bounced off the walls, raced to the ceilings, and back down again like a Ping-Pong ball let loose. She turned to where I had made the noise and began to make her way toward me, high heels on the wooden floor echoing loudly.

Joan and Helena had set up a table for me to sit behind on the far side of the room and, much to Joan's disappointment, they stepped outside to give me privacy. As Orla approached me, I felt starstruck. I couldn't believe that this person had stepped out of my "Missing" photographs and was now a living, breathing person walking directly toward me.

"Hello," she said with a smile, her Cork accent still strong despite her time here.

"Hello." My voice came out as a whisper. I cleared my

throat and tried again. I looked down at the list of names on the table before me. I would have to do this twelve times today, and then again with Joan and Bernard. The thought of seeing all these people thrilled me, but the idea of having to discuss such delicate topics so subtly was draining me already. I had asked Helena earlier once again why on earth it was that I couldn't just let everybody know without having to carry out this charade.

"Sandy," she had said so firmly that I needn't have even heard a reason, "when people want to get home they get desperate. For them to learn that you found your way here while looking for them would cause them to believe that they can leave with you. Life wouldn't be worth living here with a few hundred people trailing your every move."

She had a point. So here I was, playing the role of casting agent and owner of an acting agency, about to wind a conversation about every member of their family and friends into a Hamlet soliloquy.

I had had one more question for Helena. "Do you think that I *can* lead the people out of here and bring them home?" I had been wondering if that was my purpose for being here, because I was convinced I wasn't staying. The typical victim belief: *This can't happen to me, not me of all people.*

She smiled sadly, and once again I needn't have heard her response because her face said it all. "Sorry, Moses, I don't think so." But before I dissolved completely she quickly added, "But I think you are here for a reason and that reason is, right now, to share your stories with everyone, to tell them about their families and how much they're missed. That's your way of bringing them home."

I looked up at Orla, who was sitting before me anxiously awaiting my next move. It was time to bring her home.

She was twenty-six years old now and she looked like she'd hardly changed at all. Nearly six years had passed since she had gone missing. Six years I'd spent looking for her. I knew her parents' names were Clara and Jim and they had divorced two years ago. I knew she had two sisters, Ruth and Lorna, and a brother, James. Her best friends were Laura and Rebecca, who was also known as "Fly" because of her regular forgetfulness to zip up her fly. Orla was studying art history at Cork University when she went missing. Her debs dress was purple, and the scar across her left eyebrow was from when she'd fallen off her bike on vacation in Bantry when she was eight. She lost her virginity when she was fifteen at a house party, to Niall Kennedy, the guy who worked at the local video store, and she secretly crashed her parents' car when they were away for a week in Spain but had it repaired on time and they still don't know it to this day. Her favorite colour is lilac, she loves pop music, played the piano until she was fourteen, had secretly dreamed of becoming a ballet dancer since the age of six, yet never once took a class, and she had been here for five and three quarter years.

I looked at her and didn't know where to start. "So, Orla, tell me a bit about yourself."

I watched her as though in a trance, watched the lips I'd seen only in photographs open and close, her face animated, *alive,* and I listened to her words. The sing-song tone of her Cork accent, the way her long blond hair moved as she spoke. I was enthralled.

When she got to the part about studying in college I saw my chance to jump in. "Art history in Cork University?" I repeated. "I know someone who studied the same year as you."

"Who?" She almost jumped off her seat.

"Rebecca Grey."

Her mouth dropped open. "No way! Rebecca Grey is one of my best friends!"

"Really?" I noticed everything was still in the present. Rebecca was still her best friend.

"Yeah! That's so weird, how do you know her?"

"Oh, I met her brother Enda a few times. He's friends with friends of mine, you know how it is."

"What's he doing now?"

"Actually, last time I saw him was at his wedding a few months ago. I think I may have met your mum and dad there too."

She was silent for a moment and when she spoke again her voice was hushed and shaken. "How are they?"

"Oh, they were in great form, I was talking to one of your sisters, Lorna, I think."

"Yes, Lorna!"

"She was telling me that she got engaged."

"To Steven?!" She bounced up and down on her seat clapping her hands excitedly.

"Yes," I said and smiled. "To Steven."

"Oh, I knew she'd take him back." She laughed with tears in her eyes.

"Your older sister was there with her husband. She was heavily pregnant, I noticed."

"Oh." A tear fell from her eye and she quickly wiped it away. "What else, who else did you see? Did my mum and dad say anything? What did they look like?"

And so I brought her home.

A half hour had passed and Joan coughed rather loudly to let me know another audition applicant had arrived. We hadn't even noticed Joan enter the hall and I looked at my wrist to check the time, forgetting that my watch was still lying somewhere on the road leading out of the village. The familiar feeling of irritation scratched at my body as I thought of it being somewhere yet not being able to find it. I looked up to see the next person I was due to meet, Carol Dempsey, nervously wringing her hands as she stood by Joan, and my irritation disappeared. I became scared all over again.

"I'm sorry, our time is up," I said to Orla.

Her face fell and I knew she had all of a sudden been whisked away from home and transported and plonked back to the reality of where she was.

"But I haven't even auditioned," she panicked.

"It's OK, you've got the part," I whispered and winked.

Her face lit up as she stood, leaned over, and grasped my hand in her two hands. "Thank you, thank you so much."

I watched her leave with Helena, her head awash with a million new thoughts of stories from home. So much to think about now, new thoughts and new memories all raising new questions and a new longing for home.

Carol sat before me. A mother of three, housewife, from Donegal, forty-two years old and a member of the local choir, who went missing while on her way back from choir practice four years ago. She had passed her driving test a week before her disappearance, her husband had celebrated his forty-fifth birthday with the family the night before, and her youngest daughter's school play was opening the following week. I looked at her mouselike face, timid and shy, her brown limp hair tucked behind pink ears, a purse clasped in her hands on her lap, and I instantly wanted to take her home.

"So, Carol," I said gently, "why don't we start off by you just telling me a bit about yourself."

Later in the day, we all sat around in a circle in the grand Community Hall. I faced the stage and the thousands of handprints decorating the backdrop, "Strength and hope," I repeated to myself. Strength and hope had got me through today; I was still on a high from meeting my idols, but knew I would quickly become drained. As usual, as soon as everybody had taken their places, I had chosen to stand back and observe, outside of the circle. Old habits die hard. Helena had called out to me and the chorus of fifteen other voices joined in, coercing me to sit down. I took a seat, aware that I was joining a group, something I had run from doing all of my life. I slowly sat down, all the time battling with my legs, which wanted to run out the door, and my mouth, which wanted to make an excuse to leave.

After I had spoken to everybody individually, Helena

had come up with the idea of everybody getting to know one another better by sharing the experiences of where and when they had gone missing. She was calling it a team-building workshop, all to help the production, but I knew she was really doing it for me, to help me with my continuous search of understanding where we all are and how we got here.

One by one, the people explained how they had arrived here. It was an emotional experience. Some had been here only a few years, others more than a decade, yet the realization of never returning home was still raw. There were tears from many but, as usual, none from me. It was as though by the time my tears worked their way from my heart to my eyes, they had evaporated and drifted into the air as sad vapors instead. I was fascinated to hear what had happened after they left the scenes that I had examined so many times and arrived here. It was all so simple. I had followed unnecessary routes, suspected all the wrong people, scrutinized every single inch of the road they were last seen on. It was pointless because all they did was wander off here.

While it was painful for the missing, knowing that they wouldn't be returning home, it was a lot better than the alternative. I wished Jenny-May Butler was here, I wished Donal Ruttle was here, I wished the others on my list and the thousands of others that go missing every year were here. I prayed that harm hadn't come to Jenny-May. I prayed that, if it had, it had been quick and painless. But mostly I prayed that she was here.

I was captivated as I watched all of these people. I was

a stranger to them but they were best friends to me. I had so many stories of theirs I wanted to tell them, that I knew and understood and had laughed at and could identify with. There were so many people they knew whom I wanted to tell them I'd met and laughed with. There were situations that I knew they'd been in that I wanted to tell them I shared. The complete opposite to how I was in life. I wanted to join in, swap stories, and belong.

There was a silence and I realized all eyes were on me.

"Well?" Helena asked, adjusting her lemon pashmina around her shoulders.

"Well, what?" I asked, looking around in confusion.

"Aren't you going to tell us your story of arriving here?"

I felt like telling them I'd been here long before them all. But I didn't. Instead I politely excused myself from the hall.

Later that night, I sat in the eatery at a quiet table with Helena and Joseph. Candles flickered on every table, birds-of-paradise sat in small tin buckets in the center. We had just finished an appetizer of wild mushroom soup and piping hot brown bread, and I sat back in my chair, already full, and awaited my main course. The eatery was quiet on this Wednesday night, people choosing to go to bed before their early starts at work the next day. Each of the people taking part in the production had been granted time off from their work, their involvement in the arts seen to be enough. We were to spend all day, every day, rehearsing in order to meet the deadline of next Sunday, when Helena had already assured the cast and community the dress rehearsal would be. This was a task that seemed highly ambitious and entirely unrealistic in my eyes, yet Helena assured me that people here threw themselves into their work and were highly productive. But what did I know?

I looked at my wrist for the millionth time since I'd lost my watch, and sighed with frustration.

"I have to find my watch."

"Don't worry." Helena smiled. "It's not like being at home, Sandy; things don't just go missing."

"I know, I know, you keep telling me that, but if that's so, well, then where is it?"

"Wherever you dropped it." She laughed, and shook her head at me like I was a child.

Joseph, I noticed, didn't smile but changed the subject altogether. "What kind of play will you do?" he asked in his deep soothing tones.

I laughed. "We have no idea. Helena managed to steer the conversation away from talk of what the actual play would be every time someone asked. I don't mean to rain on your parade but I think a week is an entirely implausible amount of time to rehearse and perfect a play."

"It will be a short one," Helena said defensively.

"What about scripts and costumes and whatever else is needed?" I asked, suddenly realizing the extent of what we would have to do.

"Don't worry about all of that, Sandy." She turned to Joseph. "There's the belief at home that old theaters are haunted because costumes and makeup are always reported or rumored to go missing. Well, it's true, they do go missing but it's not due to ghosts, not of the pilfering kind, anyway, because the finest costumes show up here daily. Bobby will have everything we need," she said calmly.

"She has thought this all through." Joseph smiled affectionately at his wife.

"Oh, the thinking is all finished, dear. It has already been decided. We are going to stage *The Wizard of Oz*," Helena said grandly and proudly, swirling her red wine and taking a sip.

I started laughing.

"Why is it funny?" Joseph asked, amused.

"It's *The Wizard of Oz*," I stressed. "It's not a play, it's a musical! It's what children do in school shows. I thought you'd come up with something a bit more cultured, like a Beckett play or O'Casey," I argued. "But *The Wizard of Oz* . . . ?" I wrinkled my nose.

"My, my, I think we have a snob on our hands." Helena tried not to smile.

"I'm not aware of this *Wizard of Oz*." Joseph looked confused.

I gasped. "Neglected child."

"It's not something that was shown all the time in Watamu," Helena reminded me. "And if you hadn't left rehearsals so early today, Sandy, you would have learned that we are not doing a musical version. It is an adaptation written many years ago by Dennis O'Shea, a fine Irish playwright who has been here for two years. He heard about what we were doing and brought it to me this morning. I thought it was perfect, and so it has already been cast and the first few scenes blocked. Mind you I had to tell them that it was you that had made the decision."

"You cast them in *The Wizard of Oz*?" I said, totally unimpressed.

"What is it about?" Joseph asked, intrigued.

"Sandy, you do the honors," Helena said.

"OK, well, it's a *children's* movie," I stressed to Helena, "made in the thirties about a little girl called Dorothy Gale who is swept away in a cyclone to a magical land. Once there, she embarks on a quest to see the wizard, who can help her return home. It's ridiculous to ask a group of adults to do it." I laughed, but realized no one was laughing with me.

"And this wizard, does he help her?"

"Yes," I said slowly, feeling it odd the story was being taken so seriously. "The wizard helps her and she learns that she could have returned home the whole time. All she had to do was tap her ruby heels together and say 'There's no place like home, there's no place like home.'"

He still didn't laugh. "So she returns home in the end?"

There was a silence and I finally understood why. I nodded slowly.

"And what does she do while she's in this magical land?"

"She helps her friends," I said quietly.

"It doesn't seem such a silly story to me," Joseph said seriously. "One the people here will very much like to see."

I thought about that. In fact, I thought about it all night, until I was dreaming of ruby slippers and cyclones and of talking lions and houses that fell on witches, until the phrase "There's no place like home" was echoing so loudly and continuously in my head that I woke up saying it aloud and I was afraid to go back to sleep.

28

I stared up at the ceiling, at the point right above my head where the white paint had bubbled and cracked over the wood. The moon was sitting perfectly framed in the window of the family room I was sleeping in. Blue light was cast through the glass, causing an exact reflection of its window squares to appear on the chunky wooden table. There was no moon in the window on the table, I noticed, just a ghostly reflection of pale blue.

I was wide awake now. I felt for my wrist to check the time and remembered again my watch was gone. My heart started to pound as it always did when something of mine was missing; I would immediately become restless and ache to start looking. My hunts were like an addiction, the pre-search feeling like a craving. A part of me was possessed and became obsessed with not resting until my belongings were found. There was very little anybody could do when I was in that mode; there was very little that could be said or done to cause me to screech in my tracks. The people with me always used to tell me it was lonely for them when I left them like that all of a sudden. Everybody I was with was always the victim; didn't they know that it was lonely for me, too?

"But the *pen* is not your missing object," Gregory would always say to me.

"Yes, it is," I would grumble, while rooting in my bag, nose practically touching the bottom.

"No, it's not. When you search you are trying to fulfil a *feeling*. Whether you have the pen or not is completely irrelevant, Sandy."

"It is not irrelevant," I would shout back. "If I have no pen, well, then, how can I write down what you are about to tell me?"

He reached into the inside pocket of his jacket and handed me a pen. "Here."

"But that isn't *my* pen."

He would sigh and smile as he always did. "This idea of searching for lost things is a *distraction*—"

"Distraction, distraction, distraction, distraction. Never mind me; *you* are obsessed with saying that word. You saying the word distraction is *your* distraction from saying anything else," I spluttered angrily.

"Let me finish," he said sternly.

I stopped rooting immediately and listened to him, feigning interest.

"This idea of searching for lost things is a distract . . ."— he stopped himself—"is a way of avoiding dealing with something else that's lost in your life *within you*. Now shall we start searching for what that is?"

"A-ha!" I smiled, happily extracting my pen from the bottom of my bag. "Found it!"

Unfortunately for Gregory, the craving never reared its ugly head anytime we would try to search within me.

If there had been a ten-foot wall surrounding the house, I would have scaled it. There was no barrier to my search scenes; all they did was become invisible hurdles. Gregory did have one good thing to say about my searching, and that was that he had never seen stamina and determination quite like it. And then he ruined the compliment by saying what a pity it was that I didn't pump that energy into other areas of my life. Still, somewhere in his comment I sensed praise.

The clock on the family-room wall read 3:45. I threw back the covers in the deathly silent house and began rummaging through Barbara Langley's suitcase of eighties nightmare clothes. I settled on a black-and-white sailor-style top, black drainpipe jeans, and flat black pumps. All I needed was an armful of bracelets, hoop earrings, and backcombed hair and I'd be dancing to "The Time Warp." But then, I already was.

Joseph and Helena seemed so sure that my watch wasn't lost; they seemed so confident that nothing could leave this place. I had to find out. I slipped out of the house silently so as not to wake the family. Outside, the weather was mild. I felt like I was walking around a toy village in the snowy mountains of Switzerland; little wooden chalets with window boxes and candles in the windows to help light the way and welcome new wanderers. All was quiet outside. The crackling and the snapping of branches could be heard from the forest as people made their way to the village for the first time. People

who'd probably found themselves there during an inno-
cent walk to the shop or a stroll home from the pub. I felt
safe in the village, protected by people intent on picking
up where they left off and moving on.

I walked out of the village, following the dusty road
that ran alongside the fields. The sun was rising over the
trees in the distance, casting orange hues over the blue
light, like a giant orange squeezing its colorful juice over
the villages, the trees, the mountains and fields, and allowing the liquid light to flow like a stream down the
pathways.

In the distance I saw a figure rising and stooping in
the center of the road. He stood up and his height and
physique revealed him to be Joseph. His figure was jet
black against the rising sun that was the giant orange sitting on the top of the road, looking like it was about to
roll down to us, squashing all in its path. I was just about
to approach him when he got down on his hands and
knees and began brushing the dusty floor. I jumped into
the woods and hid behind a tree, watching him. He'd
beaten me to it; I realized he was searching for my
watch.

The beam from a flashlight shot through the trees and
made its way toward me. I quickly ducked, wondering
where on earth it was coming from. Joseph stopped what
he was doing to look up at the light. It disappeared, he
continued searching, and I continued to watch him,
wanting to see what he would do when he came upon the
watch. But he didn't find it. After an hour of very determined searching, I think Gregory would agree, Joseph

finally rose to his feet, placed his hands on his hips, shook his head, and sighed.

A chill ran through me. It wasn't there, I *knew* it.

Before Jack went home on Wednesday night, he returned to the estuary to see if Sandy's car had upped and gone over the past twenty-four hours.

Gloria had been delighted to learn that he was planning on seeing a psychiatrist, although she was a little confused, to say the least, as to why he had to travel to Dublin for a session. Still, he hadn't seen her so happy in a long time and it showed him how bad he must have been lately. He could almost hear her thinking and planning a wedding, babies, christenings, and who knows what else, as he told her. However, she was misguided in thinking the counseling was directly for him. He had no intention of wanting to be cured of wanting to find his brother. To him it was no sickness.

It was dark outside, pitch-black among the trees down by the Shannon Estuary where owls hooted and creatures moved around in the undergrowth. He took his emergency flashlight out of his car and as he switched it on, he saw various startled glowing eyes freeze and then dash back into the bushes. Sandy's Ford Fiesta was in its place, untouched since he'd last been there. He shone the light around the trees, at the pathway that led farther along the estuary. A pleasant walk for bird watchers and nature lovers or a jogging path for Sandy? He walked toward it, deeper into the forest where he had looked so many times over the last few days. His inexperience had previously led him to look out for footprints, as if they would be any help to him. He walked farther, enjoying seeing creatures leap out of the line of the light into the distance, and he shone the light up into the trees and watched as it found its way up to the sky.

A trail appeared on his left. He stopped walking and immediately stopped trying to work out what was niggling at him. He'd never noticed that trail before. He shone the light up the trail: more trees and blackness were at the end. He shuddered and moved the light away again with the intention of returning in the light of day to wander up the track. As he shone the torch in another direction, shining metal caught his eye and disappeared again. He quickly searched around with the light, afraid whatever it was would vanish. His eye fell upon a silver watch, lying among the long grass beside the trail to his left. He bent to pick it up with his heart thumping in his chest, an image suddenly appearing in his mind.

It was the memory of Sandy bending to pick up her watch at the garage a few mornings ago.

29

"Hello, I hope I've called the correct number for Mary Stanley." Jack spoke into the answering machine. "My name is Jack Ruttle. You don't know me but I've been trying to get in touch with Sandy Shortt, whom I know you were recently in contact with. I know this seems like a strange phone call, but if you hear from her or have any idea where she has gone, could you please contact me on the following number . . ."

Jack sighed and tried another number. All around him on this sunny day in Dublin, people were lying out on the grass of St. Stephen's Green. Ducks were waddling around his bench, searching for bits of bread people had dropped while feeding them. They quacked, pecked, and hopped back into the glistening water, distracting him momentarily. After spending more than an hour trying to find his way around Dublin's system of one-way streets, and then being stuck in traffic jams, he'd finally managed to find a parking space around St. Stephen's Green. He had an hour to spare before his session with Dr. Burton, something he was growing increasingly nervous about. Jack wasn't good at discussing his feelings with anyone at the best of times, never mind an entire hour of searching his brain for pretend worries with a psychiatrist, all just to find information about Sandy Shortt. Columbo he was not, and he was growing tired of trying to find indirect ways of getting answers.

He had been calling through the list on Sandy's phonebook all morning, leaving messages with all those who had contacted her over the past few days and those she had made appointments with in previous weeks. He wasn't getting anywhere; so far he'd left six voice messages, he'd spoken to two people who were extremely guarded about giving out any information, and he'd listened for far too long to her fuming landlord, who seemed more upset about not being paid yet that month than where Sandy was.

"Let me warn you now, sonny, before she breaks your heart," he'd growled. "Unless you want to be hanging around for days on end, waiting for her, then I suggest you cut your ties with her now. You're not the only one, I can tell you that." He'd laughed heartily. "Don't be fooled by her. She brings them back all the time, thinking none of us hear her. I'm right above; I hear her comings and goings, if you'll pardon the pun. You mark my words; she'll turn up here in a few days wondering what all the fuss was about, probably thinking she was gone for two hours instead of two weeks. She does it all the time. But if you do see her before then, tell her to get that money to me ASAP or she'll be tossed out on her arse."

Jack sighed. If he was going to give up, now was the time to do it. But he couldn't. Here he was in Dublin, a few minutes away from meeting someone who, he imagined, knew more about what went on in Sandy's head than anybody else. He didn't want to pack it all in and head home to . . . nothing. His idea of Sandy was changing. Through their conversations on the phone he had painted a picture of her in his mind: organized, businesslike, in love with her job, chatty, personable. The more he dug around into her life, the more that image of her altered. She was still all of those things, but more. She was becoming more real to him. This wasn't a phantom he was chasing; she was a real, complex, layered person, no longer just the helpful stranger he'd spoken to on the phone. Maybe Garda Turner was right, maybe she'd just had enough and was hiding from the world for a while, but that was something her counselor would surely know.

Just as he was about to dial another number, his phone rang.

"Is that Jack?" a woman asked quietly.

"Yes," he replied. "Who is this?"

"This is Mary Stanley. You left a message on my phone about Sandy Shortt."

"Oh, yes, Mary, hello. Thank you so much for returning my call. It was a peculiar message, I know."

"Yes." She was guarded, just as the others had been, unsure of this strange man who was looking for their friend without any viable reason whatsoever.

"You can trust me, Mary. I mean no harm to Sandy. I don't know how well you know her, if you're a relative or friend, but let me explain myself first." He told the story of how he contacted Sandy, arranged to meet her, passed her at the petrol station, and his efforts since he had lost contact with her. He left out the reason for his meeting her, feeling that wasn't relevant. "I don't want to raise any alarm bells," he continued, "but I've been calling people she seems to have maintained close contact with, just to see if they've seen or heard from her lately."

"I received a phone call from a Garda Graham Turner this morning," Mary said, and Jack wasn't sure if it was a question or a statement. It was probably both.

"Yes, I contacted him, I'm concerned for Sandy." Jack had called Garda Turner that morning and told him about discovering Sandy's watch, hoping it would make him sit up and take notice. It obviously had.

"I'm worried too," Mary said, and Jack's ears pricked to attention.

"How did he know to call you?" Jack asked, meaning, Who are you? How do you know Sandy?

"Who else was on your call list?" she asked, ignoring his question, sounding lost in thought.

He flicked open his notepad. "Peter Dempsey, Clara Keane, Ailish O'Brien, Tony Watts—do you want me to keep going?"

"No, that's enough. You got your hands on a list of Sandy's?"

"She left her phone and address book behind. They were the only ways I could look for her." Jack tried not to sound guilty.

"Did somebody you know go missing?" Her tone wasn't soft but it wasn't harsh either. He was taken aback by the question, asked so directly as though missing people happened all the time.

"Yes, my brother Donal." A lump swelled in Jack's throat every time he mentioned his brother.

"Donal Ruttle, yes, that's right. I remember reading that in the paper," she said, and was quiet again in thought. "All those you've mentioned are people whose family members have gone missing," Mary explained, "including me. My son, Bobby, has been gone for three years."

"I'm very sorry," Jack said softly. It would make sense that all of Sandy's recent contacts were work-related; he had yet to come across any friends of hers.

"Oh, don't be sorry. It's not your fault. So let me get this straight, we all enlisted Sandy to help us find our loved ones and now you're enlisting us to help you find Sandy?"

Even though Jack was on the phone, his face blushed. "Yes, I guess so."

"Well, whether the others have replied to you yet or not, I don't care. I'll speak for them. You can count us all in. Sandy's very special to us all; we'll do everything we can to help find her. The quicker we find her, the quicker she can find my Bobby."

They were Jack's thoughts exactly.

Unable to sleep for the remainder of the night, I lay awake pondering the whereabouts of my watch. My head was dizzy with possibilities, for after finding myself here, there were now a plethora of places I could imagine it inhabiting. Just as I was picturing a world where watches ate, slept, and married one another with grandfather clocks as heads of state, pocket watches as the intellectuals, waterproof watches that inhabited the waters, diamond watches the aristocracy, and digital watches the mere workers, Joseph's creeping into the house stopped me. I had observed him for what I guessed was a further hour walking back up and down the road looking wide-eyed and fierce in his attempts to find my watch. I now knew what I looked like during my searches, focused and in the zone, completely unaware of all life around, particularly oblivious to a person hiding behind a tree not far away.

A half hour after I'd returned to my bed, Joseph made his way quietly, but not quietly enough, into the house. I pressed my ear to the wall as I tried to hear the mumblings between him and Helena in the room next to me. The timber was warm against my cheek and I closed my eyes, momentarily hit by a pang of homesickness and a longing for the warm heaving chest I used to rest my head upon in bed. Then there was silence and, feeling like a caged lion, I decided to slip out of the house before anybody stirred again.

Outside, the market stalls were being set up for another busy day of trading. There was the colorful sound of banter mixed with birdsong, laughter, and shouting as crates and boxes were being unpacked and stacked. I closed my eyes, hit by my second longing for home that day, and imagined myself as a child walking hand in hand with my mother through the organic farmers' markets in the Market Yard in Carrick-on-Shannon, the scintillating smell of the fruit and vegetables, so ripe and vibrant, enticing everybody to touch, smell, and taste. I opened my eyes again and was back here.

I arrived outside the Lost and Found building and

noticed how the carvings on this building were more playful: two odd socks, one yellow-and-pink polka dot and the other purple-and-orange stripes. I stood thinking of Gregory and me at my good-bye dance at school and I laughed. A face appeared in the window, a very familiar face, and I immediately stopped laughing, feeling as though I'd seen a ghost. He was young, nineteen by now, if I calculated correctly. He gave me a cheeky grin, waved, and disappeared from the window and appeared at the now open door like the Cheshire cat. So this was the Bobby from Lost and Found that Helena and Wanda had mentioned.

"Hello." He leaned against the door frame with his shoulder, crossed one leg over the other and held out his two hands. "Welcome to Lost and Found."

I laughed. "Hello, Mr. Stanley."

His eyes narrowed at my knowing his name but his smile widened. "And you are?"

"Sandy." I'd heard he was a character, always acting the joker. I had watched countless home videos of him performing for the camera from the age of six all the way up to sixteen, just before his disappearance. "You were on my list," I explained, "for auditions yesterday, and you didn't show up."

"Ah!" Realization dawned on him yet he still continued to study me curiously. "I've heard about you." He stopped leaning against the door frame and coolly made his way down the steps with his hands in his pockets. He stopped directly on front of me, folded his arms, then placed one hand to his chin and began to circle me slowly.

I laughed. "What have you heard about me?"

He paused behind me and I twisted my upper body around to him. "They say you know things."

"They do?"

"They do," he repeated, and continued strolling around me. When he had come full circle he stopped and folded his arms again, twinkles dancing in his blue eyes. He was everything his mother had boasted. "They say you're the soothsayer of Here."

"Who are *they*?" I asked.

"The . . ." He looked around to make sure nobody was listening; he lowered his voice to a whisper. "*Auditionees.*"

"Ah." I nodded smiling. "'Them."

"Yes, *them*. We have a lot in common," he said mysteriously.

"We do?"

"We do," he repeated. "They say, *they* being"—he looked left and right again before whispering—"the *auditionees*, say you're the person to go to if you want to know things."

I shrugged. "Maybe I know some things."

"Well, I'm the person to go to if you want to *get* things."

"Well, that's why I'm here." I smiled.

He became serious. I think. "Which one? You're here to get something or to let me know something?"

I thought about that but didn't answer aloud. "Aren't you going to let me inside?"

"Of course." he smiled and dropped the act. "I'm Bobby," he said, and held out his hand. "But you already know that."

"I do." I smiled. "I'm Sandy Shortt," I took his hand

and shook it. It felt limp and I looked up to see his face that had paled.

"Sandy *Shortt*?" he asked.

"Yes." My heart beat nervously. "Why, what's wrong with that?"

"Sandy Shortt from Leitrim, Ireland?"

I let go of his limp hand and swallowed. I didn't answer. It seemed that I didn't need to. Bobby took me by the arm and led me to the shop. "I've been expecting you." He looked over his shoulder one last time to see that no one was watching before dragging me inside and closing the door.

Then he closed the shop.

30

Leading away from St. Stephen's Green, Leeson Street was a fine Georgian street largely intact. The buildings, once grand homes housing the aristocracy, now mainly housed businesses: hotels, offices, and the basements were home to Dublin's "Strip," a chain of thriving nightclubs and strip clubs.

A brass plate beside the grand black Georgian door announced the building to be Scathach House. Jack took the seven concrete steps up to the door and came face to face with a brass lion's head with a ring clasped between his teeth. He was just about to grasp it and rap it against the door when he noticed a collection of buzzers to the right of the door: modern day's ugly invention mingled with the old. He looked up Dr. Burton's clinic; it was on the second floor, a PR agency at the bottom, a solicitor's office at the top. He was buzzed upstairs where he waited in an empty reception area. The receptionist smiled at him and he felt like shouting, I'm not here for *me*, there's nothing wrong with *me*, I'm *investigating*!

But he smiled back instead.

Magazines adorned the table, some a few months old,

others a year old. He picked up one and self-consciously flicked through the pages, reading about a member of the royal family of an obscure country who lay across beds, couches, kitchen tables, and pianos in the favorite rooms of her house.

The door to Dr. Burton's office opened and Jack quickly disposed of the magazine.

Dr. Burton was younger than Jack had imagined, mid-to-late forties. He had a tight beard, light brown, speckled with silver in places. He had piercing blue eyes, was five eleven, Jack guessed, and was dressed in jeans and a tan corduroy jacket.

"Jack Ruttle?" he asked, looking at him.

"Yes." Jack stood and they greeted each other with a handshake.

The office was busy, the style of furniture and design eclectic with a packed bookshelf, a full desk, a line of filing cabinets, a wall of academic credentials, nonmatching rugs, a chair, and a couch. The place had character. It suited the man who sat before him in the chair taking his personal details.

"So, Jack." Dr. Burton finished filling out the form and crossed his legs, focusing all his attention on Jack. Jack fought the urge to run out of the building. "Why is it that you have come here today?" he asked.

To find Sandy Shortt, he wanted to say, but instead shrugged and shifted uncomfortably in his seat. He wanted to just get this all over and done with right now. How on earth was he going to find out about Sandy through making up lies about himself? He hadn't fully thought this through, assuming that everything would fall into place as soon as he'd walked into Dr. Burton's office. What was it they said in the movies when the shrinks asked them questions? *Think, Jack, think.* "I'm under a lot of pressure," he said a bit too confidently, pleased with himself for answering a question.

"What kind of pressure?"

What *kind*? Was there more than one kind? "Just the normal kind of pressure." He shrugged again.

Dr. Burton frowned and Jack feared he'd got the question wrong. "Is it due to work or—"

"Yeah." He jumped in, "It's work. It's really"—he searched his brain—"pressurizing."

"OK." Dr Burton nodded. "What is it that you do?"

"I'm a stevedore in Shannon Foynes Port Company."

"And what brings you to Dublin?"

"You."

"You came all the way to see me?"

"I had to visit a friend too," he said quickly.

"Oh, OK." Dr Burton smiled. "So what is it about work that you find so pressurizing? Talk to me about it."

"Uh, the hours." Jack made an under-pressure face which he thought was convincing. "The hours are so long." He was silent then and he clasped his hands together on his lap and nodded and looked around the room.

"How many hours do you work a week?"

"Forty." He spoke before thinking.

"Forty hours aren't more than average, Jack. Why is it you feel that you can't cope with these?"

Jack's face flushed.

"It's OK to feel that way, Jack. Perhaps we can get to

the root of why work is bothering you, if it is indeed work that is bothering you . . ."

Dr. Burton continued talking while Jack tuned out and looked around the room for signs of Sandy, as if she would have scribbled her name across the wall before she left. Jack realized Dr. Burton was staring at him in silence.

"Yes, I think that's it," Jack said, nodding, and looked at his hands, hoping he had said something suitable.

"And what's her name?"

"Whose name?"

"Your partner, the person at home you're having difficulties with?"

"Oh, Gloria," he said, thoughts switching to her at home and how delighted she was that he was here today, spilling his heart out, when in the reality he wasn't even listening. The more he thought about it, the angrier he began to feel inside.

"Do you talk to her about your feelings of stress and pressure?"

"Oh, no." Jack laughed. "I don't talk to Gloria about that kind of thing."

"Why not?"

"Because she always has an answer, she always has a way to fix me."

"You don't want that?"

"No." He shook his head. "*I* don't need to be fixed."

"What needs to be fixed?"

He shrugged, not wanting to be dragged into this discussion.

Dr. Burton left a long silence and Jack felt the pressure of having to fill it. "It's what's going on around us that needs to be fixed," he finally answered.

Dr. Burton waited for more.

"And . . ." He stalled a bit, then said, "So that's what I'm trying to do."

"You're trying to fix what's going on around you," he repeated.

"That's what I just said."

"And Gloria's not happy with this."

Dr. Burton was being paid an extortionate amount of money for this, Jack thought incredulously. "No." He shook his head. "She thinks I should move on and forget about everything." He hadn't actually meant to say any of that, but it hadn't hurt and he still hadn't given anything away.

"What does she want you to forget about?"

"Donal," Jack said slowly, not sure whether to continue or not. Maybe if he explained, Dr. Burton would agree with him and he would finally have someone on his side. "The rest of the family are the same. They want to forget him, let him go, leave him behind. Well, I don't think like that, you know? He's my brother. Gloria looks at me like I'm crazy when I try to explain."

"Did your brother Donal pass away?"

"No, he didn't," Jack said, as though that was ludicrous, "but you would think he had. He's only missing. *Only*." He laughed angrily, rubbing his face tiredly. "I sometimes think it would be easier if I knew he was dead."

There was a silence and Jack felt the need to fill it again. He thumped his fist against his hand with every point he delivered. "He went missing last year on the night of his twenty-fourth birthday." *Thump.* "He took cash out of the ATM on O'Connell Street at three-oh-eight A.M. on Friday night." *Thump.* "He was seen on Arthur's Quay at three thirty A.M." *Thump.* "And after that no one saw him again. How can you let that go?" he asked. "How can you decide to keep on living life when your brother is somewhere out there and you don't know where he is or if he's hurt and needs you? How the hell is everything supposed to become normal?" He became angry now. "How does anybody expect you to be bothered to do forty hours of pointless work a week, putting cargo on a ship? Boxes I don't even know what's in them, and send them to places I've never been and never will be in. Why is that more important than finding my brother? How can you *not* look around you in all directions, trying to find him every time you're outside? Why is it everywhere I go and everyone I ask that I'm met with the same answers?"

His voice raised even louder now. "Nobody *saw* anything, nobody heard anything, nobody *knows* anything. There are *five million* people in this country, there are one hundred and seventy-five thousand of them living in Limerick, fifty-five thousand of whom are living in Limerick city. How the hell didn't *somebody*, even *one* person, see my brother, *somewhere*?" He stopped shouting now, out of breath, his throat sore and his eyes full of tears he was adamant he wouldn't let fall.

Dr. Burton allowed the silence to lengthen. He allowed Jack to gather himself and his thoughts and ponder all that he had blurted out. He went to the water cooler and returned with a plastic cup for Jack.

Jack sipped the water and thought aloud: "She sleeps a lot you see. The times when I need her, she's asleep."

"Gloria?"

Jack nodded.

"Do you have difficulty sleeping?"

"I've so much going on in my head, I've so many papers to look through and reports to go over. Things people said go through my head over and over again, and I just can't switch off. I have to find him. It's like an addiction. It eats away at me."

Dr. Burton nodded understandingly. Not in a patronizing way that Jack had thought would be the case, but as if he had a *real* understanding. It was as though Jack's problem was now *their* problem, and it was time for them to figure it out together.

"You're not the only person that feels like this and lives like this, you know, Jack. This is exactly the kind of behavior expected after a trauma such as yours. Were you advised to speak to a counselor after your brother's disappearance?"

Jack crossed his arms. "Yeah, the guards mentioned something, and every day leaflets and fliers landed on my hall floor about joining groups of other 'sufferers,' they called them." He waved his hand dismissively. "Not interested."

"It's not just a waste of time you know. You would

realize that there are many people in your position suffering from the same effects of losing someone"—and he said more to himself—"or even suffering from losing *things*."

Jack looked at Dr. Burton with confusion, "No, no, you've got me wrong, I can deal with losing *things*, absolutely fine, it's missing family members that I've the problem with. My siblings have lost a brother too, and not one of them feels the way I do. I can't imagine anything worse than sitting in a group and having the same conversations as I do at home."

"Gloria seems supportive of you. You should appreciate that. I'm sure it's been difficult for her to lose Donal, but remember not only has she lost him, she's lost you. too. Show that you appreciate her. I'm sure that would mean a lot to her." Real emotion slipped into Dr. Burton's voice and he stood up and walked over to the other side of the room to get himself a cup of water. When he came back, he was back to his cool self. "Do you love her?"

Jack was silent, then shrugged. He didn't know anymore.

"My mother used to say listen to what your heart tells you." Dr. Burton laughed, lightening the mood.

"Was she a psychiatrist too?" Jack smiled.

"As good as." Dr. Burton laughed. "You know, you remind me of someone, Jack, someone I know very well." He smiled lightly, sadly, and then returned to his former self. "So what are you going to do?" He checked his watch. "Bearing in mind we only have a few minutes left to tell me."

"I've already started to do something about it." Jack suddenly remembered why he was here and saw a way in.

"Talk to me." Dr. Burton leaned forward, resting his elbows on his thighs.

"I found someone in the Yellow Pages, an agency, a *missing-persons* agency," he stressed.

Dr. Burton didn't flinch. "Yes?"

"I got in touch with this woman and we spoke at length about her helping me to find Donal. We arranged to meet last Sunday in Limerick."

"Yes?" He leaned back in his chair, slowly, poker-faced.

"Funny thing is, we passed each other at a gas station on the way and then she never turned up at the meeting point." He shook his head. "I really believed and still believe this person has the ability to find him."

"Really?" Dr. Burton's tone was dry.

"Yes, really. So I started looking for her."

"The missing-persons person?" he stated, deadpan.

"Yes."

"And did you find her?"

"No, but I found her car and I found my brother's files in her car, and her phone, her datebook, her wallet, and a bag full of labeled clothes all with her name on them. She labels everything."

Dr. Burton began to fidget in his chair.

"I was so worried about her. I am *still* worried about her because I believe this woman has the ability to find my brother."

"So you're fixing your obsession onto this other woman," Dr. Burton said a bit too coldly.

Jack shook his head. "She said to me on the phone once that the one thing that would be more frustrating than not being able to find someone would be not being found. It's her wish to be found."

"Perhaps she just wandered off for a few days."

"The garda I contacted said the very same thing." Dr. Burton's eyebrows rose at the mention of involving the police. "I contacted a lot of people who know her and they also said the same thing." Jack shrugged.

"Well, then, you should listen to those people. Leave it alone, Jack. Try to concentrate on dealing with your brother's disappearance before you start worrying about another one. If she's been gone a few days and hasn't been in touch, maybe it's for a reason."

"I wasn't bothering her, Doctor, if that's what you're implying. There are a few of us that are worried so we've arranged to meet up and do something about it."

"Maybe she does this a lot," he said. "Maybe there's nothing at all wrong with her and she's gone off on her own for a few days."

"Yeah, maybe. But it's been four days since I've seen her and more days since anybody else has, unless I find somebody that tells me differently. If that's the case, then I'll back off and get on with my own life, but I don't think she's *wandering,* as so many people have said." He spoke gently. "I just would really love to find her, to thank her for the encouragement she's given me, for the hope of finding Donal that she has helped me to feel. That hope she's given me has allowed me to realize that I could find her too."

"What makes you think that she's missing?"

"I'm listening to my heart on this one."

Dr. Burton smiled grimly at having his words thrown back in his face.

"And in case my heart isn't proof enough for you, there's also this." Jack reached into his pocket and gently placed Sandy's silver watch on the table.

31

It had been three years since I'd seen Mr. Burton. From a distance I could tell that time had aged him well. From a distance it appeared that time hadn't aged either of us. From a distance everything was perfect and nothing was altered.

I had changed my clothes six times before leaving the bedsit. Feeling mildly pleased with my appearance, I had made my way to Leeson Street for the fourth time that month. I had danced in the halls when I had received his business card. I had skipped down the stairs like a fourteen-year-old on a Monday morning, knowing what and who lay ahead of me that day. I had run from Harold's Cross to Leeson Street, I had taken the steps up to the grand Georgian door in twos, and I had then frozen as my finger hovered above the intercom button and had quickly retreated to the other side of the road. Close up, it was a completely different picture.

I was no longer the schoolgirl coming to him for help. Now I didn't know who I was, running *from* help. I sat across the road on two more occasions, unable to cross over, instead watching as he arrived in the mornings, left in the evenings, and everything else in between.

I sat on the concrete steps on the fourth visit, elbows on my knees, fists under my chin, staring at all the feet and legs rushing by on the sidewalk. A pair of tan shoes beneath a pair of blue jeans crossed the road. They walked toward me. I expected them to pass me by and enter through the door behind me, but they didn't. One step, two steps, three steps up they stopped and sat down beside me.

"Hi," the voice said softly.

I was afraid to look up but I did. I came face to face with him, blue eyes as bright as the day I first laid mine on him.

"Mr. Burton." I smiled.

He shook his head. "How many times do I have to tell you not to call me that?"

I was about to call him Gregory when he said, "It's *Doctor* Burton now."

"Congratulations, *Doctor* Burton," I smiled. I examined his face, taking all of him in.

"Do you think this week you could move away from these steps and make it inside the building? I was getting tired of watching you from a distance."

"Funny, I was just thinking that sometimes it's easier to see things from a distance."

"Yes, but it's impossible to hear."

I laughed.

"I like the name of the building." I looked over at the brass plate with the SCATHACH HOUSE engraving.

"I came across it advertised for rental in the paper. I thought it was perfect. A good-luck sign, perhaps."

"Perhaps. I don't suppose you're any closer to that bridge we discussed."

He smiled and searched my face, took all of me in, and shivers ran through me.

"If you let me take you out for lunch, we could see where we are. That's if your boyfriend doesn't mind."

"Boyfriend?" I asked, confused.

"The follically unchallenged young male who answered the door to your place a few weeks back."

"Oh, him." I shook my head. "That was just . . ." I paused, unable to remember his name, "Thomas," I lied. "We're not together."

Mr. Burton laughed, stood up, and held out his hand to help me up. "My dear Sandy, I think you'll find his name was Steve, but not to worry, the more men's names you forget, the better it is for me." He placed his hand lightly on the small of my back and I felt a jolt of electricity race through my body. He guided me across the road. "Can we go into my office for just a moment? There's something I want to give you first."

He introduced me proudly to his receptionist, Carol, and brought me into his office. It smelled of him, it looked like him, everything about it was Mr. Burton, Mr. Burton, oh, Mr. Burton. I felt like I was wrapped in a gigantic hug, embraced in his arms as soon as I stepped in and sat on his couch.

"It's a bit better than the one we used to have, isn't it?" He smiled, retrieving something from a desk drawer and bringing it over.

"It's beautiful." I looked around and breathed in his scent.

Suddenly he was nervous. He sat opposite me. "I was supposed to give this to you last month when I called round, for your birthday. I hope you like it." He slid the box across the veneer cherry table. The box was long, red, and velvet. I took it in my hands as though it were the most fragile thing I'd ever held, and I rubbed my fingers along the soft furry velvet. I looked at him; he was nervously eyeing the box. I opened it slowly and held my breath. A silver watch glistened inside.

"Oh, Mr. Bur—" I started to say, and he grabbed my hand, stopping me.

"*Please*, Sandy. It's Gregory now, OK?"

It's Gregory now. It's *Gregory* now. It's Gregory *now*. A choir of cherubs sang in my ear.

I nodded, smiling. I took the watch from the box and wrapped it around my left wrist, fiddling with the clasp, still stunned by the unexpected gift.

"If you look at the back, you'll see your name is engraved." With shaking hands, he helped me turn it over. There it was, SANDY SHORTT. "May it never go missing."

We smiled.

"Don't force it," he warned, watching me trying to close it. "Here, let me help you," he said just as the clasp made a snapping sound between my fingers.

I froze. "Did I break it?"

He moved to the couch beside me, all fingers and thumbs as he tried to fix it, his skin brushing against mine and everything, *everything*, melting inside of me.

"It's not broken but the clasp is loosened. I'll have to

take it back and get it fixed." He tried to keep the disappointment from his voice but failed miserably.

"No!" I stopped him from taking it off me. "I love it, I want to keep it on."

"It's too loose, Sandy. It may open and fall off."

"No, I'll keep my eye on it. I won't lose it."

He looked unsure.

"Just for today at least, let me wear it."

"OK." He stopped fiddling with it and we both finally stayed still and looked at one another.

"I'm really giving you this to help you with your time-keeping. Three years without contact are not allowed to pass again."

I looked down and twisted the watch around my wrist, admiring the links of the wristband, the mother-of-pearl face. "Thank you, Gregory." I smiled, loving how the word felt in my mouth, on my tongue as I said it. "Gregory, Gregory," I repeated a few more times as he laughed, loving every moment of it.

I let him take me out for lunch and we saw where we were.

Lunch was as close to a disaster as it could possibly have been. We consumed enough food for thought to last us our lifetimes. If either of us had any ridiculous notions that this could be the beginning of something special—and we most certainly did—we were brought to earth by the realization that we were right back where we finished off. Or very possibly right back to Gregory having to walk over razor-sharp grass blades. I was Scathach and my heart was on Scathach's island in all her and its fierce extremities. I had worsened by the years.

Yet I didn't ever, not for one day, take my watch off. There were times when it fell, but we all do that. It was put back where it belonged, where I felt and knew it to belong. That watch symbolized an awful lot. The positive side to our learning lunch was that it confirmed that we felt inextricably linked to each other, as if there was an invisible umbilical cord joining us both, allowing us to feed off one another, helping us to grow and give one another life.

Inevitably there was the flip side: that we could tug on the cord whenever we liked, twisting it and knotting it, not caring enough that our twisting and knotting had the ability to choke and suffocate each other slowly.

From a distance everything was great; close up, things were completely different. We couldn't fight the effects of time; how it alters us, how with each year an extra layer is glazed upon us, how every day we are something more than we were. Unfortunately for me and for Gregory, it was glaringly obvious that I was something and somebody far less than who I once was.

32

Bobby closed the door of Lost and Found quietly behind us, as though the sound would bring the stall owners outside to a stunned silence. I wasn't sure if this behavior was just another part of his dramatics but I sensed with a mild panic that it wasn't. Bobby let go of my clammy hand and scuttled off into an adjoining room without a word, closing the door behind him. Through the slit I could see his shadow flickering as he darted by the light, furiously rooting around; moving boxes, scraping furniture across the floor, clinking glasses, making every possible sound, each sound introducing a new conspiracy theory in my suspicious mind. Finally I averted my eyes from the doorway and looked around the room.

I was faced with walnut shelves floor to ceiling high, like in the old grocery stores of decades ago. Baskets were filled to the brim with knickknacks, tape, gloves, pens, markers, and lighters. Others were filled with socks with a handwritten sign excitedly announcing the sale of actual *pairs*. There were dozens of clothes racks lining the center of the shop, the men's and women's sections separated, everything color-coordinated, styles, eras labeled with dates from the fifties, sixties, seventies, and up. There were costumes, traditional clothing, and wedding dresses. (Who loses a wedding dress?) On the opposite wall there was a selection of books, and before that there was a counter displaying jewelry: backs of earrings, single earrings, some pairs Bobby had matched up despite the difference in their appearances.

There was a musty smell in the shop; everything was secondhand, used, had a history. Thin T-shirts had depth, had layers glazed upon them. There wasn't the same atmosphere as in a shop of shiny new things. Nothing was squeaky clean and young and innocently ready to learn. There were no books unread, no hats not yet worn, no pens not yet held. The gloves had held the hand of an owner's loved one, the shoes had walked distances, scarves had wrapped, umbrellas had protected. These objects knew things, knew what they were supposed to do. They had experience of life and lay in baskets, folded on shelves, and hung on racks ready to teach those who wore them. Like most of the people here, these objects had tasted life and then saw it slip away. And like most people here, they waited until they could taste it again.

I couldn't help but wonder about who was looking for them now, who was tearing their hair out to find their favorite earrings. Who was grumbling and searching in the bottom of their bag for another lost pen? Who was on their cigarette break only to find their lighter was missing? Who was already late for work and couldn't find their car keys that morning? Who was trying to hide from their spouse the fact that their wedding ring had disappeared? They could look and look till their eyes were sore, but they would never find. What a time for me to have such an epiphany. Here in Aladdin's cave of lost possessions far away from home. *There's no place like home* . . . the phrase taunted me again.

"Bobby," I called, inching closer to the doorway and shutting out the voice in my head.

"Just a minute," came his muffled reply, followed by a bang, followed by a profanity.

Despite my nerves, I smiled. I ran my finger along a walnut dish cabinet, like the kind you'd expect to contain the good silverware and crockery. Here it contained hundreds of photographs of smiling faces from all over the world, over the decades. I picked up one of a couple standing in front of Niagara Falls and studied it. It looked like it was taken in the seventies; it had the yellowy tint that could be obtained only by being dipped in time. Two fortysomethings in wide flares and raincoats, one second caught and contained among a lifetime of seconds. If they were alive now, they too would be in their seventies with grandchildren looking on and waiting patiently as they leafed through their photo albums, looking for the picture to recall their trip to Niagara. Secretly wondering if they had imagined it all, whether that second among a lifetime of seconds had been true at all, while grumbling to themselves, "I know I have it here somewhere . . ."

"Nice idea, isn't it?"

I looked up to see Bobby watching me from the doorway. After all his rummaging in the next room, he had nothing in his hands.

"Last week, Mrs. Harper found a wedding photo of

her cousin Nadine, whom she hadn't seen for five years. You wouldn't believe her reaction when she came across the photo. She sat there all day just staring at it. It was a group photo of everyone at the wedding, you see; her entire family was there. Imagine not seeing your family for five years and then suddenly coming across a recent photo of them? She only came in looking for socks," he said with a shrug. "It's times like that when I feel useful around here."

I put the frame of the couple down. "You said you were expecting me." I said it more harshly than I meant to, but I was scared.

He unfolded his arms and placed his hands in his pockets. I thought he was finally going to take something out of them and give it to me but instead he left them there. "I've been here for three years now." He had the same haunted face as everyone else had when they recalled the memory of arriving here. "I was sixteen years old. Two years to go till I finished school, ten years to go till I planned on growing up. I had no idea what I wanted to do with my life. I figured I'd still be at home annoying Mum until she forced me out and made me get a proper job. In the meantime I was happy being the joker at school and having my boxers washed and ironed. I didn't take many things seriously." He shrugged and then repeated, "I was only sixteen."

I nodded, not knowing where this was going. Wondering why on earth he said he'd been expecting me.

"I didn't know what to do when I first arrived here. I spent most of the time on the other side of the woods trying to find a way out. But there's none." He took his hands out of his pockets and made a clear signal. "I'll tell you that now, Sandy, there's *no* way out of here and I've seen people drive themselves demented trying to find a way." He shook his head. "I soon realized I had to start life here. I had to, for once in my life, take something seriously." He shifted uncomfortably in his stance. "It happened when I was looking for some clothes to wear. I was rummaging through all the gear outside, feeling like a homeless man at a junkyard. I came across a sock that was bright orange, glowing from under a business file I imagine someone was fired that morning for losing. It was so bright I couldn't help but wonder how on earth someone had managed to lose something so luminous, something that so clearly stood out from the crowd. But the more I looked at it, the better it made me feel about myself turning up here, because before, I thought it was my fault. I thought it was my complacency that led me to wind up here. I thought that if I'd paid more attention in school and had stopped messing around so much, that I could have prevented myself from coming here."

I nodded. I knew that very same feeling.

"The sock made me feel better because it was the brightest thing I'd ever seen." He laughed. "It was even *labeled* for Christ's sake, and I just knew that it was bad luck and *only* bad luck on both our parts for ending up here! There was nothing I could have done to avoid ending up here, no more than the sock could have done. I felt sorry for the person who'd labeled it, put their address on it, who'd basically done everything to prevent it from going missing. So I kept it to remind myself of that feeling, of that day I stopped blaming myself and every-body else. A *sock* made me feel better." He smiled. "Fol-low me." He went back into the adjoining room.

The next room was much the same as the shop, with walls lined with shelving units, though it was much smaller and was piled high with cardboard boxes, by the looks of it, used for storage.

"Here's the sock." He gave it to me and I held it in my hands. It was small, that of a child, and was of towel ma-terial. If Bobby thought the sock was going to have the same effect on me as it did on him, he was wrong. I still wanted out of here and blamed myself and everybody else for putting me here.

"After a few weeks of being here, I found myself help-ing newcomers to find clothes and anything else they needed when they arrived. So I eventually opened this place up. Mine is the only store in this village where you can get everything all under one roof," he said proudly. My lack of enthusiasm caused his smile to disappear and he continued his story. "Anyway, as part of owning and running this place, I have to go out every day and collect as many useful things as possible. I pride myself on being the only place that sells actual pairs of shoes and socks, matching outfits, and such like. Other people just gather what they find and display them. I search for the other half—kind of like a matchmaker," he added with a grin.

"Go on," I urged, sitting on an old torn chair that re-minded me of my first sessions with Mr. Burton.

"Anyway, the orange sock wasn't much of a big deal at all until I found this." He leaned over and took a T-shirt from a box beside him. Again, it appeared to be that of a child. "And *that* wasn't even a big deal until I found this." He placed another odd sock on the floor before me and studied my face.

"I don't get it." I shrugged, throwing the orange sock down to the floor.

He continued to take out the contents of the cardboard box in silence and laid them out on the floor before me while my mind worked overtime trying to decipher the code.

"I thought there was more in this one, but anyway, that's the lot," Bobby said finally.

The floor was almost covered in items of clothing and accessories and I was about to stand up and demand he start talking sense when I finally recognized a T-shirt. And then I recognized a sock, a pencil case . . . and then handwriting on a piece of paper.

Bobby stood by the empty box, excitement flashing in his eyes. "You get it now?"

I couldn't speak.

"They're all labeled. The name 'Sandy Shortt' is written on every single thing you see before you."

I held my breath, looking furiously from one item to another.

"That's just *one* box. They're all yours, too," he said excitedly, pointing to the corner of the room where five more boxes were stacked up. "Every time I saw your name I collected the item and stored it. The more things of yours I found, the more I became convinced that it was only a matter of time before you would come to collect them yourself. And here you are."

"Here, I am," I repeated looking at everything on the

floor. I got down on my knees and ran my hand across the orange sock. Although I couldn't remember it, I could imagine my frantic searches that night while my poor parents watched on. That was the beginning of it all. I took my T-shirt in my hands and saw my name written on the label in my mother's handwriting. I felt the ink with my fingertips, hoping that in some way I was connecting with her. I moved on to the piece of paper with my messy teenage handwriting. Answers to questions on *Romeo and Juliet* from school. I remember doing that homework and being unable to find it in class the next day. The teacher hadn't believed me when I couldn't find it in my schoolbag; he'd stood over me in a silent classroom and watched me root in my schoolbag, my frustration clearly growing, and yet his failure to recognize that genuine frustration had meant punishment homework. I felt like grabbing the page and running back to Leitrim, bursting in on that teacher's class and saying, "Here, look, I told you I had done it!"

I touched every item on the floor, the memory of wearing them, losing them, and searching for them coming to mind. After I'd seen every item from the first box, I raced over to the next on the top of the stacked pile in the corner. With shaking hands, I opened the box. Staring up at me with his one eye was my dear friend, Mr. Pobbs.

I took him out of the box and held him close to me, inhaling him, trying to get the familiar scent of home. He had long ago lost that and was musty like the rest of the belongings here, but I clung to him and squeezed him to my chest. My name and phone number were still visible on his tag, the blue felt pen of my mother's writing blurred now.

"I told you I'd find you, Mr. Pobbs," I whispered, and I heard the door behind me gently close as Bobby stepped out of the room, leaving me alone with a head and a room full of memories.

33

I don't know how long I'd been in the storeroom. I had lost track of all time. I looked out the window for the first time in hours, feeling cross-eyed and tired from concentrating on my possessions for so long. My *possessions*. I actually had belongings in this place. They brought me that bit closer to home, momentarily linking the two worlds, blurring the boundaries so that I didn't feel so lost as I touched and held things I once held in my place, near the people I loved. Especially Mr. Pobbs. So much had happened since I'd seen him. Johnny Nugent and a thousand other Johnny Nugents had happened. It seemed that the night Mr. Pobbs disappeared from my bed, an entire team of Mr. Wrongs had taken his place.

Joseph walked by the window and I sat back and watched as he strode confidently in his white linen shirt with sleeves rolled to just below his elbows and trousers rolled above the ankles of his sandaled feet. He always stood out from the crowd. He looked like somebody important who oozed dominance and power. He spoke little, yet when he did he chose his words carefully. When he spoke, people listened. His words moved from whispers to songs, never anything in between. Despite the strength of his physical demeanor, he spoke softly, which made him all the more superior.

The bell on the shop's front door rang again. The door squeaked and closed.

"Hello, Joseph," Bobby said cheerfully. "Did my Wanda not want to see me today?"

Joseph laughed lightly and I *knew* Bobby was funny to have made him laugh. "Oh that girl is so in love with you. Do you think she wouldn't be here if she knew I was here?"

Bobby laughed. "How can I help you?"

Joseph's voice lowered as though he knew I was here and I immediately pressed my ear against the door.

"A watch?" I heard Bobby repeat loudly. "I have lots of watches here."

Joseph's voice was lowered to inaudible again and I *knew* it was terribly important for his voice to be so hushed. He was talking about *my* watch.

"A silver watch with a mother-of-pearl face," I heard Bobby say and I was thankful for his habit of repeating people. Their footsteps on the walnut floor got louder and I prepared to move away from the door in case it was opened.

"What about this one?" Bobby asked.

"No, it would have been one you had found yesterday or this morning," Joseph said.

"How do you know?"

"Because it went missing yesterday."

"Well, I don't know how you could know that." Bobby laughed awkwardly. "Unless you've been talking to someone from the other world, which I'm highly doubtful of."

There was silence.

"Joseph, this watch is exactly what you've described." I could hear the confusion in Bobby's voice.

"It's not the one I want," Joseph said.

"Did you see it somewhere? On somebody? Perhaps you could tell them to visit me so I get an idea of what you're looking for. If I come across it, I'll save it for you."

"It is the very watch I saw somebody wearing, that I'm looking for."

"Someone from Kenya? Years ago?"

"No, from Here."

"Here," Bobby repeated.

"Yes, Here."

"Did somebody from Here give it to me?"

"No, it went missing."

Silence.

"It can't have. They must have misplaced it."

"I know, but I saw it with my own eyes."

"You saw it *disappear*?"

"I saw it on her wrist and she didn't move an inch from her place and then I saw that it was gone from her wrist."

"It must have fallen off her."

"Yes, it did do that."

"So it's on the ground."

"That's the funny thing," Joseph said drily and I *knew* it wasn't funny at all.

"But it can't ha—"

"It did."

"And you thought it would show up here?"

"I thought you may have found it."

"I didn't."

"I can see that. Thank you, Bobby. Speak of this to no one," he warned, giving me a chill. Footsteps began to move away.

"Hold on, hold on, Joseph. Don't go yet! Tell me, who lost it?"

"You don't know her."

"Where did she lose it?"

"Halfway between here and the next village."

"No," Bobby whispered.

"Yes."

"I'll find it," Bobby said determinedly. "It has to be there."

"It's not." Joseph raised his voice to a normal tone but for him it was loud. From the way that he said it, I *knew* that it was not.

"OK, OK." Bobby backed down, still not sounding like he believed it. "Does the person who lost it know that it's gone? Maybe she knows where it is."

"She's new here." That said it all. That meant *she doesn't understand a thing*, and he was right, I didn't, but I was learning fast.

"She's new?" The tone in Bobby's voice had changed. I recognized that and was sure Joseph would too. "Maybe I can talk to her and get the exact description."

"I have given you the exact description." Yes, he noticed it. Footsteps moved toward the door again, the door squeaked, and the bell rang.

"Was there a name on the watch?" Bobby called out at

the last minute, and the squeak of the front door stopped. It closed again, and footsteps got louder as they neared me again.

"Why do you ask?" Joseph's voice was firm.

"Because sometimes people engrave names, dates, or messages on the backs of watches." Bobby sounded nervous.

"You asked me if there was a name. Why did you specifically ask about a name?"

"Some watches have names engraved on them." His voice went up an octave in defense. "I should know." He tapped on glass and I guessed it was the jewelry cabinet.

There was a funny atmosphere outside, I didn't like it.

"Let me know if you find the watch. Be quiet about it, you know how people would react if they found out that things from Here were going missing."

"Of course, I understand it might give them hope."

"Bobby . . ." Joseph warned, and a chill ran through me.

"Yes, sir," Bobby said smartly.

The door squeaked, the bell rang, and it was closed again. I waited a while to make sure Joseph didn't come back in. Bobby was silent outside. I was about to stand up when Joseph walked by the window again, closer this time, staring at the building suspiciously. I quickly ducked and lay flat on the floor, wondering why on earth I was suddenly hiding from Joseph.

Bobby opened the door and looked down at me. "What on earth are you doing?"

"Bobby Stanley," I said as I sat up, brushing the dust off me, "you have a *lot* of explaining to do."

He took me by surprise and folded his arms across his chest. "And so have you," he said coolly. "Want to know why I wasn't at your auditions? Because nobody told me about them. Want to know why? Because around here everybody knows me as Bobby *Duke*. Ever since the day I arrived here, I haven't told *anybody* that my name is Bobby Stanley. So how did you know?"

34

"M r. Le Bon, I assume," Dr. Burton addressed Jack, leaning back in his chair and folding his arms.

Jack reddened but he was determined not to back down or be dismissed from Dr. Burton's company as a raving lunatic. He leaned forward. "Dr. Burton, there are *many* of us who are trying to find Sandy—"

"I don't need to hear any more." He pushed his chair back, grabbed Jack's file from the coffee table, and got to his feet. "Our time is up, Mr. Ruttle. You can settle the fee outside with Carol." He spoke with his back turned as he made his way to his desk.

"Doctor—"

"Good-bye, Mr. Ruttle." His voice rose.

Jack took the silver watch in his hands and stood. He spoke quietly but quickly while he had the chance. "Can I just say that a garda by the name of Graham Turner may contact—"

"Enough!" Dr. Burton shouted, slamming the file down on the desk. His face reddened and his nostrils flared. Jack froze and was immediately silenced.

"You obviously haven't known Sandy very long *or*

intimately. Taking that into consideration, it's glaringly obvious that it's absolutely no business of yours to go snooping around in her life."

Jack opened his mouth to protest but he was beaten to it again.

"But," Dr. Burton continued, "I believe that you and your group are genuine and so I will tell you this before you take things any further with the police." He battled visibly with his anger. "I'll tell you what the Gardaí will tell you if they start calling around. I'll tell you what Sandy's own family will tell you." His anger rose again and he ground his back teeth. "And what every single person who knows her will tell you, and that is this: that *this*," he said, and threw his arms up helplessly in the air, "is what Sandy does."

Jack tried to speak again.

"*All* of the time," he shouted. "She floats in and floats out, leaves things behind, sometimes she collects them, sometimes she doesn't." He placed his hands on his hips, his chest heaving with anger. "But the point is, she'll come back again. She always comes back."

Jack nodded and looked down at the ground. He started to cross the room to leave.

"You can leave her things here," Dr. Burton added. "I'll make sure she gets them and thanks you on her return."

Jack slowly lowered the rucksack of her belongings to the ground by the door and quietly stepped out, feeling like a scolded schoolboy, but at the same time feeling sympathy for the schoolmaster who had chastised him. It wasn't Jack he was angry at. It was the breeze that came and went, blowing sporadic gusts of hot and cold air from puckered lips, kisses that tickled and air that smelled sweet, but who at the snap of her fingers inhaled it all back in an instant. It was Sandy he was mad at. And himself, for his eternal wait.

Jack left Dr. Burton, hands on hips, staring out the Georgian window, grinding his jaw. Jack closed the door softly behind him, locking the atmosphere inside. It was far too precious to allow to creep into the reception for the awaiting people to sense. It would remain locked in the office, hovering around Dr. Burton while he took the time to process it, deal with it, allow it to cool, and then eventually dissipate.

The receptionist, Carol, looked at Jack with worry, not sure whether to be frightened of him or sorry for him at the screaming she had heard inside. Jack placed his credit card on the counter and reached down to her desk to pass her a piece of paper.

"Could you please tell Dr. Burton that if he changes his mind, here's my phone number and the address of the meeting point later today?"

She read the note quickly and nodded, still defensive of her boss.

He entered his PIN into the machine and retrieved his credit card. "Oh, and please give him this, too." He placed the silver watch on the counter. Her eyes narrowed as he walked away.

"Mr. Ruttle?" he heard her say as he reached the door. A man reading a car magazine looked up at the mention of the peculiar name.

Jack froze and turned to her slowly. "Yes?"

"I'm sure Dr. Burton will be in contact soon."

Jack laughed lightly, "Oh, I'm not too sure about that." He moved to leave again and she cleared her throat, trying to get his attention. He walked back to her desk.

She leaned forward and lowered her voice. The man took the hint and went back to reading his magazine.

"It's usually just a few days each time. The longest was almost two weeks but that was at the beginning. This is by far the longest in a while," she whispered. "When you find her, tell her to come back to . . ." She looked sadly at the door to Dr. Burton's office. "Well, just tell her to come back."

As quickly as she'd spoken, she stopped, took the watch from the counter, placed it in a drawer, and carried on typing. "Kenneth," she called, ignoring Jack now. "Dr. Burton will see you now. Go right in."

It's difficult beginning a relationship with someone you were never allowed to know anything about.

Our relationship to date had been based on me, and I was finding it hard to make the transition to it suddenly being about the both of us. Every week our meetings were centered on how *I* was feeling, what *I* had done that week, what *I* thought and what *I'd* learned. He was allowed to access my mind whenever he wanted, that was the sole reason for our relationship; for him to delve into my mind and try to figure me out. And to try and stop me from trying to figure him out.

A more serious relationship, a more *intimate* relationship was proving to be the opposite. I had to remember to ask him about him, and to remember that he couldn't now know everything that was inside my head. Some things had to be held back, for safekeeping, for self-preservation, and in a way, I lost my confidant. The closer we got, the less he knew about me, the more I learned about him.

An hour a week had been intensified and roles had been reversed. Who'd have thought Mr. Burton had a life beyond the four walls of the old school. He knew people and did things that I never knew about; things that I was suddenly allowed to know about but wasn't sure whether I wanted to. How could a person historically incapable of sharing a bed *and* a head not need to run from all of that? Sure, I went missing for days at a time.

No, the age gap didn't matter, it had never mattered. The years weren't the problem; it was the time that was the fault. This new relationship existed without a ticking clock. There was no long hand to dictate the end of a conversation; I could not be saved by the proverbial bell. He could access me at all times. Of course I ran.

There's a fine line between love and hate. Love frees a soul and in the same breath can sometimes suffocate it. I walked that tightrope with all the gracefulness of an elephant, my head weighing me to the side of hate, my heart hoisting me to the side of love. It was a wobbly journey and sometimes I fell. Sometimes I fell for long periods of time, but never for too long.

Never for as long as this.

I'm not asking to be liked. I've never yearned to be

liked, nor am I asking to be understood; I've never been that, either. When I behaved that way, when I left his bed, let go of his hand, hung up the phone, and closed his door behind me, even *I* had difficulty liking me, understanding me. But it's just how I was.

How I *was*.

35

B obby stood at the door of the stockroom, arms folded across his chest, a scowl on his face.

"What?" I scrambled to my feet and towered over him. He didn't seem so confident now that I'd risen to my full six-foot-one height. He dropped his hands by his sides and looked up at me. "Your name *isn't* Bobby Stanley?"

"No, according to everybody else here, my name is Bobby Duke," he said defensively, accusingly, childishly.

"Bobby *Duke*?" I rubbed my face in frustration. "What?" I repeated. "The guy from the cowboy movies? Why?"

"Never mind the *why*." His face reddened. "I think the issue here is that you are the only one who knows my real name. How?"

"I know your mother, Bobby," I said softly. "There's no great mystery, it's as simple as that." The past few days had consisted of secrets, mysteries, and little white lies. It was time to stop all that, for now anyway. All I wanted to do was meet the people I had been searching for, tell them all that I knew, and then bring them home. That is what I would do. While contemplating all this I suddenly noticed that Bobby had gone completely silent and had whitened ever so slightly.

"Bobby?" I said.

He didn't speak, just backed away a little from the doorway.

"Bobby, are you OK?" I asked a little more gently.

"Yeah," he said, not looking at all OK.

"You're sure?"

"I kind of knew that," he said quietly.

"What?"

"I kind of knew that you knew my mum. Not just when I first opened the shop door this morning and you called me Mr. Stanley and not just when everybody from the auditions told me that you knew so much, but I kind of knew when I kept finding all of your things." He looked beyond me to my lost life, scattered on the floor. "When you're on your own, you look for signs. Sometimes you make them up, sometimes they're actually there, but most of the time you can't tell the difference between the two. I believed in this one the most."

I smiled. "You're exactly as she said you'd be."

His lower lip trembled and he tried to stop it. "Is she OK?"

"Apart from missing you like crazy, she's OK."

"Ever since Dad left it was always just her and me. She's on her own now; I hate that she's on her own." His voice went up and down as he tried to control it.

"She's never alone, Bobby; she has your uncles, aunts, and grandparents. Besides she brings anyone and everyone who'll listen into her home and goes through photo albums and home videos of you. I don't think there's one person in Baldoyle who hasn't seen you score against St. Kevin's in the finals."

He smiled. "We could have won that match had it not been . . ." His voice trailed off.

I continued for him: "Had it not been for Gerald Fitzwilliam getting injured in the second half."

He raised his head and looked at me, light in his eyes. "It was Adam McCabe's fault," he tutted, and shook his head.

"He should never have been put in midfield," I said, and he laughed. He laughed that loud, cartoon laugh that I'd heard so many times in the home videos, the laugh that his family spoke about so much. The high-pitched, addictively funny sound that instantly made me giggle.

"Wow," he said, followed by a breath. "You know her *well*."

"Bobby, believe me, you don't need to know your mother well to know that."

Jack sat in Mary Stanley's home, drinking coffee and watching home videos of her son, Bobby.

"See this bit here." Mary inched forward suddenly in her chair, coffee spilling over the side of her mug and falling onto her blue jeans. "Ah." She jumped back, making a face, and Jack leaped forward thinking she'd burned herself. "That's where it all went wrong," she said angrily.

Jack realized she was still referring to the television and he sat back on the couch.

"See him?" she pointed at the TV, spilling coffee again.

"Watch yourself," Jack warned her.

"I'm fine." She rubbed her leg without looking. "This is where it all went wrong. We could have won that match had it not been for him." She pointed again. "Gerald Fitzwilliam, getting injured right there in the second half."

"Mmm," Jack replied sipping his coffee and watching the amateur footage of the match jumping up and down on the screen. Most of the time all he could see was a blur of green followed by closeups of Bobby's head.

"It was Adam McCabe's fault," she tutted, and shook her head. "He should never have been put in midfield."

Bobby brought me up a small winding staircase, which led to his residence above the shop. I sat waiting for him in his living room on an impressive leather couch I imagined somebody had impatiently waited to be delivered, for longer than the average four-to-six-week period. He brought me in a glass of orange juice and a croissant and my ravenous stomach gurgled in thanks.

"I thought everybody was supposed to eat in the eatery," I said, attacking the fresh croissant, which flaked in my hands.

"Let's just say the chef has a soft spot for me. She has a son my age back home in Tokyo. She slips me food every once in a while and I occasionally tease her, disgust her, and do other son-like things."

"Charming," I murmured, face covered in pastry.

Bobby was staring at me, his food untouched on his plate.

"Whapft?" I said with a mouthful of food. He continued staring and I quickly swallowed. "Is there something on my face?" I felt around.

"I want to hear more," he said sombrely.

I looked sadly to the remainder of food on my plate, wanting so much to finish it but knowing by the look on Bobby's face that I owed it to his mother to start talking fast.

"You want to know about your mum?" I washed down the crumbs with orange juice.

"No, I want to know about you." He got comfortable on the couch while I watched him, suddenly uncomfortable, with my mouth agape.

"I was told you ran an acting agency. Was it through the agency that you became friends with my mum?"

"No, not really."

"I didn't think so."

"What do you mean by that?"

"You don't run an acting agency do you? You don't seem like the type."

My mouth dropped open and I felt oddly insulted. "Why, what *type* of person usually runs an acting agency?"

"People that aren't like you," he said, but with a smile. "What do you really do?"

"I search," I said, smiling. "I hunt."

"For talent?"

"For people."

"For talented people?"

"I suppose everybody I look for has a talent of some sort, although I'm not too sure about you." Bobby looked confused and I decided to drop the awkward humor and place my trust in him. "I run a missing-persons agency, Bobby."

At first he looked shocked. Then, as the realization hit him, he began to smile, the smile grew into a grin, the grin worked its way into laughter, laughter became the addictively funny sound I knew so well, and then I was laughing too.

Suddenly he stopped. "Are you here to bring us all home or are you just visiting?"

I looked at his hopeful face and immediately felt sad. "Neither. I'm stuck here too, unfortunately."

At moments when life is at its worst there are two things that you can do: 1) break down, lose hope, and refuse to go on while lying facedown on the ground banging your fists and kicking your legs, or 2) laugh. Bobby and I did the latter.

"OK, here's what you have to do. *Do not* tell anybody else this news," Bobby said.

"I haven't. Apart from Helena and Joseph, nobody else knows."

"Good. We can trust them. The idea for the play was Helena's?"

I nodded.

"Clever move." His eyes glistened mischievously. "Sandy, you really need to be careful. People were talking this morning at the eatery."

"People don't usually talk at the eatery?" I joked, tucking into the remainder of my croissant.

"Come on, this is serious. They were talking about you. The group of auditionees must have told their friends and their families here about what you'd told them, who in turn told a few other people, and now *everybody's* talking."

"Is it really that bad that they know? I mean, what harm will it do if they all know I used to look for missing people?"

Bobby's eyes widened. "Are you crazy? The vast majority of people here are settled and wouldn't go back to their old ways if you paid them, and not just because money is of absolutely no use to them here. But there are a number of people, the kind of people that are how I was when I arrived. These people haven't found their feet yet because they are still trying to find their way out. Those people will latch onto you like you don't know what and you'll be wishing you'd never opened your mouth."

"Helena said the very same thing to me. Did that happen before?"

"*My god*, did it happen before. Well not *exactly* the same circumstances." He waved his hand dismissively and dropped the dramatics. "Years ago, before I even arrived here, some old guy claimed that some of his things kept going missing. If you ask me it was his mind more than anything. Well, as soon people heard, there wasn't a toilet he could go to without company. He was followed absolutely *everywhere*. When he went to the eatery, people flocked to his table; they followed him to the shops and even waited outside his home. It was madness. Eventually he had to give up his job because huge numbers would shadow him."

"What was his job?"

"He was a postman."

"A postman? Here?" I screwed up my face.

"What's so odd about that? We need postmen here more than anywhere. People need to get letters, messages, and packages to others in surrounding villages, because even though we have telephones, televisions, and computers, there's no network or service on any of them, just static and a lot of fuzz. Anyway he couldn't keep cycling into villages with a trail of people behind him. Villagers were giving out about it but the people who followed him thought he was miraculously going to find his way out of here."

"And what happened?" I asked, now on the edge of my seat.

"They all drove him crazy, even more crazy than he already was. There was nowhere he could go in privacy."

"Where is he now?"

"I dunno." Bobby appeared suddenly bored by the story. "He disappeared. He's probably a few towns away or something. Joseph would know, as they were very close. You should ask him."

A chill entered my body and I shivered.

"Are you cold in here?" Bobby asked, incredulous. "It's always so hot upstairs, I find. I'm absolutely sweating." He picked up our plates and glasses.

He may have acted cool, but I saw him. I saw him from the corner of my eye, giving me a long, long look before he exited the room. He wanted to see if his seed had been planted. He needn't have worried. It had.

36

"Come on, we can walk and talk at the same time," Bobby said, standing and grabbing my hand to pull me up.

"Where are we going?"

"To rehearsals, of course. Now more than anything, you have to keep up this play lark. People will be keeping their eyes on you whether you notice it or not."

I got chills again and shuddered. Once downstairs, Bobby started throwing clothes at me.

"What are you doing?"

"People will take you a lot more seriously if you stop dressing like Sinbad the Sailor." He handed me a gray pinstriped pair of trousers and a blue shirt.

"These are the correct sizes," I said, looking through the tags, impressed.

"Yes, but I did not take into account the very long legs." He bit his lip, looking down at me.

"The bane of my life." I rolled my eyes, handing the trousers back.

"No problem, I've got just the thing!" He ran off down to the end of the shop. "This entire rack is for people with very long legs." He rooted through the hangers, while I looked at the clothes like a kid in a candy store. Never, *never* had I come across such a luxury.

"My God, I think I might be happy here after all." I ran my fingers along all the clothes.

"Here you go." He handed me what looked like exactly the same trousers, but longer. "Put them on quick. We don't want to be late for rehearsals."

We stepped outside into the bright sunny day, my eyes aching after being hidden away in the darkness of the musty walnut building. It was noisy with the business of trade going on. People were shouting, bargaining, laughing, and calling out in all different languages, some I had never heard before. A small group of four women turned to stare at Bobby and me as he locked up the shop. I stood on the porch in my new clothes, feeling on display, as they whispered to one another.

"There she is," I heard one whisper very loudly, so loudly I wonder how on earth she thought I wouldn't hear her. One nudged another and she was pushed forward, stumbling toward us as we made our way down the steps.

"Hi." She stopped us in our tracks.

Bobby went to move around her but she stepped to the left, blocking us again.

"Hi," she repeated, looking at me and ignoring Bobby.

"Hi," I responded, aware that the group she had emerged from was watching.

"My name is Christine Taylor?"

Was that a question?

"Hi, Christine."

Silence.

"I'm Sandy."

Her eyes narrowed as she searched my face, hunting for my recognition of her.

"Can I help you?" I asked politely.

"I've been here for two and a half years?" she asked again.

"Oh, I see. That's"—I looked to Bobby, who raised his eyes to heaven in response—"well, that's quite a while, isn't it?"

She studied me again. "I used to live in Dublin?"

"Really? Dublin's a very nice city."

"I have three brothers and one sister?" She tried to refresh my memory. "*Andrew* Taylor?" Eyes searched my face. "*Martin* Taylor?" Silence. "*Gavin* Taylor?" Silence. "My sister is *Roisín* Taylor?" Searched again. "She's a nurse in Beaumont Hospital?"

"I see . . ." I nodded slowly.

"Do you know any of them?" she asked hopefully.

"No, I'm sorry, I don't." I really didn't. "It was nice to meet you, though." We started to move away when she grabbed my arm. "Hey!" I yelped, trying to shake her off. Her grip tightened.

"Hey, let go of her." Bobby stepped in.

"You know them, don't you?" she said, moving closer to me.

"No!" I said, stepping back, her grip tightening on my arm.

"My mam and dad are Charles and Sandra Taylor." She spoke more quickly now. "You probably know them too. Just tell me ho—"

"Get *off* me!" I pulled my arm violently away from her as the crowd around us quieted and turned to stare.

That stopped her talking and she turned to her friends, who stared back, assessing me.

"I'm sorry, but we're late for the rehearsals. We have to go now." Bobby took me by the sore arm and pulled me away. In shock, I allowed him to pull me along, half running, half walking through the crowd, feeling eyes boring into me as we passed.

We finally reached the Community Hall and there was a small line forming at the door.

"Sandy!" one person called out. "There she is! Sandy!" Others began to call out and swarmed around me. I felt Bobby tugging me again, I was pulled backward and the door to the Community Hall slammed behind me. The cast of the play, who sat in a circle, all turned to stare at me and Bobby, who stood panting with our backs pressed up against the door.

"Well," I said, catching my breath, as my voice echoed around the hall, "is this the bloody twilight zone or what?"

Helena jumped up, "Said Dorothy as she landed in Oz. Thank you, Sandy, for sharing her first line with us," she said quickly as horrified faces transformed to understanding nods. "It will be a modern twist on an old story," Helena explained. "Thank you, Sandy, for sharing that with us *so* dramatically."

Mary finally pressed STOP as Bobby's first-grade school play ended and she ejected the videotape Jack had secretly fantasized about burning for the last two hours. He knocked back the remainder of his cold coffee in a bid to stay awake.

"Mary, I really have to get back to Limerick tonight," he hinted, looking at his watch. In all the time he had spent in her company, there hadn't been one mention of Sandy. He felt he was being broken in first, being inducted into Mary's life before they could move on to other matters. All around him in the living room, framed photographs cluttered every surface. Bobby as a newborn baby, Bobby as a toddler, Bobby on his first bike, Bobby on his first day of school, Bobby on the day of his Holy Communion, his Confirmation, decorating a Christmas tree, Bobby in freeze-frame, leaping into a swimming pool on a summer holiday. From bald, to bleached-blond, to mousy-brown hair. No teeth, to missing teeth, to metal train tracks. There were no clocks in this room, time was imprinted in every picture and suspended as if forbidden to tick on from the last photograph; Bobby and Mary on his sixteenth birthday.

Thirty-eight-year-old Mary lived in an apartment above her charity shop, which consisted of clothes, shoes, books, knickknacks, home accessories, and everything else you could imagine. The shop was musty from the smell of second- or third-hand clothes, dusty books that had been well thumbed, and old toys that had been outgrown and outlived. Above was the space that Mary had shared with Bobby all of his sixteen years.

Mary stood up. "More coffee?"

"Please." Jack followed her to the kitchen, where he found more photographs dotting the walls, lining the windowsill. "Aren't any of the others I called coming to the meeting?" Jack had been expecting a small gathering.

"They can't make it on such short notice. Peter lives in Donegal with his two young children and Clara and Jim live in Cork, although they've recently divorced so the chances of getting them in the same room will be slim. It's sad really. Their daughter, Orla, has been missing for six years. I think it's that that drove them apart." She poured more coffee. "Things like this, huge dramatic changes in life, have the magnet effect. They either drive people apart or bring them together. Unfortunately the former happened in their case."

Jack immediately began thinking of Gloria and how this magnetic event had repelled them apart.

"I've no doubt everybody will pitch in to help, though, once we need them for something specific."

"Sandy helped all of these people?"

"Sandy *helps*, Jack. She's not gone yet. She's a Trojan worker. I know you didn't get the benefit of actually seeing her in action, but she keeps in touch with us every week. Even after all these years, she gives us a weekly call to let us know if there's any news. Most of the time, and particularly more lately, the phone calls have been to see how we are."

"Did anybody hear from her this week?"

"Nobody."

"And that's unusual?"

"Not *entirely* unusual."

"I've been told by a few people that it's not unusual for her to lose contact and just disappear for a while."

"She disappeared all the time, but she'd still ring us from her hiding places. If there's one thing Sandy is committed to it's her work."

"It sounds like it's the only thing."

"Yes, I wouldn't be surprised if that's true." Mary nodded. "Sandy gave, *gives*"—she corrected herself—"very little away. She's a pro at not talking about herself. She never mentions family or friends. *Not once,* and I've known her for three years."

"I don't think she has any," Jack said, sitting at the kitchen table with a fresh mug.

"Well, she has us." Mary joined him. "You didn't get anywhere with Garda Turner?"

Jack shook his head. "I spoke to him today. There's really nothing he can do if relatives and friends are saying that this is normal behavior. Sandy's not a danger to herself or others and there's nothing suspicious about her disappearance."

"There's nothing suspicious about a deserted car with all her belongings left inside?" Mary asked in surprise.

"Not if it's what she does all the time."

"But what about the watch you found?"

"The link on it was broken, she apparently often drops it."

Mary tutted and shook her head. "That poor girl is going to be punished for all her previous odd behavior."

"I'd love to talk to her parents, see what they think about the whole thing. I have such a hard time dealing with the fact that five days without hearing from a family member isn't something to be worried about." Jack knew inside that this was all entirely possible. He hadn't been particularly close to Donal or with the rest of his family, for that matter. Apart from Judith, they would often go for weeks without hearing from one another. It was his mother who had raised the alarm bells after three days.

"I have their address, if you want." Mary left the table to rummage around in a kitchen cabinet. "Sandy quite surprisingly asked me to send something to her there." Her voice was muffled from inside the press. "I think she was stranded with the family for Christmas one year and was desperately looking for some work to save her." She laughed. "But isn't that what Christmases are all about? Here it is." Her head finally emerged.

"I can't just drop in unannounced," Jack said.

"Why not? The worst they can do is not talk to you, but it's worth a try." She handed him the Leitrim address. "You can stay here tonight, if you like. It's far too late for you to be traveling to Leitrim and then on to Limerick."

"Thanks, I might even stay in Dublin a bit longer tomorrow to see if Sandy shows up to another appointment she made." Jack smiled, looking at a photo of a young Bobby dressed as a dinosaur for Halloween. "Does it get any easier?"

Mary sighed. "Never easier, but a little less hard, perhaps. It's always at the forefront of my mind, every single waking and sleeping moment. The hurt begins to . . . not quite disappear, but it's as though it evaporates so that it's always there in the air around me, ready to rain down when I least expect it. Then when the hurt goes, anger takes its place; when the anger runs out of steam, loneliness steps in to take over. It's a never-ending circle of emotions; every lost emotion being replaced by another.

The same isn't so for sons, unfortunately." She smiled wryly. "I used to love the great mysteries of life, the uncertainties, the not-knowing. I always thought it was so necessary to our journey." She smiled sadly. "I'm not so enthusiastic about that anymore."

Jack nodded and they both got lost in thought for a while.

"Anyway, it's not all doom and gloom." Mary perked up, "Hopefully, Sandy will do what she always does and return home in the morning."

"With Bobby and Donal in tow," Jack added.

"Well, here's hoping." Mary raised her mug and clinked it with Jack's.

37

J ack slept in Bobby's box bedroom that night, surrounded by posters of sports cars and half-naked blondes. On the ceiling were miniature stars and spaceships that once illuminated brightly in the dark but, like Bobby's presence, now merely emitted a faint glow. Stickers that had been stuck to the door and the discolored wallpaper had been torn off, leaving He-Man without his sword, Bobby Duke without his cowboy hat, and Darth Vader without his helmet. The earth's solar system was displayed on the navy blue duvet cover, every planet and place to be seen but the one Bobby was in.

A writing desk was piled high with CDs, a CD player, speaker phones and magazines containing yet more cars and women. Few school books were piled up in the corner, their place of importance low on the scale. Above the desk, shelves burst with more CDs, DVDs, magazines, and football medals and trophies. Jack doubted anything had been altered since the day Bobby had left this room and never come back. Jack placed his hands on as few items as possible and tiptoed on the carpet, not wanting to leave his imprint behind. Everything in this room was precious and existed only as a museum.

Peeking out from between the posters of cars and naked glamour models was *Thomas the Tank Engine* wallpaper. Just beneath the surface lay childhood with only a thin layer to separate it from adolescence. It was the room of someone no longer a boy but not yet a man; of someone in a place between innocence and realization, on the path of discovery.

Jack once again felt as he had earlier while in the house. He felt trapped in a time that wasn't allowed to move on. The door plate reading BOBBY'S ROOM: KEEP OUT! had been heeded and the door had been firmly shut, leaving everything inside, all the treasured items locked away as though the bedroom were a safe. Jack wondered whether Bobby was elsewhere now, living his life, whether he had moved on from the image Mary was fighting to hold on to or whether his journey had ended. Was he forever to exist in time as no longer a boy and not yet a man, in an in-between place as an in-between person with nothing fully whole, nothing fully realized?

He thought of his own refusal to let go of Donal and what Dr. Burton had said to him about replacing one search, which had reached a dead end, with another. He supposed in theory he was refusing to let go, but he was adamant that it wasn't due to an unwillingness and inability to move on. He shook away the thought that he was in any way similar to Mary, hanging on to memories and being stuck eternally in a moment that had long since passed. He pulled the duvet over his head and hid from the stars on the ceiling and galaxy above him. Realistically, his search for Sandy wouldn't find Donal, but something in his heart, in his mind was driving him forward.

Tomorrow would be Friday, and Sandy, if she didn't wander back into her life, would have been missing for six days. He needed to make the decision now whether it was the moment to pull back, to open the door of his life and allow the trapped time and memories to escape, to move on and catch up on all it had missed. Or he could go full steam ahead with this search, peculiar and out of the ordinary though it might be. He thought about Gloria at home, the nothingness he felt toward her, his life, and their future, and he decided that he, like the Bobby that still inhabited the room he lay in, was embarking on a journey of discovery. He heard Mary switching off the television and unplugging appliances in the kitchen. A gap in the curtains welcomed a sudden light to seep through into the bedroom, shining a ruler of yellow light onto a poster of a red Ferrari. Realizing it was the porch light, Jack was engulfed by a strange sort of calm and he watched the light on the wall until his eyes became heavy.

He awoke at eight forty-five the following morning to the sound of his phone ringing.

"Hello?" he croaked, eyes looking around and momentarily thinking he'd traveled back in time to his teenage years and was waking up at home in his mother's house. His mother . . . he felt a pang of loneliness for her.

"What the hell are you doing?" his sister Judith asked

angrily. In the background he heard babies crying and dogs barking.

He groaned. "Waking up."

"Yeah?" she said sarcastically. "Beside whom?"

Jack turned to his right and looked at the blonde wearing not much more than a cowboy hat and boots. "Candy from Houston, Texas. She likes horseback riding, homemade lemonade, and taking her dog Charlie for walks."

"What?" she shrieked, and a baby cried louder.

Jack started laughing. "Relax, Jude. I'm in the bedroom of a sixteen-year-old boy. There's no need to worry."

"You're *what*?"

Could he hear gunshots?

"JAMES, TURN THAT TV DOWN!"

"Ouch." Jack moved his head away from the phone.

"I'm sorry, did that noise from *hundreds of miles away* disturb you?" she said in a huff.

"Judith, why are you so tetchy today?"

She sighed. "I thought you were only going to Dublin to meet with the doctor."

"I was but I thought I'd ask around a bit more before I head home."

"This is still about the missing-persons woman?"

"Sandy Shortt, yes."

"What are you doing, Jack?" she asked softly.

He rested his head back against Babs from Down Under's nether regions. "I'm putting my life back together."

"By tearing it apart first?"

"Remember when we used to do the Humpty Dumpty jigsaw together every Christmas?"

"Oh dear, he's lost his mind," she sang.

"Humor me. Do you remember?"

"How can I forget? The first year it took us till March to finish it and all because Mum cleared it off the good room's dining table in a panic when Father Keogh paid one of his surprise visits."

They both laughed.

"After Father Keogh had left, Dad came in to help us start again, remember? He taught us to separate all the pieces, turn them all face up first and *then* get to work putting them together."

"And they said 'All the king's horses and all the king's men.'" She sighed. "So you're gathering all your pieces."

"Exactly."

"My philosophical baby brother. What happened to trips to the pub and fart jokes?"

He laughed. "That's still inside me somewhere."

She turned serious. "I understand what you're going through and I understand what you're doing, but do you have to do it all on your own without telling anybody anything? Can't you at least make it back home for the festival this weekend? I'm going tonight with Willie and the kids, there's an outdoor band playing and some games for the kids with the usual fireworks display on Sunday night. You've never missed one before."

"I'll try to get there," Jack lied.

"I don't know where Gloria gets her patience from. She seemed so cool about you staying on, but you're certainly testing her. Are you deliberately trying to push her away?"

Jack was about to launch into another defense of himself but stopped and thought about it for a change. "I don't know," he said, sighing. "Maybe. I don't know."

"Good morning," Mary sang, knocking on the door.

"Come in," Jack called out, wrapping the bedclothes around him.

There was a rattle and a few clinks as the handle lowered and Mary pushed open the door with a tray filled with breakfast.

"Wow," Jack said, eyeing the food hungrily.

Mary laid the tray down on the writing desk. She didn't move any magazines or CDs, preferring to allow the tray to rest dangerously on the edge of the desk. Nothing was to be touched. Jack was surprised she had allowed him to sleep in the bed at all.

"Thanks, Mary, everything looks great."

"You're very welcome. I used to love treating Bobby occasionally to breakfast in bed." She looked around the room, wringing her hands together. "Did you sleep well?"

"Yes, thanks," he replied politely.

"Liar," Mary said, moving toward the door. "I haven't slept through one single night ever since Bobby disappeared. I bet you're the same."

Jack just smiled, grateful to hear he wasn't the only one.

"I have to go open the shop now, but take your time. I've left a towel in the bathroom for you." She smiled, took one more haunted look around the room, and was gone.

Jack was glad he'd made a note of all of Sandy's future appointments before handing her diary over to Dr. Burton. For today she had written "YMCA Aungier Street. 12 Noon—Room 4." There was no mention at all of what the occasion was, but he noted that she had attended it, or at least made a note of it, once every month. He decided it was best not to call ahead but to go straight there.

He entered the building ten minutes after twelve, thanks to Dublin's dire traffic he had yet to account for in his travel time. There was no one behind the counter at reception, so he leaned over the desk looking left and right and called out, but to no avail. He was faced with many doors and notice boards advertising fitness classes, child care, computer classes, counseling services, and youth work programs. What was behind door number four? he wondered. He seriously doubted it was another counseling service but whatever it was he hoped it wasn't a fitness class. Computers, he hoped for; he could do with learning about computers. He rapped lightly on the door, looking for signs of what was inside and hoping, *hoping* it was Sandy.

The door opened and a lady with a kind face answered.

"Hello," she said with a smile, her voice almost a whisper.

"Sorry to interrupt," Jack whispered. Whatever was going on behind the door, it was certainly being done quietly. Yoga—he hoped it wasn't yoga.

"Don't worry, people are welcome regardless of the time. Do you want to join us?"

"Em, yes . . . I was actually looking for Sandy Shortt."

"Oh, I see, did she recommend this to you?"

"Yes," he replied, nodding emphatically.

She opened the door wider and a circle of people turned to stare. No mats, he thought with relief, no yoga. His heart beat wildly as he looked for Sandy, wondering if she could see him before he'd spotted her. And if she was looking at him now, would she recognize him? Would she be angry he had found her, hiding in her burrow, or would she be thankful, relieved someone had noticed her absence?

"Welcome. Come and take a seat." The woman held her arm out toward the circle while somebody unstacked a chair from the side of the small room and brought it to the circle. Jack walked toward them searching from face to face for a sign of Sandy. The circle grew larger as he neared, the movement like an umbrella being opened slowly. He sat down with trepidation. Sandy wasn't there.

"As you can see, Sandy unfortunately isn't with us today."

"Yes, I see that." He ground his back teeth together and the familiar pain began to throb at the back of his mouth.

"I'm Tracey," the woman said.

"Hello." Jack cleared his throat nervously as heads turned to stare at him, assess him, study him, analyze his every awkward move. "I'm Jack."

"Hello, Jack," they all responded in unison and he paused, his eyes widening in surprise at the hypnotic tone of their voices. There was a long silence as he shifted uncomfortably in his seat, not at all sure what it was he was supposed to be here for.

"Jack, would you prefer it if the others spoke first this week and maybe next week you can tell us your story?"

His *story*? He looked at everybody else; some had notepads and pens in their laps. To one side of the room was a white board with the words WRITTEN ASSIGNMENT circled at the top. From that circle stemmed the words FEELINGS, THOUGHTS, CONCERNS, IDEAS, LANGUAGE, EXPRESSION, TONES, among so many others he couldn't take them all in, and finally he came to the conclusion that it was more than likely he was in a creative-writing class.

"Sure," he replied with relief, "I'd like to listen to everyone else first."

"OK, Richard, can you start off for us by letting us know how you got on this month."

"Here, I find that this helps," a woman beside Jack whispered and handed him a pamphlet.

"Thank you." He left it on his lap and decided to wait until Richard had finished his story before reading through it. Richard's story was a rather absurd tale about an instantly unlikable man and his constant fear of acting on violent impulses. He droned on, painfully and miserably reciting the tale of how an equally painfully miserable man constantly felt overly responsible for the safety of others, to the point that he was afraid to drive out of fear he would run over someone with his car. At times, Jack shook his head and laughed out loud thinking it an obvious, however slightly dark, comedy, but he quickly stopped after receiving numerous odd looks from the group.

Minutes—which felt like hours—later, the room was still echoing the incessant droning of Richard's story, each word sounding twice in Jack's ears, which were already bored from hearing them the first time. As the story moved toward being just plain depressing, with the main character's behavior the cause of the loss of his wife and child, Jack finally tuned out and began to read the pamphlet scrunched beneath his clammy hands.

His relaxed body stiffened as he finally concentrated on the cover of the thin glossy booklet. Hot waves of color spread from his neck all the way to the top of his strawberry-blond head within seconds as he read WELCOME TO OBSESSIVE COMPULSIVE ANONYMOUS.

Jack sat quietly through the remainder of the meeting, feeling embarrassed to be there and generally ashamed by his earlier behavior during Richard's story. Keeping his head down when the hour was up, he filed out of the room, hiding among the rest of the members.

"Jack!" Tracey called out and he froze. He stopped walking and allowed everyone to file past him, watching their faces as they prepared to leave their safety net and battle the world and all its demons, alone. He also saw Dr. Burton, who was waiting outside the room, arms folded and a face like thunder. Jack took a few steps back into the room toward Tracey.

Tracey caught up to him and held out her hand to shake his. "Thank you for coming today," she said with a smile. "You know your coming here was the first step in helping to heal yourself. It's a rocky journey; it will be difficult, but please know that we are all here to help you through it." Jack heard Dr. Burton laugh mirthlessly. "The twelve steps that we mentioned earlier, as originated by Alcoholics Anonymous, and adapted for OCA, *can* bring relief. I've seen that they can reduce and even eliminate our obsessions and compulsions, so do come again next month." Tracey patted his arm encouragingly.

"Thanks." He cleared his throat awkwardly, feeling like an impostor.

"Do you know Sandy well?" she asked.

He winced, disliking being asked the question in Dr. Burton's company. "Kind of," he said uncomfortably, clearing his voice.

"If you see her, tell her to come back to us. It's unusual for her to miss a meeting."

Jack nodded again and felt glad now that Dr. Burton was within earshot. "I'll do my best."

"Hear that?" he said to Dr. Burton as soon as Tracey was out of earshot. "She says it's unusual for Sandy not to be here. I wonder where she is."

38

I went to the OCA meetings every month. I went because every month that I was there I knew it was another month of deserving to be with Gregory.

"Sandy!" I could hear Gregory calling my name. I was downstairs in his house, half-naked at ten past two in the morning, rooting through my overnight bag that I'd placed, as usual, by the front door when I'd walked in.

"Sandy!" he called again.

There was a thump and the floorboards above me creaked as he climbed out of bed and crossed the bedroom. My heartbeat quickened and my search became more frenzied. Feeling a pressure now that Gregory was making his way toward me, I turned my bag upside down and spilled the contents to the floor. I picked items up, tossed them aside, shook out all my clothes, went through the pockets, laid them flat on the floor, and ironed each point firmly with the palm of my hand, trying to feel for the hidden lump.

"What are you doing?" His voice was suddenly behind

me and I jumped. My heart thudded and adrenaline raced through me as I felt like I'd been caught in the act, as though I'd been doing something criminal like stealing or immoral like cheating on him. I hated that he made me feel what I was doing was wrong. It was that same look in his face that I had run from in others, the look that strangely hadn't chased me away from him yet. Not completely, anyway, although I had run a few times.

The aftershave I bought for him each of the six Christmases we had been together filled the room. I didn't respond to him, I just laid my navy blue garda uniform out on the carpet, feeling each point for unusual bumps.

"Hello?" he sang out. "I was calling you."

"I didn't hear you," I replied.

"What are you doing?"

"What does it look like?" I replied calmly, running my hand down the length of the navy blue nylon trouser leg.

"It looks like your clothes are being given a deep massage." I felt him move further into the room and he sat down before me on the couch, wrapped in the robe I'd bought for him this Christmas, wearing tartan slippers I'd bought for him the previous. "I'm rather jealous," he murmured, watching me smoothing down the pockets.

"I'm looking for my toothbrush," I explained, emptying the contents of my wash bag onto the floor.

"I see." He watched me. He just sat there quietly and watched me, yet this made me feel uncomfortable. His disapproving eyes on me made me feel as if I was sitting on the floor doing drugs instead of merely looking for something. A few minutes passed, searching without results.

"You know that you have a toothbrush upstairs in the bathroom already?"

"I bought a new one today."

"The old one won't do?"

"The bristles are too soft."

"I thought you liked soft bristles." He ran his hand through his tight beard.

I smiled for his sake.

He watched me for a little while longer.

"I'm going to make a cup of tea, do you want one?" He had the same method as my parents; they too used to keep an easy tone in their voices to pretend to me that everything was all right, to stop me from picking up negative vibes and panicking because something was lost. When I was younger that's what I thought. Now that I was older, I had learned from Gregory that it wasn't me he was trying to lighten the atmosphere for; it was himself. I stopped searching and watched him move around the adjoining kitchen as though he made cups of tea at two o'clock every morning. I watched him playing house and pretending that his on/off girlfriend was perfectly normal and correct to be sitting on the carpet half-naked while emptying her bag for a toothbrush she already had sitting in a cup holder upstairs. I watched him pretending to himself, smiling as I fell in love with another flaw I never knew existed within him.

"Maybe it fell out in the car," I said, more to myself.

"It's raining, Sandy. You don't want to go out now, do you?"

He needn't have asked, he knew the answer but he was still playing along with his own game. Pretending now, that his full-time, eternally faithful girlfriend was going to risk running out into the wet night to look for something. How unusual, how frightfully odd, how attractively kooky. Such fun.

I looked around the living room for a jacket or blanket to throw on. There was none. In this state, although I appear calm on the outside, inside I'm running around, screaming, shouting, looking in all directions, anxious to go, go, go. To run upstairs and throw some clothes on would take too long, would take precious minutes away from finding. I looked at Gregory, who was pouring the boiling water into a witty mug I'd got him for the previous Christmas. He obviously saw the desperate search in my eyes, the silent longing for help. He played it cool, as usual.

"OK, OK." He held his hands up in surrender. "You can have the robe."

I actually hadn't thought of his robe.

"Thanks." I got to my feet and walked to the kitchen.

He undid the belt and coolly shrugged it off his shoulders, and handed it to me, standing dressed now only in his tartan slippers and the silver chain I had given him for his fortieth birthday the previous year. I laughed and took the robe from him, but he held on to it, the robe firmly in his grasp. He turned serious.

"Please don't go outside, Sandy."

"Gregory, don't," I mumbled, tugging on the robe, not wanting this discussion again, not wanting to go through the same thing all over again, fighting about it, talking in circles, resolving nothing and apologizing for nothing but the insults fired between the main issues.

His face crumpled. "Please, Sandy, *please* can we just go back to bed. I'm up in four hours."

I stopped tugging on the robe and looked at him, standing before me naked but revealing more in the look on his face alone. Whatever it was about that face, about the way he looked at me, the way he yearned for me not to leave him, the way it seemed so important that I be with him rather than away, something inside me stopped fighting.

My grip relaxed on the robe. "OK." I gave in. *I gave in.* "OK," I repeated more to myself this time. "I'll go to bed."

Gregory looked surprised, relieved, and confused all in one glance, but he didn't push it, he didn't question it, he didn't want to ruin the moment, spoil the dream and chase me away again. Instead he held my hand and we went back upstairs to bed, leaving the clutter of my scattered clothes and wash bag on the floor by the door. It was the first time I'd turned my back on the situation and headed in the other direction. It was apt that it was Gregory leading me.

In bed I laid my head on his warm heaving chest, felt his heartbeat beneath my cheek and his breath on the top of my head. I felt loved and secure and thought everything in my life couldn't possibly be any more perfect and wonderful. Before he fell asleep, he whispered to me to remember that feeling. At the time, I thought he was referring to us being together, but as the night slowly moved on for me and the niggling returned, I knew he had meant for me to remember the feeling of walking away and the reason that led to that decision. I needed to hold on to that, store it in my memory and call upon it whenever the moment raised its ugly head.

I was restless that night. I only meant to go back downstairs and tidy my belongings away. And then when I had done that, I only meant to go out into the wet night to search my car. But then when it wasn't there, I forgot the feeling that I'd tried to hold on to while in Gregory's arms and Gregory's bed.

He woke up alone that morning and it pains me to imagine his thoughts when he felt around the bed and his hand rested on the cold sheets. Meanwhile, as he was asleep in his bed pretending in his dreams that I was alongside him, I had returned to a cold bedsit to find my toothbrush still in its packet, lying on the table. For once I got no solace from finding. I was emptier after finding the toothbrush than I had been before. It seemed the more things I found when I was with Gregory, the more I lost inside. I was alone in bed at five in the morning after leaving the warm bed of a man I loved, and who loved me. Of a man who would, as a result, no longer take my calls. A man who after thirteen years of wanting to learn all there was to learn about me had finally given up and wanted to know me no longer.

For a while, I gave up on him too until I became too lonely, too tired, and my heart became too sore from pretending I cared more about a whole series of nothings with nobodies rather than a single episode of *something* with *somebody*. I told myself that morning to hold on to that feeling, to remember the foolishness of leaving warmth to walk alone in the cold, the ridiculous loneliness of leaving something for nothing.

He took me back on one condition. That I recognize my problems and attend a monthly meeting of a group called the OCA. The first thing you learn while in OCA is that you can't be in OCA for anybody else but yourself. It was a lie from the very beginning. Every extra month I attended the meeting was another month spent with Gregory, a happier Gregory, who was content knowing I was taking steps, twelve to be precise, to recover. He pretended to himself again because it was obvious to everyone that there had been no change in my behavior. I knew in my heart that I wasn't the same as the others in the class. I felt it absurd that he would think I was among the likes of those who scrubbed and cleaned themselves for hours at night before going to bed until they almost bled, and hours in the morning before going to work. Or the woman who made tiny slits with a blade on her own arms, or the man who touched, counted, arranged, and hoarded every little thing that came into his path. I wasn't like them. My *dedication* was confused with obsession. There was a difference. *I* was different.

Years and years of going to the meetings and I was still the same as the twenty-one-year-old who sat on the concrete steps opposite Dr. Burton's office building every week, with my elbows on my knees, chin rested on my hands, watching the world pass by as I waited to cross the road.

Every single time, Gregory crossed over for me and met me on my side. I realize now, I don't think I ever met him in the middle. And I don't think I ever once said thank you for that.

But I'm saying sorry now, I shout it a thousand times

a day from this place that he can't hear me from. I say thank you and sorry and I scream it through the trees, over the mountains, pour my love into the lakes, and I blow kisses in the wind, hoping that they will reach him.

I went to the OCA meetings every month. I went because every month that I was there I knew it was another month of deserving to be with Gregory.

I missed it this month.

39

After returning from an afternoon rehearsal at the Community Hall, Bobby and I sat around the pine table with Helena and Joseph in their home. Wanda sat opposite me, her head of messy black curls just about visible over the table, and her arms pulled up in a giant effort to clasp her hands together, imitating how I was seated. Joseph had just announced that the council had called a meeting for tomorrow night, which for reasons known only to the others around the table was a cause to become quiet and allow an atmosphere of impending doom to fall over us.

I don't know why, but I found the day-to-day running of this place comical. I didn't and couldn't take their world and their issues seriously, however important they were. I hid my smile beneath my hand as I watched them worriedly looking at one another. I was completely detached from the problem, thankful that whatever was happening was happening to them and not me. It was as though their problems weren't mine because I was an outsider of my own choosing, and I would do my utmost to remain in that position. Anything to avoid having to deal with the harsh reality of settling here. There seemed to be very little choice involved in that reality. So my feeling while I sat at the table was that my time here would be too short-lived to have to care about whatever it was that affected their world. *Their* world, not mine. Nobody had spoken for a while so I tried to break the frosty atmosphere.

"So what's such a big issue that would cause a meeting to be called?"

"You," Wanda said perkily, and I could tell her legs were swinging under the table from the way her shoulders rocked.

A chill went through me. I chose to ignore her, annoyed that a child was allowed to sit in on our conversation without being silenced, annoyed that she had transformed me from black sheep to piggy by snatching me from the outside where I felt comfortable and plonking me right in the middle of the equation. I looked to the faces around the table, still glancing worriedly at one another but still not speaking. The only one willing to look me in the eye was Wanda.

"What makes you say that?" I questioned the five-year-old, taking the fact that nobody had corrected her as either because it was the general consensus or they were ignoring her because she was bonkers. I hoped for the latter.

"From the way that everyone was staring at you when we walked from the Community Hall to here."

"That's enough now, sweetheart," Helena said gently.

"Why?" Wanda looked up at her grandmother. "Didn't you see how they all stopped talking and made way for her? It was like she was a fairy princess." She revealed her gummy smile. Yep, bonkers.

"OK." Helena patted her on the arm to signal her to stop. Wanda was quiet and I could tell her legs were still.

"The meeting is being called about me." I absorbed this. "Is this true, Joseph?" I very rarely, if at all, got nervous for anything and, at the idea of this, curiosity was the only emotion that stirred within me. And yet it was still mixed with the bizarre feeling of thinking it was all very cute and twee. A funny little happening in a funny little place.

"We don't know that it's about you." Bobby leaped to my defense. He looked at Joseph. "Do we?"

"I have been told nothing."

"Do people regularly call meetings about new arrivals? Is that normal?" I asked. I squeezed the stone that was Joseph, for water.

"Normal." He threw his hands up in the air. "What do we know of normal? What does our world and the old world, the world who thinks it knows it all, really know of normal?" He stood up and loomed over us.

"Well, do I need to be worried?" I asked, hoping now that he could at least reassure me.

"*Kipepeo*, one never *needs* to be worried." He placed his hand on my head and I felt his warmth soothe my pounding headache. "We will be at the Community Hall at seven P.M. tomorrow. We shall test our understanding of normality then." With a small smile he drifted out of the room. Helena followed him.

"What did he just call you?" Bobby asked, confused.

"*Kipepeo*," Wanda sang, her legs swinging wildly again.

I leaned into the table and Wanda momentarily looked startled. "What does that mean?" I asked rather aggressively, but I was anxious to know.

"Not telling you." She pouted and crossed her arms across her chest. "Because you don't like me."

"Don't be silly. Of course Sandy likes you," Bobby said stupidly.

"She *told* me she didn't."

"I'm sure you misheard her."

"She didn't," I explained, "I told her directly." Bobby looked shocked, so I made an attempt to wave the white flag. "Well, tell me what *kipepeo* means and I might like you."

"Sandy!" Bobby exclaimed.

I shushed him. Wanda mulled it over. Slowly but surely her face began to crumple. Bobby kicked me in the leg and I leaned forward. "Wanda, don't worry about it." I tried to soften my voice as much as I could. "It's not your fault that I don't like you." In the background Bobby tutted and sighed. "If you were ten years older, it's very possible that I could like you."

Her eyes lit up. Bobby shook his head at me. "What age will I be then?" she asked, kneeling excitedly on her chair and leaning forward on her elbows on the table to get closer to me.

"You'll be fifteen."

"Nearly the same age as Bobby?" She was hopeful.

"Bobby is nineteen."

"Which is four years older than fifteen," Bobby explained politely.

Wanda seemed delighted by this and gave him another shy gummy smile.

"But I'll be twenty-nine when you're fifteen," Bobby
explained, and I saw her face fall. "Every time you get
older, I get older." He laughed. He was confusing her
fallen face with a lack of understanding and he continued. "I'll always be fourteen years older than you, you
see." As I watched her face falling along with the penny
in her mind, I signaled for him to stop.

"Oh," she whispered.

Your heart can break at any age. I think that's when I
started liking Wanda.

I hated going to sleep in the place they called Here. I
hated the sounds at night that drifted into the atmosphere from home. I hated to hear the laughter, I wanted
to block my nose to the smells, close my eyes to the people wandering in from the woods for the first time. I was
afraid each noise would be me, I was afraid each sound
would be a part of me forgotten. Bobby and I shared that
fear. We stayed up late into the night talking about the
world he had left behind: music, sport, politics, and everything in between, but mostly we spoke about his
mother.

Jack returned to Mary Stanley's house after leaving Dr.
Burton at the OCA meeting. Once again angry words
had been shared between them, the doctor firing threats
of stalking charges and everything he could think of to

make Jack back off from his search. After wandering around Dublin city for the afternoon, he had left a voice-mail on Gloria's phone telling her he wouldn't be home for another few days; that it was complicated but that it was important. He knew she would understand. He had postponed his trip to Leitrim to visit Sandy's parents after being warned off by Dr. Burton. Instead, he hoped to share his thoughts and concerns with Mary before he moved on with his search. He needed to know whether to continue or not. He needed to know if he was chasing his own shadow, whether there was any purpose to him searching for Sandy if those who knew her well weren't concerned.

Mary had welcomed Jack to stay with her for another night and they sat in her living room once again watching a video of Bobby performing in his sixth class school play, *Oliver.* He noticed Bobby had an unusual laugh, a loud chuckle that came from deep inside him, causing everyone around him, including the audience, to smile. Jack found himself with a grin on his face as Mary turned off the tape.

"He seemed like a happy lad," Jack commented.

"Oh, yes." She nodded enthusiastically, sipping on her coffee. "He was that, indeed. He was always cracking jokes, always acting the class clown and letting his words get him into trouble and his laugh get him out of it. People loved him." She smiled. "That laugh of his . . ." She looked at a photograph on the mantelpiece, Bobby's face a picture of delight, his mouth wide open mid-laughter. "It was infectious, just like his grandfather's."

Jack smiled and they studied the photo.

Mary's smile faded. "I have a confession to make, though."

Jack was silent, not sure he wanted to hear it.

"I don't hear that laugh anymore." Her voice was almost a whisper, as though if she said it any louder it would make it true. "It used to fill the house, it used to fill my heart, my head, all day, every day. How can I not hear it anymore?"

From the faraway look in her eyes Jack could tell she wasn't asking him for a reply. Then she shook her head as if failing to hear it again.

"I remember how it used to make me *feel*. I remember the atmosphere just one simple giggle would evoke in a room. I remember people's reactions. I can see their faces and the impact the sound made on them. I can hear it on the videos when I play it back, I can see it on his face in photographs, I hear versions of it, I suppose, echoes of it in other people's laughter. But without all those things, without the photographs, videos, and echoes, when I'm lying in bed at night, I can't remember it. I don't hear it, and I try to, but my head becomes a jumble of the sounds I've made up and the sounds I've recalled from memory. But as much as I search and search, my memory of it is missing . . ." She looked over at the photo on the mantel again, cocked her ear as though listening for the sound. Then her body seemed to collapse into itself as she gave up.

Bobby and I were both tucked up on the couch in Helena's home. Everybody had gone to bed, apart from Wanda, who had sneaked back in and was hiding behind the couch, overexcited by the fact that her dear Bobby was staying the night in her house. We knew she was there but ignored her, hoping she would get bored and go to sleep.

"Are you worried about the meeting tomorrow night?" he asked.

"No, I don't even know what reason I have to be worried. I don't see what I've done wrong."

"You haven't done anything wrong but you know things, you know too much about people's families for everybody's comfort. They will want to learn how and why."

"And I'll tell them I'm a hugely sociable person. I move around the Irish social scene talking to friends and family of missing people," I said drily. "Come on, what are they going to do to me? Accuse me of being a witch and burn me at the stake?"

Bobby smiled lightly. "No, but you don't want your life being made difficult."

"They couldn't possibly make it any more difficult. I'm living in a place where lost things go. How bizarre is that?" I rubbed my face wearily and muttered, "I'm definitely going to need some serious counseling when I get back."

Bobby cleared his throat. "You're not going back. You need to get that out of your head for a start. If you say that at the meeting you'll definitely be asking for trouble."

I waved him off, not interested in hearing that again.

"Maybe you could start writing your diaries again. It looked like you enjoyed doing that."

"How do you know I wrote diaries?"

"Well, because of the diary in one of your boxes back at the shop. I found it down by the river just at the back of the shop. It was dirty and damp but when I saw your name written on it I brought it back to the shop and spent a lot of time restoring it," he said proudly. On my lack of reaction he quickly added, "I promise I didn't read it," he lied.

"You must be thinking of somebody else." I forced a yawn. "There wasn't a diary there."

"There was." He sat up. "It was purple and . . ." He trailed off trying to remember it.

I began to pull on a thread on the hem of my trousers.

He snapped his fingers and I jumped in fright, feeling Wanda behind the couch jumping, too. "That's it! It was purple, kind of a suede material that was ruined because of the damp but I cleaned it up as much as I could. Like I said, I didn't read it but I did open up the first few pages and there were doodles of love hearts all over it." He thought again. "Sandy loves . . ."

I pulled on the thread more.

"Graham," he continued. "No, it wasn't Graham."

I tightly wrapped the fine filament around my baby finger watching my skin squeezing through, watching the blood being caught.

"Gavin or Gareth . . . Come on, Sandy, you must remember. It was written so many times I don't know how you could forget the guy." He kept on thinking aloud while I kept on pulling the thread, wrapping it tighter and tighter.

He snapped his fingers again and said, "Gregory!

That's it! Sandy loves Gregory. It was written all over the inside of the book. You must remember it now."

I spoke quietly. "It wasn't in the boxes, Bobby."

"It was."

I shook my head. "I spent hours going through everything. It's definitely not there. I would have remembered it."

Bobby looked confused and irritated. "It was bloody well there."

With that, Wanda gasped from behind the couch and jumped up.

"What's wrong with you?" I asked, seeing her head popping up between mine and Bobby's.

"You've lost something else?" she whispered.

"No, I haven't." I contradicted her but felt a chill again.

"I won't tell anyone," she whispered, her eyes wide. "I promise."

There was a silence. I fixed my eyes on the black thread that kept on coming. Suddenly and completely inappropriately, I heard Bobby laugh loudly, one of his finest, loudest laughs I had heard from him yet.

"The situation is hardly very funny, thanks, Bobby."

Bobby didn't reply.

"Bobby," said Wanda in a childish whisper that ran down my back.

I looked up at Bobby, noticed the deathly pale of his face, his mouth hung open as though the words that had run from his vocal cords had chickened out last minute, refused to jump, and instead stood on his lips in fear. Tears formed in his eyes and his bottom lip trembled and

I realized the laughter hadn't come from his mouth at all. It had floated from there to Here, carried on the wind, over the treetops and into this place, landing somewhere among us. While I attempted to process all this, the door to the living room was pushed open and Helena appeared sleepy-eyed in her robe, her hair tousled and her face a picture of worry. She froze at the door while she studied Bobby, making sure she had heard correctly. His look said it all, and she charged at him, holding her arms out. Plonking herself on the couch, she held his head to her chest and rocked him as though he were a baby while he cried and mumbled through his tears how he'd been forgotten.

I sat on the other end of the couch and kept on pulling the thread. It kept on coming, unraveling more and more with every minute spent in this place, unable to stop this fine thread from detaching itself from the seams.

40

I have found that the many imbalances within our individual lives result in an overall more worldly balance. What I mean is that no matter how unfair I think something is, I need only look at the bigger picture to see how, in a way, it fits. My dad was right when he said that there was no such thing as a free meal: *Everything* comes at a cost to others, most of the time at a cost to ourselves. Whenever something is gained, it has been taken from another place. When something is lost, it arrives elsewhere. There are the usual philosophical questions: Why do bad things happen to good people? Within every bad thing I see good, and, likewise, within every good thing I see bad, however impossible it is to understand it or see it at the time. As humans we are the epitome of life; in life there is always balance. Life and death, male and female, good and bad, beautiful and ugly, win and lose, love and hate. Lost and found.

Apart from the Christmas turkey my dad won in the Leitrim Arms pub quiz when I was five years old, my dad had never won anything in his life. The day Jenny-May Butler went missing was the day that my dad won £500 on the lotto scratch cards. Maybe he had a good thing owed to him.

It was a summer day. There was only one week left before we were to go back to school and I was dreading even the thought of it, but apart from the anxiety for the week ahead, without having to get up every morning for school over the past few months I had lost all sense of time. Weekdays were the same as weekends. For a few months a year, the dreaded Sunday nights were the same as Friday and Saturday nights. This night was a Sunday night but, unusually for this time of year, it was a dreaded one. It was six forty P.M., still bright, the cul-de-sac was busy with kids playing, just like me, forgetting what day it was but knowing that whatever day it was, it sure was a great one because tomorrow would be exactly the same. My mother was in the front garden with my grandma and granddad getting the last few warm evening sun-rays. I was sitting at the kitchen table anxiously waiting for the doorbell to ring. I was drinking a glass of milk and watching the clothes in the washing machine go around and around, trying to identify each garment that flashed by, just to occupy my mind.

My dad had eyed me warily as he came back and forth from the TV room to the kitchen, grabbing food he wasn't supposed to be eating while on his new diet. I didn't know whether he was trying to scope me out or whether he was eyeing me to see if I had noticed him stealing food. Either way he'd asked me three times already what was wrong, and I'd just shrugged and told him nothing. It was one of those occasions when telling someone wouldn't make it any better. He checked on me from time to time, noticing how I'd jumped when the doorbell rang (only my mum, who had forgotten to put the door on the latch). He made a few faces at me to try to make me laugh, cramming a few biscuits into his mouth all at once to pretend he was entertaining me and not his stomach. I smiled for his sake; he seemed happy enough with that and then moved into the TV room again, this time with a lemon square up his sleeve.

You see, I was waiting for Jenny-May to call around.

She had challenged me to a game of King/Queen. It was a game we used to play on the road with a tennis ball. Each person stood in the boxes that were drawn on the road with chalk and then the idea was to bounce the ball first in your own box before passing it into someone else's. They had to do the same and if they missed it, if they failed to bounce it in their own box first or if the ball went outside the lines, they were out. The idea was to try to make it to the box at the top, which was the King's box, which was where Jenny-May was for the duration of the game. Everybody used to always say how wonderful she was at playing the game, how amazing and brilliant and talented and fast and precise and how gag, gag, make me puke, she was. My friend Emer and I used to watch the games from our wall. We were never allowed to play because Jenny-May wouldn't let us. I merely commented to Emer one day that one of the reasons Jenny-May always won was because she always *started* in the top box. This meant that she didn't have to work her way up like everybody else did.

Well, somebody somewhere overheard, and word got back to Jenny-May what I'd said and the next day, when

Emer and I were sitting on the wall kicking our heels against the bricks and flicking ladybirds from the pillars to see how far they'd go, Jenny-May marched up to us with her hands on her hips, surrounded by her posse, and demanded I explain myself, which I did. Red-faced and flustered at being answered back at, she challenged me to a game of King/Queen. As I said, I'd never played this game before and I knew all too well that Jenny-May was good; all I'd meant was that she wasn't *as* good as people were saying. There was something about Jenny-May that made people see more in her than there actually was. I've come across a few people like that in my life and they always make me think of her.

She was clever, though. She made sure that everyone knew that if I didn't show up, then she would automatically become the champion, and I suddenly wished my dreaded visit to Aunty Lila was a day early.

Word spread among everyone in the road that Jenny-May had challenged me to a game. They were all going to turn out and sit on the curb to watch, including Colin Fitzpatrick, who was way too cool to hang out on our road. He used to go skateboarding with the people around the corner whom no one else had the privilege of hanging out with. Word was that even the skateboard gang were all coming to watch.

I barely slept a wink the night before. I got out of bed, put my runners on with my nightdress, and went outside to practice King/Queen up against the garden wall. It wasn't much use because the ball kept hitting against the stippled back wall and sent it flying in all the wrong directions. Plus it was so dark I could hardly see it.

Eventually Ms. Smith from next door opened her bedroom window and stuck out her head, which was covered in hair curlers which I thought was odd because the next morning her hair was straight, and she sleepily asked me to stop. I went back to bed but didn't sleep much, and when I did, I dreamed of Jenny-May Butler being lifted onto everyone's shoulders wearing a crown while Stephen Spencer, who was on a skateboard, pointed a nail-varnished finger at me and laughed. Oh, and I was naked.

It was my challenge with Jenny-May that alerted her parents to the fact she was missing. During the summer months we all had complete freedom. We stayed outside together all day playing, rarely going inside and sometimes having lunch in one another's house. So I don't blame her parents for not noticing she hadn't been around all day. Nobody blamed them because I knew they all understood. They all knew deep down that it could have happened to them too, that it could have been their child no one had noticed not being around for a few hours that day.

Jenny-May's house and mine were directly opposite each other. Mum and my grandparents had come back inside now that the sun had finally disappeared behind the Butlers' house. I knew everybody was gathering on the curb waiting for me and Jenny-May to leave our houses and meet in the middle. I saw my dad look out the front window and then back at me. I think he finally understood what was wrong and gave me a small smile. Then he put biscuits on the table and sat with me, munching away.

Eventually, as it struck seven P.M., everybody outside

began chanting. Some voices called for me but they were drowned out by chants for Jenny-May. Maybe it was equal but I seemed to hear only her name. All my life, I've heard her name louder than my own. Suddenly there was a big cheer and I assumed Jenny-May had left her house. Then the cheering stopped, there was chattering, then it got quieter and then it was completely silent. Dad looked at me and shrugged. The doorbell rang. I didn't jump this time because something didn't feel quite right. Dad patted my hand. I heard Mum answer the door, her voice as friendly and chirpy as ever. Then I heard Mrs. Butler's voice, not so friendly, no singsong tone. Dad recognized it too, and left the table to join them in the hall. Voices turned to concerned tones.

I don't know why, but I couldn't leave the table. I just sat there thinking of ways to get out of the challenge but at the same time having the strange feeling that I wouldn't need an excuse. The atmosphere had changed—for the worse, I sensed—but I had that relieved feeling like arriving at school to find out the teacher's sick and not for one second worrying about the teacher. A few minutes later the kitchen door opened and Dad, Mum, and Mrs. Butler came in.

"Honey," Mum said softly, "do you, by any chance, know where Jenny-May is?"

I frowned, confused by the question even though it was perfectly straightforward. I looked back and forth to all their faces. Dad was looking at me with concern, Mum was nodding at me encouragingly, and Mrs. Butler looked like she was going to cry. She looked like her entire life depended on my answer. I suppose it did, in a way.

When I didn't answer immediately, Mrs. Butler spoke quickly. "The kids outside haven't seen her all day. I thought maybe she would be with you."

I knew it was wrong but I felt the sudden urge to laugh at the idea that Jenny-May would have spent the day with me. I just shook my head. Mrs. Butler called around to all the neighbors to see if they'd seen her daughter. The more doors she knocked on, the more I could see how her face changed from embarrassment to steely determination and then to fear.

I've seen mothers' faces in shopping centers when they turn around and notice their child isn't with them. I studied their faces so intently, completely fascinated by it, because I don't recall ever seeing that look on my mum's face. Not because she didn't love me, of course, but because I was always so tall and out of place there was no way she could lose me. I used to try to get lost sometimes, just to see her face. I would close my eyes, spin around, and choose a direction to head in. Other times I deliberately waited for her to turn the corner into the next aisle in the supermarket. I would shiver by the frozen food and count to twenty until I felt she was far enough away, but most of the time I would turn the corner and there she would be, studying the calorie content on the back of food packages, not having even noticed my absence. If she ever did notice the lack of my shuffling lanky body trailing behind her, no more than five minutes would pass before she found me. She needed only to look up and she'd see my head above the clothes racks or look down to spy my awkward oversized feet poking out from behind a shelf.

From viewing other mothers, I see how the first casual glance over their shoulder changes to panic, how
their movements become quicker, head, eyes, limbs darting around, then their abandoning shopping carts in
search of the only thing that truly feeds their soul. The
fear, the panic, the dread, the drive. They say a mother
has the strength to lift a car if it means saving her child.
I think that week Mrs. Butler could have lifted a bus just
to find Jenny-May. As it got into the second month she
looked as though she could barely lift her own eyes above
ground level. Jenny-May had taken a big chunk of her
with her, too.

It turned out that I was one of the last to see her.
When Grandma and Granddad arrived at noon that day,
I opened the door to welcome them in and Jenny-May
cycled past. She turned to look at me and gave me a look.
One of her looks that I hated so much. A look that could
wither you instantly. A look that said "I'm better than
you and you are going to lose today at King/Queen and
then Stephen Spencer will know what an incompetent
lanky idiot you are." I looked over my grandmother's
shoulder as I hugged her and watched Jenny-May cycling
down the road with her head held high, her chin back
and nose in the air, and her blond hair falling to the
small of her back. I did what anyone in my situation
would have done. I wished she would disappear.

That day my dad won £500 in the lotto scratch cards.
He was so delighted, I could tell. He sat down in the
kitchen with me and tried not to smile, but I could see
the corners of his lips curling. We could hear Mrs. Butler
crying in the next room with my mother. He placed his

hand over mine and I knew he was thinking right then that he was so lucky, what a lucky father to win money in the lotto and still have his daughter when people like Mr. and Mrs. Butler were suffering so much. I, in turn, was glad that I hadn't gone missing and due to Jenny-May's no-show I was now the undisputed champion of King/Queen. I'd also made some new friends now that Jenny-May wasn't around to tell them not to. Things were going great for my family and life couldn't possibly be any worse for Mr. and Mrs. Butler. My parents stayed up late those nights talking and thanking God how they had been blessed.

But something inside me felt different. Jenny-May's last stolen glance had taken a part of me with it. That day, Mr. and Mrs. Butler weren't the only parents to lose a child.

Like I said, there's always balance.

41

Despite Dr. Burton's threats and protestations, Jack had decided to continue with his mission and make the journey to Leitrim after all. Another night spent in young Bobby's room had awoken the drive within him to find Donal, not that it had needed much of an awakening. It was the part of him that was constantly wide-eyed and alert, searching around for answers, clues, and meaning with every beat of his heart. He was still clinging to the idea that finding Sandy was his way out. She was the medicine his overworked mind needed in order to rest. Why exactly, he didn't know, but he had rarely felt such instincts for something in his life. It was as though the part of him that had been lost along with Donal had been replaced by a strengthened sense. He was like a blind man being led by his heightened sense of smell; by touch he could orient himself; by sound he could listen to his heart. When Jack had lost Donal, he had lost his vision but he'd gained a new sense of direction in his life.

He didn't know what he was going to say to Sandy's parents when he saw them, if indeed they were home or if they would even give him the time of day. He just kept on following the invisible internal compass that had replaced Donal. At noon he found himself sitting in his car around the corner from the housing estate where they lived, taking deep breaths. It was a Saturday but the small cul-de-sac was quiet. He got out of the car and strolled down the small street, trying to look inconspicuous but feeling and knowing he was completely out of place on the tranquil road, the only moving piece on a chessboard.

He stopped outside number four, where there was a small two-door silver car in the drive that glistened to within an inch of its life. The front garden was immaculate and was a hive of activity for bees and birds. All the summer flowers were out in their glory, colors of every shade, sweet honey scents, jasmines and lavenders. The grass was an even inch in height all around, the border where it met the soil a razor-sharp line that looked like it could cut any petal that dared to fall. A hanging basket overflowing with petunias and geraniums hung from outside the porch door. An umbrella stand sat inside, Wellington boots and fishing gear beside that. By the entrance a gnome hid under a willow tree holding a sign saying WELCOME. Jack relaxed slightly. Here were the boarded-up windows, barking dogs, and burned-out car from his worst-case scenario fears.

He opened the lemon-colored gate, which matched the front door and window frames, like a perfectly edible candy house. There was no creak; just as he suspected. He walked up the even flagstones, not a weed peeking up between the stones. He cleared his throat and pressed the doorbell, its tinkling sound also nonthreatening. He heard footsteps, saw a shadow through the obscured glass get closer to the door. Despite the friendly appearance of the woman he assumed to be Sandy's mother, the arrival of a strange man on her doorway demanded the porch's sliding door remain closed.

"Mrs. Shortt?" He smiled and gave her the least threatening face he could.

She seemed to relax a bit more and stepped into the porch area, the sliding door still a barrier. "Yes?"

"My name is Jack Ruttle. I'm very sorry to disturb you at home but I was wondering if Sandy was here?"

Her eyes moved fleetingly over him, quickly surveying the man who looked for her daughter and then she slid the porch door open. "You're a friend of Sandy's?"

He doubted saying no would get him any further, but would probably result in the closing of the door once again. "Yes," he said, smiling. "Is she here?"

She smiled back. "I'm sorry Mr. . . . what did you say your name was?"

"It's Jack Ruttle, but just call me Jack."

"Jack," she said pleasantly, "she's not here. Is there anything I can help you with?"

"I don't suppose you could tell me where she is?" He kept smiling, knowing it had the potential to be far more of an awkward moment, a perfect stranger interrogating a mother on the whereabouts of her child.

"Where is she?" she repeated thoughtfully. "I don't know, Jack. Would she want me to tell you where she is?"

They both laughed and Jack shifted uncomfortably. "Well, I'm not sure how I could possibly convince you of that." He held his hands out, admitting defeat. "Look, I don't know what I was expecting when I got here but I just thought I'd take a chance. I'm very sorry for bothering you. Could I leave a message for her? Could you tell her that I'm looking for her and that . . ." He paused and tried to think of something that could convince Sandy to crawl out of her hiding place if she was in that house listening to him right now. "Could you tell her that I can't do this without her. She'll know what I'm talking about."

She nodded, studying him all the while. "I'll pass the message on."

"Thank you." There was a pause and Jack prepared to wrap it up.

"You're not a Leitrim boy, by the sounds of it."

He smiled. "Limerick."

She mulled that over. "She was going to visit you last week?"

"Yes."

"The one thing I do know about my daughter, she rang me on her way to Glin, was it?" She smiled and it faded quickly. "She was looking for someone of yours?"

Jack nodded, feeling like a teenager faced by a nightclub bouncer and hoping by his silence he would be allowed in.

Mrs. Shortt was quiet while she pondered what to do. She looked up and down the road. A neighbor across the road raised a garden glove to her and she waved back. Perhaps feeling less threatened, she made her decision. "Come inside," she said, and motioned to him, moving away from the door, heading back down the hall.

Jack looked up and down the road. The neighbor watched him reluctantly step into the house. He smiled awkwardly. He could hear Mrs. Shortt in the kitchen clattering cups and plates. He heard the kettle go on. The inside of the house was as immaculate as the outside. The front door led directly into the living room. It smelled of furniture polish and fresh air, as though all the windows had been left open for the scents of the garden to rush inside. There was no clutter. The carpet was vacuumed, silver and brasses gleamed, wood shone.

"I'm in here, Jack," Mrs. Shortt called out, as though they were life-long friends.

He went through to the unsurprisingly gleaming kitchen. The washing machine was running, RTE Radio 1 was on in the background, and the kettle was building up its crescendo to boiling point. From the kitchen there were French doors that led out to the back garden and again it was as well maintained as the front, with a large birdhouse, currently accommodating a greedy-looking robin singing between each peck at the seeds.

"You have a lovely home, Mrs. Shortt," Jack said, taking a seat at the kitchen table. "Thank you for the kind invitation."

"You can call me Susan, and you're welcome." She filled the teapot with boiling water, covered it with a tea cozy and waited. Jack hadn't had tea like that since his mother used to make it. Despite welcoming him into her home, Susan was still on guard and stood by the counter with one hand on the tea cozy, the other fiddling with a tea bag. "You're the first friend of Sandy's to call by since she was a teenager." She looked deep in thought.

Jack didn't know how to respond to that.

"Everybody after that knew better." She smiled. "How well do you know Sandy?"

"Not well enough."

"No," she said more to herself, "I didn't think so."

"Every day that I search for her, I learn something new about her," he added.

"You're searching for her?" She raised her eyebrows.

"That's why I'm here, Mrs. Shortt—"

"Susan, please." She looked pained. "I look around for Harold's mother and the scent of cabbage when I hear that name. Everything was cabbage, cabbage, cabbage with that woman." She laughed at the memory.

"Susan." He smiled. "The last thing I came here to do is worry you, but I was due to meet with Sandy last week, as you mentioned. She didn't show up and since then I've done everything to try to contact her." He deliberately left out the details about finding her car and phone. "I'm sure she's fine," he insisted, "but I really want—" He started again. "I really *need* to find her." Sending Sandy's mother into a panic was the very opposite of his intentions and he held his breath awaiting her response. He was relieved if not a little shocked to see a tired smile crawl onto her face but it gave up, collapsing in a sad heap before reaching her eyes.

"You're right, Jack, you certainly don't know our Sandy well enough." She turned her back to him to pour the tea. "Now let me teach you another thing about my daughter. I love her very much but she has the ability to hide as expertly as a sock in a washing machine. No one knows where it goes, just as no one knows where *she* goes, but at least when she decides to come back, we're all here, waiting for her."

"I've heard that from everyone this week."

She whisked around. "Who else did you speak to?"

"Her landlord, her clients, her doctor . . ." His voice trailed off guiltily. "I really didn't want to have to call on you about this."

"Her doctor?" Susan asked, not minding at all that she had been left until last. She was more interested in the mention of her daughter's doctor.

"Yes, Dr. Burton," Jack said slowly, not sure whether to reveal Sandy's private information to her mother.

"Oh!" Susan tried to hide a smile.

"You know him?"

"Do you know by any chance if it's *Gregory* Burton?" She tried to hide her excitement but failed miserably.

"That's him, but he isn't so keen on me, in case you're talking to him."

"Indeed," Susan said thoughtfully, not hearing what he'd said. "Indeed," she repeated with her eyes alight, answering a question Jack wasn't privy to. She was clearly delighted, but remembering Jack was in the room, she composed herself, intrigue taking the place of a mother's excitement. "Why is it that you want to find Sandy so much?"

"I was worried about her when she didn't turn up to meet me in Glin, and then I was unable to contact her, which made me even more concerned." It was partly true but it sounded lame and he knew it.

Susan appeared to know it too. She raised her eyebrows and spoke in a bored tone. "I've been waiting for three weeks for Barney the plumber to come and fix my sink but I haven't yet planned on visiting his mother."

Jack looked absentmindedly at her sink. "Well, Sandy *is* looking for my brother. I even got in touch with a member of the Gardaí in Limerick." He felt his face flush as Susan let out a sound of surprise. "Graham Turner is his name, in case he calls."

Susan smiled. "We called the police on three occasions at the beginning but we've learned not to, now. If Garda Turner asks around he'll know not to continue with his investigations."

"He's already done that," Jack said grimly, and then he frowned. "I don't understand all this, Susan. I can't understand where she's gone. I can't fathom how she can disappear so cleverly without anyone knowing where she is, without anyone *wanting* to know where she is."

"We each have our hiding places and we each put up with the little quirks of the people we love." She rested her head on her hand and seemed to study him.

He sighed. "That's it?"

"What do you mean?"

"That's it? Just let people vanish? No more questions asked? Come and go as you please? Flutter in and out. Disappear, reappear, and disappear again? No problem!" He laughed angrily. "Nobody worry about a thing! Don't bother caring about all the people at home that love you and that are worrying themselves sick to death about you."

There was silence.

"You love Sandy?"

"What?" He screwed his face up.

"You said . . . Never mind." She sipped her tea.

"I've only ever spoken to Sandy on the phone," Jack said slowly. "There was no . . . relationship between us."

"So by finding my daughter, you find your brother?" He didn't have time to answer the question. "Do you think your brother's hiding place is the same as Sandy's?" she asked boldly.

And there it was. A complete stranger, someone who had met him no more than ten minutes before, had summed up the ridiculous notion behind his frantic search, in one question. Susan allowed a few moments to pass before offering, "I don't know the circumstances of your brother's disappearance, Jack, but I know he's not in the same place as Sandy. Here's another lesson," she said softly, "a lesson Harold and I have learned over the years. No one ever finds the other sock in the washing machine, not through actively looking, anyway." She waved her hand dismissively. "Things just turn up. You can drive yourself crazy trying to find them. It doesn't matter how neat and tidy you keep your life, it doesn't matter how organized things are." She paused and laughed sadly. "I'm a hypocrite, I somehow pretend to myself that a tidy house will make Sandy come home more often. I think, if she can just *see* everything, if she can see that everything is in order and has its place, then she won't have to worry about things going missing." She looked around the spotless kitchen. "Anyway, it doesn't matter how much, how often, or how closely you keep an eye on things because you can't control it. Sometimes things and people just go." She waved her hand through the air on the last word. "Just like that." Then she placed the comforting hand over his. "Don't destroy yourself trying to find out where."

They said their good-byes at the door and Susan, trying to hide her embarrassment, said, "Talking about things turning up, if you do come across Sandy before we do, tell her I found her purple diary with the butterflies. It was in her old bedroom. Unusual, because I've cleaned out that wardrobe dozens of times but never came across it." She frowned. "Anyway, it would be important for her to know."

She looked up and waved again across the road and Jack turned to see a woman similar in age to Susan. "That's Mrs. Butler," she said, although it was of no importance to Jack. "Her daughter Jenny-May went missing when she was ten years old, the same age as Sandy. Such a lovely little girl, an angel, everyone said."

Jack, suddenly interested, studied the woman some more. "Did they find her?"

"No," Susan said sadly, "they never did, but she has left that porch light on every single night for twenty-four years hoping she'll come home. She'll barely go away on holiday, she's so afraid she'll miss her."

Jack slowly walked back to his car, feeling odd, different, as though he had switched bodies with the man who had only an hour ago entered the Shortt household. He stopped walking, looked to the sky, and contemplated all that he had learned through meeting Sandy's mother. He smiled. And he cried as relief washed over him like a waterfall raining down. Because for the first time in a year, he felt like he could finally stop.

And start living again.

42

Bobby was in no mood to discuss hearing his laughter enter this atmosphere the previous night, but he needn't have spoken a word because it was clear that the air had been let out of his once ballooned spirit and all that was left was its deflated shell. It broke my heart to see him that way, to see a bird that had once soared now lie defeated on the ground, a broken wing stopping his flight. The few times I had attempted to raise the issue, the more still he lay wounded. There wasn't a whimper, there wasn't a tear; it was his silence that screamed the words he couldn't or wouldn't voice. It appeared he was going to concentrate on my problems until he felt fit to deal with his own. Not an altogether alien method of dealing with life, for me.

"Why do you always leave your bag by the door?" Bobby spoke for the first time as we entered his shop.

I looked to where Bobby was staring to see my bag, or dare I say, Barbara Langley's bag, that had been quite absentmindedly placed beside the door. Like a cowboy in a western who parked his horse up by the saloon door, it was to enable a swift departure from any situation. To help ease the feelings of claustrophobia I would feel in the rooms and company of those I wasn't altogether comfortable with, my parents included. Gregory included. My own home included. Rarely were there places I would keep my bag on my person. I would look to the door, see my bag, and feel secure knowing there was a way out, and there, as proof, were my belongings not far from that exit to freedom.

I shrugged. "Just habit." How all of my life's complications and complex idiosyncrasies could be reduced to a shrug and two words. How nothing words could be.

Bobby wasn't in the mood to question me any further and we returned to the storeroom containing my boxes of belongings.

"So," I said, breaking the silence as I looked to Bobby, who was staring as though lost, as though he had never before encountered this room. "What are we doing back here?" I asked.

"We're going to empty your boxes."

"Why?"

He didn't respond, not because he was ignoring me but because I think he didn't hear me. There was so much more for him to hear now. He began emptying the top box, placing Mr. Pobbs very carefully on the floor. He lined up each item in a row from wall to wall, then moved to the next box and did the same. I helped him though I didn't understand why. After twenty minutes, my belongings from Here were lined neatly in six rows across the walnut floor. I looked down at each item and couldn't help smiling. Each one, from the impersonal—the stapler—to the personal—Mr. Pobbs—all opened the doors to previously locked-away memories.

Bobby was looking at me.

"What?"

"Do you notice anything?"

I looked back to the floor, running my eyes along the rows. Mr. Pobbs, stapler, T-shirt, twenty odd socks, engraved pen, work file I got in trouble for losing . . . Was I missing the point? I turned to him questioningly.

"What about the passport," he stated lifelessly.

I looked back to the floor, smiling already. When I was fifteen years old my parents had arranged for us to go to Austria on a hiking holiday but the night before we were due to travel, my passport was nowhere to be found. I hadn't wanted to go away at all. I had been complaining about the trip for months. A week away had meant missing two sessions with Mr. Burton, but not only that, any fear, any irrational phobia, tends to affect normal daily life. I stopped enjoying trips away due to my fear of losing things, and if something was lost in a place like Austria, a place I had never been to, a place I would more than likely never return to again, well then, how on earth was I supposed to find anything again? The night I lost my passport I had a quick change of heart. The two sessions with Mr. Burton were forgotten. All of a sudden I wanted to find the passport and I wanted to go on the trip. Anything that meant not missing another possession in my life.

The trip was canceled as it was too late to get a replacement or temporary passport, but for once my parents were genuinely as flummoxed as I was, and had searched as frantically as I had. Finding it here after all those years, tattered and worn and complete with gawky photograph of me at age eleven, had been an incredible moment. But as I looked around the floor my smile faded. It was no longer there.

I stepped over the rows of items, kicking some in my rush to get to the cardboard boxes where I frantically searched. Bobby left the room to give me my space, or so I thought, but he returned with a Polaroid camera. He motioned for me to step aside, which I did without question. He pointed the camera at the ground, took a photograph, extracted the square photo, shook it, examined it, and then slid it into a plastic folder.

"I found this camera years ago," he explained, sadness echoing in his words. "It's difficult to find the cartridges that go with it. I don't even know if they make them anymore, but now and again, I come across boxes of the right ones. I have to be careful with the photographs I take; I can't waste them. I don't mind being careful but it's difficult to know which second among a lifetime of seconds is more special. Often when you realize how precious those seconds are, it's too late for them to be captured because the moment has passed. We realize too late." He was silent for a moment, lost in thought, frozen as though his batteries had run out. I touched his arm and he looked up, surprised to see me in the room. He looked down at the camera in his hands, surprised to see it there too. Then he rebooted. The light returned behind his eyes and he continued, "This is how you refill it. Take photos of these items on the floor every morning from now on." He handed it to me and added before walking away, "And then I suggest you start taking the other photos."

"What other photos?"

He stopped at the doorway and suddenly looked even younger than his nineteen years, like a lost little boy. "I don't know much about what goes on around here, Sandy. I don't know why we're all here, how we all got here, or even what we're supposed to be doing. I never knew that when I was at home with my Mum either." He smiled. "But as far as I can see, you followed all your belongings here and now, day by day, items disappear. I don't know where they're going, but wherever that is, I suggest that when you find yourself there, you have proof that you were ever here. Proof of us." His smile weakened. "I'm tired now, Sandy. I'm going to go to bed. See you at seven for the council meeting."

43

Barbara Langley hadn't much in the way of clothes suitable for community meetings, most likely because the doomed New York holiday, which resulted in the loss of her luggage more than twenty years ago, didn't call for being put on trial by an entire community. But then again, you never know.

I chose to stay away from rehearsals at the Community Hall, knowing that my presence there later would be enough and that Helena had the play I really wasn't interested in being involved in all under control. I passed the day by covering the shop for Bobby, who had quite understandably decided to stay in bed the entire day. I busied myself; I *pleasured* myself rooting around the long-legged people's section, diving into bargain buckets with all the ferocity of a bear that had stumbled upon a picnic park. Excitedly I pulled out outfits I dreamed of having at home. Ecstasy-fueled purrs escaped my lips as I tried on shirts with sleeves that reached my wrists, T-shirts that covered my belly button, and trousers with hems that fell to the floor. A tingle rushed through my body each time the feel of fabric covered an area of skin so used to being bare and exposed. What a difference an inch of fabric made. Particularly on a cold morning standing at the bus stop stretching the sleeves of a favorite sweater just so it covered a racing, angry pulse. That small inch, insignificant to most, everything to me, was the difference between a good day and a bad, internal peace and outward loathing, denial and the realization of an overwhelming albeit temporary desire to be like everyone else. A few inches shorter, a few inches happier, richer, content, warmer.

Every once in a while, the bell over the door sounded, and just like the end of my playtime at school, the climax would come to an abrupt end. The majority of shoppers that day had come to the shop with one goal in mind: to have a look at me, the one they had heard about, the one who knew things. People from all nations would lock eyes with me, hoping for recognition, and, when there wasn't any, would leave, disappointment weighing heavy on their shoulders. Each time the bell rang and another pair of eyes bored into mine, I became more nervous for the evening ahead, and no matter how hard I wanted to prevent the many clocks on the wall from ticking, the hands raged on and the night was suddenly upon me.

It seemed the entire village had decided to attend the council meeting at the Community Hall. Bobby and I pushed our way through throngs of people slowly filing toward the giant oak door. News of somebody with the capacity to know all about families at home had caused people of all nationalities, races, and creeds to flock by the hundreds to the building. The hot orange sun was disappearing behind the pine trees, giving the effect of strobe lighting as we walked briskly alongside them. Above us, hawks circled low in the sky, dangerously skimming the treetops. Around me, I felt eyes on me, watching, waiting to pounce.

The carvings of people shoulder to shoulder, upon the giant doors, parted and bodies began to file in. The theater had been transformed from the informal arrangement of rehearsal hours. I felt deceived, realizing it was more than it had originally appeared to be, capable of more than it had shown itself to be, and now here it was, elegantly dressed, standing upright and proud, royalty when I had thought it a servant. Hundreds of rows of seats led from the stage, the red velvet curtains pulled back by a chunky golden twist with tassels bowing, their overturned heads of hair skimming the ground. On stage rows of representatives sat on tiered seating, some wearing their countries' traditional costumes, others choosing modern dress. There were three-piece suits next to embroidered *dishdasha,* sequined *jellabahs,* silk kimonos, *kippas,* turbans and *jilbab,* bead, bone, gold and silver jewelry, women in elaborately patterned *khanga,* upon them Swahili proverbs offering pearls of wisdom I could not understand, and men in fine *hanbok.* There was everything from *khussa* shoes to Jimmy Choos, Thousand Mile sandals and flip-flops to polished leather lace-ups. I spotted Joseph in the second row wrapped in a purple gown with gold trimming. The vision was stunning, the mixture of fine cultured clothes side by side a treat. Despite my feelings on the evening ahead, I lifted the Polaroid camera and took a photo.

"Hey!" Bobby grabbed the camera from my hands. "Stop wasting the cartridges!"

"Wasting?" I gasped. "Look at that!" I pointed to the stage of representatives from all nations, sitting grandly overlooking the sea of villagers, who watched them expectantly, desperately awaiting news of the old world they had left behind. We sat in seats halfway up the auditorium to ensure I wasn't in the first row for the firing line. We spotted Helena toward the front of the room, desperately scouring the crowds with an alarming look of concern or fear, I couldn't tell which. Assuming it was us she was looking for, Bobby waved at her wildly. I couldn't move. My body sat frozen in this new fear I was experiencing, in a theater that had very quickly become filled with the noise of hundreds of people becoming louder and louder in my ears. I glanced over my shoulder. Dozens more stood at the back of the hall, blocking the exits, unable to find seats. The banging shut and locking of the gigantic doors reverberated around the room and everybody instantly fell silent. The breathing of the man behind me was loud in my ears, the whispering of the couple in front of me like a loudspeaker. My heart began a drumbeat of its own. I looked at Bobby for reassurance I didn't get. The harsh lights from above didn't allow anybody or their reactions to hide. Everyone and everything was revealed.

Helena had been forced to take her seat when the door had shut and silence had ensued. I tried my best to keep thinking that this was a silly little place, a figment of my imagination. It was all a dream, unimportant, not real life. But no matter how much I pinched myself and tried to zone out, the atmosphere pulled me back in, leaving me with the foreboding sense that this was as real as the beating of my heart.

A woman walked up the outside aisle with a basket of earphones. They were taken by the person at the end seat and passed along the rows like a church collection. I looked to Bobby questioningly and he demonstrated, plugging the headphone set into a socket in the chair in front. He placed them over his ears as a man stood before the microphone on stage. He began speaking Japanese, not a word of which I could understand, but I was so transfixed by the scene before me I failed to remember to put my earphones on. Bobby elbowed me and I jumped, quickly placing them over my ears. A heavily accented English voice offered the translation. I had missed the beginning of his announcement.

". . . this Sunday evening. It's rare that so many of us all gather together. Thank you for the wonderful turn-out. There are a few reasons why we are here tonight . . ."

Bobby elbowed me again and my headphones came off. "That's Ichiro Takase," he whispered. "He's the rep president. It changes person every few months."

I nodded and the headphones went back on again.

"Hans Liveen wishes to speak to you about the plans for the new mill scheme, but before we address that we will deal with the reason why so many of you have attended this meeting. Irish Representative Grace Burns will speak to you about this."

A woman who appeared to be in her fifties stood from her seat and made her way to the microphone. She had long wavy red hair, her features were pointed as though chiseled from a rock, and she was dressed in a sharp black business suit.

I removed my headphones.

"Good evening, everybody." Her accent placed her from the north of Ireland, Donegal. Many of the non-Irish English speakers put their headphones back on for the translation. "I'll make this brief," she said. "I was approached this week by many people from the Irish community with news that a newcomer from Ireland had information on various villagers' families. Despite the rumors, this of course isn't unusual, given Ireland's size. I was also told that an item belonging to this person, I understand that it's her watch, has gone missing," she said in her matter-of-fact tones.

People who understood English immediately gasped, although the majority of them were surely aware of this rumor already. A few seconds later, there was a second gasp as the interpreters translated. Murmuring began in the hall and the Irish representative held her arms up to silence everyone. "I understand this news has had an effect on the entire village. News like this disrupts our attempts for normal living and we are keen to put the rumors to rest."

My heart began to beat a little less dramatically.

"We've called the meeting tonight to assure you that the matter is in hand and it will be dealt with. As soon as it is, we will immediately inform the community, as we always do, as to the outcome. I believe this newcomer is among us tonight," she announced, "and so I wish to address this person."

Instantly my heart began to palpitate again. People around me looked about, murmuring, jabbering excitedly in foreign tones and eyeing one another suspiciously, accusingly. I looked to Bobby in shock. He gaped back at me.

"What will I do?" I whispered. "How do they know about the watch?"

The nineteen-year-old in him shrugged, eyes wide.

"We all think it's best to deal with this privately and quietly so that the person can remain anonymous—"

There was a heckling of boos from the crowd, some people laughed, and my skin crawled.

"I see no cause or need for dramatics," Grace continued in her official, no-nonsense tone. "If the newcomer could just present us with the alleged missing item, then this will be dropped and forgotten once and for all so that the congregation can get back to spending their valuable time in their usual greatly productive ways." She smiled cheekily and there were chuckles from around the room. "If the person in question could familiarize themselves with my office tomorrow morning and bring the watch with them, then this can be dealt with swiftly and privately."

More boos by members of the audience.

"I'll take a few questions on this and then we will move on with the more important matter of the plans to build farther past the wild farm." I could tell she was being deliberately blasé about the whole thing. An entire village had turned out to hear about me, about how I knew intimate details of people here and their family members. In a few sentences she had brushed it all under the carpet. People looked around at each other unhappily and I sensed a storm brewing.

Many people raised their hands and the representative nodded to one. A man stood. "Ms. Burns, I don't think it's fair that this matter be dealt with privately. I think it's clear from the turnout tonight that this issue is more important than the manner of how you have chosen to address it, which is a deliberate attempt at playing down the significance." There were a few claps. "I put forward that the person in question, whom I know to be a woman, show us the watch right *now*, right here, *tonight* so that we can see it with our own eyes and therefore allow the matter to be dropped and for our minds to be put at rest."

There was a healthy applause to this suggestion.

The representative looked uncomfortable; she turned to look at her colleagues. Some nodded, some shook their heads, others looked bored; some shrugged and left it up to her.

"I'm concerned only with the welfare of the person in question, Mr. O'Mara," she addressed him. "I hardly see it fair that she has arrived here only this week and is also faced with this. Her anonymity is vital. Surely you can appreciate that."

This wasn't so strongly supported by people, but there was a light round of clapping from a few dozen and I silently thanked them and cursed Grace for confirming my sex.

An elderly woman standing beside the man speaking

from the audience shot up out of her seat. "Ms. Burns, our well-being is more important, and the well-being of all the villagers. Isn't it more important that if once again we have heard rumors of somebody's belongings going missing we have a right to know if it's true?"

There were noises of support from among the crowd. Grace Burns held her hand up to her forehead to block the harsh stage lights in order to see the person belonging to the voice. "But, Catherine, it *will* be revealed to you tomorrow after the person has come to me. Whatever the outcome, it will be dealt with appropriately."

"This doesn't just affect the Irish community," a Southern American male voice called out. Everybody looked around. The voice came from a man standing at the back. "Remember what happened the last time there were rumors of things going missing?"

There were mumbles of agreement, and nods.

"Everybody here remember a guy called James Ferrett?" he shouted now, addressing the hall.

There were loud murmurs of yes and heads nodded.

"A few years ago he told of the very same thing happening to him. The representatives did the same thing then as they are doing now," he addressed the crowd, who were unfamiliar with the story. "Mr. Ferrett was encouraged to follow the same procedure as our anonymous woman tonight and instead he disappeared. Whether it was to join the rest of his belongings or whether it was the work of the reps, we will never know."

There was an uproar at this but he shouted over the noise. "At least let us deal with it now before the person in question has a chance to escape once again without us learning about what is happening. It's not as though any harm will come to her and it's our duty to know!"

There was huge applause to this. The entire community erupted. They didn't want to lose another opportunity of finding a way back. The rep was quiet for a while as the hall chanted around her. She made a motion for silence and the crowd died down.

"Very well," she said loudly into the microphone and those two words bounced around my heart until I thought I would faint or laugh, which one I wasn't sure.

I looked to Bobby. "Please pinch me." I smiled. "Because this is all so ridiculous I feel as though I'm in one of those awful nightmares you laugh about the next day."

"It's not funny, Sandy," he warned. "Don't tell them anything."

I tried to hide a smile, yet my heart pounded.

"Sandy Shortt," the representative announced, "could you please stand up?"

44

After Jack had left Sandy Shortt's family home, he drove to the Leitrim Arms, the local bar in the small village. Despite the early hour, the pub was dark, lit by too few dusty wall lights, natural light blocked out by dark burgundy stained-glass windows. The floor was uneven, flagged with stones, and the wooden benches were covered with paisley cushions with foam spilling from the sides. There were a total of three men in the bar; two at opposite ends of the counter, pints in hand, necks craning to see the horseracing on the small television suspended from a bracket from the ceiling. The barman held court behind the counter, arms resting on the taps, head up, eyes glued to the race. There was anxious expectation painted on each of their faces, a monetary interest in the outcome obvious. The commentator's thick Cork accent speedily documented a second-by-second account of the race, speaking so fast, everybody couldn't help but hold his breath, adding to the atmosphere of suspense.

Catching the barman's attention, Jack ordered a pint of Guinness and chose to sit in the quiet snug at the far end of the bar, away from everyone. He had something important to do.

The barman took his gaze away from the television, choosing profession over obsession, and gave his pouring of the perfect pint his complete attention. He held the glass at a forty-five-degree angle close to the spout, preventing large bubbles from forming in the head. He pulled the tap fully open and filled the glass 75 percent full. He placed the pint on the counter, allowing the stout to settle before filling the rest of the glass.

Jack took Donal's police file out of his bag and placed it on the table before him, spreading out the pages one last time. This was his good-bye. This was the end, the final glance at all he had studied every day for the past year. The end of the search, the beginning of the rest of his life. He wanted to raise a glass to his brother one final time, one last drink together. He ran his eyes over the police reports, the long hours of dedicated police time. Each page reminding him of the ups and downs, the hopes and disappointments of the previous year. It had been long and hard. He laid out the witness statements in a row, the reports from all of Donal's friends who had been with him that night. The anguish and tears, lost sleep and despair that had gone into trying to remember every last blurred detail of the night.

Jack placed Donal's photograph on the tall stool opposite him. One final pint with his brother. He smiled across at him. *I've done my best, Donal; I promise you I've done my best.* For the first time, he believed it. There was no more he could do. With that thought came great relief. He looked down again at the pages before him. Alan

O'Connor's face stared back at him from the passport photo attached at the corner. Another broken man, another life almost destroyed. Alan was far from reaching the point Jack had arrived at that day. Jack had lost his brother, a brother he didn't know as well as he should have, but Alan had lost his greatest friend. He glanced at the statement he'd read a thousand times, if not more. Alan's full detailed account of the doomed night matched the accounts of Andrew, Paul, and Gavin, and the three girls they had met at the fast-food restaurant, though they had trouble remembering the beginning of their night, never mind the early hours of the next morning. The language of the report was awkward, stilted, and foreign. It lacked emotion, relayed only the facts of the matter, times and places, who was there and what was said. No feelings to convey the fact that a group of friends had been torn apart by the incident of this one night. The one night that changed a lifetime of nights.

Andrew, Paul, Gavin, Shane, Donal, and I left Clohessy's on Howley's Quay at approximately 12.30 on Friday night. We went to the nightclub The Sin Bin in the same building . . . Jack skipped the details of what happened inside the club. Andrew, Paul, Gavin, Donal, and I left the club at approximately 2 A.M. and walked two blocks to SuperMacs on O'Connell Street. Shane had met a girl in the nightclub that none of us knew and went home with her . . .

He skipped a few lines.

All of us sat down in a booth on the right-hand side of the chipper closest to the counter, to eat our burgers and chips. We got talking to three girls who were also in the chipper. We asked them to join us and we all sat in the booth. There were eight of us; me, Andrew, Paul, Gavin, Donal, Collette, Samantha, and Fiona. Donal sat on the outside, on the edge of the seat beside Fiona and opposite me. We made plans to go back to a party at Fiona's house . . . Jack skipped to the most important part. I asked Donal if he was going to the party and he said yes and that was the last conversation we had that night. He didn't tell me he was leaving the chipper. I started talking to Collette and when I turned around Donal was gone. That was at 3 A.M. approximately.

They had all relayed the same story. It was just a normal lads' Friday night out. Pub, nightclub, chipper, nothing out of the ordinary for them to remember; just the fact that their best friend went missing. Each of Donal's friends relayed different final conversations, nobody noticed him leave the chipper apart from the girl named Fiona, who was sitting beside him, and she only noticed that he was not beside her when she turned around and saw him walking out. She said he had fallen against the door frame as he left, and a few girls by the door had seen him and laughed. Later, none of these girls could offer any more information than just that. As the place was full of people all thrown out of nightclubs at the same time, the CCTV did not film the booth that Donal had been seated at. The lines forming at the counter and the pockets of people standing around unable to get a table blocked the booths. Still, there was nothing to see but Donal walking out, bumping his shoulder on the door frame as everyone had witnessed. CCTV filmed him at the nearby ATM where he withdrew €30, he was seen again stumbling down Arthur's Quay, and then his trace was lost.

Jack thought back to the last time he had spoken to Alan and felt guilty for putting him under such pressure to try to remember more. Alan had clearly already been squeezed for every last drop of detail of the night by the Gardaí. Jack had felt that in some way his brother going missing was his fault, that as an older brother there was something that he should have done, was supposed to do to make it right. His mother died feeling that same responsibility. Was there anyone that didn't blame themselves? He recalled his conversation with Alan, how only a few days ago he had admitted the same.

I hope you find him, Jack. I keep going back over that night again and again, wishing I'd left with him.

On the counter, the creamy head of the Guinness began to separate from the dark body. It was still foggy but was becoming clearer.

I keep going back over that night again and again, wishing I'd left with him.

Jack's heart caught in his throat. He fumbled through the pages to find Alan's statement again.

We made plans to go back to a party at Fiona's house. I asked Donal if he was going to the party and he said yes and that was the last conversation we had that night. He didn't tell me he was leaving the chipper.

The barman topped off the pint by pushing the tap forward slightly, allowing the head to rise just above the rim.

Jack sat up straight, focused his mind, didn't lose his head. Thoughts began to rise to the top and he felt close to something. He kept reading and rereading the police report while simultaneously going over in his mind the conversation with Alan from only days ago.

The stout didn't overflow or run down the glass.

Jack controlled his breathing and kept his fear contained.

The barman delivered the pint to the snug and hesitated at the entrance, unsure of where to put the Guinness with the table a mess of papers.

"Just put it down anywhere," Jack said. The barman made a circular motion with the pint in the air, trying to decide where to plant it and finally brought it down to the table, rushing back to where the men where shouting at the television, urging their horse on. Jack's eyes moved down the ruby-black belly of the body of the pint, right down to the base of the glass. The barman had placed it on Alan's statement, next to the sentence he had read over and over again. Everything was drawing him back to that sentence.

I asked Donal if he was going to the party and he said yes and that was the last conversation we had that night. He didn't tell me he was leaving the chipper.

Jack was trembling but he didn't know why. Shaking, he raised the glass into the air and smiled wobbly at his brother's photo. He put the glass to his lips and took a big slug of the thick liquid. At the same time the warm stout slid down his throat, the memory of Alan's next sentence fired itself at him.

I really thought he'd be OK getting a taxi down that way, you know?

The Guinness caught in his throat and he began to cough, leaning away from the table to hack it up.

"You OK?" the barman shouted over.

"Yes! Go on, ya boya!" The two men in the bar celebrated the victory of their horse, clapping their hands and cheering, giving Jack a fright.

Jack's mind ran through a million excuses, defenses, mistakes, and whether he'd misheard. He thought of Sandy's diary entry to visit written in red capital letters, he thought of the worried face of Mrs. O'Connor. *You think he done something wrong?* She knew. She had known all along. Chills ran through him. Anger fired through his veins. He slammed the pint down on the table, the white ring left on the inside of the glass. His legs went weak as rage and fear took over his body.

He didn't remember leaving the pub, he didn't remember calling Alan, and he didn't remember driving back to Limerick in record time to meet him. Looking back on those hours there was very little he knew about that night other than what people told him. The one thing he did recall was Alan's forlorn voice now ringing constantly in his head: *I keep going back over that night again and again, wishing I'd left with him. I really thought he'd be OK getting a taxi down that way, you know?* The contradicting voice from his statement shouted even louder: *I asked Donal if he was going to the party and he said yes and that was the last conversation we had that night.*

The last conversation we had.

He had lied. And why would he do that?

45

I stood up from my chair and the eyes of thousands of people turned to look at me, study me, form opinions, judge, hang me, and burn me at the stake. I spotted Helena in the front row, clearly distressed by how this was all playing out. Her hands were clasped tightly to her chest as though in prayer and her eyes glistened with welling tears. I smiled at her, feeling sorry for her. For *her*. She nodded at me encouragingly. Joseph, on the stage, did the same. I wasn't sure what to fear and I suppose that's why I didn't. I didn't understand what was going on, why it mattered so hugely that something of mine had gone missing, why something that seemed so positive could be turned into something so negative. The one thing I did understand was that those who had been here longer than I was were fearful for me, and that was enough. Already over the last few days, life had been even more uncomfortable for me with people following me around, questioning as to whether I knew their families. I wasn't keen on it getting any worse.

The representative fixed her eyes on me. "Welcome, Sandy. I know it doesn't seem fair to do this so publicly but you have witnessed the reason for having to do it this way."

I nodded.

"I must ask you, this rumor of your belongings going missing." She paused, clearly not wanting to ask the question for fear of the answer. "Could you please confirm how this isn't true?"

"You're leading her!" one man shouted out, and others hushed him.

"This is not a courtroom," the rep said angrily. "Please allow Ms. Shortt to speak."

"The rumor," I said, looking around to the thousands of faces, some of which were listening to the translation of my words in their headphones, "is most definitely not true." There was a babble of voices again so I raised my voice. "Though I do understand where it has come from. I was waving to somebody and my watch flew from my wrist and landed in the nearby field. I enlisted some people to help me find it. It's really not a big deal."

"And they found it," said Grace Burns, unable to hide the relief from her voice.

"Yes," I lied.

"Show it to us!" one man shouted out, and a few hundred more agreed.

Grace sighed. "Are you wearing this watch now?"

I froze and looked down at my bare wrist. "Em . . . no, because the clasp broke as it fell to the ground and it hasn't been fixed yet."

"Bring the watch!" a woman shouted.

"No!" I shouted back, and everyone quieted. I felt Bobby look at me in surprise. "With respect to you all,

I feel that this whole thing is no more than a ludicrous witch hunt. I have given you my word that my watch has not gone missing and I refuse to continue with this charade by bringing it here to masquerade around the hall. I haven't been here long enough to understand why it is exactly you are all behaving this way but if you all wish to welcome me here, as you should, then please allow my word to be enough."

That didn't go down well.

"Please, Ms. Shortt," Grace said worriedly. "I suggest the best thing for you to do is to leave the hall and retrieve the watch. Jason will accompany you." A man dressed in a black suit, lean and slenderly built, with a posture so perfect it could only have come from the army, arrived at the end of my row. He held his arm out toward the door.

"I don't know this man." I grasped at straws. "I'm not going with him."

Grace looked confused first, and then wary. "Well, you have to bring the watch to us whether you like it or not, so who would be the best person to accompany you?"

I thought quickly. "The man beside me."

Bobby jumped to attention.

Grace strained her eyes to see, there was a flash of recognition, and she nodded. "Very well, they will both go with you. We will move on with the session while you're gone."

The Dutch representative took to the stage to talk about the plans for more mills, but nobody took any notice of him. All eyes were on us as we walked down the long aisle of the hall. People who stood at the back parted for us and we were swallowed up through the huge doors. Once outside, Bobby gave me big eyes, not wanting to speak in front of our companion.

"We have to collect my watch from Bobby's shop," I explained calmly to Jason. "He was supposed to fix the clasp for me."

Bobby nodded, finally understanding.

We arrived outside the door of the Lost and Found shop, the brightly colored odd socks decorating the front. It was dark outside now, the village like a ghost town with everybody in the Community Hall waiting for me, waiting for news of whether it was possible to leave Here or not.

"I'd like to wait here for Bobby." I stopped walking and stayed on the veranda looking out to the black forest. Jason didn't say anything, but stood back with his hands joined before him and waited with me.

"What are you, secret service?" I teased, looking him up and down. He didn't smile, just looked away. "*Matrix* bad guy? Man in black? Johnny Cash uber-fan?" He didn't answer. I sighed. "Are you here to make sure I don't run away?" I asked him.

He didn't answer.

"Would you shoot at me if I did?" I said smartly. "Asking you to accompany me," I tutted. "What do they think I am, a criminal?" I turned to him. "Just for the record, I don't appreciate you being here."

He stared straight ahead.

Bobby interrupted the uncomfortable silence, banging the door behind him. "Right, got it."

I took it from his hand and examined it.

"Is that yours?" Jason spoke for the first time, studying my face.

It was silver with a mother-of-pearl face but that's where the similarities ended. Instead of a linked bracelet it was chunky, instead of a rectangular face, this was round.

"Yep," I said confidently. "That's my watch, all right."

Jason took it in his hands and wrapped it around my wrist. It was hugely oversized even for my wrist. "Bobby," Jason said, rubbing his eyes wearily, "get her another watch. One that fits, this time."

We both looked at him in surprise.

"*That's* what I'm here for," he said smartly, returning to his spot on the veranda.

Bobby quickly headed back to the shop and Jason called after him, "Oh, and make sure the clasp is broken. You said you weren't wearing it because it was broken, right?"

I nodded, still silent.

"Well, that shut you up," he said, looking back out to the forest.

Jason, Bobby, and I walked back quickly to the Community Hall in silence, me holding the watch tightly in my hands. Just before Jason pulled open the door, I stopped him.

"What happens now?" I asked, anxiety building up inside me.

"Well, I assume you go in there and . . ." He thought

aloud about it and finally shrugged his shoulders. "And lie." He pulled the door open and thousands of faces turned to look at us.

The Dutch representative's speech immediately went quiet and Grace Burns moved forward to the microphone. Anxiety was written all over her face. Bobby and Jason stayed at the door, Bobby nodded encouragingly and I began to walk forward up the long aisle to the stage at the top. If I hadn't been so uneasy I would have laughed at the irony of it. Gregory would have done anything to get me up the aisle, and his gift of the watch had finally succeeded.

I reached the top and handed the watch to Grace. She studied it, but I questioned how on earth she was to know whether it was my watch or not. It all seemed so ridiculous. It was all an act. To make those who were unsettled here feel more secure so they wouldn't rise up and demand to find a way out.

"How do we know it's her watch?" one person shouted out, and I rolled my eyes.

"Her name is engraved on the back!" someone shouted, and my blood turned cold. There were only a few people who knew that. I looked immediately to Joseph, but from the look on his face I knew it wasn't him. He was looking angrily at Helena, who was looking even more angrily to . . . Joan. Joan sat in the front row with a red face, beside the man who had shouted out. She must have overheard. She looked apologetically to Helena and me. I looked away, not knowing how to feel, not truly knowing what any possible outcome could be.

"Is this true?" the representative looked at me.

"I assure you it's true," the man shouted out again.

My face said it all, I'm sure.

She turned the watch over to look for my name at the back. She seemed pleased. "SANDY SHORTT is engraved on the back."

There was a loud sigh and more talk within the audience.

"Sandy, thank you for cooperating. You may leave now and enjoy your life here with us. I hope people will be more welcoming toward you from now on." She smiled warmly.

Stunned, I took the watch, unable to believe that Bobby had managed to engrave my name in such a short space of time. I quickly walked back down the aisle while people clapped and smiled at me, some apologizing, others still not convinced and probably never would be. I grabbed Bobby by the hand and led him out of the hall.

"Bobby!" I laughed once we were a safe distance away from the Community Hall. "How the hell did you manage that?"

Bobby looked horrified. "Manage what?"

"To engrave my name so quickly!"

"I didn't," he said in shock.

"What?" I turned the watch over. A clear metallic back stared back at me.

"Come on, let's get inside," Bobby said, unlocking the door to the shop while looking around him uncertainly.

In the shadows there was a noise and Jason stepped out.

I jumped.

"Sorry to startle you," he said in his robotlike tone.

"Sandy." Emotion slipped into his voice and his body loosened as he stepped into the light of the porch. "I just wondered if you knew my wife, Alison?" he asked awkwardly. "Alison Rice? We're from Galway. Spiddal." He swallowed hard, his aggressive appearance softened and vulnerable, concern written all over his face.

Still taken by surprise at his sudden appearance, I ran the name through my mind a few times. Not familiar with it, I shook my head slowly. "Sorry."

"OK." He cleared his throat and straightened up, the hardness returning as though the question had never passed his lips. "Grace Burns wanted me to tell you that she requests a meeting with you in her office first thing in the morning." And he disappeared back into the darkness.

Jack felt the anger pumping through his veins. The muscles in his face twitched as they jumped around under his skin, psyching themselves up for the big fight. He tried to control his breathing, control his temper. His back teeth felt like they'd been ground to the bone on the drive there. His cheeks were hot, and throbbed along with the rest of his body. He clenched and unclenched his fists while walking through the crowded Limerick city pub.

He spotted Alan sitting alone at a small table with a pint before him, a stool sat in front of him waiting for Jack. Alan looked up and waved, a smile stretched across his face, and in that face Jack could see the ten-year-old who used to drop by to their house every day. He prepared to fire himself at Alan but stopped. Instead he diverted to the toilet, where he stood at the sink, splashing water on his face, panting as though he'd run a marathon. It was all he could do to stop himself reaching out and wanting to kill Alan himself.

What had he done? What on earth had Alan done?

The week that Jenny-May Butler went missing, the Gardaí came to Leitrim National School. We were all especially excited because it was rare that our principal graced our humble selves with his presence, particularly in our classrooms. As soon as we caught sight of his stern, accusing face, butterflies fluttered in everyone's stomachs, each of us instantly hoping we weren't in trouble even though we knew we'd done nothing wrong. But such was his power. Our main reason for excitement was due to him disrupting our religion lesson to whisper loudly into Ms. Sullivan's ear. Loud whispering in the classroom by teachers always meant something important was happening. We were allowed to abandon our studies that morning and told to line up in a single file at the door with our fingers on our lips. For teachers, our placing our fingers on our lips didn't usually have the desired effect, the finger not being a suitable silencer as it was indeed a finger, not a zipper, and it was, more important, our own finger, which we had the ability to remove at any stage. But that day when we entered the school hall, none of us said a word, because at the top of the very unusually silent room were two members of the Gardaí Síochana. One woman and one man, dressed head to toe in navy blue.

We sat on the floor in the middle of the hall with the other fourth classers. Up at the front were junior and senior infants. The older you were, the further back you were allowed be. The sixth always coolly took their places in the back row. Very quickly the hall was filled. The teachers lined up against the walls on the outside aisles like prison wardens, and every now and then clicked their fingers with an angry face at someone who was whispering or who was trying to make themselves more comfortable on the cold and slightly dirty gym floor, but who was seen to be fidgeting too much.

Our principal introduced the two guards to us, explaining that they were from the local garda station and were here to talk about a very important issue. He told us that we would be asked questions by our teachers later in class about what they had said. I looked over at our teachers when he announced this and noticed a few suddenly straightening themselves up to listen. Then the male garda began talking, he introduced himself as Garda Rogers and his colleague Garda Brannigan, and while he slowly walked the width of the front of the room with his hands behind his back, he explained how we shouldn't trust strangers, how we shouldn't get into their cars, not even when they tell us that our parents have told them to collect us. That made me think of refusing to get into my uncle Fred's car on Wednesday afternoons when he collected me, and I almost laughed out loud. He told us that we should always speak up if we notice someone getting friendlier than they should. If someone approaches us or we witness anybody else being approached, we should tell our parents or teachers straightaway. I was ten years old and I remember thinking about when I was seven and I saw Joey Harrison being collected by a weird man at school. I told my teacher at the time and she reprimanded me because it was his dad and she thought I was being rude.

Also, for those of us at ten years of age, almost eleven, this safety talk was old news, but I supposed that particular safety talk was especially for the five- and six-year-olds who sat in the front rows of the hall picking their noses, scratching their heads, looking at the ceilings. A front row of little grasshoppers. At that point I had no desire to join the guards. It wasn't that day's free lesson in safety that set off my ambition; it was the odd socks. I also knew the talk was because of Jenny-May's disappearance that week. Everybody had been acting weirdly about it all week. Our teacher had even left the classroom in tears a few times whenever her eyes fell upon Jenny-May's empty seat. I was secretly delighted, which I knew was wrong, but it was the first week of peace I'd gotten at school for years. For once I didn't feel Jenny-May's balls of paper hitting my head as she blew them through a straw, and whenever I answered a question in class I didn't hear sniggers behind me. I *knew* that a really terrible and sad thing had happened but I just couldn't *feel* sad.

We said a prayer in class every morning for the first few weeks after she went missing, for Jenny-May's safety, praying for her family and praying that she would be found. The prayer got shorter and shorter as the weeks went by, and then suddenly one Monday, when we came back after the weekend, Ms. Sullivan just left out that prayer without mentioning a thing. Everybody's desks were rearranged in a different shape in the room, and *bam!*, everything went back to normal. I found that even weirder than Jenny-May going missing in the first place. I spent the first few minutes of that day looking at everybody reciting their poems like they were crazy, but the teacher chastised me for not learning the poem I had spent two hours learning the night before and she picked on me for the rest of the day.

After Garda Rogers had finished his safety talk, it was Garda Brannigan's turn to talk more specifically about Jenny-May. She spoke in softer tones about how, if anybody knew anything or had any information about something they saw over the last few weeks or months, they should go to Room Four beside the staffroom, as she and Garda Rogers would be there for the day. My face burned because I felt like she was talking directly to me. I looked around, in paranoia, feeling as though this entire event had been staged just for me, to confess all that I knew. No one looked at me oddly, apart from James Maybury, who picked a scab on his elbow and flicked it at me. Our teacher clicked her fingers at him, which had little effect, as the damage had already been done and he wasn't afraid, nor did he care much about clicking fingers.

When the talk was over we were once again encouraged by our teachers to go to Room Four to talk to the Gardaí, and then we were given our lunch break, which was a stupid idea because nobody was going to bother missing time playing in the yard by going to the guards. As soon as we got back into our classroom and Ms. Sullivan told us to take our math books out, hands suddenly shot into the air. People just suddenly seemed to remember vital evidence. But what else could Ms. Sullivan do? And so the Gardaí found themselves with a very long line of students of all ages outside their door, some of whom had never even met Jenny-May Butler.

Room Four was nicknamed the Interrogation Room, and the story of what went on inside became more and more exaggerated with each pupil that left and rejoined his friends. There were so many pupils with alleged information that the guards had to come back the next day, but not without a stern announcement to each class that although everybody's help was very much appreciated, garda time was very precious and students should only go to Room Four if they had something very important to tell them. By the second day, I had already been refused access to Room Four by my teacher twice on account of the first request to go taking place during the history lesson and the second during Irish.

"But I like Irish, Miss," I protested.

"Good, then you'll be happy to stay," she snapped, before ordering me to read an entire chapter aloud from the book.

I had no alternative but to raise my hand during art class on Friday afternoon. *Everybody* loved art class. Ms. Sullivan looked at me in surprise.

"Can I go now, Miss?"

"To the toilet?"

"No, to Room Four."

She looked surprised but finally took me seriously and I was given permission to leave art class to the sound of *ooooooooh* from everybody else.

I knocked on the door to Room Four and Garda Rogers opened the door. He must have been six feet tall. At ten years old I was already very tall, at five foot five, and I was happy finally to see someone tower over me, even if he was intimidating, dressed in a garda uniform, and I was about to confess to him.

"Another math class?" He smiled broadly.

"No," I said so quietly I could barely hear myself. "Art."

"Oh." He raised his thick caterpillar eyebrows with surprise.

"I'm responsible," I said quickly.

"Well, that's good, but I don't think missing one math class makes you irresponsible, although don't tell your teacher I said that." He touched his nose.

"No," I said, taking a deep breath. "I mean I'm responsible for Jenny-May going missing."

This time he didn't smile. He opened the door wider. "Come on in."

I looked around the room. It was nothing like the rumors that had been going around the last two days. Jemima Hayes said that someone told her friend that someone told her that someone hadn't been allowed to leave the room to go to the toilet and had to pee in his pants. The room was nonthreatening, with a couch up against one wall, small table in the center, and a plastic school chair opposite that. There was no sign of a wet chair.

"Sit down there." He pointed to the couch. "Make yourself comfortable. What's your name?"

"Sandy Shortt."

"You're tall for your age, though, aren't you, Miss Shortt?" He laughed, and I smiled politely even though I'd heard it a million times. He stopped himself laughing. "So, tell me, what makes you think you were responsible for Jenny-May's disappearance, as you called it?"

I frowned. "What do *you* call it?"

"Well, we don't know for sure if . . . I mean there's nothing to suggest . . ." He sighed. "Just tell me why you think you're responsible." He motioned for more.

"Well, Jenny-May didn't like me," I began slowly, suddenly becoming nervous.

"Oh, I'm sure that's not true," he said kindly. "What makes you think that?"

"She used to call me a lanky slut and throw stones at me."

"Oh." He fell silent.

I took a breath. "Then last week she found out that I told my friend Emer that I didn't think she was as good at King/Queen as everybody thought she was and she got really angry and stormed over to me and Emer and challenged us to a game. Well, not *us* actually, because she didn't say anything to Emer, just me. She doesn't like Emer either but she doesn't like me more, and I was the one that said it so we were supposed to play this game the next day, me and Jenny-May, and whoever won meant that they were the undisputed champion and nobody could say that they weren't good because the fact that they'd won would prove it. She also knew that I fancied Stephen

Spencer and she always used to shout stuff at me just so he wouldn't like me, but I knew that she liked him too. Well, it was obvious because they French-kissed in the bushes at the end of the road a few times for dares but I don't think that he really liked her and maybe he's happy she's gone now too, so he'll be left alone, but I'm not saying I think he did anything to make her disappear. Anyway, the day we were supposed to play King/Queen I saw Jenny-May Butler cycling past my house down the road and she gave me a bad look and I knew she was going to beat me that day at King/Queen and that things would be even worse than they already were and—" I stopped talking and pursed my lips, not sure whether to say what I felt next.

"What happened, Sandy?"

I gulped hard.

"Did you do something?"

I nodded and he moved in, shuffling his backside closer the edge of his chair.

"What did you do?"

"I . . . I . . ."

"It's OK, you can tell me."

"I wished her away." I said it quickly, like pulling a bandage from my skin, quick and easy.

"I'm sorry, you what?"

"I wished her away?"

"Whisht? Is that a weapon of some—"

"No, *wished*. I *wished* that she'd disappear."

"Ah." Realization dawned and he sat back slowly, in his chair. "I understand now."

"No, you're just saying that you do but you don't really.

I really did wish for her to be gone, much more than I've ever wished for anything to be gone in my whole entire life, even more than when Uncle Fred stayed over in our house for a month after he split up from Aunt Isabel and he smoked and drank and stunk the place out and I really wanted him gone but not as much as I wanted Jenny-May gone, and a few hours after me wishing that, Mrs. Butler came over to our house and told us she was missing."

He leaned forward again. "So you saw Jenny-May a few hours before Mrs. Butler came over to your house?"

I nodded.

"What time was this at?"

I shrugged.

"Is there anything that could remind you of what time it was? Think back, what were you doing? Was there anybody else around?"

"I had just opened the door to my grandma and granddad. They came over for lunch and I was giving Grandma a hug when I saw her cycling by. That's when I made the wish." I winced.

"So, this was lunchtime. Was she with anyone?" He was on the edge of his seat now, ignoring my concern over my wishing her away. He asked question after question about what Jenny-May was doing, who she was with, how did she look, what was she wearing, where did it look like she was going, lots of questions over and over again until my head hurt and I could barely think what the answers were anymore. It turned out that I was such a good help to them because I was the last person to see her that I was allowed to go home early that day. Another benefit to Jenny-May's disappearance.

A few nights before the Gardaí came to the school I had begun to feel guilty about Jenny-May disappearing. I watched a documentary with my dad about how one hundred fifty thousand people in Washington, D.C., all arranged to think positive thoughts at the same time and the crime rate went down, which proved that positive and negative thinking had a real effect. But then Garda Rogers told me that it wasn't my fault Jenny-May Butler was gone, that wishing for something to happen didn't actually make it happen, and so I became a lot more realistic after that.

And there I was, standing outside the office of Grace Burns twenty-four years later, about to knock on the door and feeling exactly the same as when I was ten. I had that same feeling of being responsible for something beyond my control but I also held the belief in some childish way that ever since I was ten years old, I had been secretly, silently, and subconsciously wishing I'd discover a place like this.

48

"Jack, is everything OK?" Alan asked, as soon as Jack had taken his seat opposite him at the low bar table. Concern was written all over his face and doubt crept in on Jack again.

"I'm fine," Jack replied, putting down his drink, settling on the stool, trying to keep the anger out of his voice, feeling confused.

"You look like shit." His eyes dropped to Jack's leg, which was bouncing away steadily.

"Everything's OK."

"You're sure?" Alan narrowed his eyes.

"Yeah." He took a slug of Guinness, his mind going back to the memory that had hit him with his last taste. Alan's lie.

"So, what's up?" Alan said, back to his usual nature. "You sounded on the phone like there was a fire. Something important to tell me?"

"No, no fire." Jack looked around, avoiding eye contact, doing everything he could do to stop himself from throwing a punch. He needed to approach this properly, and tried to relax. His leg stopped bouncing, he leaned in to the table, and stared into his pint. "It's just this past week I've been looking for Donal, and it's brought everything back, y'know?"

Alan sighed and stared into his pint too. "Yeah, I know. I think about it every day."

"About what?"

Alan looked up quickly. "What do you mean?"

"I mean, what kind of things do you think about every day?" Jack tried to take the interrogative tone out of his voice.

"I don't know what you mean. I think about the whole thing." Alan frowned.

"Well, *I* think about how I wish I'd been there that night, how I wish I'd known Donal better because if I had then maybe . . ." Jack said, holding his hands up. "Maybe, maybe, maybe. Maybe I'd know where to look, maybe I'd know the places or people he went to for safety or for privacy. Anything like that, you know? Maybe there were some people he was running from, people he got involved with. We didn't talk much about private things and every day I think about the fact that if I'd been a better brother maybe I'd have found him. Maybe he'd be sitting right here beside us having a pint."

They both naturally looked to the empty stool beside them.

"Don't think stuff like that, Jack. You were a good bro—"

"Don't," Jack interrupted, raising his voice.

Alan stopped in surprise. "Don't what?"

Jack looked him directly in the eyes. "Don't lie."

Fear and uncertainty entered Alan's face and Jack

knew his intuition was correct. Alan looked around the room anxiously but Jack stopped him. "You don't need to tell me I was a good brother because I know I wasn't. Don't lie to make me feel better."

Alan seemed relieved by this answer. "OK, you were a shit brother." He smiled and they both laughed.

"As much as I've been giving myself a hard time for not being there that night, deep down I know that even if I'd been there, the same thing probably would have happened. Because I know you had his back; you've always had his back."

Alan smiled sadly into his pint.

"Last time we talked, you blamed yourself for not leaving with Donal that night." Jack picked up a soggy beer mat and slowly began peeling the outer label off. "I know what it's like to blame yourself: it's not good. I've been going to see some people, to help sort my head out." He scratched his head awkwardly. "They told me all this stuff about blaming yourself was normal. I thought it'd be important to tell you that. Over a pint."

"Thanks," Alan said quietly. "I appreciate that."

"Yeah, well . . . at least you got to have a conversation with him before he left, right?"

Alan's face showed that he wasn't sure where this was going, but Jack's voice was still nonthreatening and he'd managed to calm himself completely now, to ignore what he guessed.

"You're lucky. The rest of the lads didn't notice him leave."

"I didn't either." Alan began fidgeting.

"No, you did," Jack said casually. "You said so last week."

He took another slug of Guinness and looked around casually. "Busy here, isn't it? Didn't think it would be, so early in the evening." He looked at his watch: six P.M. It felt like days since he had met Sandy's mother, not hours. "Last week you said you wished you'd left with him and you thought he'd be safe getting a taxi down that way."

Alan looked uncomfortable. "I didn't—"

"You did, man," Jack interrupted and laughed. "I may be losing my mind but I do remember that. I was happy to hear it, though."

"Yeah?"

"Yeah," Jack said, nodding happily, "because it meant that he didn't just wander off, you know. He let someone know, and it also makes sense what he was doing walking in that direction. That must make you feel better. The other lads, they're frustrated with themselves for not noticing. They blame themselves for not seeing him leave. At least you don't have that on your head."

Alan was fidgeting. "Yeah, I suppose so." He took his bag of tobacco out of his shirt pocket. "I'm going outside for a smoke. I'll be back in a minute."

"Hang on a minute," Jack said casually. "I'll finish off this pint and go out with you."

"You don't smoke."

"I took it back up," Jack said, though it was a lie. The last thing he wanted was for Alan to disappear. He would only get one chance to do this. "Why is it so busy this evening?" he said, looking around.

Alan relaxed. "I dunno." He took out the skins and began to sprinkle the tobacco inside. "It's a Saturday, I suppose."

"Should we get a taxi down by Arthur's Quay to-night?" Jack asked casually. "I left the car at home."

"What do you mean?"

"That's where you told Donal to go for a cab, isn't it?"

Alan snorted and swallowed, cleaning his nostrils, making a sound but not answering the question. He slowly rolled the cigarette between his hands; Jack could see he was thinking. Trying to work it all out in his head.

"It's probably not such a good idea to recommend it to anyone now," Jack said a little too angrily.

Alan stopped playing with his cigarette and looked at Jack. "What's going on, Jack?"

"There are a few things running through my mind." He scratched his forehead with his thumb and noticed his fingers tremble with anger. Alan looked up and saw them too. His eyes narrowed. "I lost contact with the woman who was helping me look for Donal," Jack explained, hearing his voice shaking but having no control over it. "And that's driven me half insane. But mostly what's bothering me"—he spoke through gritted teeth—"is the fact you told the guards and my family and everyone that would listen that you hadn't noticed Donal leave. Then last week you told me that you *had* noticed him leave. In fact, you'd even spoken to him. In fact, you'd even told him which way to go for a taxi."

Alan's eyes got wider and wider as Jack spoke. His hands began to fidget more, he moved uncomfortably in his seat and a bead of sweat formed above his top lip.

"It doesn't make sense, Alan. And it might not even be a big deal, but can you tell me why you lied for an entire year about the fact you told my brother, your best friend, to walk to an area, for a taxi, that would cause him to disappear?" The anger began to rise, and the volume of his voice with it.

Alan started to tremble. "I had nothing to do with it."

"With what?"

"With Donal going missing. I had nothing to do with it." He went to stand up but Jack reached out and pushed him down by the shoulder. The bag of tobacco spilled to the carpet. Jack kept his hand there firmly, holding him down.

"Well then, who did?" he said angrily.

"I don't know."

Jack dug his fingers into Alan's shoulder blade. He was just skin and bone.

"Jesus Christ, do we have to do this here?" Alan said in pain, trying to squirm out of Jack's grasp but failing.

Jack leaned in and said, "Do what here? Is there someplace else you'd like to go? The garda station maybe?"

"I didn't do anything," Alan insisted. "I swear."

"Then why did you lie?"

"I didn't lie," he said with big wide eyes, looking like he'd never told the truth in his life. "I don't exactly have a clean sheet as it is. I thought the guards would think I'd something to do with it."

Their faces were only inches apart now. "Tell me the truth."

"I have."

"He was your best friend, Alan; he was always there for you."

"I know, I know," he interrupted, holding his trembling

nicotine-stained fingers to his head. Tears began to form in his eyes and he stared down at the table, his whole body shuddering.

"You can either tell me and make me understand, or I go to the guards," Jack threatened.

It felt like hours before Alan built up the nerve to speak again, "Donal got involved in something," he said, so quietly Jack had to move his head even closer. Their heads were practically touching now.

"You're a liar."

"I'm not a liar," Alan's head shot up, and Jack could see for once he was telling the truth. "I was working for these lads—"

"What lads?"

"I can't say."

Jack reached across and grabbed his collar. "Who are they?"

"I'm helping you as much as I can, Jack," Alan croaked, color rising quickly in his face.

Jack loosened his grip slightly, enough for Alan to be able to breathe, and listened.

"They brought Donal in to program some stuff onto their computer. I suggested him as he'd got his degree and all, but he saw and heard a few things he shouldn't have and they got angry. I told them he wouldn't say a word but Donal was threatening to talk."

"About what?" Anger was firing through Jack. He couldn't believe after one year of searching, the answer was right here at home, the truth resting with his brother's best friend.

"I can't tell you that," Alan said through gritted teeth,

spittle spilling from the sides of his mouth. "I couldn't talk Donal out of snitching. He was trying to get me on the straight and narrow, but he didn't understand how serious they were. He wouldn't listen." His entire body trembled and Jack's eyes filled as he waited. Alan's voice broke and the shame was evident as he whispered, "They were only supposed to knock him around a bit, warn him off, give him a scare."

It was as though red powder fell before Jack's eyes. The anger pumped violently within him. "And you walked him straight into it." His voice was hoarse. Jack jumped out of his chair, pushed his hand up against Alan's throat and forced him off his chair. He fell back against the wall, and the mirror behind Alan's head smashed with the force. The pub was silenced and people leaped out of the way of the two men. Jack threw Alan's head hard against the wall again. "Where is he?" he hissed, his face up against Alan's.

Alan made choking sounds and Jack squeezed his grip tighter. Alan tried to speak and Jack remembered himself and loosened his grip. "Where is his body?"

When he got his answer, he let go of Alan's throat and backed away, dropping him from his grip as if he were a dirty rag. He allowed Garda Graham Turner, who had been sitting nearby, to take over, and Jack left the pub to find his brother. This time he could say good-bye properly. This time the brothers would both finally be at rest.

49

"Hello, Sandy." Grace Burns smiled at me from behind her desk. Her office was a cubbyhole at the back of a planning office. Inside were models of buildings and layouts of future plans for the surrounding lands.

I took a seat before her desk. "Thank you for saving me from the angry mob last night," I joked.

"No problem." But her smile quickly faded. "Tell me what's really happening, Sandy. Is your watch missing?"

After talking to Joseph, Helena, and Bobby late into the night about what was the best thing do, they all agreed that I should lie. I didn't agree.

"Yes, it's missing," I responded. Her eyes widened and she sat up straight in her chair. "But the last thing I want to do is make a big deal of it," I warned. "I cannot explain how it disappeared, just as I can't explain how I arrived here. No amount of questions from your colleagues or scientists or people who consider themselves to be experts can help this situation. I don't want that G.I. Joe following me around anymore either. I don't know anything. You must give me your word that you won't spread this news because I will not be co-operative."

"I understand," she said. "In the time that I've been here there have been a few people I know of who have reported the same thing, but we have been unable to learn anything, just as all of our studies have had little success in discovering how we arrived here. The people I knew of either moved out of town because word got out and life became too difficult under the gaze of everybody in the village, or else it was a false alarm and they found whatever it was they thought they'd lost. The two people that we did actually have the opportunity to work with closely just couldn't provide us with anything solid to work on. They knew nothing about why and how it was happening and most of us have realized that it's an impossible thing to understand."

"Where are they now?"

"One passed away, the other is living in another village. You're definitely sure your watch is gone?"

"It's gone," I assured her.

"Is this the only thing that has disappeared?"

This is where I chose to lie. I nodded. "And believe me, there's no better person at searching than me." I looked around her room while she studied me.

"What is it that you do back home, Sandy?" She rested her chin on her hand and gazed intently at me, trying to solve the puzzle in her own mind.

"I run a missing-persons agency."

She laughed first, but her smile faded when she realized she was laughing alone. "You search for missing people?"

"And help people reunite, find long-lost relatives, adopted parents, adopted children, that kind of thing," I rattled off.

Her eyes widened with each example. "So your case is certainly very different from the others I spoke about."

"Or it's coincidental."

She mulled that over but didn't comment. "So that's how you know so much about the people here."

"Only some people. Only the people in the play. By the way, the dress rehearsal is on tonight. Helena wanted me to invite you." I remembered how Helena had hammered it into my head before I left the house that morning. "It's *The Wizard of Oz* but it's not a musical, Helena is stressing to everybody. It's just her and Dennis O'Shea's interpretation." I laughed. "Orla Keane is playing the role of Dorothy. I'm actually quite looking forward to it." I realized this, as I said it, for the first time. "The idea for the play was initially just my way of having a chance to talk to the potential cast without raising suspicions. We thought it would be far cleverer than knocking on doors and relaying stories of home, but perhaps we should have put a bit more thought into it. I didn't realize how quickly people talk here."

"Word gets around fast," Grace replied, still in a daze. She leaned in further and said, "Were you looking for someone in particular when you arrived here?"

"Donal Ruttle," I said, still hoping I'd find him.

"No." She shook her head. "The name isn't familiar."

"He's now twenty-five years old, from Limerick, and would have arrived here last year."

"He's definitely not in *this* village, anyway."

"I don't think he's here at all, I'm afraid," I thought aloud, feeling instant sympathy for Jack Ruttle.

"I'm from Killybeggs in Donegal, I don't know if you know it . . ." Grace leaned forward again.

"Of course I do." I smiled.

Her face softened. "I'm married here but my maiden name is O'Donohue. My parents were Tony and Margaret O'Donohue. They have passed away now. I saw my dad's name in the obituaries in a newspaper I found six years ago. I've kept it." She glanced over at her wall cabinet. "Carol Dempsey," she started up again. "You know Carol. She's in the play too, I believe. Well, she's a Donegal woman too, as you well know, and she informed me of my mother's death when she arrived a few years ago."

"I'm sorry to hear that."

"Yes, well . . ." she said gently. "I'm an only child," she explained, "but I have an uncle Donie who moved to Dublin a few years before I arrived here."

I nodded along with her, waiting for the story to begin, but she fell silent and watched me. I shifted uneasily in my chair, realizing she was giving me information about her life to refresh my memory.

"I'm sorry, Grace," I said softly. "That might have been before I set up the agency. How long have you been here?"

"Fourteen years." I must have looked at her with such pity because she quickly explained, "I love it here, don't get me wrong. I have a wonderful husband and three gorgeous children and I wouldn't go back in a heartbeat, but I was just wondering . . . I'm sorry." She sat upright again and composed herself.

"It's OK. I'd want to know too," I said gently, "but I'm not familiar with the people you've mentioned. I'm sorry."

There was a silence and I thought I'd upset her, but when she spoke again she seemed fine.

"What made you want to find missing people? It's such an unusual career."

I laughed. "Now, there's a question." I thought back to when it all began. "Two words," I said. "Jenny-May Butler. She lived across the road from me when I was a child in Leitrim, but she went missing when she was ten."

"Yes." Grace smiled. "Jenny-May is as good a reason as any. What a character."

It took me a moment to catch what she'd said. My heart leaped into my throat with the surprise. "What? What did you say?"

50

"Come on, Bobby!" I yelled, poking my head in the door of Lost and Found.

"What?" he shouted from upstairs.

"Bring the camera, get your keys, lock up, and let's go. We've got to go!" I allowed the door to swing shut and paced up and down the veranda, Grace's words still ringing in my ears. She knew Jenny-May. She had given me directions. I had to go to her *now*. My excitement had gone way past boiling point and was overflowing, spilling from me as I waited impatiently outside for Bobby. I needed him to show me the way to Jenny-May's home in the forest, yet I didn't have the patience to explain what it was I wanted.

Bobby arrived at the door, looking bewildered. "What the hell are you doing—" He stopped as soon as he saw the look on my face. "What happened?"

"Get your things, Bobby, quick." I pushed by him into the shop. "I'll explain on the way. Bring the camera." I hopped around him as he clumsily tried to gather his things, trying to keep up with the speed with which I was barking my orders. By the time he had finished locking up I was power-walking down the dusty street, aware that even more eyes were on me now, after the community gathering last night.

"Wait, Sandy!" I heard him panting behind me. "What the hell happened to you? It's like you've a rocket shoved up your arse!"

"Maybe I have." I smiled, racing on.

"Where are we going?" He jogged alongside me.

"Here." I thrust the page of directions at him and kept walking.

"Hold on. Slow down," he said, trying to read it and run alongside me at the same time. One of my strides equaled two of his but I kept walking nonetheless. "Stop!" he shouted loudly in the market area, and others turned to stare. I finally stopped. "If you want me to read this properly you have to tell me what the hell is happening."

I spoke faster than I had ever spoken before in my life.

"OK, I think I got all that," Bobby said, still slightly confused, "but I've never been in this direction before." He studied the map again. "We'll have to ask Helena or Joseph."

"No! We've no time! We have to go *now*," I whined like an impatient child. "Bobby, I've been waiting for this moment for the past twenty-four years of my life. Please do not delay me now when I'm so close."

"Yes, Dorothy, but it will take a bit more than following the yellow brick road," he said sarcastically.

Despite my frustration, I laughed.

"I understand your haste but if I try to bring you to

this place it will be another twenty-four years before we get there. I don't know this part of the woods, I have never heard of this Jenny-May person, and I don't have any friends who live that deep. If we get lost, we're in big trouble. Let's just go to Helena for help first."

Although he was almost half my age, the boy made sense, and so I grudgingly stomped my way to Helena and Joseph's house.

Helena and Joseph were sitting on the bench in the front of their house, enjoying the relaxing atmosphere of Sunday lunchtime. Bobby, sensing my urgency, rushed straight to Helena and Joseph while Wanda jumped up from the ground where she was playing and ran to me.

"Hi, Sandy," she said, grabbing my hand and skipping alongside me as I walked toward the house.

"Hi, Wanda," I said in a bored tone as I tried to hide my smile.

"What's that in your hand?"

"It's called Wanda's hand," I said.

She rolled her eyes. "No, the *other* hand."

"It's a Polaroid camera."

"Why?"

"Why is it a camera?"

"No. Why do you have it?"

"Because I want to take a photograph of somebody."

"Who?"

"A girl I used to know."

"Who?"

"A girl called Jenny-May Butler."

"Was she your friend?"

"Not really."

"Well then, why do you want to take a photograph of her?"

"I don't know."

"Is it because you miss her?"

I was about to say no when I stopped myself. "Actually, I did miss her, very much."

"And are you going to see her today?"

"Yes." I smiled, grabbing Wanda under her armpits and swinging her around, much to her delight. "I am going to see Jenny-May Butler *today*!"

Wanda began laughing uncontrollably and sang a song she pretended to know about a girl called Jenny-May, which she clearly was making up on the spot, much to my amusement.

"I'm going to come with you," Helena said, breaking into Wanda's song, giving her a kiss on the top of her head. I took a photo of the two of them when they weren't looking.

"Stop wasting the cartridges," Bobby barked at me, and I snapped his face too.

"No, Helena, I don't expect you to come." I waved the photos in the air to dry before placing them in my shirt pocket. "You've got the dress rehearsal tonight. That's more important. Just explain to Bobby where it is." I began to get jittery again.

She looked at her watch and I had a pang of longing for mine. "It's just after one. The dress rehearsal isn't until seven; we'll be back in time. And besides, I want to go with you." She touched my chin lightly and winked. "This is far more important, plus I know exactly where we're going. This clearing is not much farther on from where you and I met last week."

Joseph made his way to me. He held out his hand. "Safe trip, *Kipepeo* girl."

I took his hand with confusion. "I'm coming back, Joseph."

"I should hope so," he said, and placed his other hand on my head. "When you get back I shall tell you what a *Kipepeo* girl is." He smiled.

"Liar," I said, narrowing my eyes.

"Right, let's go," Helena said, throwing a lime green pashmina over her shoulders.

We set off in the direction of the woods, Helena leading the way. At the edge of the woods a young woman appeared, looking dazed and confused as she gazed around the village.

"Welcome," Helena said to her.

"Welcome," Bobby said happily.

She looked with confusion from their faces to mine. "Welcome," I said and smiled, pointing her toward the registry office.

The routes Helena chose were cleared and well-traveled trails. The atmosphere reminded me of the first few days I had spent alone in these woods, wondering where I was. The scent of pine was rich, mixed with moss, bark, and damp leaves. There was the foul smell of rotting leaves mixed with the sweet floral scents of the wildflowers. Mosquitoes hovered in small areas, darting in circular motions together. Red squirrels bounced from branch to branch, and occasionally Bobby stopped to pick up an item of interest in our path. We couldn't walk fast enough, as far as I was concerned. Yesterday I had thought the prospect of finding Jenny-May an impossibility; today I was going back the way I had come, to actually see her.

Grace Burns had explained that Jenny-May had arrived in the village with an elderly Frenchman, who had been living deep in the woods for years. She had knocked on his door seeking help when she had first arrived all those years ago. Seldom in the forty years he had lived Here had he ventured to the village, but twenty-four years ago he arrived at the registry office with the ten-year-old girl named Jenny-May Butler, who insisted on him being her guardian—the only person she trusted. Despite his desire for solitude, he agreed to care for her, choosing to remain in his home in the woods but making sure Jenny-May went back and forth to school every day and formed and maintained friendships. She became fluent in French, choosing to speak it when in the village, which meant that few of the Irish community were aware of her true roots. Jenny-May cared for her guardian until his dying day, fifteen years ago, and she decided to remain in the home he made hers, outside of the village, rarely venturing to the village herself.

After twenty minutes, we passed the clearing where I had met Helena and she insisted on stopping for a break. She drank from the canteen of water she had carried with her and passed it to Bobby and me. I didn't feel the heat or the thirst on this hot day, though. My mind was focused on Jenny-May. I wanted to keep moving, keep walking until we reached her. After that, I had no idea what would happen.

"God, I've never seen you like this before," Bobby said,

staring at me oddly. "It's as though you've ants in your pants."

"She's always like that." Helena closed her eyes and fanned her perspiring face.

I paced up and down beside Helena and Bobby, hopping around, kicking leaves, and trying desperately to channel the adrenaline that was rushing through me. Feeling more anxious with every second they spent with me, they finally felt under pressure to move again, which I was glad of, but felt guilty about.

The next part of the journey was farther than Helena had thought. We walked for another thirty minutes before seeing a small wooden cabin in a clearing in the distance. Smoke was puffing from the chimney, following the direction of the tall pines until it overtook them, going where they couldn't go, up and out in the cloudless sky.

We stopped walking as soon as we saw the cabin in the distance. Helena was red in the face and tired, and I felt more guilty for bringing her on such a journey on this hot day. Bobby was looking at the cabin rather disappointedly, probably hoping for something far more luxurious than this. I, on the other hand, was more pumped up than ever. The sight of the humble home before me took my breath away. It was the home of a girl who had always boasted about wanting so much more, yet, to me, the sight of it was a dream, a perfect pretty little picture. Just like Jenny-May.

Tall pines stood protectively on two sides of the house. In front there was a little garden amid the large clearing with small bushes, pretty flowers, and what looked from afar to be a vegetable patch or herb garden. Mosquitoes and flies, when hit by the sun, looked like symbiotic creatures circling in the air, pockets of them scattered throughout the area. Streams of sunlight shone down through the trees, spotlighting center stage.

"Oh, look," Helena said, handing the water to Bobby as the front door of the cabin opened, and out of it came a little girl with white-blond hair. Her laughter echoed around the clearing and was carried over to us on the warm breeze. My hand went to my mouth. I must have made a sound, though I didn't hear it, because Bobby and Helena immediately looked to me. Tears welled in my eyes, as I watched the little girl, no older than five, exactly like the little girl I began my first day of school with. Then a female voice called from the house and my heart thudded.

"Daisy!"

Then a male voice: "Daisy!"

Little Daisy ran around the front garden, giggling and twirling, her lemon dress floating around her on the wind. Then from the front door, a man stepped out and began to chase her. Her giggling turned to screams of delight. He made terrifying noises behind her, teasing how he was going to catch her, which made her scream with laughter even more. Finally he caught her and spun her around in the air while she screamed "More, more, more!" He stopped when both were out of breath and he carried her in his arms back toward the house. Just outside the door he stopped and turned around slowly to look straight at us.

He called into the house. We heard the female voice

again, but not her words. He stood there looking directly at us.

"Can I help you?" he called, holding his hand to his forehead to shield the sun from his eyes.

Helena and Bobby looked to me. I stared at the man and the child in his arms, speechless.

"Well, yes, thank you. We're looking for Jenny-May Butler," Helena called politely. "I'm not sure if we're at the right place."

I had no doubt we were at the right place.

"Who is looking for her?" he asked politely. "I'm sorry, I can't see you from here." He began to take a few steps forward.

"Sandy Shortt is here for her," Helena called.

Immediately a figure appeared at the door.

I heard my large intake of breath.

Long blond hair, slim and pretty. The same but older. My age. The child in her was gone. She wore a loose-fitting white cotton dress and was barefoot. She held in her hand a tea cloth, which fell to the floor when she held her hand to her forehead to block out the sunlight, and her eyes fell upon me.

"Sandy?" Her voice was older but the same. It quivered and was uncertain, displaying fear and joy all at the same time.

"Jenny-May," I called back, hearing exactly the same tone in my voice.

Then I heard her cry as she slowly started to walk toward me and I heard myself cry as I took steps toward her. And I saw her arms reaching out and felt mine do the same. The distance between us grew smaller, the idea of her being before me becoming more real. Her sobs were loud; mine too, I was sure. We cried like children as we walked toward one another, studying faces, hair, bodies, and remembering, good things and bad. And then we were within each other's grasp and we fell into each other. Crying and hugging, moving to look at each other's face, wiping tears from each other's cheek, and then holding on again. Never wanting to let go.

51

"Jack," Garda Graham Turner said with surprise, "what are you doing back here? We won't have results back from forensics for another few days, and I promise you we'll contact you with the news."

Time had got to Donal's body before them, and had spared it no mercy. He had yet to be officially identified, though Jack and his family knew in their hearts it was Donal. Fresh and decaying flowers were found on the site that Alan had visited each week of the year. He had confessed his true story to police the previous night but had refused to give the names of the gang involved. Over the next few months he would stand trial, and Jack was glad his own mother wasn't around to see the man she helped raise take part in the blame for the murder of her baby.

After discussing the night's events with his family, it was the early hours of the morning before Jack returned to Foynes. The town was still celebrating the festival with all the energy of its opening hours. He ignored the sounds of music and singing, and went into the bedroom to find Gloria lying asleep in bed. He sat beside her on the bed and watched her, her long black lashes resting on the tops of her rosy cheeks. Her mouth was slightly open, soft sounds of her breath causing her white chest to heave gently up and down. It was that hypnotic sound and sight that compelled him to do what he hadn't done for a year. He reached out to her, placed his hand on her shoulder, and gently woke her from her slumber, finally inviting her into his world. When they had talked all night about the past year and all he had learned in the past week, he finally felt tired and joined her in her sleep at last.

"I'm not here about Donal," Jack explained, sitting down in the station on Sunday evening. "We need to find Sandy Shortt."

"Jack." Graham rubbed his eyes wearily. His desk and the surrounding desks were covered in paperwork, and phones rang all around him. "We've been through this."

"Not in enough detail. Now listen to me. Maybe Sandy got in touch with Alan and he panicked. You never know. Maybe they arranged to meet and he got nervous she was getting close to the truth and maybe he did something. I don't know what. I'm not even talking about murder. I know Alan's not capable of that but—" He paused. "Actually," he said, his pupils dilated with anger, "maybe he did. Maybe he got desperate and—"

"He didn't," Graham interrupted. "I've been through it over and over again with him. He doesn't know anything about her, he had never even heard of her. He had no clue about what I was talking about. All he knew was what you told him, that some unknown woman was helping you find Donal. That's all." He looked Jack in the eyes and softened his tone. "Please, Jack, give up on this."

"Give up? Like everyone told me to when I was looking for Donal?"

Graham shifted in his seat uncomfortably.

"Alan was Donal's *best friend* and he lied about what happened to him for *one year*. He's in enough trouble already. Do you think he's going to bother telling us about what he could have done to some woman he cares nothing about? Was I not right about Alan the first time?" Jack raised his voice.

Graham was silent for a long time, biting down on his already nonexistent nail as he quickly made a decision. "OK, OK." He closed his tired eyes and focused. "We'll start searching the site where her car was left."

52

I have thought about that moment with Jenny-May long and hard for many hours, days, and nights but I have no words for the time that we spent together that day. It was far too big for words. It was more important than words; it had more meaning than just words.

We stole away from the cabin, leaving Bobby, Helena, Daisy, and Jenny-May's husband, Luc, to chat among themselves. We had a lot to say to each other. To explain our conversations would not do the moment justice because we talked about nothing. To explain how I felt, watching an older version of the pretty photo embedded in my memory come alive, would fall short of the enormity of my delight. Delight not good enough a word. Relief, joy, pure ecstasy still not even close.

I filled her in on local people she once knew who were doing things of no interest to anybody but her. She told me about her family, her life, all that she had done since I had seen her. I told her of mine. Not once did we speak about her treatment of me. Does that seem odd? It didn't then. It wasn't important. Not once did we mention where we both were. Does that seem odd too? Perhaps, but that wasn't important either. It wasn't about then, or where, it was just about now. This moment, today. We didn't notice the hours go by, we barely saw the sunset and the moonrise. We didn't feel the heat leave our skin and the evening breeze cooling it. We felt nothing, heard nothing, saw nothing but the stories, sounds, and visions of our own minds, which we filled each other with. It is nothing to others but so much to me.

But it is perhaps enough to say that a part of me was set free that night, as I sensed was the case for Jenny-May. We never said it to each other, of course. But we both knew.

53

Helena had to get back to the village for the dress re-hearsal, and so while they said their good-byes, Jenny-May and I put our heads together and looked up to the camera in my hand and smiled. I took the photo and slid it into my shirt pocket. Jenny-May turned down her invitation to see the play, preferring to stay home with her family. We said we would meet again but we made no arrangements. Not out of any bad feeling between us, but because I felt it had all been said, or not said but under-stood, and she probably did too. To know she was there was enough, and for her to know I was around probably was too. Sometimes that's all people ever really need. Just to know.

We borrowed a flashlight from Jenny-May, as the sun was hiding behind the tree, leaving us bathed in blue light. Helena led the way back to the village. Eventually I could see the lights in the distance. Feeling dizzy with happiness, I took the photos from my pocket to study them once more while walking. I retrieved two and felt around for the third. It was gone.

"Oh, no," I moaned, and stopped walking, immediately looking to the ground.

"What's wrong?" Bobby stopped walking and called to Helena to stop.

"The photograph of me and Jenny-May is gone." I started to walk back the way we had come.

"Hold on, Sandy." Bobby followed me, looking at the ground. "We've been walking for almost an hour now. It could be anywhere. We really have to get back to the Community Hall for the play; we're late as it is. You can take another photo with her tomorrow when it's bright."

"No, I can't," I whinged, straining my eyes to see the ground in the evening light.

Helena, who so far hadn't said a word, stepped forward. "You dropped it?"

That made me stop and look up at her. Her face was serious, her tone grave.

"I assume so. I doubt it leaped out and ran away on its own."

"You know what I'm talking about."

"No, I definitely dropped it. My pocket is open, see?" I showed them the shallow breast pocket. "Why don't you two just go on ahead and I'll look around here for a little while."

They looked unsure.

"We're less than five minutes away. I can see the pathway back, we're so close." I smiled. "Honestly, I'll be OK. I have to find this photo and then I'll go straight to the Community Hall to see the play. I promise."

Helena was looking at me oddly, obviously torn between helping me and helping the cast prepare for their dress rehearsal.

"I'm not leaving you on your own," Bobby said.

"Here, Sandy, you take this flashlight. Bobby and I will be able to see our way from here. I know it's important for you to find it." She handed over the flashlight and I thought I saw tears in her eyes.

"Helena, stop worrying!" I laughed. "I'll be OK."

"I know you will, sweetheart." She leaned over and, taking me by surprise, planted a quick kiss on my cheek and gave me a quick, tight hug. "Be careful."

Bobby smiled at me over Helena's shoulder. "She's not going to die, you know, Helena."

Helena slapped him playfully over the head. "Come on with me. I need you to bring all the costumes over from the shop ASAP, Bobby! You promised I'd have them yesterday!"

"Well, that was before David Copperfield here was called to the Community Hall!" he defended himself playfully.

Helena glared at him.

"OK, OK!" He backed away from her. "Hope you find it, Sandy." He winked at me before following Helena back down the path. I heard them nagging and teasing one another for a while until the sounds of their voices disappeared and they entered the village.

I turned around and immediately started scanning the ground. I could pretty much remember the way we had come. It seemed to be one main pathway. Very rarely did we come across a choice of others, and so with my eyes peeled to the ground, I made my way back deeper into the forest.

Helena and Bobby rushed around backstage, fixing costumes, last-minute broken zippers and tears, going over lines with nervous cast members, and giving final pep talks to a panicked crew. Helena hurried out to her seat in the auditorium beside Joseph before the performance began and finally relaxed for the first time in the last hour.

"Is Sandy not with you?" Joseph asked, looking around.

"No," Helena said, staring straight ahead, refusing to look at her husband. "She stayed behind in the forest."

Joseph took his wife's hand and whispered, "Along the Kenyan coast where I come from, there is a forest called the Arabuko-Sokoke Forest."

"Yes, you've talked about it," Helena acknowledged.

"There, there are *kipepeo* girls, butterfly farmers who help keep the forest preserved."

Helena looked up at him, finally learning the meaning of the nickname. He smiled. "They are known as guardians of the forest."

"She stayed in the forest to find a photograph of her and Jenny-May. She thinks she dropped it." Helena's eyes began to fill and Joseph squeezed her hand.

The curtains on stage parted.

At times I thought I saw the white of the photograph glowing in the moonlight and I would wander off the track to search among the weeds and undergrowth, chasing small birds and creatures away with my flashlight. After half an hour I was sure I should have reached the first clearing by now. I shone the flashlight all around me, looking for something familiar, but it was just trees, trees, and more trees. But then again I had been walking far more slowly and so it would take me longer to get there. I decided to keep walking in the same direction. It was black now, and around me owls hooted and creatures moved in their natural habitat, startled to find me where I didn't belong. I didn't plan on being there much longer. I shivered, the cool evening now turning to cold. I shone the flashlight straight ahead, deciding that I'd dropped the photograph closer to Jenny-May's house than I thought.

"Where am I?" Orla Keane stepped onto the stage as Dorothy Gale, looking around the community hall that, for the night, was a grand theater. Hundreds of faces stared back at her. "What is this strange land?"

Thirty minutes later, sweating, panting, and dizzy from jogging around in different directions, I recognized the first clearing up ahead. I stopped running and leaned over to hold on to a tree, to steady myself and catch my breath. I breathed a sigh of relief and was taken aback by the realization I'd been more anxious about being lost than I'd thought.

. . .

"I need a heart," Derek cried out. "I need a brain," Bernard announced theatrically. "And I need courage," Marcus said quietly in his bored tone. The audience laughed as they all hopped off with Dorothy stage right, arm in arm.

It was brighter in the clearing, the moon shining down without the trees acting as a shield. The floor of the clearing was blue and in the center I could see a small white square sheet glistening. Despite my tiredness and the pain in my chest, I began to run toward the photograph. I knew I was out longer than I had intended to be and I had promised Helena I would be there for her. A mixture of emotions rushed through me as I felt such pressure to find the photograph and to be there for Helena and my new friends. I wasn't concentrating as I stupidly ran at top speed in the dark, in Barbara Langley's heeled shoes. I landed unevenly on a rock and felt my ankle twist. The pain shot up my leg, forcing me off balance. The ground came up to meet me quickly before there was anything I could do to stop it.

"You mean I had the power inside myself to go home all the time?" Orla Keane said innocently. The audience laughed.

"Yes, Dorothy," Carol Dempsey, dressed as the good witch Glinda, said, in her usual gentle tones. "Just click your heels together and say the words."

Helena grabbed Joseph's hand more tightly and he squeezed back.

Orla Keane closed her eyes and began to click her heels together. "There's no place like home," she said, pulling everyone into her mantra. "There's no place like home."

Joseph looked across at his wife and saw a tear roll down her face. He raised a thumb to stop it from dropping from her chin. "Our *kipepeo* has flown."

Helena nodded, and another tear fell.

I felt everything go from under me, my head smashed violently against something hard. I felt the pain shoot down my spine and everything went black.

On stage Orla Keane tapped her ruby slippers together one last time before disappearing in a puff of smoke, compliments of Bobby's firecrackers. "There's no place like home."

54

"I don't think she's here." Graham walked toward Jack in the wooded area of Glin. In the distance, fireworks were going off over Foynes as the village celebrated the last few moments of the Irish Coffee Festival. They both stopped to look up.

"I have a feeling you might be right," Jack finally admitted. They had spent the last few hours searching the scene where Sandy had deserted her car and, despite the fact it had fallen dark mid-search, Jack had insisted they continue. These were not practical searching conditions and he could see the others checking their watches. "Thanks for letting me try," Jack said as they walked along the pathway back to the car.

Suddenly there was a loud crash; a sound as though a tree had come down. A thud and a female cry. The men both froze and each looked at the other.

"Which way did that come from?" Graham asked, spinning around, shining his flashlight in every direction. They heard groaning coming from farther up on their left and all involved rushed to find her. Jack's flashlight fell upon Sandy, lying on her back, her leg looking dislocated, blood on her hand and staining her clothes.

"Oh, my God." He rushed forward and kneeled down by her side. "She's here!" he called to the others, and they hurried over crowding around her.

"OK, let's move back, give her space." Graham radioed for an ambulance.

"I don't want to move her. Her head is bleeding heavily and it looks like her leg's broken too. Oh, God, Sandy, talk to me."

Her eyes fluttered open. "Who are you?"

"I'm Jack Ruttle," he said, relieved she'd opened her eyes.

"Keep her talking, Jack," Graham said.

"Jack?" Her eyes widened in surprise. "Are you missing, too?"

"What? No." He frowned. "No, I'm not missing." He looked at Graham worriedly. Graham made motions to keep her talking.

"Where am I?" she asked in confusion, looking around. She tried to move her head and called out in pain.

"Don't move. An ambulance is on its way. You're in Glin, in Limerick."

"Glin?" she repeated.

"Yes, we were supposed to meet here last week, remember?"

"Am I home?" Her eyes filled with tears, which quickly fell over her mud-streaked face. "Donal," she said suddenly, stopping her tears. "Donal wasn't there."

"Donal wasn't where?"

"I was in this place, Jack. Oh, my God, this place where all the missing people were. Helena, Bobby, Joseph, Jenny-May, oh, my God, Helena's play. I'm missing her play." Tears fell quickly now. "I need to get up." She struggled to move. "I have to go to the dress rehearsal."

"You have to wait for the ambulance to come, Sandy. Don't move." He looked back to Graham. "She's delusional. Where the hell is the ambulance?"

Graham radioed again. "On its way."

"Who did this to you, Sandy? Tell me who did this and we'll get them, I promise."

"Nobody did." She looked confused. "I fell. I told you I was in the place . . . where's my photograph, I've lost a photograph. Oh, Jack, I've something to tell you," she said softly now. "It's about Donal."

"Go on," he urged.

"He wasn't there. He wasn't in . . . the place with everyone else. He's not missing."

"I know," Jack said sadly. "We found him this morning."

"I'm so sorry."

"How did you know?"

"He wasn't there, with all the missing people," she mumbled, her eyes fluttering closed.

"Stay with me, Sandy," Jack said, with urgency in his voice.

My eyes opened to bright white, and my lids felt heavy. I looked around, but my sockets were sore. My head pounded. I groaned.

"Sweetheart . . ." My mum's face appeared from above.

"Mum." I instantly began crying and she reached out her arms to hold me.

"It's OK, sweetheart, it's OK now," she said soothingly, while smoothing down my hair on my head.

"I've missed you so much." I cried into her shoulder, ignoring the pulsing pain around the rest of my body.

Her patting stopped when I said that, the shock of my words freezing her, and then it slowly began again. I felt Dad kiss the top of my head.

"I missed you, Dad." I continued crying.

"We've missed you too, love." His voice shook as he spoke.

"I found the place," I said excitedly, the sounds and visions around me still blurred and faraway. My own voice was muffled. "I found the place where all the missing things go."

"Yes, sweetheart, Jack told us," Mum said in a worried tone.

"No, I'm not mad, I didn't imagine it. I was really there."

"Yes." She hushed me. "You need to rest, sweetheart."

"The photographs are in my shirt pocket," I said, trying to explain all the details clearly, but it felt muddled in my head. "It's not my shirt pocket, it's Barbara Langley from Ohio's. I found it. I put them in my pocket."

"The guards didn't find anything, honey," Dad said quietly, not wanting anyone else to hear. "There aren't any photographs."

"They must have fallen out," I mumbled, getting tired of trying to explain. "Is Gregory here?" I asked.

"No, shall we call him?" my mother asked excitedly. "I wanted to call him but Harold wouldn't let me."

"Call him" was the last thing I remember saying.

I awoke in my childhood bedroom and stared at the same floral wallpaper I was forced to look at all throughout my teens. I had hated it then. I couldn't wait to see the back of it, but now it gave me a strange sense of comfort. I smiled, feeling delighted to be home for the first time in my life. There was no bag by the door, no feeling of claustrophobia or fear of losing things. I had been at home now for three days, catching up on sleep and resting my injured and weary body. I had broken my leg, twisted my ankle, and had ten stitches on the crown of my head, but I was home and I was happy. I often thought of Helena, Bobby, Joseph, and Wanda, and felt a longing to be with them but knew that they would understand what had happened, and wondered if they perhaps understood the entire time.

There was a knock on the door.

"Enter," I called.

Gregory peeked his head around, then entered with a tray of food in his hands.

I groaned. "Not more food. I think you're all trying to fatten me up."

"We're trying to make you well again," he said somberly, placing the tray on the bed. "Mrs. Butler brought you the flowers."

"That's so sweet of her," I said gently. "Do you still think I'm crazy?" I asked.

I had told him about where I had been as soon as I had felt well enough to explain it properly. My parents had also obviously asked him to talk to me about it as it was issue number one on the agenda, although he was keen not to take the role of counselor. Not anymore. That was then, this is now.

He avoided the question. "I spoke to Jack Ruttle today."

"Good. I hope you apologized."

"I definitely apologized."

"Good," I repeated, "because if it wasn't for him I would literally be lying in a ditch somewhere. My own boyfriend didn't care enough to join the search party," I said, in a huff.

"Honestly, Sandy, if I joined a search party every time you disappeared . . ." He had meant it as a joke but it changed the mood.

"Well, it won't be happening again."

He looked unsure.

"I promise, Gregory. I've found what I was looking for." I reached out to touch his cheek.

He smiled but I was sure it would take time before he'd truly believe me. The past few days I had questioned whether I believed myself.

"What did Jack say on the phone?"

"That he went back to the place where he'd found you to look for the photographs you've been talking about, and he didn't find anything."

"Does *he* think I'm crazy?"

"Probably, but he still loves you because he's convinced you and your mum helped him find his brother."

"He's a sweet guy. If it wasn't for him . . ." I repeated, just to annoy Gregory.

"If you didn't already have a broken leg, I'd break it for you," he threatened, but then became serious again. "You know how your mum received a phone call from the Sheens? The people who bought your grandparents' house all those years ago?"

"Yes." I tore the crust off a slice of toast and put it in my mouth. "I thought that was weird. I can't believe they were ringing to tell her they were moving."

Gregory cleared his throat. "Actually . . . well, that's not why they called; your dad concocted that story."

"What? Why?" I put the toast down, no longer hungry.

"He didn't want to worry you."

"Tell me, Gregory."

"Well, your parents may not agree with me but I think it's important you know that they'd actually called to say that they'd found a teddy bear belonging to you. A Mr. Pobbs, lying underneath a bed in the spare room with your name embroidered on his striped pajamas."

I gasped. "Everything's turning up again."

"They found this particularly unusual because they had used that room as storage for a number of years and only turned it back into a bedroom last month. They had never noticed the teddy bear before."

"Why didn't anyone tell me?"

"Your parents didn't want to upset you again, with you talking about this missing place and—"

"It's not a missing place, it's a place where missing people and things go," I said angrily, realizing once again how stupid it sounded.

"OK, OK, calm down." He ran his fingers through his hair and leaned his elbows on his knees.

"What's wrong?"

"Nothing."

"Gregory, I know when something's wrong with you. Tell me."

"Well." He wrung his hands together. "After their phone call I gave further thought to your . . . theory."

I rolled my eyes with frustration. "What disorder do you think I have now?"

"Let me finish," he said, his voice raised, and an angry silence fell between us. After a while he spoke again. "When I was emptying your hospital bag I found this in your shirt pocket."

I held my breath as he removed something from his top pocket.

The photograph of me with Jenny-May.

I took it from his hands as though it were the most fragile thing in the world. Trees framed the photograph.

"Do you believe me now?" I whispered, running my finger over her face.

He shrugged. "You know how my mind works, Sandy. For me this kind of thinking is nonsensical." I looked to him angrily. "*But*," he said firmly before I had a chance to snap, "this is very difficult to explain."

"That's good enough for now." I accepted what he said, holding the photograph close to me.

"I'm sure Mrs. Butler would want to see that," he said.

"Do you think?" I was unsure.

He thought about it. "I think she's the only woman

you could show it to. I think she's the only woman you *should* show it to."

"But how could I explain it?"

He looked at me, spread his hands apart and shrugged. "This time, you're the one with the answer."

55

Sometimes, people can go missing right before our very eyes. Sometimes, people discover you, even though they've been looking at you the entire time. Sometimes, we lose sight of ourselves when we're not paying enough attention.

Days later, when I was feeling fit enough to venture outside on my crutches, under the gaze of Gregory and my parents, I hobbled my way across the road to Mrs. Butler's house with the photograph of her daughter in my pocket. The lantern-shaped porch light provided a warm orange glow above the door and drew me in, like a moth to a flame. I took a deep breath and knocked on the door, once again feeling a responsibility and knowing that I'd wished for this moment my entire life.

We all get lost once in a while, sometimes by choice, sometimes due to forces beyond our control. When we learn what it is our soul needs to learn, the path presents itself. Sometimes we see the way out but wander farther and deeper despite ourselves; the fear, the anger, or the sadness preventing us from returning. Sometimes we prefer to be lost and wandering; sometimes it's easier. Sometimes we find our own way out. But regardless, always, we are found.

Acknowledgments

Huge thanks to Peternelle van Arsdale, Ellen Archer, and the Hyperion team.

Thank you, Marianne Gunn O'Connor, for continuing to inspire and motivate me. Also thanks to the incredibly supportive Pat Lynch and Vicki Satlow, and thank you to Dermot Hobbs and John-Paul Moriarty.

Special thanks to David, Mimmie, Dad, Georgina, Nicky, and all my family; Kellys, Aherns, Keoghans, and of course, the witches of Eastwick—Paula Pea, Susana, and SJ.

Thank you to all those who read my books—for the greatest motivation of all.

©Kieran Harnett

Cecelia Ahern is the author of the international best-sellers *PS, I Love You*; *Love, Rosie*; and *If You Could See Me Now*. Foreign rights to her novels have been sold to more than forty countries, and film rights have been bought by Walt Disney Pictures and Warner Bros. She lives in Dublin.